RED SPIRIT

Also by Humphrey Hawksley

Ceremony of Innocence
Absolute Measures
Dragon Fire

with Simon Holberton

Dragon Strike

RED SPIRIT

Humphrey Hawksley

HEADLINE
FEATURE

First Published in 2001
by HEADLINE BOOK PUBLISHING

A HEADLINE FEATURE hardback

10 9 8 7 6 5 4 3 2 1

British Library Cataloguing in Publication Data

Hawksley, Humphrey
Red spirit
1.Suspense fiction
I.Title
823.9'14[F]

hardback 0 7472 2275 4

Typeset by
Letterpart Limited, Reigate, Surrey

Printed and bound in Great Britain by
Mackays of Chatham plc, Chatham, Kent

HEADLINE BOOK PUBLISHING
A division of Hodder Headline
338 Euston Road
LONDON NW1 3BH

www.headline.co.uk
www.hodderheadline.com

To my son and his mother

All men must die, but death can vary in significance

Mao Zedong, *Selected Works, Vol. III*, p. 228,
'Serve the People', 8 September 1944

As soon as the First Emperor became king of China, excavations and building had been started at Mount Li, while after he won the empire more than seven hundred thousand conscripts from all parts of the country worked there. They dug through three subterranean streams and poured molten copper for the outer coffin, and the tomb was filled with models of palaces, pavilions and offices, as well as fine vessels, precious stones and rarities. Artisans were ordered to fix up crossbows so that any thief breaking in would be shot. All the country's streams, the Yellow River and the Yangtse were reproduced in quicksilver and by some mechanical means made to flow in a miniature ocean. The heavenly constellations were shown above and the regions on the earth below. The candles were made of whale oil to ensure their burning for the longest possible time.

The Second Emperor decreed: 'It is not right to send away those of my father's ladies who had no sons.' Accordingly, all these were ordered to follow the First Emperor to the grave. After the interment, someone pointed out that the artisans who had made the mechanical contrivances might disclose all the treasure that was in the tomb; therefore after the burial and sealing up of the treasures, the middle gate was shut and the outer gate closed to imprison all the artisans and labourers, so that no one came out. Trees and grass were planted over the mausoleum to make it seem like a hill.

Extract from the *Shi Ji*, the Records of the Grand Historian, by Sima Qian, 104–92 BC, translated by Yang Hsien-yi and Gladys Yang, Foreign Language Press, Peking, 1979.

1

Chapter One

The hot unventilated study was long and narrow, wedged between two rooms, with his workplace at one end. Beside the door was a small window through which sunlight fought its way in on dusty rays, split up randomly by slatted blinds. The desk where he sat was swathed in darkness. In between was nothing, just worn floorboards, an old carpet, shelves of books pressed up against both walls and a woman on her knees, her head lowered, letting out soft, short cries.

'It is all right to feel the pain,' said Wu Tian in barely more than a whisper from behind his desk. 'It's all right to cry.'

She was no more than forty, a farm worker from the countryside, with a red, weather-blown face. She held her hands across her face like a guard against further affliction.

'But tell me, why did your son steal the petrol?' said Wu Tian. His face was impassive but his question cut through the room like a cold command. He rolled a pen back and forth along the top of his desk.

'He was in love with a girl from the village,' said the mother. A hand left her face to touch the edge of an eye, then returned. 'He wanted to marry her and start a new life. But our family had no security and no money to help him.'

'And when was your commune abolished?'

'Six, seven years ago,' she said. Her uncertainty showed in the flickering of her eyes. 'Maybe eight, I am not sure. Does it matter?' She looked behind her, where Li Yi was standing, his hands folded across his small barrel chest.

'It doesn't matter,' said Li Yi.

'No, it doesn't matter,' repeated Wu Tian.

'When we had a commune, we didn't have these problems,' she added quickly.

Wu Tian stood up and brushed down the collar of his blue tunic. 'You were right to come to me. It is appalling how the peasant classes are being treated.'

As Wu Tian walked round to the front of his desk, the woman's eyes shifted between fear and gratitude. 'Your son will be freed. He did not have the protection of the real China. The poor people are helpless under the new government. You see now how the money ideology has left you with nothing, not even your pride. Now get up off your knees, comrade, and face me like an equal.'

The wiry figure of Mok flitted across the room. He touched the woman's elbow, helping her up, then left her alone and returned to the shadows.

'Our new leaders know nothing of the havoc they are wreaking on this country.' Wu Tian walked towards her and placed his hands on her shoulders. 'Now go. Your son will be with you soon. We will give you money for the wedding.'

As she left, Wu returned to his desk. The queue outside stretched back through the university campus. Wu Tian prepared for the next session, but Li Yi closed the door and bolted it.

'Sally Parsons starts drilling tonight,' Li Yi said softly.

Wu Tian's face became deathly grey, as if it had been rubbed with damp ashes.

Ko Guo's headlights were barely able to cut through the thick winter fog. Sally cupped her hands round a glass of hot tea; the printed face of Mao Zedong on the side stared knowingly up at her. Right now, she loved China, loved Mao, loved Ko and loved every tiny detail of her life. Particularly, she loved the Emperor Qin Shi Huang, whose extravagance might give her a small place in archaeological history. Except if she was honest with herself, she hoped it would be the biggest damn place available in the late twentieth century.

When she had faxed her boss, Jack Messent, she had made sure it was just past midnight so the fax showed Monday,

4

23 January 1989, in China but arrived in an empty office at just past noon on Sunday, 22 January 1989, in New York. By the time he got it, it would be too late to stop her. Paul was safely in bed, watched over by Ko's wife. And Ko, his loyalty stretched to a thread, was still hanging in there. Her preparation work over the past winter weeks was finished. They had just picked up the probe and monitor from her office underneath the museum. She waited for Ko to slow at the entrance so she could take another sip of her tea.

Instead, the shooting started, two shots from the driver-side back window out of a black Toyota Crown which was speeding towards them. Shots backwards. Not at Ko and Sally.

Ko braked, threw the car into reverse and backed it off the road. The Toyota skidded, scraping on the gateposts, the gunman firing again, on automatic, at the car behind.

Ko crouched behind the steering wheel. But Sally had to watch, one hand across her mouth, the other hot with spilt tea from the Mao mug. 'It's a police car,' she whispered, prompting Ko to peek out as well.

'Probably bandits stealing the terracotta warriors,' said Ko, and as the tail lights of both cars vanished into the fog, Ko eased forward back onto the road. 'You want to carry on?'

'Yes,' said Sally too quickly. *Go home. Go back to Paul*, a voice cried inside her. *It's not worth it.* 'Of course,' she added. *This is China. Not America. For God's sake, Sally Parsons, grow up.* 'Yes, go on, Ko, please. It's nothing to do with us.'

As Ko pulled up by the tomb, the mountains rose ghost-like from the flat countryside and the wind blew ice-cold across the frost-dead fields. It howled around the car like a wild spirit. Flecks of hail hit the windows like pellets, flattening and smearing as the ice melted against the warm glass.

The headlights picked out wooden shacks, and then Ko and Sally saw a peasant bundled up in quilted cotton, sitting on an upturned box, back to the road, staring at the great burial mound ahead of them. Sally wondered if it was a mother about to abandon a newborn baby to the night.

'It's the madman. I haven't seen him for months,' said Ko, flashing his headlights to frighten him away.

'How d'you know he's mad? There's a lot of homeless people in China nowadays.'

For a moment the figure was caught in Ko's lights. 'Why else would he be out here?'

'Not as lucky as you, maybe.'

Ko shrugged. The figure shuffled away, his head protruding from the folds of cloth like a turtle, his eyes dancing back towards the car. Soon he was out of the arc of the headlights and hidden in the blackness. Ko pulled up by the kiosks, full of tourist trinkets but locked up for the night.

'Ko, you stay here,' said Sally, zipping up her jacket and wrapping her scarf tight round her neck and lower face.

'You'll be all right?'

'I'll be fine.' Only scientists, atheists or the homeless would venture out on a night like this, she thought.

Outside the car, the southerly wind swept down from Mount Li whose rich deposits of gold and jade were the reason why the mausoleum had been built here. Sally lifted out her knapsack with her flashlights, blanket, food, digging gear. The monitor and connection leads made it heavy. She hitched the bag on her back, as high as possible so the weight didn't drag down on her shoulders, then she banged the top of the car boot. Ko opened it from inside the car. Sally began to speak, but a roar of wind round the side of the burial mound drowned her words. She lowered her head against it, went to his window and knocked on it, until Ko got out.

They lifted out the box which contained the probe, and Sally set it up on its wheels. Ko, smiling like a fat Buddha, held the flashlight with both hands to keep it steady.

Sally pulled the box behind her, the wheels trundling like a rubbish cart on a pavement. It was heavy, but she had expected that and had marked the closest places to the path where she could carry out the surveys.

Pomegranate trees rose from the edge of the path ahead of her, leafless and stark. As she began to climb through them, the contours of the tomb became clearer. Against the starless night sky, she could make out the rounded edges of the mound rising two hundred feet up ahead of her. The howl of the wind, less confined higher up, had dropped. The higher she climbed, the quieter it became, until it sounded distant and harmless. Up here, with flatlands below and mountains behind, the still, cold air of winter froze and preserved the tomb in a silent, timeless world of its own.

Halfway up the concrete steps, Sally hauled the probe off the path and onto a narrow farmers' dirt track between the fruit trees. She stopped, braked the wheels and slid her knapsack to the ground.

A smell of smoke hung in the air, drifting in from fires far away, and it suddenly reminded Sally of winter at home, when smoke curled up the chimney and her family spent Christmas fighting and competing as the logs in the fireplace spat sparks and embers.

Everyone who knew Sally thought she was a success. But if they looked closer, she was convinced they would discover what she herself already knew: that she had never quite hit the mark. She was bright, but not brilliant, striking but not beautiful, determined but not hard-edged. She had something about her of the innocent caught up in the maelstrom of the world, a loving mother and a grateful daughter, but not perfect enough for her life to be free of guilt.

With Richard around, she now hoped a loving relationship might finally be within her grasp. But, strangely, she was only completely at ease when she was working as an archaeologist and felt the simple thrill of piecing together history from digging in the ground.

Sally had been barely ten when she worked out a scheme to persuade her reluctant father to take her to Peru to see the Inca ruins. They were living in Arlington, Virginia, then. It was before her father had done his first tour in Vietnam and he was working at the Pentagon. He didn't much like travelling any-where, and Sally quickly understood that the normal childhood tricks of tears and tantrums would not persuade him. So she devised a system of earning points for good deeds done, setting an impossibly high target which her father thought she would never achieve. She hauled out the rubbish, visited sick relatives, cleaned his competition crossbows, played him at chess, tended the garden, washed the car, painted the house, and every Sunday she wrote down her weekly points, and got her father to sign it.

A year later, she announced that she had earned enough for an air ticket, hotel and sightseeing, and showed him her hours to prove it. Her reluctant but proud father honoured the deal – and booked the tickets.

While in Peru, Sally told her parents she wanted to be an archaeologist and so began another long and skilful campaign of persuasion which brought her to where she was now, half frozen to ice on the slopes of a two-thousand-year-old burial mound in the middle of China.

It had taken months to persuade Jack Messent to give her the probe used two years earlier in 1987 to photograph inside the Great Pyramid of Khufu in Egypt. She worked at night when the tourists were gone. Just before the New Year, she had set up an airlock over her target area and drilled her first hole through the surface of the tomb into one of the outer chambers of the mausoleum.

That had been a night of disappointment and mixed blessings. As the drill broke through the soil, there was no change of air pressure. She fed in the hose and pumped up samples of air at different levels on the way down, seven inches below the surface, then thirty-seven, and lastly eighty-seven. She captured the air in three separate canisters, filled a fourth with air from outside, and shipped them back to New York for analysis.

The measurements of chlorofluorocarbons and carbon dioxide confirmed her worst fears: the air inside the ancient chamber was not substantially different from the air she was breathing. It meant the tomb's hermetic seal had been broken. Someone or something had already been in there. But there had been an upside. She had been able to get permission to carry out the second stage of her experiment of lowering a miniature camera into the chamber.

Messent had been nervous from the outset. 'Sal,' he fussed, 'I just don't feel right about this. Are you absolutely sure that what you're doing is legal? I don't get how the Shaanxi provincial government can overrule the National Cultural Relics Bureau. They're based in Beijing, for Christ's sake.'

But Sally had her own arguments ready. 'Listen,' she said patiently, 'I'll set up an airlock before each drilling, OK? The drill holes will only be three inches in diameter. When I'm done, I'll seal them up again. This is exploration, Jack. Not excavation.'

That was just before Christmas, and, in the end, she had won.

Sally pulled her woollen hat down so her hair wouldn't fall into her eyes as she worked. She started the engine, which spluttered to life like a generator. In the frosty silence it sounded unnaturally loud.

The drill plunged into the soil like a corkscrew. It sank further and further through the clay until, seven yards down, it broke through the first level, spinning on thin, stale air. She sealed the hole, set up the tiny airlock antechamber just beneath the surface, and then prepared the camera and lights.

Her equipment had been designed by the space and nuclear power industries, then adapted by archaeologists. A bundle of fibreoptic cables produced vivid, cold light, which meant she could illuminate the inside of the chamber without raising the temperature. She attached the camera to the probe, checked the picture on her monitor and fed it down into the chamber.

The first images on her monitor were grainy and reminded her of when she was pregnant with Paul and saw his first ultrasound scan, wriggling around in her womb, eight years ago.

She turned the camera and peered at the changing images – a collapsed wall, rubble, and beyond that a pillar or perhaps a statue, rising up to the ceiling of the chamber the camera was in. She shifted the lens again.

The mausoleum and its outer chambers were meant to be a replica in miniature of the empire of Qin Shi Huang, who more than two thousand years earlier had created a unified Chinese nation. Briefly, she allowed herself to close her eyes, forget about the cold and envisage the world which might be here, the one described in the *Shi Ji*, the Records of the Grand Historian, the first work written on that period: the constellations, the rivers reproduced in mercury, crossbows charged with poisoned arrows to ward off intruders. She might find ceilings embedded with jewels, beautifully preserved terracotta horses and decorations of

9

birds and animals and women celebrating Qin Shi Huang's love of life. Or Qin himself, laid out on an island, ringed by a lake of mercury, his skeleton draped with lavish burial robes preserved by the dry air of central China.

She allowed herself time to imagine because this was what it had all been about. She had to slow her hopes in case it didn't work, and it had all been for nothing. Minutes from now, she might discover the treasures of Qin Shi Huang or she might see only debris and ash left by underground flash fires ignited by methane deposits centuries ago.

Slowly, as the camera worked its way round the chamber, she let the excitement envelop her. She identified at least one face of a terracotta warrior, and what could have been part of a horse's armour. She zoomed in on what looked like an arm snapped off a standing archer, and his weapon, also broken in two, lying a couple of feet away.

At the western end of the chamber, she thought there was a door, wide and high enough for a human being to walk through. On the floor was a small red oblong shape, half hidden under what looked like a rafter of burnt wood. It looked oddly out of place.

On the wall were paintings of animals, deer, dogs and horses, and, amazingly, what could have been architects' diagrams, sketches of rooms and tunnels, drawn as the builders had worked.

She had become so transfixed that she hadn't noticed how the cold was beginning to get to her. She stamped her feet, banged her hands together, then settled down to record the chamber, noting each angle and shot. Once back in the office, she would examine it all more carefully, and establish how much closer she was to the fabled burial spot of China's first emperor.

Even this was enough for Sally to prove her point, for here in one of the very outer chambers to the mausoleum were archaeological treasures matching anything else in the world.

No one except Sally had ever seen them.

As Ko drove back towards Xian, Sally stared out of the window, not at the old China they had come from but the industrialised

China of concrete and factories. They were just about to enter the dark rain-stained tunnel on the Huaqing road when she saw a bundle on the ledge ahead, lit up just for a second by the lights of an oncoming vehicle.

'Ko, stop the car,' Sally said urgently. But Ko accelerated past it. Sally banged her hand on the back of his seat. 'Stop the goddamn car or I'll never ride with you again.'

Ko pulled over and stayed put with his hazard lights on while Sally ran back. The ledge was narrow and half swathed in shadow, tricky to get to.

She lifted the child from the ledge, felt the cold face. Sleeping? She couldn't tell. The baby was wrapped up badly. A girl, unwanted by her parents, left to be found? Or to freeze and die before morning, without nothing more said?

She walked quickly and carefully back to the car. Ko had the door open for her and the vacuum flask of warm milk ready. Sally felt the baby girl's breathing. She held her, rocked her, soothed her, saw the little eyes open, fed her the milk on her finger, and sang a Chinese song about a mother's love for her daughter.

Ko pulled out and they headed to the orphanage. He didn't need to be told. They'd done it many times before. Every time, on the way back from her night's surveying of the tomb, Sally looked. They didn't always find an abandoned baby, but they had saved enough to make Ko feel uneasy. One day it might be Ko himself who had to leave his baby girl on a ledge. He was only allowed one child and, with his wife pregnant, there might be nothing else for Ko to do unless she gave him the son they both so badly wanted. Sally had set herself a mission to ensure that Ko did not leave his baby to die if it was a girl.

As they got closer to the centre of Xian, police were directing traffic away from an accident. It was the same Toyota Crown they had seen earlier, now smashed into a lamp post, its windows shattered and a man slumped over the steering wheel.

'Keep driving,' said Sally.

When they had passed it, Ko lit a cigarette, using both hands to shield the match against the blast of hot air from the heater and steering briefly with his large belly on the bottom of the wheel.

11

He drew deeply on the tobacco and rubbed his fingers on one of the laminated Mao cards hanging from the mirror.

Exhibit 17 – Audio Tape Evidence
Federal Court, Pearl Street
Manhattan
December 16th 1989

'She's put the camera into the mound.'
'And?'
'She hasn't seen it. Not even close. She'll want to go to New York before doing any more.'
'Let her go, then.'

Chapter Two

Sally had never had time to arrange for Paul to meet Julie Maddox, so when she told him he was to stay with her for a couple of nights, he kicked up a stink. It was a real blinder, locking himself in his room, bursting into tears, then taking off on his bicycle so that Sally and Ko had to fetch him back.

They caught up with him a mile and a half down the road, where the paved-over potholes gave way to icy craters on a track of rubble, and Paul's mountain bike could handle it better than the taxi. Sally, remonstrating out of the window, pleaded with him to pull up.

'I don't like Julie Maddox,' he yelled at her, fists gripping the handlebars.

'Paul, honey, you haven't even met her.'

'Neither have you.' The tyres slipped on some ice, but he caught the bike on the way down and saved himself from falling.

'You'll have a great time with her.' Sally got out of the car. 'She runs a neat place for kids whose parents are away.'

'Why's she safer than staying with Mrs Ko?'

'Mrs Ko's having a baby.'

Paul straightened up his bike. 'Why didn't you ask me first? Instead of just telling me. You always said we were a partnership.'

This was when it got really bad, when she just wanted to give up the balancing act and take Paul home to Southampton. She walked over to him and put her hands on his shoulders. 'I'm sorry. OK, honey? Mommy's been too busy at work.'

Paul shook his head, refusing to budge. 'Just because she's

having a baby doesn't mean I can't stay here.'

'It's a difficult pregnancy, hon. Sometimes new moms have a hard time.'

Paul threw back his head. 'But the baby's not coming till the summer.'

'Yeah, but sometimes it's difficult right at the beginning, when it starts to grow in her tummy.'

Paul shivered a bit. They were both getting cold, standing in the middle of the road. 'OK. So this is the deal,' he bargained. 'I stay with the Kos this time. Then when you get back we'll go meet Mrs Maddox. If I like her, I'll stay with her when you go away again.'

Sally looked over towards Ko. 'Just a couple of days?' she asked in Chinese and Ko nodded. 'OK, darling. A deal,' Sally relented, smiling because she couldn't hide her pride that her seven-year-old son was so bright. 'Now follow us back.'

The Kos were fine, and Paul felt at home with them. Sally rented one side of their house. Paul had decorated his room with pictures of bicycles and fighter planes and his window looked out onto the back garden, over the chicken pen and the wire run for the litter of puppies. Whenever Sally had to be away, Ko and his wife looked after Paul like the son they didn't have.

One thing was for sure, she had to go to New York. She didn't want to move any further on the tomb without showing Jack Messent her pictures. With the time difference, she could fly out and come back in two nights. But as Richard was in New York, she would give it an extra night.

Apart from her sister Cait, Richard had been the first person to understand why Sally ended up in China. As soon as she told him about training as an archaeologist in the mid-seventies, he'd said, 'That's about as chauvinist and tough a profession as any woman could choose. Is that why you're here in China?'

He'd got it in one. The glory was all in Egypt. But Sally would not have been thought smart enough or fraternal enough to get anything decent there. No one wanted China because you couldn't get access. And if you couldn't dig, you couldn't discover.

Nor had Richard thought anything strange about Sally living as a single mother, cheek by jowl with a taxi driver and his wife.

'My father thinks I'm stupid, crazy and selfish,' she'd told him.

Richard pondered it for a moment, then said, 'I can understand that. He's probably afraid for you, a little jealous and full of admiration.'

She was taller than Richard by half an inch, but then she had got used to being a thread's width under six feet in China, with a mane of flaming red 'foreign devil' hair. Most of the time her hair fell over her face because her head was constantly lowered to talk to people. The prominent chin, cheekbones and forehead were all very much Sally, and her nose was perhaps her most striking feature, thin-boned, curving delicately and wider at the nostrils. Best of all was the skin. Sally had beautiful skin, but it was the skin of a redhead which, when Richard painted her, had taken days to get right with oils.

Her awkwardness – all arms and legs, her mother had said – would be all right if she were a long-maned racehorse. But she did have something of a wild mare about her, as her mother would remind her when her father was giving her a hard time. Her pointed chin gave her an air of determination which put a lot of men off. Nowadays, anything could be seen as a threat, even a decent chin.

Richard had come along after a period of celibacy. Eighteen months? Two years? She didn't like to count. She had been in Beijing giving a talk on the tomb. Richard was a diplomat working in the American Embassy. They'd got on well from the start, moved easily around each other, had interests in common as well as separate ones. Richard was interested in what Sally had to say about archaeology, and he taught Sally about music. He had an amazing collection and was switching from vinyl to compact disc. She helped him catalogue his collection and taught him about filing for an archive. It was quiet, homely and fun, the sort of thing that dating agencies put five stars next to.

She had let him end the celibacy. It wasn't frightening or a game-play, or savage ten-times-a-night stuff. It was just very nice, and she wanted more. After a time, Paul had accepted

Richard and become part of their relationship, and one evening, when Richard had asked, she told him about Bill Cage.

'How does that saying go? Good men do things for you, bad men do things to you,' she'd said. 'I guess I let him do a lot of things to me which didn't turn out so well.'

'But he gave you Paul,' said Richard.

And, as ever, that pulled Sally back together. However dreadful Bill Cage had been, he had helped her produce the most gorgeous little boy. Her thoughts had tumbled round in a cycle, as they always did when it came to Cage and Paul and her, and she wondered if she hadn't been too hard on Cage. Then she ejected those thoughts and closed off her mind. Paul was half Cage and half her, and she shuddered when she thought how she had almost had an abortion. When love goes wrong, you come down hard. It's nature's way of sorting things out.

Now she was going to build a life with Richard, a guy who realised people needed plans, needed kindness, needed humour, needed all those things to keep going in life.

She called Richard and left a message on his answer machine at work. Called him at home, left another message. It cost her a fortune long distance from Xian in central China to New York on the US east coast but it made her feel good to know there was someone waiting for her – that is, apart from Jack Messent and his money men.

On the second try, she managed to get through to Jeff Binsky, her old China tutor. The first time there had been an answer machine, so she left a message to say she would be in New York. But she knew he was a sly recluse and was probably in and would pick up the phone if she begged. She began her second message: 'Jeff, I know you're there. Come on, Jeff, take your head out of your book and come talk to me . . .'

Her wheedling worked. Binsky picked up the phone. 'Now tell me, Sally, exactly when will you be in this city?'

'The day after tomorrow. In the evening. Are you free?'

'You have other appointments, I presume.' His black terrier, Manchu, yapped in the background. 'You are not coming to America just to see your ageing tutor.'

Sally laughed. 'No. I have a meeting with Jack Messent and the trustees.'

'Then come see me after your meeting. Not before. You can tell me about it. And, if you will, there's a little something I would like you to do for me . . .'

Chapter Three

The Archaeological Institute of America had booked Sally a hotel, but she had not planned to stay there. The idea had been to be with Richard in his split-level apartment on 89th Street between Central Park and Columbus. Except there was no answer from his home or office. She even got a cab to pass by the apartment and saw that the lights were off, no one at home. So she took the hotel room, feeling miserable. She called, got the answer machine again and said, 'Richard, where the hell are you? If you haven't got any messages before, I'm in New York.'

To console herself, she called Cait, but had to leave another message. 'Hi, Cait, it's Sal. I'm in town for a couple of nights. Any chance of meeting up tomorrow evening?' She would like to have seen Helen, too. But Helen had her hands full with kids and there wouldn't be time. And Mom was away in Southampton, she'd catch up on another trip.

Fuck Richard, she told herself, thinking that that was just what she wanted to do. If Richard turned up, she would drop everything; any healthy heterosexual female archaeologist on a visit to the real world from China would do the same. In the event, she slept alone and fitfully, in an impersonal, stuffy hotel room where the heater rumbled through the night like an old fishing trawler.

Next morning, as she made her way to the meeting, the weather had become ferocious, so the streets were still in darkness. It was eight in the morning and the cabs had gone to ground. Rain began to fall in heavy drops, then tiny white bits of hail which covered the ground like snow. On came headlights,

18

up went umbrellas, and Sally stumbled on with the cold cutting through her face, eyes watering with the wind and her spine and shoulders chilled to the marrow.

Shortly after nine, she walked into the foyer of the American Institute of Archaeology with her beige suede trouser suit blotched with dark patches of rain and water dripping off her soaking coat. Her pass had expired and she had to be escorted upstairs by a security guard.

The lift was taking so long coming that she asked the guard, 'Jerry, you heard of the terracotta warriors?'

'Nope,' he said stolidly.

'What do you know about China?'

'Communism. I hear there are a billion communists in China.' The lift arrived and Jerry stabbed the button for the tenth floor.

'Anything else?' Sally went on.

Jerry was unsettled. 'Mao. He was the dictator there. But he's dead now, I believe.'

'He sure is,' she murmured. The elevator slowed and stopped. 'I expect most people don't think much about China, do they?'

'It is far away, ma'am.'

The institute's offices were decked out with vases and masks, aerial photographs, blown-up maps and portraits of distinguished past members. Sally wasn't among them yet. OK, she was distinguished, but not quite distinguished enough. With the money they spent on the offices, she thought caustically, they could have sent twenty Sallys out to China.

Messent bumbled towards her, his face full of panic. It didn't worry Sally. Jack would panic trying to get a table in a diner.

Sally and Jack went back a long way. He had been a listening ear when she and Bill Cage were living in New York and Paul had just been born. And he had helped her through her messy split, getting her to China with Paul, as far away from Cage as she could get. And Sally had been on the end of the phone for him, through hours of his ramblings about his drink problem, his wife's infidelities, his stalled career. She never could work out how he made it to finance director.

'Hi, Jack,' she greeted him. 'Have I got a surprise for you!'

'I got your fax. I hope it's been worth it.'

'Didn't you trust your golden girl? I got some great shots.'

He seemed more nervous than ever, talked in a hushed whisper as if the world was listening. 'Better show me this stuff before we go in.'

She rested her briefcase on the window ledge by the elevator, unzipped it and pulled out two large brown envelopes. 'I made you copies,' she said. 'You haven't told them why I'm here, have you?'

Messent shook his head. 'I told them you were in town for family reasons. They think we're saving money by bringing the annual assessment meeting forward.'

'Do they know about the probe?'

'Not yet.'

She let Messent look at the images without comment, enjoying the smile that spread across his face, like a father with the first snap of his kid. She liked Messent's whistle through his teeth and the way he jerked his head round to check no one was looking over their shoulders.

'Before I asked for the probe, I took echo soundings until I identified a hollow area close to the surface,' she explained. 'I took the main tourist path up from the east, cut off to the south until I was over the area we think covers the mausoleum. Then I used the electrical resistivity prod and came up with a more defined area, which was almost certainly a burial chamber. That's your second set of images. Luckily, it's a damp winter and I'm working through clay. But those nights up there were freezing, Jack, I tell you. And I witnessed a shoot-out the other morning.'

Messent looked up. 'Sal, you be careful. Who's shooting who?'

'The police caught a gang trying to steal the warriors and sell them.'

Messent nodded. 'You be careful,' he said again, fingering each photograph delicately at the edges. 'And don't mention that in the meeting. It'll give them another excuse to pull you out.'

'Pull me out? What are you talking about?'

'Just keep cool, Sal. Nothing's been decided yet. It's just that

20

they don't think they've seen any results yet.'

'Don't you call this a result?' Sally demanded, leaning across Messent to tap the picture he was holding. Impatiently, she pulled out another one. 'See. I blew this one up. That, Jack Messent, is a kneeling crossbow warrior. A little crushed, sure, but that's how the terracotta warrior army is these days. A kneeling crossbow warrior,' she repeated. Out came another photograph. 'Look at this, Jack. Virtually intact. The wheel of a chariot. OK, so this chamber is on the outer circle of the main mausoleum, and it's got the same stuff in it as we've already found down in the three pits—'

'Don't say it like that,' said Messent.

'Like what?'

'You're not dealing with archaeologists, Sal. You're dealing with our sponsors. These are business types. Don't say it's the same stuff. You have to have different stuff, new stuff. Or they won't understand it. Do you have new stuff?'

'Sure,' said Sally breezily, then stopped herself. She didn't want to tell anyone about it yet, not even Jack. 'But I'm not sure what it is yet. As soon as I've worked it out, you'll see it. Jack, they certainly are not going to close me down now.'

Just as Messent was shaking his head at Sally's combative tone, the elevator doors opened. He stuffed the photos into the envelope and handed it back to Sally.

'Listen, Sal,' he said hurriedly. 'I have to tell you, this isn't going to be any kind of a pushover.' Then he stepped forward, adjusting his tie, smile obsequious, hand outstretched. His voice changed as they moved towards the meeting room.

'Well, this is Dr Sally Parsons . . . Sally, I'm not sure you've met . . .'

And she hadn't. Damn him! There were three of them, two men and a woman, unfamiliar faces. Why was Jack just marching her in there without briefing her?

The conference room was huge and they gathered down at one end of the table. Sally ended up next to a tall barrel-chested man, well into his fifties, named Craig Eliot, 'With one "l" and one "t",' he insisted as he shook Sally's hand. 'I'm from Commerce Bank. We're re-evaluating our cultural donation strategy.' He pulled a chair out for her. 'Your file says your first name is Sarah, not Sally. Is that correct?' said Eliot as they sat down.

'Sure is,' said Sally, watching Eliot make a note. 'Dad called me Sally from the moment I can remember.' Eliot glanced across at her. Nothing in his expression indicated he wanted the ice to break between them. So Sally played the game. 'Dad said I was a little girl who had too much fun to run with the name Sarah. What do you think, Mr Eliot? Was he right?'

'I think that is a family matter,' replied Eliot, retreating back into his notepad.

The woman took a seat opposite Sally, arranged her papers, then leaned across the table, her handshake firm, masculine even, but soft compared to the callused and scarred skin of Sally's own hands.

'Dr Parsons, I'm Hazel Watson from the State Department. It's an honour to meet such a legend in her field.' She was a chic, middle-aged brunette, competitive with the men around her. She tapped her index finger on her red clipboard as she spoke, showing off a long, glossy maroon fingernail.

'State Department?' queried Sally, eyeing Messent.

'Sure. Foreign policy works in a strange way. With President Gorbachev's reforms in the Soviet Union, we're reviewing all elements of our relationship with China. You're working on a very high-profile and sensitive project.' She tried a winning smile. 'It has nothing to do with money. That's these guys' department. I have more of a sitting-in role.'

Next to Hazel Watson was a grubby little man in a crumpled brown suit, with a button missing from his shirt. He said cordially, 'Simon Beard, trustees' representative.'

'What happened to Peter Ormond?' said Sally, referring to the trustees' chairman whom she usually dealt with. She had never heard of Simon Beard.

'I'm standing in for Peter,' he said. He made a note, then looked up with a smile. 'Hope they fixed you up with a hotel and everything.'

'Sure. Great. It's fine,' lied Sally. At least they didn't ask about Richard.

Messent sat at the end, next to Beard, his shoulders slumped and his podgy face red with enough broken blood vessels to map central China.

Sally flipped her hair back as if she was swatting a wasp, put her elbows on the table and rested her chin on cupped hands. 'I'm ready,' she said lightly.

She thought it would be the trustees' representative, Beard, who spoke first but Craig Eliot took the cue.

'Dr Parsons, as with most things in business, this is about money,' he said. 'We know the annual review isn't due yet, but I have to warn you the news isn't good. Our charitable donations are finite and, unless you have something remarkable to report, a decision has been taken to end the funding for your work with the terracotta warriors in China at the end of this review year in May. You've been in China more than three years now, and all of us here appreciate what you have done out there.'

'You've been remarkable, Sal,' muttered Messent.

'But the harsh truth is that your access is limited,' continued Beard. 'The Chinese block most of your attempts at real excavation. So we feel the money would be better spent elsewhere.'

'Like where? Where else would be a better place to spend my paltry salary?' Sally pushed out her chair and crossed her legs. Watch it, she chided herself silently. Don't antagonise them just yet.

'North Africa. We're hoping for an agreement with the Sudan,' said Beard.

'The East Germans are there. You wouldn't get near anything interesting.'

'Or Latin America,' interjected Messent. 'You have to admit we haven't even scratched the surface there.'

Sally glowered at him. Jack might have his own job to protect but he was getting close to betraying their friendship. 'You know how much I cost? I doubt my monthly salary even matches what this meeting cost to set up. I live in a two-bedroom apartment. The rent's about as much as a cab fare across Manhattan. Jack and I cut a deal so that I pay half of Paul's school fees. Paul's my son,' she added quickly, smiling at Watson, who looked like the type of woman who would put on plastic gloves to change a diaper. 'I get an economy fare back home once a year. That's

23

less than a thousand dollars. My medical insurance is what it would be here. What I'm saying is that my little project in China doesn't exactly break the bank.'

'Dr Parsons,' said Beard, 'perhaps you could tell us, in your own words, exactly what you think in reality you would be able to achieve over the next year, if funding were to continue.'

This was the moment she had been waiting for. 'The terracotta warrior army was discovered by peasant farmers fifteen years ago, just outside of Xian in central China. The warrior army is a mile across fields from Qin Shi Huang's mausoleum. The whole area is an incredible site, more than two thousand years old and simply one of the most remarkable archaeological discoveries ever made. I work in all three pits, and we estimate there are some eight thousand warriors, made up of archers, kneeling and standing, warriors in battle robes, cavalrymen and horses. No two are the same; every one of them is unique. And I'm the only American allowed to work there.'

'I'm sorry to interrupt,' said Eliot, 'but I'm not clear how this contributes to the lives of the American people.'

'Excuse me?'

'The lives of the American people,' Eliot repeated. 'The brief from my board of directors is to allocate funding according to the contribution it can make to American cultural life.'

'America hadn't been discovered in the year two hundred and ten BC,' said Sally. Immediately, she checked herself. She was being too sarcastic.

'Yes, we're aware of that,' said Beard, as if he had read her thoughts.

She gave a small, nervous laugh. 'I'm not sure if I get this. You are suggesting that the United States pulls out of work on the greatest archaeological discovery this century. I can't believe I'm hearing this. Listen.' She leaned forward, her face alight with passion. 'The terracotta army was built to protect the tomb of the Emperor Qin Shi Huang, the man who first unified China. We are learning so much about the skills of that era. The workmanship is truly remarkable. For example, I've been helping to restore one of the Emperor's chariots, and we found they even put on an umbrella holder, with a lock and key for keeping

24

it in place. Before working on the warriors we would never have imagined such intricate engineering and science existed that long ago.'

'An umbrella holder,' Eliot snorted. 'Three and a half years, and you give us an umbrella holder.'

'I think there's been a bit more achievement than that, Craig,' said Beard. He looked at Sally. In another place, at another time, his could have been a kindly face.

'Qin was like Napoleon,' she said.

'Or George Washington,' offered Messent.

'Or Adolf Hitler,' said Eliot. 'Didn't Hitler try to unify Europe?'

Sally unfolded her arms, spread her hands flat out on the table and stared at Eliot. 'Qin built the Great Wall. You must have heard of the Great Wall, Mr Eliot. It's the wall you can see from the moon.' She didn't have a notepad, like the others, not even a pen to fiddle with, so she eyeballed Craig Eliot, smiling and glaring at the same time. Since he didn't react straightaway, she tossed back her head so that her hair bounced and fell back again on her shoulders.

By the age of thirty-three, Sally had learnt that if ever she needed the playing field levelled, she could at least take advantage of a man's testosterone. Eliot looked like the sort of guy who didn't care how much grey matter a woman had between her ears, provided her legs were long enough and her breasts round enough.

'I think Craig is trying to identify the pay-off,' said Beard.

'The what?'

'Yes.' Eliot referred to his notes. 'You have been out there for three and a half years and there's nothing in the file to say that you have given us any more than we would have got in our normal cultural exchanges with the Chinese.'

Sally glanced at Messent, looking for support, but he gave none. Eliot tapped his pen on the table, making a sound like a slow, dripping tap.

Watson spoke for the first time, slapping her hand lightly on the table. 'Come on, guys. Anyone would think we were talking about the end of the world. Let's all loosen up. Dr Parsons has been doing a great job. We all know that, and deep down I expect we're all a little jealous of her achievements.'

'Thank you,' said Sally. She hooked her hair behind her ear. 'You know, if we pull out we'll lose our toehold on China's archaeological heritage – to the Soviets.'

'Or the French, the Germans, the Japanese,' said Eliot. 'I don't find that convincing.'

'When Gorbachev visits, the Soviets are going to sign a cultural exchange deal, just like the one we have,' said Sally.

'Nixon signed ours,' said Eliot, uninterested.

'Gorbachev's signing theirs,' snapped Sally. 'He's going to Xian in May.'

'I didn't even know that Gorbachev was going to China,' said Beard. 'Shows how deep my head is in the sand.'

'The announcement's due on February third,' said Watson.

Sally nodded. 'He's visiting the terracotta army. Climbing to the top of the tomb.'

Watson glanced sternly towards Sally, unhappy that she knew, but said nothing.

'I can't see how it matters what Gorbachev does in Xian,' said Eliot. 'The Soviets don't have the excavation technology we have. There's no way they can compete.'

'They can if we're not there,' retorted Sally.

'Simon,' said Watson, 'what would happen, in the archaeological world, if the Chinese suddenly opened up this tomb for anyone who wanted to excavate?'

'Putting my Egypt bias aside, I would say it would be one of the biggest archaeological developments in the last half century, certainly in my career.'

'It would dwarf the discoveries of Tutankhamen,' said Sally. 'I don't get a sense you understand anything about Qin Shi Huang. The only thing we know about this tomb is what is written in a book called the *Shi Ji*, the Records of the Grand Historian. Imagine if John Kennedy had been buried in a mausoleum decorated with all the trappings of America in the early sixties – nuclear missiles, Marilyn Monroe, Jackie, the Vietnam War, the glamour of Washington's Camelot – and two thousand years later you had a chance to dig it up and find out exactly what made the most powerful nation on earth tick. If you had the chance to be the first person to get a look at it, would you just throw it away?'

Beard chuckled. 'A far-fetched but interesting parallel.'

Sally lifted her briefcase onto the table. 'If we stay with it, we could have the first bite. Don't you guys get that?' She pulled out the pictures and passed them around, in no particular order. Eliot shuffled through them sceptically and pushed them across the table.

Sally kept talking. 'Over the time I've been in China, I've been able to build up influential contacts and I managed to get permission—'

'Can you elaborate on your contacts?' Hazel Watson interrupted.

Sally flinched. She didn't want to. She damned herself for boasting about it. 'There's a guy who works in the Shaanxi provincial government. He really wants to—'

'Name?'

'Sorry?'

'The name of this man.'

'Li Yi. At least that's what's on his business card.'

Watson wrote it down. 'Go on. You were saying.'

'Excuse me?' said Sally hesitantly, wondering why Watson was suddenly so interested and aggressive.

'You were saying who he was.'

Sally checked her temper. 'Li Yi works for the Shaanxi provincial government. He's involved in bringing in foreign investment, and he's very keen that we get into the tomb so that it'll become a world-famous tourist site. That's how he managed to get me permission to carry out a kind of keyhole endoscopic photographic survey inside one of the burial chambers around the mausoleum. He hopes that he might be able to persuade the government to allow a full-scale excavation.' She stared at Watson and couldn't help herself. 'Is that all right, Hazel, or do you need more? He's happily married with two children, speaks fluent English and German, and I believe some of his family even live here in New York.'

'And he's your main contact?' asked Watson.

'Correct,' said Sally with a note of finality. She leant across and pointed at the picture Eliot was holding. 'See this, Mr Eliot?' She looked from Eliot to Watson. 'This is a facial ornament for a horse. And here, lower down, this heart-shaped shield – it's tiny, you can barely see it – this could be from the girth worn round a horse's belly.'

'This is all very interesting,' said Watson dismissively. 'Why don't you leave these with us and we'll be in touch.'

'I'm sorry?'

'Leave these with us, we'll discuss them and get back to you,' repeated Watson.

Sally shook her head. 'But you're not qualified. None of you is an expert on Chinese history. You have no idea what they could mean.'

'With all due respect, Dr Parsons . . .' began Beard.

Sally drew out another photograph. 'Do any of you know about the machine-tooling of mixed metals during the rule of Qin Shi Huang?'

'Sal, please,' Messent pleaded.

Sally put the photograph in the middle of the table. She might have looked tough and uncompromising, but she knew if she didn't keep going she would just burst into tears. After all the effort, the nights on the tomb, they were going to take her pictures and let her know. 'This is a thirty-inch dagger blade. This kind of metal engineering was not seen in the West for another thirteen hundred years—'

'Sal,' tried Messent again, 'we're all on tight schedules. We do need time to go over it. We'll be in touch.'

'But you need me to explain what they mean,' pressed Sally. 'No one – let me stress this, no one – has yet been inside this tomb. It is the great unknown of the archaeological world.'

'You've put your point of view most eloquently, Dr Parsons,' said Watson. 'Now, if you'll excuse us . . .'

Calming herself, Sally called Cait from the foyer. Cait was a child psychologist, and sounded as if she was between clinics. 'Can you hold all my calls for a couple of minutes?' Sally overheard her saying, then a door closed and the noise from the children stopped.

'I'm so glad you called,' Cait said. 'Listen, Bill's been in touch with me. And before you say anything, he hasn't broken any court order because, technically speaking, although I'm your sister, I'm also a third party and that's what the judge said – he must contact you only through a third party.'

'What does he want?'

'He wants . . .' Cait hesitated. 'Now, you're not going to get angry or unreasonable?'

'No. I'm fine. Just go ahead.'

'He wants to see you.'

'Well, I don't want to see him.' Just as everything seemed to be going right, some demon was trying to screw up her professional and personal life all at once. Upstairs they were plotting against her and the thought of seeing Bill Cage again filled her with dread.

'Let's meet at six,' said Cait. 'Dad's in town. He might drop by as well.'

Chapter Four

Bill Cage took a table right at the end of the narrow coffee shop, his view of the building on the corner of Grand and Lafayette obscured only by a pole of scaffolding.

Across the road was the Sun Mei Food Market, the name emblazoned in red on a bright yellow sign. Next door to that was the Foo Wah Bakery, and beyond that Chinese figures, wearing hooded anoraks, lined up at a fruit stall. It was cold outside. Well below zero.

Cage was two blocks across the old frontier between China-town and Little Italy. Except everything around here was Chinese and not Italian, which would explain why the Italians were so pissed off. He had his eyes on the big windows, blue hoarding and fire escapes of the block across the road, and he tried to order a coffee just as a bell rang behind the counter.

'Anton, I hear you, OK?' shouted the waitress. 'Please, give me a break and get me down two over easy with toast.' Cage reckoned she was early forties, Filipina, which made her kind of Latin-Chinese. 'You want breakfast?' she yelled across at him.

'Black coffee,' said Cage.

'Black coffee I can do.' She walked over with the pot and poured it for him, eyeing him strangely, not quite sure what he was.

Cage didn't enlighten her. 'Thanks,' he said, running his hand across the front page of the *New York Times* to flatten it.

A new customer came in and diverted her attention. 'Oh my God, Jamie,' she said, embracing him. 'It's been so long. Where have you been?'

Cage glanced up as a window-cleaning dock was lowered down the side of the building opposite, settling halfway between the third and fourth floors. Lined up on the street outside was a Mercedes van marked up as a carpet-cleaning company, then two unmarked cars, an Oldsmobile and an old Ford Pinto. He identified five watchers on foot: a guy in a grey Italian suit; a girl in jeans; a couple necking; and a motorcycle dispatch rider. Lastly, a FedEx van drew up, and he wondered what FedEx would have thought about that. It wasn't the way he would have done it, but then this wasn't his operation.

Cage glanced across at the Chevrolet Suburban Discoverer parked next to the ticket booth at the Early Bird Parking Ground. It had been there two days now, with just two guys watching it from the second floor of the Sun Yee Beauty Salon, Hair, Nail and Sun Care.

The apartment block was clean but the vehicle was as dirty as hell. One thing Cage knew about was dirty cars. He could spot them, spot the people looking after them, and he was looking at one right now. What he wasn't sure about was if the morning would end up going his way.

It had started before six with a phone call which woke Cage, then a meeting in the office of Robert H. Leonard, the willowy black agent who was handling Cage while he settled in.

'She kept a capsule of cyanide up her ass, and she chewed it this morning, an' now our stool pigeon's dead and we're short of staff,' Leonard began. He tapped his pencil on the open page of his crossword book, leaning hard back in his chair and looking at Cage for answers.

'And you want me to do what?' Cage asked.

Leonard pushed the crossword book to one side and pulled a file off his in tray. 'This is your file, Captain Cage. I don't know you well, don't know why the hell you've been given to us, but in your file it says you came close to infiltrating the Teochiu Triads back in nineteen eighty-four. Those are the guys who run most of the dope from the Golden Triangle, right? And it seems they're a lot smarter than the Mafia families because they've developed a new kind of heroin, a type which gets round the needles and the AIDS scare, because the addicts get the same rush smoking it as injecting it. In the past two years the Chinese share of the New York heroin market is eighty per cent and rising.' Leonard slapped his hand down on the file, brought out a photograph of a New York cop and handed it to Cage.

'Captain Al Freni. Used to work for the mob. Now defected to the Teochiu. He's about to earn his spurs by taking delivery of a shipment of heroin at an apartment on the corner of Grand and Lafayette. His life expectancy anywhere isn't considered high, but for this morning he's our man.' More photographs came out and a map of Manhattan. 'Our stool pigeon was meant to have been in this coffee shop. Freni was to have come in, dropped a bunch of keys into her pocket. She was to head up and open up the apartment. Once we find the dope, we pick up Freni.'

'Why'd she do it?' said Cage.

'She was a mule. A junky. She was gang raped by the goons up on the Burma border. Got HIV. Got pregnant. You wouldn't want to hear her story. But if it's motive you're looking for, it wasn't missing in her.'

'You believe that?'

'You know something I don't know, Cage, tell me straight off. Don't jerk around asking questions.'

'They wouldn't give her a key. They wouldn't give her the job,' Cage said softly.

Leonard whistled through his teeth and looked at his watch. 'Don't think we've got time to contradict the thinking of a basket full of US law enforcement agencies. What I need is not new theories but a new stool pigeon.'

'Does Freni know her?'

'No. But he knows it'll be a Chinese woman. We've got no female Chinese undercover agents available, no one who speaks Chinese.'

'I'll do it,' said Cage.

Leonard shot Cage a bad look. 'I said don't jerk me around. You mix with Chinese. Do you know anyone you can pick up the phone and—'

'I'll do it,' Cage said again.

'She's a woman, for Christ's sake. You gonna dress as a woman?'

Cage shook his head. 'No, but if I dress as a man dressed as a woman, it'll be fine.'

So he had put on a blue raincoat over navy blue trousers and a wig of dark hair which tumbled to his shoulders. He was thin and tall, and his Chinese features gave him elegance and grace. He lightly applied lipstick, smearing it a bit to give a look of carelessness, dulled his eye colour with contact lenses and paled his skin with a thin layer of make-up.

The van window went down and a cigarette was flipped out, still burning, leaving a trail of sparks. The driver's fingers tapped the wheel as he looked across to the coffee shop. Cage spotted the radio scanner fixed above the windscreen, tiny green lights flashing.

Two more vans drew up. One was marked up with the logo of a plumbing company. The other was telephone. Three vans in all now. The guy in the suit ran up the steps into the block. The motorcyclist kick-started the machine. The back door handle on the plumber's van started to move.

Cage saw Freni walk into the coffee shop just as a shot was fired across the street and two cops ran over. A woman next to the window knocked over her cappuccino and stood up, screaming. A cop was outside the coffee shop door, his back to the glass, a black shape, bulging with a Kevlar vest, yelling at people to stay away.

Cage was up, clustering with the other customers, keeping an eye on Freni. Then he saw Leonard, wearing a long, expensive, brown raincoat, buttoned once in the middle. He had one hand inside the coat, making Cage wonder if he was carrying.

Freni came up next to Cage and dropped a package into his pocket, heavier than a bunch of keys. He moved away, pushed through the door and brushed by the cop like he owned him. Cage put his hand in and felt a ring with just two keys on it, then – shit – a piece. He wrapped his hand round it, touching the trigger guard, the snub barrel, checking the safety without thinking.

Leonard was still out there, ignoring Freni.

The cop blocking the doorway turned with a weapon.

Another cop ran across the road and pushed straight through the door into the coffee shop. Cage knew they were coming for him. You get a sense about these things. He brought the pistol out of his pocket and smashed it into the cop's face. Cage dropped the piece, a thud on the floor, and hurled himself among the civilians. Another cop had his weapon raised but couldn't do anything. Couldn't shoot Cage among the customers. Three cops moved in from across the street towards the coffee shop.

The only way out was through them. The customers cleared a path for him, opening a channel. Fear does that to people. Being nice and terrified at the same time. Shoulder turned. Head down. Arms punching. Screaming too, just like everyone else. Cage ran at the cops like a madman, smashed straight through them, taking them by surprise. Sirens everywhere.

Another shot from somewhere. Cage rolled. Saw feet. Policemen's boots. Then the double crack of a police pistol.

Leonard was down. He fell elegantly, his raincoat flapping out like a parachute just landed. Hand flat to break the fall, but no strength, so the wrist went back on itself. Bystanders stepped back, hands to mouth. No one helped him. They were frozen in horror. They'd never seen someone shot before; didn't realise they're still human till they're dead.

Cage got to his feet. He couldn't see how bad Leonard was hit. But they had ambulances and hospitals in New York. Leonard would be fine. Or dead. Cage couldn't change it either way. He had to keep moving.

A cop lunged at him, and Cage levelled him, then headed towards the crowd so they couldn't shoot without risking an innocent. A police car, siren wailing, headed straight for him, and Cage ran, still moving like a drag queen, forgetting it didn't matter any more. He was fifty yards getting out of range. Racing left, he looked for a quieter sidewalk.

Cars parked both sides. Sidewalk narrow. A woman, fur coat and walking stick. Another innocent. Mother with a pushchair. Cage kept going, expecting a bullet. Turned right into a wider road. He tore off the wig, threw off the coat, dumped the handbag, leaving a trail like a hooker on a whorehouse floor.

While running, he pulled out glasses and put them on, then switched to the spring of a man – his limbs loosened up, no more sway. Glancing over his shoulder, he saw nothing. They had fifty cops back there and not one was chasing.

He kept going west along Broome Street, then cut down Watts until he got to the Hudson River where he slowed to a walk, north along West Street, a big, wide dangerous road. But Cage was alone, a man again. When he knew for sure they weren't following him, he hailed a cab.

He got out way uptown, past West 80th, waited ninety minutes as arranged with Leonard, then called the number he'd given him.

'Cage, well done, man,' Leonard answered, like nothing had happened. 'Everything went fine. Just fine.'

'Nothing went fine,' said Cage.

'We got him cold, man. We've got Freni and a whole lot more with him.'

'You're not shot?' Cage's voice had an edge to it, more anger than curiosity.

Leonard laughed. 'Me, man? Agent Robert H. Leonard? Shot? Never. But they think I'm shot. Shot with a thirty-eight, and a bent cop shooting a straight cop is a big offence, so they're singing like fucking canaries.'

Freni was a bulldog of a man whose beat covered the area of Little Italy just north of Canal Street.

An FBI agent called Harvill conducted the interview. Leonard's blood-stained raincoat was draped over the back of a chair next to him. Cage, Leonard and other agents watched from another room. Like Leonard had predicted, Freni was talking.

'The Chinks are trying to take on the families. I plead with you guys, don't be brain dead over this. You just don't understand what happens when you take on the families. Most of the cops in Little Italy have an arrangement.'

'Then why don't you tell us how it is, Captain Freni.'

'C'mon, don't look so fucking surprised. They've had an arrangement with the families since before Prohibition, and they don't want to work for any fucking Chinks. So I'm telling you, you don't straighten this out, there won't be a fucking NYPD any more.'

'Why not, Captain?' asked Harvill coolly. 'Perhaps you could explain it to me in the most simple terms possible.'

'The Chinks, they run their restaurants, they pay their taxes, like they're fucking angels. The Chinks are good at that, and you guys, fucking FBI, don't even know what's going on.'

'That's why we're asking for your input,' said Harvill.

'I've told Castello he has to get tough with the slant-eyes or they'll take over the whole of fucking New York. Fucking world more like, if we don't watch them. There's a billion of them out there, and what I tell the Castellos, 'cause it's their ground they're moving into, I tell them to go into one of their restaurants and push their skinny fucking asses into their chairs, pick up a set of fucking chopsticks and stick them in their eyes and say, you little cock-sucking communist piece of yellow shit, you stay in your rice paddy and keep outta my olive grove. You savvy? That's what I tell them, 'cause there's no fucking way the New York Police Department can handle a turf war between the Chinks and the Italians.'

'And what did Castello say?'

Freni blinked hard, shutting his eyes and screwing up his face, as if he hadn't expected the question. When he finally answered, he was slower, his voice softer. 'Castello is a cautious man. He likes to think he's a modern man but he doesn't understand that sometimes you have to bang heads in the old-fashioned way.'

Harvill handed a cigarette to Freni who let Harvill light it for him. 'Don't get me wrong. I want to get rid of organised crime just like the next cop. It's a fucking cancer. But we know the families. They're Americans. We don't know the slant-eyes. That's what makes them so fucking dangerous. They have Chinatown. But they want more. The only way to do it is say, 'Outta my fucking olive grove! You savvy?' Freni let out a throaty, deep laugh and jabbed the air with imaginary chopsticks.

'And that's what you were doing, was it, Captain?'

'That is exactly what I was doing. I was going to bust their heroin racket so hard they would never think of crossing the line again. And it was working until you mother-fuckers turned up.'

Leonard was at his desk working on the book of crossword puzzles when Cage walked in, just like he was that morning. Leonard's face appeared to have escaped the tumult of the world. He was a tall, strong man, yet he carried himself lightly. He muttered about the crossword clues while Cage sat on the other side of his desk.

'The car's dirty,' began Cage.

'Maybe.'

'We should bring it in. Now.'

Leonard didn't answer. Cage was used to silences and he let it last more than three minutes before speaking again. 'We need to trace the stuff in the car back to China. It's the only way to end it.'

'China,' muttered Leonard, as if he was testing a word. 'You're serious?'

'Never been more serious in my life.'

Leonard dropped his pencil onto the desk, flipped the book to one side and leaned back. 'We're not allowed to operate in China.'

I wasn't allowed to operate in Cambodia, Angola, Sudan, thought Cage. But he held back. 'My kid's there,' said Cage softly, which interested Leonard, because he looked at Cage curiously, then flipped open his file which was still on his desk.

'Paul, right?'

Cage nodded.

'Seven years old, and you haven't seen him since he was three. His mother is—'

'Dr Sally Parsons, a distinguished archaeologist specialising in China,' interrupted Cage.

'What were you doing mixing with good people like that, Captain Cage?'

Cage stayed quiet and Leonard read in silence, turned the page, then stabbed his finger down. 'Got it. She took out a court order on you. You can't contact her or your son unless you do it through a third party. Preferably a lawyer, it says here. You did something so terrible to that woman, she had to do that? You beat her up? Committed marital rape . . .'

'We weren't married.'

'OK, you weren't married. But something happened that she took Paul and got about as far away from you as she could get. You didn't give a shit because you were busy working in all sorts of shit holes around the world. Operations are classified, so you bottle it all up. You slug your commanding officer and get thrown out of the Marine Corps. I'm the sucker in the FBI who has to take you on because you speak half a dozen Asian languages and can help us stop a war between the Chinese and the mob. And you did all right today, Cage, I'll give you that.'

'Thank you, sir.'

Slowly, Leonard turned a page. 'You're half Chinese and half white. Do you know which half?'

'My mother was Chinese.' What did he mean 'was'. She is Chinese. She's not dead until he knows she's dead.

'You've had some bad luck, haven't you, Cage? You were taken out of China as a baby, adopted, then your new mother turned into a drunk and your father's in jail.'

'Wall Street fraud,' said Cage.

'I think I remember the case. You should have run to us instead of the Marine Corps. You might not be in such a mess. How did you meet Dr Parsons?'

'Language school.' Knew it straight off that he wanted Sally. Never stopped knowing it.

'How come you were learning with her?'

'I volunteered. Evening classes. It was my own thing.'

'Before you joined the classified world?'

'Right.'

'So you dated. How long did you live with Dr Parsons for?'

Still living with her. Think of her every day. Cry myself into the abyss. 'We had an apartment on East Thirty-sixth from nineteen eighty-one to eighty-four.'

'Did she know your work?'

'No, sir.'

'Difficult, not being able to tell. What did you do? Drink?'

'Yes.'

'Beat her.'

'No.'

'Beat Paul?'

'No.' No, damn you, Leonard. Don't push it.

'Lie?'

'Of course.'

'Fuck around?'

'Not much.'

'Far away, alone . . .'

'A couple of times. It wasn't a habit. I loved Sally. She was smart enough to know I was lying.'

'But not smart enough to guess what you did for a living.'

'How would any woman feel if they knew the man they'd shacked up with went out and killed for a living?'

'So she didn't know, but she stopped trusting you and threw you out.'

'That's about it.'

'And it still hurts.'

'Not enough to cloud my judgement, sir.' The symptoms came and went: insomnia, drinking, fighting, short temper. Straight after Sally and Paul had gone, he had managed to bring himself back under control. But he was slipping again, becoming drawn and distant. He cried at movies too much and couldn't laugh any more. That was the real symptom – the inability to laugh. He had been born an outcast. He didn't want to live as one, and he yearned to belong.

Leonard dropped the cover of the file shut. 'Are you trying to screw me over, Cage? Are you trying to use this drugs shit to get to China and harass your girl again?'

'No, sir.'

'My advice is: hang out with us, don't push the walls, and in a couple of years your lapse of judgement in the Marine Corps will be forgotten. You have to learn to be a team player as well as a good player.'

'The Teochiu are serious,' said Cage. 'They'll fight the Italians here in New York. I don't know much about the NYPD, but Freni had a point.'

'Go on,' said Leonard.

'The Teochiu are disciplined,' said Cage. 'More disciplined than the Italians, the Koreans, the Vietnamese, the Turks or the Japanese. A Teochiu makes a move, it'll be on orders from above. There are no freelancers, no loose cannons. So if they do something to start a mob war in New York, it's going to come right from the top. The Teochiu are run from mainland China. You want to stop them, you have got to go there and get the evidence. For them, the US is the prize. It has the customers, the money, the politicians and the power. To break them, you have to send someone to the source, someone who can become one of them.'

'You did it before, right? But in the jungle with refiners and shippers.'

'This time it has to be higher.'

'And you reckon you can do that for us?' said Leonard. 'Just you against all those fucking Chinese? I can see where you're coming from, Cage. But I can't allow it.'

'Then I tender my resignation as of now.'

Leonard rolled his pencil back and forth across his desk. 'And you'll go straight back to a military prison. You're not thinking straight.'

'And once you accept my resignation,' Cage continued as though Leonard hadn't spoken, 'I will have the perfect cover.'

'Sally and Paul?'

'And the search for my natural parents.'

Leonard whistled through his teeth. 'I'll be honest, I can't read you, Cage.'

Cage didn't answer. He'd worked it through, measured Leonard, taken the risk.

Leonard's rolling of the pencil got slower and slower. 'Once I accept your resignation . . .' Leonard repeated.

'You will not be responsible for anything I do. Let me have access to your facilities here in the States. Give me a few weeks and I'll have a pretty good idea of who's running the show in China. After I've done all that, I can resign and catch the plane before the assault rap and law courts catch up with me. Once in China, I won't have any contact with the embassy. I'll keep in touch with you by calling you at home – whatever you like –

something untraceable. If it goes wrong, you never even knew it was happening.'

Leonard threw his head back, laughing. 'You, Cage, are one hell of a cool dude, but you don't have much of a life now, do you?'

'No, sir, I don't.'

Chapter Five

Jefferson Binsky opened the door, wearing green socks, brown cord trousers, a maroon sweater and a yellow polka-dot bow tie. 'Sally, my God, you're drenched!'

Sally's hair was dripping and, now she had stopped walking, the wind from Riverside Drive was cutting through her damp clothes like ice. He shook her hand. Binsky never kissed. 'Come in. Come in, and warm yourself,' he urged.

The room stretched from front to back, its walls heavy with books. As Binsky led Sally down to the kitchen in the basement, Manchu leapt up at her, yapping and nuzzling her upper thighs and buttocks.

'Manchu, get down!' yelled Binsky. Deferred by the damp, Manchu settled for sniffing at her ankles. 'Don't mind him, his bark is worse than his bite.'

'He hasn't bitten yet,' laughed Sally.

Binsky stopped on the staircase and turned to her, his bright blue eyes studying her. Then he led her round the final twist of the stairs to the kitchen, where a log fire was burning. Sally headed straight for it, squatting down, her hands held out to the flames.

'I can make you coffee, the finest and most expensive filtered coffee in the house,' offered Binsky. 'You can have tea, if you prefer. I also have red wine, which compared to the coffee is not so expensive, but neither is it cheap. Or you could have some malt whisky from the Scottish Highlands to warm your sodden soul. And – remiss of me not to have mentioned it at once – I do have a clean T-shirt upstairs and a sweater, if you want to change.'

'The fire's fine,' said Sally. 'But coffee and a glass of wine would be lovely.'

'You want both and you shall have both. All free of charge.'

The front window of the kitchen looked out onto a wall of concrete. Sally could see the ankles of pedestrians walking past on the street above them. Rain dripped down noisily onto the tiny yard, making Binsky's scruffy little kitchen seem even cosier. Two Chinese garden chairs stood in each corner by the window, and a cluster of mugs, wineglasses and plates, standing on a tea towel, had been pushed to one end of the dark wood dining table.

As her professor, all those years ago, Jefferson Binsky had fought hard for Sally and she had always been grateful to him. While her father carped and criticised, Binsky encouraged. When her father was difficult with money, Binsky argued for Sally to get a scholarship. And when Sally felt like quitting, Binsky enchanted her with stories of China. Without Binsky's enthusiasm, she might have ended up as a gofer in Peru or Egypt. He had steered her towards a place where she might shine. She had been aware of China as a country of dictators, communism, executions and labour camps. Like the rest of America, she disapproved. Yet Binsky accepted China as it was, neither praising the system nor damning it. His stories were of emperors and of the forging of a civilisation.

'So, did the meeting go well?' Binsky swivelled to address the dog. 'Manchu, get to your basket and shut up.' Manchu obeyed.

Sally frowned. 'Maybe. They say they'll let me know. I left them with the photographs I took inside the tomb—'

'My God, how did you manage to do that?'

Sally smiled. At least Jeff recognised her achievement. 'With a probe like the kind they've been using in Egypt. It's a camera on a rod, which you slide into the ground, and it takes pictures of whatever is inside. I now have the first pictures ever taken from inside the tomb of the Emperor Qin Shi Huang.'

'Ah, so my most intelligent and rebellious pupil pulled a rabbit out of her hat, did she? Sponsors love rabbits. They are naturally mean people who feel bad about themselves. Being generous alleviates some of their pain, but they have to be told why. Now, warm yourself, my dear, and tell me all about it.'

Sally found herself obeying as if she was back at college. She squatted close to the fire, rubbing her hands together.

'This probe, is it legal to use in China?' asked Binsky.

'Absolutely. It's called non-destructive exploration. It wasn't excavation. The local Shaanxi government issued me a permit to *explore*, so long as I don't disturb anything.'

Binsky walked round from the kitchen counter with a bottle of wine and a corkscrew. 'And how did you get the probe, firstly from your mendacious little institute, and secondly into China?'

'I have a contact in the Shaanxi government, a real wheeler-dealer called Li Yi, who really wants information about what's in the tomb. He thinks he could make a killing on tourism if it was opened. And I twisted Jack Messent's arm. Told him here was a chance to make or break his own career. By the way, I gave Jack your number in case there was news from the meeting.'

Binksy suddenly put the unopened wine bottle down on the table. 'I clean forgot. He's called already. Wants you to get back to him straightaway.'

Binsky fiddled in the kitchen while Sally talked to Messent, her face becoming darker by the second. She kept flicking her hair out of her eyes. 'So if it wasn't Eliot, who was it?' She closed her left hand into a fist, opened and closed it repeatedly. 'But Watson was on my side – our side . . . Two-faced bitch. How could she do that? . . . Jack, I only just got here. How long did they spend looking at those pictures? Thirty seconds? . . . What's the point of having a meeting with someone who can be overruled? . . . No, Jack, I'm not even thinking about pulling out. Paul's in the middle of his school year . . . No, I'm not accepting any goddamn deadlines. This is archaeology, not a TV quiz show.'

She hung up and looked at Binsky, furious. 'I lost,' she said.

'So I deduced.' He handed her the wine bottle. 'Open this, then we'll commiserate.'

Sally twisted the opener viciously into the cork. 'But why wouldn't they want me to keep working? I am the only person in the world to have taken those pictures.'

'You will probably find it is not all as it seems,' Binsky said seriously.

'And what's that supposed to mean?' The cork came out with a dull pop and Sally passed the bottle back to Binsky.

'China is a tricky beast, and you've done brilliantly to have got as far as you have. But there is always something more. This Watson, who is he?'

'He's a she. From the State Department.'

'Why the State Department?'

'She said my work could become so high profile that they wanted to keep an eye on it.'

'And the others?'

'The trustees' representative, a new guy called Simon Beard. He says he worked in Egypt, but I've never heard of him. The other was Craig Eliot from our main commercial sponsor. And Jack.'

'I'd put my money on Watson.' He poured wine into two glasses. 'Governments always have the key. We think it's not so, but it is . . .' Binsky's sentence faltered and Sally wasn't sure whether he had finished or not.

'And?' she prompted.

'If you're to win, you need something that Watson wants. I don't know, but I think this could be Jefferson Binsky's chance to help his star pupil just one more time.'

Just for a second before he looked away, Sally saw something troubling in his face. Fear.

Binsky stood up and walked round the small table, rearranging the chairs. He flicked specks of dust off the seats, then put away the crockery and cutlery, wiping each piece with a tea towel before slipping it into place. He poured the sludge from the coffee machine into the garbage bin underneath the sink, banging the filter against the side to get the coffee grains out. He was both meticulous and distracted – a knife ended up in the fork tray, a saucer on a pile of side plates. He didn't speak. Sally turned in her chair to watch the fire, putting on another log without asking, and Binsky didn't seem to notice. He left her and went upstairs. Sally got up and went and stood by the window looking out on the grey, rain-stained concrete.

A fizz of static from above her head startled her. It was followed by the clunking of metal, the click of a button, a cough and then a rasping voice projected with difficult breathing and awkward pacing.

Binsky came downstairs with a portable cassette player in one hand and a pile of papers in the others. He put them on the table, moving the wineglasses, as if not to have done so would have been disrespectful to the manuscript in his hand. From the middle of the pile, he pulled out a sheet of paper, marked with a yellow slip stuck to the top of the page. 'Read that,' he whispered. 'And listen.'

Sally sat down and heard a voice, listening to the voice, echoing as if it was being recorded in an empty room. She recognised the educated Chinese spoken by elite Communist Party officials in Beijing.

'You should see the dead horses too, draped in armour of jade, bronze and copper, fine leather bits in their teeth, the weapons of their riders fallen and scattered around them.'

Sally looked up at him sharply. Binsky stopped the tape. 'Six months ago, five cassettes arrived out of the blue, addressed to me and delivered by FedEx.' He leant over her and pulled out another marked page from the pile. 'I've spent months translating them and I'm convinced they're authentic. This is from another section altogether.' The faltering voice started up again and Sally read the page Binsky gave her.

'Immediately after death, Lenin was frozen, which had an adverse effect on the body tissues, causing patches of wrinkles, reddening of the skin, the nose darkening and the eyes sinking into their sockets. It was Vorobiov who created the balsamic liquid solution that eventually preserved Lenin's body. The formula was based on glycerine and potassium acetate and Vorobiov used it to preserve anatomical specimens at Kharkov University. I was asked to find the formula so that it could be used for Mao. But it was impossible.'

Sally dropped the sheet onto the table and pushed back her chair. 'All right, Jeff. Stop teasing. Frankly, I don't give a stuff about Lenin. But the other bit about the dead horses, that sounds to me like the *Shi Ji*.'

Binsky nodded and adjusted his bow tie. 'Yes, it is. But you must be patient. This is the voice of someone calling himself Zhang Ying. That's all I know about him. Except whoever sent this knew how to find me.' He screwed up his face like an embarrassed schoolboy and covered the sheets of translation with splayed hands, as if hiding treasures from a child. 'I'm telling you about it because I want to deliver it to someone in China, a man called Wu Tian. I think he can authenticate it.'

'Does he know Zhang Ying?' asked Sally cautiously.

Binsky didn't look up. His mind was elsewhere, his eyes unblinking, almost glazed with thought. The rhythmic sound of his index finger tapping down on the wad of paper suddenly gave the room an atmosphere of madness.

'I have no idea,' he said at last. 'It's thirty-two years since I last saw him.'

'A real good friend then,' she commented, then regretted her sarcasm.

'Yes. Yes, he was,' he said thoughtfully, still tapping the papers. With his other hand he undid his bow tie and tossed it onto the chair behind. Cold sadness creased his face.

'What's wrong?' Sally ventured.

His eyes were flat and grey. Without his colourful bow tie and in the erratic light of the room, he looked frail. She was seeing Binsky without his mask, and his expression was truly miserable.

'Do you get the sense that you will never belong to China?' he asked.

'I'm not sure I want to.'

'Perhaps not. Of course.' He seemed irritated by her reply. 'Perhaps you don't want to. You want to dig up the tomb and come back to New York to receive the accolades. I am different. I am a fool. I loved China. I loved her greyness, her untouchability, her self-containment, her brooding violence. I loved the contours of her land, her vicious rivers and the unyielding harshness of her countryside. I loved her because she was so different.' He slapped his right hand loudly down on the table. 'Do you know what I mean?'

'Not quite, I think,' she replied quietly. She shifted in the chair.

'All right. Think back to your work in Xian now. I wish I had been in China when the terracotta warrior army was discovered. It is an order of advanced military science. The battle formations guarding the tomb are the same ones Qin used to unify China.'

Binsky emphasised his points by drawing shapes on the surface of the table. 'Pit Two. You have a front line, four across and three deep, of robed warriors, interspersed with officers. Then comes another formation, again, four across and three deep, of warriors and soldiers. Then the chariots, each drawn by four horses. Remember the chariots and the horses? You can see the horses neighing, their reins hanging loose, the extraordinary sense of motion, how the sleeves of the warriors seem to flutter in the wind. And the strings of the archers' bows are taut, ready to fire. You must have worked in Pit Three.'

Sally reached into her bag and brought out a small trowel. She put it on the table. 'Here you are, Jeff. Complete with clay from Pit Three, my first excavation in China. I travel with it as my lucky charm.'

Binsky picked it up, scraped some orange-brown earth off with his fingernail, brought it up to his nose and sniffed it. 'The soil of China,' he whispered reverently and put the trowel down at the end of the table.

'Think of those formations of war chariots, eight deep and eight across, eight being the luckiest number in Chinese superstition. Then, north of them, three lines of war chariots, with armoured soldiers in between. And north again, three more lines of warriors, two formations of war chariots, and then, eight lines of cavalry horses. Tell me, what was in the mind of a man who would construct something on this scale to protect his own tomb? He was a man of supreme authority, we know. A man of vision. A man with the ability to plan. He was meticulous. Not only did he wage war and unify his territory, he also imposed uniform weights and measures and currency. He unified the written script of the Chinese language, doing it all by force and dictatorial authority. His laws were unforgiving, but just. He raised taxes like a bureaucrat and sought his own immortality like a god. He guarded the southern borders of his empire with three hundred thousand men, used half a million labourers to put up the Great Wall, another three quarters of a million to build your beloved tomb, and let tens of thousands die where they worked in order to get the job done.

'The hills trodden by tourists gazing at the Great Wall are filled with the crushed bones of his victims. Yet it is called a wonder of the world. But what did Qin care for the dead? Supreme rulers spare no thought for the sufferings of others. Theirs is a higher level of consciousness, which is why lesser mortals like you and me devote our lives to uncovering their greatness.'

'You know, Jeff, I think your devotion and mine are totally different.'

'How so, Sally? How so?'

'I love my work. The history. But you seem to love, I don't know, something deeper, something invisible, that I can't see.'

'Exactly. Exactly,' Binsky enthused. 'We are not just looking for the secret of how Qin forged the lethal metal of his swords, or how the engineering of his crossbows was thirteen hundred years ahead of any other weapon invented. We are seeking the very soul of a man who would build such a tomb, and whose beautiful concubines would robe themselves in glorious splendour, and let themselves be walled up to die of suffocation and starvation around his putrefying corpse. A man who would let his workers finish the final magnificent artefact, then have them herded in, with their horses, to die alongside the concubines. There is something about such figures which is magnetic.'

'So it's not just China, then.'

Binsky paused to sip his wine. 'What I'm talking about is something enormously powerful, the ability to create a cult, a movement, some kind of fanatical surge which changes the course of history.'

'Cult?'

'Yes. Hitler is an obvious example. Stalin, too. Pol Pot in Cambodia who wanted to recreate the Angkor empire. Marcos in the Philippines had some of it about him. But it's not just world leaders. Where was that place they all drank poison?'

'Jonestown. Nineteen seventy-nine.'

'Exactly. And who was responsible? Was it the man or his devotees? What are the conditions that cause people to follow one man so blindly?'

'But Jonestown was a one-off.'

Binsky shook his head. 'That's where you're wrong. It is in fact the most common formula for war and revolution. Let me ask the question again a little differently. What are the conditions that allow members of a society to send each other to the gas chambers or the killing fields? What are the conditions that lead to families betraying each other as they did in Mao's China? I'll tell you. It's the paranoia, the threat they see in the world around them, the craving for everlasting life, the survival by secrecy and punishment, the pride in their own cult, country, community – call it what you like. Mao, Hitler, Stalin and all the rest throw out an inspiration that galvanises all around them.'

'OK,' said Sally, not sure where Binsky was heading.

'Why are we so fascinated by men like Hitler? Isn't it because we want to know how *we* would act living under such a man?'

'Is that why you went to China?' asked Sally. She had known Binsky for years, but he had only ever brushed over his own experiences in China.

'Yes. But I had no idea then. Years from now, when you examine why you worked in China, you will discover motives you never dreamed existed. When I was young, Sally, I craved to be ruled by a man like Hitler or Qin Shi Huang, so that I could judge my own character, know whether I would rebel or obey, love or despise. I craved for a force in my life which would remove the blandness, a leader I could loathe enough to kill or love enough to worship. I needed to know, for instance, why the German people flocked to join the Nazis, how they could kill their own countrymen and think it was right. I craved to be subjected to injustices, so that I could react to them. Only when faced with impossible choices does a person really come to know himself. Don't you see what I mean, Sally?'

Sally swallowed her wine quickly. 'Yes, I understand what you're saying.'

'I first went to China when I was a little younger than you. It was nineteen fifty-six – just ten years after the end of World War

Two. I managed to get a visa as a visiting academic. Mao Zedong had been in power seven years. We had fought him in the Korean War, and now he was ruling all of China. And let me tell you, there had never been anything like it since Qin Shi Huang. It was as if Qin had been reincarnated in the form of Mao. Can you imagine how exciting that was?'

'Yes,' said Sally softly. 'Yes, I can.'

Binsky took out a handkerchief and blew his nose. 'I hated him. He was a monster. They didn't let me love him.'

'Who didn't?'

'The Chinese. The Americans. They.'

'You wanted to love Mao?'

'I needed to test myself. To try to understand. I needed to love a man as powerful as Hitler to see if I would allow my neighbour to be dragged off in the middle of the night. Mao was the only show around at the time. I sincerely believed that what Mao was doing was right for China. But I also knew his methods were ruthless. Here was a ruler whose ambition was to change human instinct itself. Instead of loving our parents, he wanted us to betray them to the mobs. Instead of nurturing our children, we were to hand them over to the Communist Party. Instead of being loyal to our friends, we denounced them as spies and traitors.'

'But you didn't.'

'No, Sally. I didn't. I met Wu Tian instead. He showed me how it worked. He was so calm. He had neither burning love for Mao nor burning hatred. He simply believed, with a super-human passion, in the rightness of the revolution. For Wu, Mao Zedong was no more than a mechanism of the revolution. Wu had cut his teeth on the purges of land reform in the early fifties, when millions who owned great estates or even a couple of acres of land were hauled out by the mob and killed. You know what Wu did?'

'What?' said Sally.

'He set up a system to smuggle such people out of China. The revolution was the big picture, he told me, but it didn't take account of individuals. Wu's job was to save those people whom China might need again. He got me to help him. Because of my

51

visa, I could go to Hong Kong and back again once or twice. Wu had me memorise the names of people who would flee across the border. I passed them on to the British officials in Hong Kong and when they arrived they'd be looked after.' Binsky glanced out of the window.

'Then?' Sally prompted gently. 'Then what happened?'

'I had to leave. June the eighth nineteen fifty-seven.'

'Why?'

His face went dark. 'I had some personal problems. I had to go.'

'Come on, Jeff. What do you mean, personal?'

Binksy raised his hand, cutting her off. 'Just hear me out.'

'All right. So you came back to America? To Columbia?'

'I did, but I kept in touch with Wu until sixty-eight. It was the Cultural Revolution, and his wife was killed by a mob of Red Guards.' Binsky went quiet for a moment, his face drawn with memories. 'She was a very beautiful woman. An absolutely remarkable woman. Wu blamed himself, although he never said as much. I never heard from him again. I wrote several times, but got nothing back. But you have to understand what it is like living in a country like that. He will always be my friend.'

Binsky flicked through the sheets of the translation like a pack of cards. 'I've never told anyone that, Sal. Must be these tapes. I have this overwhelming need to show this to Wu Tian before anyone else. It took a while, but I tracked him down, and I even managed to send him a fax.'

He reached into his trouser pocket and brought out a computer disk. 'He's in Beijing, a professor in the Department of Marxism at the People's University of China.'

Sally took the disk and put it on the table in front of her. 'So when you got back here, to Columbia, what then?'

He smiled. 'I became what I am now.' Binsky shook his head. 'Damn rain.' He picked his bow tie from the chair behind him and began to tie it back on. 'How's Richard? Someone told me you two are getting very serious.'

Sally laughed softly. 'He's a good friend.' It wasn't a topic she wanted to get into with Jeff Binsky. Thankfully, the telephone rang. Binsky let the answer machine pick it up. They both fell quiet, listening. It was Cait. 'Dr Binsky, this is Cait Parsons, looking for Sally.'

When Sally took the phone, Cait said, 'Hi, little sister. We're waiting . . .'

Sally looked at her watch and put her hand to her mouth. 'My God! I'm on my way.'

She pushed back her chair. 'Sorry, Jeff, I have to rush.'

'Before you go, Dr Sally Parsons, listen to this.' Binsky handed her a page of translation, wound the tape on a little way and pressed the play button. The voice sounded older now and deathly tired.

'I have been into the tomb, and it is as they say, a place of unimaginable magnificence. Everything is there as described by the ancient writings of the *Shi Ji*.'

Sally started to speak, but Binksy put his fingers to his lips and fast forwarded the tape.

'We worked only at night in case the farmers saw what we were doing. The main passage, the inner passage and the burial hall had been built like a maze to confuse robbers. We dug in for fifty feet and found the entrances to four or five halls, each blocked with rocks. We had to move the rocks from every one to find the genuine hall. We found it. And I have never seen a sight like it.

'You may have heard about the rivers of mercury and the bejewelled constellations of heaven imbedded in the roof. It is all there, I can promise you, although the rivers have evaporated now and the air is thick with mercury. But even the crossbows with poisoned arrows to shoot at grave robbers like us are there. But they were old and didn't work. I could describe to you the absolute darkness inside the tomb and the noise of the fierce night winds that howled their way in, chasing us down the passages like savage dogs. The lanterns showed us the skeletons . . .'

Sally felt as if she had been struck by a sudden illness, paralysed, while keeping her senses intact. She hardly dared breathe.

'You cannot imagine how many chambers surround the mausoleum. For his burial ground the emperor re-created his earthly empire, with hunting birds and animals, gardens for his concubines, stables for his horses and offices for his state officials.

'And, if you don't believe me, I can take you there, and show you.'

The voice fell silent and the tape hissed on for a few seconds until Binsky turned off the player. He smiled, his professional mask back in place, the authority of the great professor. He handed Sally the computer disk. 'The man who wrote this has been inside the tomb of the Emperor Qin Shi Huang.' He spoke so quietly that she could hardly hear him. 'He is my gift to you, Sally. Take this disk to Wu Tian, find Zhang Ying, deliver him to Hazel Watson and you will have your prize.'

Half an hour after Sally left, and alerted by the bark of his dog, Binsky put down his book and went upstairs to answer the doorbell.

'Manchu, knock it off,' he ordered as he drew back the locks. 'Tell me, is it my favourite ex-student back again come to get the lucky trowel she left behind?'

The moment Binsky opened the door, he was hit in the mouth. As he stumbled back, the attacker stepped inside and shut the door. He kneed Binsky in the groin, struck him in the stomach, then pushed him down the narrow stairs, kicking the body to keep it moving.

He spotted Sally's trowel on the kitchen table and, holding it in both hands, struck Binsky through the right eye and embedded the trowel into his skull, twisting it round and pushing it to ensure that it would stay there and that Binsky was dead.

The attacker found the computer in the study upstairs, ripped it from the desk and smashed it on the floor.

Back down in the kitchen, he washed his hands, using just water, no soap, and dried them on a handkerchief in his pocket. He picked up the loose sheets of the tape translation and put them into a plastic bag. Then, avoiding the jittery dog, he stepped over Binsky's body and let himself out of the house.

Chapter Six

'Cait, Dad, great to see you. So sorry, I got caught up over work.' Sally handed her coat to the attendant. She hugged Cait, brushed her father's cheek with a kiss and sat down with them at the corner table.

The bar was meant to have a view over Central Park, but the evening was rain-swept and black, stretching out like a moonless night sea.

'Don't know why you girls have to work so damn hard,' said George Parsons. He was a slim, tall, attractive man in his mid-sixties.

'Just earning a living, Dad,' said Cait.

'Helen's happy enough.'

Cait glanced sideways at Sally. 'Dad, she's worn down by the kids, and she and Jack are fighting about whether to move to Dallas.'

'I provided for your mother all these years. She didn't complain . . .'

She didn't dare, thought Sally.

'Dad, you promised,' said Cait.

Sally couldn't remember a single conversation in which Colonel George Parsons Rtd and his daughters hadn't quarrelled to some extent, but she was too preoccupied with what she'd just learned from Binsky to care. 'I've named one of my terracotta warriors after you, Dad,' she said, trying to lighten things up. She turned to the approaching waiter. 'A glass of house red for me. Cait? Dad?'

'Vodka and orange with ice,' said Cait.

'I'm finishing my beer and I have to go in a minute,' said George Parsons, looking at his watch. 'If you'd come when you said you would, we would have had a chance to talk. But the snow's whipping round like a sadist out there and I don't want your mother worrying.'

'The warrior's a standing crossbow archer,' continued Sally, ignoring the complaint. 'He lives in a humidity-controlled case and I'm trying to rebuild his crossbow.' She leaned over and smiled. 'So you see, I do think about you.'

'What are you using for the cord? Dacron?' Ah! She'd won his interest.

'That's man-made, Dad. This is meant to be a genuine replica. So I'm using hemp twine wrapped around a thread of silk in the middle. From what we know, that's how they used to do it – the two-thousand-year-old equivalent to Dacron.'

George Parsons grunted. 'You were always damn good with the crossbow, Sally. You could have made the Olympics if you'd listened to your father.'

'Thanks for the compliment, you old grump.'

'You got a decent place for my grandson to live? I hope you're not turning him into a damn communist.'

Sally laughed. 'We've moved to a new place. We're sharing a house with a Chinese family.'

'What sort of people are they?'

'Well . . .' Her drink arrived and she contemplated skirting round the question. But then thought, to hell with it. 'They're good people. Actually, he's my cab driver.'

Parsons was appalled. 'You share a house with a cab driver?'

'I rent three rooms from him. It's cheap.'

'I don't know why you can't just grow up,' he growled.

'Dad . . .' said Cait.

Parsons finished his drink. 'It's no damn good for the boy and you know it, Sally. What'll you say to him when he's grown up, with no education and no childhood friends except Chinese communists?'

Sally tried to control her temper. 'I'm sure Cait is better equipped professionally to advise me on how Paul should be brought up.'

'I have to be going.' George Parsons stood up.

It was always like this, but neither of them could help themselves. Her father unerringly pushed the button which he knew would upset her, and she did the same to him.

'Sorry,' said Sally, when Cait came back from seeing him off. Cait's face was rounder than Sally's, more maternal, and her laugh lines richer. She was two years older, a more settled soul, they agreed, although her hair was just as red and unruly. Cait had come straight from a school clinic and was wearing a pair of denim overalls from China that Sally had given her, with teddy bears embroidered all over them.

Cait rolled her eyes. 'One day, you two are going to have to make your peace.'

'One day,' said Sally, sipping her wine.

'C'mon. Give him a break. Deep down, he thinks you're great.'

'I'm holding my breath for him to tell me that.'

Cait took a handful of peanuts from the bowl. 'Before we get down to business, I brought this for you.' She put a beautifully wrapped package on the table, tied with a gold ribbon with a holly leaf on it. 'A belated Christmas gift.'

Sally untied the ribbon and opened the paper without tearing it. Inside was a box and as she lifted the lid, she gasped and smiled. 'It's beautiful.'

'I couldn't resist it,' said Cait. 'It goes perfectly with your hair.'

Sally brought out a long, deep ochre cashmere scarf and put it round her neck. She pulled her hair out so it hung freely. Spontaneous generosity was typical of Cait. Sally gave her another hug. 'It's lovely. Thanks a million,' she said, feeling a little guilty that she had brought nothing to give her sister.

'I thought you might get a bit cold out in China all by yourself,' said Cait, grinning mischievously. 'Unless . . .'

'Unless what?' said Sally, running her hands down the soft wool.

'How's Richard?'

'Well, he's in New York, and I'm in New York, but I haven't seen him yet.'

'So you're very cool. Or you've split up. Or . . . What the hell happened?'

'Nothing happened,' Sally said testily. 'Honestly, it's fine.' Then she made an effort to grin as if it didn't matter. 'So, big sister, let's get to business. Bill Cage.'

'Like I said, he called me at work recently. He was very polite, very businesslike, and I now have to tell him what you think. If you give permission, he can contact you direct. That's the court ruling.'

'I know. Did you meet him?'

'Nope. But he faxed me this.' Cait pulled an envelope from her handbag. 'It's a copy of a letter from the American adoption agency, confirming that baby William Cage came from a government orphanage in Xian.'

Sally read it. She was interested, but it wasn't something she wanted to hold on to. She handed it back to Cait.

'How is he?' Sally asked.

'He sounded fine. Just said he didn't want this parent thing eating away at him, so he was headed out your way.'

'And what do you think – as a professional?'

'I think,' Cait said slowly, 'that if Paul ever found out that his dad was in Xian and that you used a court ruling to stop him from seeing his father, Paul would be real angry with you. Look, it's not like Cage beat you up or anything.'

'Cait, the guy used to disappear for weeks, sometimes months at a time. No phone call. No warning. You remember how it was. I didn't know where he was. I thought he'd left me, not just once but again and again. Then suddenly he's back in my life, climbing into bed with me, like we'd been together every night. It was weird. And when I asked him where he'd been, what he'd been doing, he made up some bullshit story. You have to live with it to understand it. I didn't even know who he was sleeping with all that time.'

'If anyone,' injected Cait.

'Who knows?'

'To be honest, I've never understood why you got out that court order.'

Sally closed her eyes and rested her glass on her lap. If there was one thing she regretted, it was bringing lawyers between herself and Paul's father. 'I needed Cage out of my life,' she said. 'He was calling me, turning up drunk at my door, wouldn't accept that it was over. Dad found me this aggressive lawyer and he insisted on the third party conditions. I feel bad about letting it happen. I'm not that sort of person and I know it hurt Cage a lot.'

Cait's hand was on Sally's arm. 'OK, Sal. That's the past. This is about the future. There are things you have to work out. Paul shouldn't stay at school in China much past ten. He has to find his role models and peer groups. Bill's turned up now, so why not try to work it all through? When your son starts asking difficult questions and when you want him to trust you, you'll be able to give him straight answers. Paul's with you for life. You have to have some sort of arrangement with his father.'

Sally kissed Cait on the cheek. 'You're right. Tell him to call me.'

It was barely eight when Sally left Cait and the night was relentless with rain and cold. She joined the scuttling figures hurrying to be safe behind the doors of their homes, weaving her way through pockets of people, avoiding the crumpled shapes of the homeless bedding down for the night. Thankfully she pushed through the glass door into the foyer of her hotel and went straight up to her room. She switched on the television, began to fix herself a drink, then changed her mind. She'd give it one more try. She called Richard and, to her surprise, he picked up on the second ring.

'Sal,' he said enthusiastically. 'Pack your things right now and come on over. No way is my favourite archaeologist sleeping in a hotel bed when she could be in mine.'

Suddenly, the world seemed a better place.

Chapter Seven

The Brownstone houses along West 89th Street were decorated with tasteful flower boxes and painted window shutters of reds, yellows and blues. But there was still a shabbiness about the area. It was getting expensive, but wasn't there yet. Through the windows, Sally saw televisions throwing out flickering hues of comfort.

Richard had a duplex, the first and second floor. A light was on downstairs, and the curtains drawn back, revealing the shapes of his furniture in the front room. He appeared at the front door with a huge smile. 'Sal, hi. Here, let me get that for you,' he said, reaching for her suitcase.

Sally dropped her purse and threw her arms round him. 'It's so very good to be here,' she whispered.

Richard looked fit, although not obsessively so. He was dressed in a dark blue shirt, the collar open, and the sleeves rolled up without cuff-links. The lamp over the door lit up raindrops on his thick, brown, swept-back hair. His blue eyes, dancing playfully, made Sally as nervous as a little girl.

'Good to see you, too. Sorry I couldn't get back to you. I was in the office all last night,' he brushed back her hair and kissed her again on the forehead. Then he guided her in and she slipped off her coat, squeezing him closer to her.

He took her hand, led her up the stairs and casually pushed open the bathroom door. Thick towels hung over the handrails. Delicious smells came from bowls of potpourri and fresh flowers. It was their first time in New York together, and she had never been in his house before. 'It's lovely,' she whispered.

'I had tenants in. But they've just left,' he explained. 'With me here, it'll soon turn into a pigsty.' He kissed her on the lips. 'Take your time, I'm fixing dinner. Just the two of us. OK?'

Sally sat on the edge of the bath and kicked off her shoes. Her cold, damp feet sank into the fur of the carpet and felt warm and at home. Downstairs, she heard Richard in the kitchen, and decided she wanted a shower, long, hot and powerful. She dropped her clothes in a heap and kicked them to the edge of the room so they wouldn't get splashed. Just after she turned on the water, and steam fogged up the mirror, music started up from a hidden speaker somewhere in the ceiling. Sally stepped under the shower, letting it envelop her. He had put on the *St Matthew Passion*, which had been playing the first night they slept together.

She picked up a fresh bar of soap and ran it over herself. She let the water wash away the suds, then soaped again and again, washing away the dirt and damp of a long day in the city. She tilted her head back and the water ran down her hair, splashing warm onto her back. She pushed her fingers through her hair like a comb, then squeezed out the shampoo in the bottle Richard had left there, and massaged it into her scalp. The noise of the water roared across her ears, mixed faintly with the music.

Steam misted the glass of the shower stall, and Sally was so sealed off from the outside that she never heard the click of the lock or saw Richard step soundlessly into the room.

When the door slid open, there was a sudden chill, but she was facing the wall. She put out a hand to reach for the shampoo again, and brushed against a human torso. She spun round, wet hair falling across her eyes so she couldn't see, and felt her arms held to her side, soft fingers stroking her skin. She let out a cry, tiny shredded sounds which flew away with the water.

Sally kissed him on the mouth, drawing him towards her.

'Sal, one thing for you to know,' said Richard, laying the table.
'And what's that?' Sally was chopping the salad.
He grinned. 'Missed you.'

61

'Did you now?' Sally laid lettuce leaves in the bowl, and sprinkled them with grated cheese.

'Missed you. Missed China. Missed Paul. Missed everything about us,' he said, draining the spaghetti and stirring in a rich-smelling sauce. 'Shall I light a candle?'

'Leave it as it is,' suggested Sally. 'I want to see you properly.' She placed the salad in the middle of the table, brushing her arm against him as he put down the steaming bowl. She turned, kissed him and squeezed his hand. 'Did you miss Ko as well?'

'Now that's a tough one.' He drew out Sally's chair for her to sit down, then brought out a bottle of red wine from the rack behind him. 'This all right for you?' he asked, showing it to her.

Sally squeezed her eyes teasingly shut. 'I'm not looking. I trust you completely.'

Richard opened it and poured. 'If we don't like it, there's plenty more.' He broke off some bread, handed her a piece in his fingers, then wiped the melted butter off his hand with a napkin.

'So, what's keeping you out of my bed and so busy?' she said.

'The Gorbachev visit to China. Everyone's terrified there's going to be a new big love-in between the Soviets and the Chinese at our expense.'

'That's exactly what I threatened them with at the assessment review meeting this morning.' She put a forkful of spaghetti into her mouth. 'They want to close me down when this year's funding finishes in May.'

'Close you down. Why, for God's sake?'

'Money. Or so they say. Gorbachev's meant to be visiting the warriors. I'm worried China will give the Soviets permission to excavate, and that's what I told the committee.'

'Not a chance,' said Richard. 'No one's been in that tomb and no one's likely to. The Chinese are too proud.'

'I drilled through with the probe.'

Richard leaned across and took her hand. 'God, Sal! Well done!'

'That's why I rushed over here. To show them the pictures.'
'And?'

'They weren't impressed.'

When they had finished eating, Sally pushed back her chair and opened her briefcase. 'I've got copies of the pictures I took. Give me your expert view. You have got to know more about China than any of those guys at the meeting.' She moved the wine bottle and spread the pictures out at one end of the table. Richard got up and looked at them with his hand on her shoulder. She picked one out. 'These are paintings of hunting birds. Qin loved hunting.' She shuffled through to another. 'See this thing, lying here? It looks like a studded belt. I'm pretty sure that's the face strap running down between the eyes of a horse.'

She moved to another picture and pulled a magnifying glass out of her purse and handed it to Richard. 'Now look at this tiny heart-shaped shield. You can see the workmanship, the way they decorated the bronze. And if you move just a fraction to your left you'll see two blades. Their tips are just touching each other.'

Richard had it in view and was nodding keenly.

'The dagger blade is thirty inches long, with a flat handle at the end, which you can just about make out. The one on the left is still fixed to its wooden shaft, which could be up to three metres long. It looks like a spear. The blade becomes gradually narrower and thinner towards the end. See the geometric progression of the curves. You would need the most sophisticated machine tool to do that kind of engineering today.' She tapped the picture. 'These blades look the same as the ones we've already tested from the warriors and we found the proportion of alloys which made up the weapons used scientific knowledge far beyond the age. They mixed precise quantities of copper and tin to give the metal hardness and tenacity. For the arrow heads, they cut down on the tin and loaded up with lead, which, of course, is poisonous.'

'This is amazing,' muttered Richard. 'How come you didn't bowl them over?'

'I wish.' Sally gave a quick laugh. 'Look closely here. This one puzzled me. It looks like a casket or a box, but tell me what you see.'

'It's soft. Difficult to tell the proportions.'

'I'm ninety per cent certain it's one of Mao's little red books,' said Sally triumphantly. She brought out a copy from her briefcase. 'What do you reckon?'

'Could be . . . could be,' murmured Richard, holding the red book with its cheap plastic cover and black-and-white photograph of Mao Zedong inside as if it was a treasure. 'First edition, nineteen sixty-six. Remarkable.'

'We know the Red Guards were around the tomb during the Cultural Revolution.'

'But this means they got inside.'

'Not exactly. This is only an outer chamber, and the hermetic seal was broken. I reckon people over the centuries have got this far before.'

'Did you tell the committee?'

Sally shook her head. 'They were looking for ancient treasures. Not modern political pamphlets.' She took the book from Richard and slipped it back into her briefcase. He pointed to the photographs. 'Still, I can't see how they can stop your funding when you have stuff like this.'

'Someone from the State Department was at the meeting. Hazel Watson. Jeff Binsky reckons she's behind it. Do you know her?'

'The name doesn't ring a bell.'

'She said mine was a high-profile job.'

'It could be,' mused Richard. 'But it still doesn't make sense to take you out of there and leave the place open, certainly if we want to contain Soviet influence in China. Did Jeff say why he thought the government was behind it?'

'You know Jeff, he was being tricky.' She suddenly closed her eyes. 'Damn it! I left my trowel on Jeff's kitchen table.'

'Your lucky trowel?'

'I was showing it off to him. It was a little joke we had between us.'

'Do you want to call him?'

'No. I'll call him tomorrow. He got me all excited playing some audiocassettes someone had sent him. There's a guy who claims he's been inside the tomb.'

'You've had quite a day. Inside the tomb? Are you sure it's for real?'

'Jeff thinks so. Having heard some of it, I think so too. This voice . . . it was so old and, well, painful. I don't think you could fake that. And if you did, why? Only nutters like me are obsessed with the tomb.' She put her hand to her mouth, talking about work but still girlish with Richard around. 'I guess I shouldn't be telling you all this.'

'And who am I about to tell?' laughed Richard.

'Don't, please. Jeff didn't say so, but I feel it's a secret. At least, I want it kept a secret.' She shrugged. 'Anyway, Jeff gave me a transcript on disk. He wants me to take it to a Professor Wu Tian to get it checked out.'

'I know of him. He's a hardliner. An old ideologue but a respected scholar.'

'I'll let you know what happens.' She got up, went round and stood behind Richard. 'I can't wait to work on it but,' she slid her hands down his chest, 'right now, I'd prefer to work on you.'

At four in the morning, Richard woke Sally. 'Sal, get dressed,' he said. 'We're leaving for JFK in fifteen minutes.'

She was dreaming deeply about fresh towels, showers and clean sheets. She rolled over to touch him, but he was standing at the foot of the bed, fully dressed, holding her clothes, her damp, grubby clothes from yesterday, asking her to put them on.

'JFK? Now? Why?' she managed, sitting up.

'I'll explain on the way.'

She rubbed her eyes. Richard moved round and sat on the edge of the bed. 'Please.'

'No. Now.' She wasn't going anywhere. 'Tell me now. What the hell is it? Look at the expression on your face. What's going on?'

'It's Jeff,' Richard whispered. He took her hand. 'He's been murdered.'

'Murdered?' Sally spoke weakly, hardly able to get the words out. 'How?'

'I just heard it on the radio,' said Richard softly. 'They found your trowel.'

'Trowel?' Her voice was strangled with shock.

'You left it behind, remember?'

Sally nodded. Her eyes shifted away from Richard, looking at the window. It was still dark outside. 'Murdered?' she said again. 'My trowel?'

'It was a break-in.' Richard unfolded her trouser suit and laid it on the bed. 'Sal, we've got to go.'

She buried her head in her hands and felt Richard's hand on her shoulder, comforting her but also coaxing her to get dressed. 'The police are going to want to talk to you. You must have been there just before he was killed.'

'Who would want to kill Jeff?' She couldn't stop the tears and she flung her arms round Richard, burying her head in his shoulder. 'He was such a sweet, lovely old man.'

'The house was broken into around six thirty or seven,' said Richard, stroking her back. 'It was ransacked and the trowel . . . whoever it was used the trowel to kill him.' Sally shivered, pushed back and stared at Richard, her eyes wet and bloodshot. 'Any minute now, the police are going to want to talk to you,' he continued. 'Whatever happens, they won't let you leave the US again for China.'

'I didn't kill Jeff.' She turned her attention to her trouser suit, leaned across and picked at a piece of dried mud at the bottom. 'I was with Cait. Then I came to see you.' Her voice was so soft it was barely audible.

'If we leave now, Sal, you can handle it back in China. The last thing we want is for Paul to be brought back here.'

'Paul? What's it got to do with Paul?'

'It's a police homicide investigation. They could keep you in the US for a week or a month. Jeff was probably killed by some drugged-out piece of garbage. I'll talk to the police here and tell them you caught the flight before hearing the news. I'll be back in China myself in a couple of weeks. If they still want to talk to you, we can arrange it through the embassy.'

Sally pulled back the duvet. Thank God for Richard, she thought. Thank God for his clear thinking. Then she thought of

Jeff Binsky, the log fire, the wine and his kindness, and she couldn't stop the tears again.

Exhibit 23 – Audio Tape Evidence
Federal Court, Pearl Street
Manhattan
December 16th 1989

'The police have found the fax Binsky sent to Wu Tian.'
'About?'
'The audio tapes. He wanted Wu to authenticate them.'
'It'll be fine. Wu's putting his own man in with them. Is that how you say it in English – putting your own man in?'

Chapter Eight

ATT: Dr Wu Tian, Professor of Marxism
       People's University

FROM: Dr Jefferson Binsky
         New York

January 19th 1989

Cover Note:

I am so, so glad I have tracked you down after all these years.
I will try to call over as soon as you get this. Please tell me
what you think. I am sending just a page and will find
someone to bring the rest to you. Tell me, is it genuine? Have
you ever heard of Zhang Ying? We have so much to catch up
on. But I am so excited you survived the interesting times.

Your dear and old friend,

Jeff Binsky

Transcript of the tape of Zhang Ying (pseudonym).
Tape 1 of 5.
Translated by Dr Jefferson Binsky
January 10th 1989

*If you ask me, I can tell you a story. I have been into the
tomb, and it is as they say, a place of unimaginable magnificence. Everything is there as described by the ancient writings
of* Shi Ji . . .

68

As Wu Tan read the fax he could have been a statue. His wide forehead didn't crease into a frown, nor did the edges of his small, almost feminine mouth quiver, as often happens when cruel men become excited. When he was angry, he could be menacing, but this was not the case now.

Yes. Wang Donxiang the bodyguard was dead. Zhang Yufeng, the train stewardess, dead as well. Jiang Qing, the wife, in jail, Li Zhisui the doctor in exile, Jeff Binsky dead too now – all the confidants and holders of the Party secrets were gone, except the one who spoke the words he was reading now.

He had read them over and over again ever since the fax had arrived. Who owned the voice on the audio tapes? What did he know? And why did he send it to Jefferson Binsky?

He thought the shadow of light passing across the doorway was Mok, coming to take him to Tiananmen Square, but instead he heard the voice of his daughter. 'Get out of the damn way, you morons,' she shouted. 'Don't you know who I am?'

Wu Tian got up, walked across and opened the door. The air outside was so cold and rasping that it made him cough. The guards' faces were inert, like the faces of dead men. When Po Ki saw him, she thrust out an envelope.

She was his only child and he had raised her from the age of eight on his own. The way she looked at him now disturbed him. She was becoming more hostile, more remote, yet the more distant she grew, the more he found himself loving her. She had become his impossible longing.

Her face was like a little girl's, big almond eyes both hopeful and threatening, a face which simultaneously carried expressions of brutality and fear. He could see so much of himself in her, though whenever he looked at her, it was her mother's face he saw.

Her name, Po Ki – Perfect Jade – had been chosen by her mother. But memories of her mother unsettled her, so she had turned her back on them and had given herself a Western name, Christine. That was the measure of her loathing for him.

'I brought this for you,' she said impatiently. 'I thought you might be interested.'

Her breath came out in bursts of cloud. She wore a black cashmere overcoat, a fur hat with earflaps, and a scarf bundled round her neck and tucked into her collar, one end trailing down her back. He could see just her mouth, nose and eyes. Snow covered the toecaps of her boots and the envelope was held in gloved fingers. He didn't take it.

Long ago, both had been full of sympathetic emotions for each other. But the years and the death of her mother had withered those emotions. Although not quite extinct, neither father nor daughter had the energy to revive them and both retreated along the easier paths of anger and blame.

'It's a note from a Westerner I'm going to fuck,' she said defiantly. Some time ago, she had told him she had slept with an American. But he didn't believe her, thinking she was only trying to upset him, threatening to draw herself away completely, something he knew she could never do. He forced himself to show no reaction, either to what she said or the crude way she said it.

They went inside. He could not remember that she had ever been in his study, and they stood awkwardly, like visitors to a library. For guests, Wu only kept folding chairs and a mah-jong table propped against the wall for his secretary to work on. Clumsily, he began pulling them out, but the legs of the chair got stuck and he didn't know how to open it.

'Don't worry. I can't stay,' said Po Ki. 'I thought you would be interested that I might be marrying an American.' The envelope again, with the hand still gloved.

'You could get married anywhere you wish, you know. The Summer Palace. The Forbidden City. I can arrange it.'

'I would never get married in *your* China.' She unwrapped her scarf and took off her hat roughly, as if irritated by the sudden indoor heat. 'I shall have my wedding in America.'

She had a boyish look, her short hair only just reaching the top of her ears. Her face was both childlike and sophisticated, her mouth wide, even sensuous. But her lips were tight and her eyes, though spirited and shining, were detached, in a sealed calm of their own. Her manner was vulnerable and at the same time hard, as if one side of her were a protection against the other. She wanted to retain human emotions but also knew the risk of doing so.

Wu didn't open the envelope. If what she told him was true, he had no cause to read it. If it was false, he would only show his weakness by being fooled into looking at it. This was not about any American boyfriend. It was about the way a daughter treated a father. He handed the envelope back. But she didn't take it, and rather than look like an idiot, Wu walked back to his desk and put it there.

'Who is he? A businessman? A diplomat? Am I worthy to meet him?'

'There is no point. You will not be invited to the wedding.'

Wu Tian stood silently in the middle of the study. It was his capsule, so far removed from the outside world that having his daughter in there seemed like an invasion. 'As a Party member and academic, I do not require to be involved in your wedding, but as a father, my absence from it will be unbearable,' he said humbly.

'I know,' she said. Her face became more difficult to read. Cruelty showed there without shame, trying to blend with other emotions. But cruelty was a raw and forceful instinct. The woman in front of him was indeed his own daughter and Wu felt proud. He could see she was struggling to show how unyielding she could be, and loved her all the more for it.

'I am going to Washington,' she said. 'General Secretary Zhao Zhiyang is sending me as his personal envoy.'

'Will you see him – your American – there?'

'Yes. I will make love to him in Washington.'

'You speak like an American now,' he said. There was disgust in his voice.

'I understand them better than I understand my own father.'

'Why? Why are you doing this?' It was an appeal, the start of a choreographed routine they both knew by heart. Whenever she was about to do something she knew would anger him, she would come and see him, usually in his house, her childhood home, where they had lived with her mother. He would be hurt by her lack of respect, plead with her to change her mind, then threaten her.

71

Her mind had become American, he thought. He would never have believed that a loyal Chinese could attend the John F. Kennedy School of Government at Harvard University, until his own daughter went. He remembered how she had come to him beforehand, defiant and provocative as she was now, to show him the air ticket, because she knew it would make him angry. That was why she was here now, five years later, to rip open the wounds again. She used her sex life, her university education, her job and her next visit to America only as weapons.

'I am doing it to make China a better place.' She sounded bored, and her words carried no conviction.

'What is the visit for?'

'General Secretary Zhao wants me to study the American style of democracy.'

'It is not suited to China.'

'Maybe it is.'

'We have copied enough from the Americans already.'

'At least the Americans did not condemn millions of people to starvation.'

If she weren't his daughter, she would not have dared to speak like that. He would never have insulted his own parents the way she did him. He had always acted for the good of China, even if it meant killing. Revolution was not a painless experience and its leaders carried a great weight of responsibility. Po Ki would not understand that, and it pained him. Yet the relationship between a daughter and a father was still stronger than the revolution. He wished it were not so, but it was.

'It has been difficult, all these years. Bringing you up alone,' he said.

'Stop it! Listen to what you're saying! You criticise me for trying to make our country a better place.' Po Ki's face became truly brutal. 'And you are wriggling away from your shame, pretending to be sorry.'

'I'm not ashamed. It is you who should be. You still need to understand why people can do such terrible things.'

She looked away, then cocked her head haughtily. 'Why should I? We have moved on. We are better people now. We don't enjoy killing our own families.'

He felt his arm draw back to strike her. She knew what made him do it and she always taunted him to draw her blood. He looked away from her, forcing himself to be calm. He could smell expensive perfume on her. 'You make it sound as if I am . . . indifferent . . . to . . .'

'Indifferent. What does that mean? What a word to use! No wonder I am marrying an American, when I see what Chinese do to their own families. Do you honestly think what you did was right?'

'The revolution was right, yes.'

She glared and walked towards him. 'Did you ever want to do anything to stop my mother being killed?'

He couldn't stop himself. He hit her just once, with the palm of his right hand, harshly, but not hard enough for the guards to hear. She began to lash out, but he caught her wrists and let her test her strength like a snake pinned to the ground. She gave up and he let her go.

'If anything fills me with shame it is the way my daughter thinks we can atone for our wrongs by dancing to the tune of America.' Wu's face was impassive and his voice was soft, sobering after the violence, letting the words alone make the point. 'Fuck your American, if that is what you want, but if you lose your Chinese spirit, you will be nothing but a prostitute.'

She wiped blood from her mouth. 'You really are sick,' she hissed. 'Just look at you. Look at the way you dress in those stupid Mao clothes, with that stupid Communist Party badge. You wear the same suit from the same system under which you committed your crime.'

Now that he had proved his power physically, he felt more relaxed. He could see that she was holding back tears. Once she had cried, she would admit her love for him and he could let her leave in peace.

Instead she surprised him. 'My lover works for the State Department,' she smirked. 'Maybe that's why I've been chosen.'

Wu didn't react. For a few seconds, silence hung between them like the underbelly of a rain cloud.

'I met him at Harvard and seduced him to rid myself of anything to do with you.'

'The system is right for China. You should listen to me on this issue.' Wu's manner was quietly reasonable. He didn't seem to be talking to his daughter any more, but to an imaginary audience of sympathisers.

'I let him into my bed because he was an American. Because he was an imperialist. I lay naked with him. And I'm going to lie naked with him again. Are you listening to me, you damp little excuse of a father?'

Wu continued calmly, 'All cultures are capable of great evil. I want you to remember that, when you live in America.'

'And now I'm going to learn from him how to govern a country properly. Not like that thug you idolise, but so that the people benefit.' She stepped back from him and cocked her head again. 'Aren't you proud of your daughter?'

'Western governments play up communism and Nazism as evils greater than they really are,' lectured Wu.

'Snap out of it, Father,' she said, goaded by his refusal to be angry. 'Aren't you furious that I sleep with Westerners?'

'Of course we make mistakes, but communism with Chinese characteristics is the correct path for the motherland. Before he died, Mao Zedong said: "I am passing the task on to the next generation. I may not be able to pass it on peacefully, in which case I may have to pass it on in turmoil."'

'Yes, I know. Mao's conversations with Hua Guofeng, Jiang Qing and others, June the fifteenth, nineteen seventy-six. Wasn't I a good girl? I learnt it all by heart, just like Daddy told me. I learnt your excuses for slaughtering innocent people. For what you did to my mother.' She tucked the scarf into her coat. 'Save your brilliant thoughts for someone else.' She put on her hat and pulled down the earflaps. 'You're nothing but a cliché. They should put you in a museum.' She spat at him, flecking him with saliva and blood. 'What did Mum do wrong, then? Deny you sex, so you killed her?'

Wu lashed out at her again, but she was ready and moved back. She held a handkerchief to her lip and walked quickly towards the door, throwing up dust from the floorboards.

'Our country is a better place,' he said quietly as she pulled open the door. The guards opened the gate to let her out into the snow.

As Po Ki stepped outside, she turned round; lingering there half in the cold sunlight and half in the warm darkness, she looked both proud and lost. He had wounded her only as much as she had let him, and she left with the look of a woman who wished to see no one and to understand nothing. Her fate was that of her generation and her culture. It was a very Chinese fate.

Wu Tian took his coat from the rack and put it on, pulled on a hat of grey cat's fur, lowered the clumsy earflaps and knotted a red woollen scarf to cover his lips, which with age had become vulnerable to chapping. Lastly, he put on his gloves.

He opened the door to an icy morning gust. Two guards, rugged up in green overcoats, signalled to Mok who started the car and drove it to the door of the building, the tyres crushing the ice.

Wu Tian viewed the winter starkness around him with a sort of contentment. The cold usually gave him a reason to stay indoors. He did not like to go out, but today he would visit the only place in China where he felt at ease with himself.

When he saw the kites above the roof of the Great Hall of the People, he asked Mok to stop, preferring to walk from a distance and to come upon it gradually. Mok warned him to be careful.

Wu shuffled along outside the Forbidden City, the heart of the Chinese world for half a millennium. Every time he needed to visit, he came by this route, so that he would pass under the rostrum of the Gate of Heavenly Peace, where Mao Zedong proclaimed the People's Republic of China on 1 October 1949. From there, he crossed into Tiananmen Square, where he could look back on the portrait of the Great Helmsman hanging above the gate. Here, in this place, he could understand the purpose of his life.

He took a few steps backwards, as he always did, to absorb the authority of the Square around him: to the east the museums of Chinese history and the Chinese revolution; to the west the Great Hall of the People with its ten thousand seats and the magnificence of Mao's vision for the motherland; in the middle, the

Monument of the People's Heroes for the fallen of the revolution; and, to the south beyond it, the Chairman Mao Memorial Hall, built in just one year and opened on the anniversary of his death on 9 September 1977.

Wu Tian gazed up at the portrait of Mao, took off his gloves and prepared to light the cigarette given him by Mok. Those in the square understood the spirit of Mao. It was not a day for casual visitors, for it was cold and the wind cut like a sickle, keeping the ice hard on the stones and causing the young men guarding the square to stamp their feet and rub their hands together in gloves too thin for the weather.

The first match broke, its phosphorous flaring, dropping to the ground and hissing. Wu Tian turned, his back to the wind, cupping his hand and bending over to give the flame the best protection. The second match took and he drew on the tobacco, coaxing it to burn. The smoke was too light for his taste, not harsh like it used to be during the war against the Nationalists when his young lungs had been used to anything, even the smoke of dried leaves, donkey dung and newspapers.

Only among these buildings and on those huge paving stones surrounded by the silhouettes of the monuments could Wu Tian understand himself once again. Sometimes the dreams were so vivid that he would wake in the night and come to the Square, empty but for guards.

Wu Tian closed his eyes and smoked. The dream from the night before was the worst for some time, because it included not only the flames and the screaming, not only the hands reaching through the window and the children, but also the aftermath – something too terrible for him to remember. Over the years he had built up barriers and routines – the Square, the cigarettes, the recitations from Mao – to protect himself from the dreams and the anger and hatred of his daughter. Po Ki hated him, and perhaps always would. But although she had been with him and had seen what he had done, she would never tell. It was a comforting thought.

He exhaled the warm smoke and walked slowly on to touch the cold stone of the Monument of the People's Heroes. He kept going until he came to the queue of peasants and workers waiting for the Memorial Hall to open. They were obedient and silent. The only colours were the flags of their villages and factories, hanging limply then picking up as gusts came and went across the square.

In his memory, the shriek of his wife tore through him. He heard her plead for him to care for their daughter Po Ki. He heard his own voice, lost in the noise of the fire and the roar of the crowd cheering the flames. In his imagination, he could see the window on fire, could see her lips moving as she begged him to love her always, even as the fire engulfed her and she died.

The cigarette was finished, almost burning his fingers. He dropped it on the ice and killed it with the toe of his shoe. He was glad Po Ki knew. Somehow it made it easier. One day, he hoped, she would understand about sacrifice and the vision of Chairman Mao and learn to love her father again.

The guard undid the lock and slid back the huge black metal gate. The queue edged forward into the Northern Hall and slowed as they passed the white marble statue of Mao. Wu Tian brought out a card from the pocket of his coat, its lamination creased, but the guard immediately recognised it. To the guard, Wu was a hunched, frail and hesitant man with trembling fingers. His was a face etched with the history of China, a face of humility and honour, and the blue stamp in the top left-hand corner, just above the name, even smudged and faded granted Wu Tian the greatest respect. It described him as a member of the Communist Party of China and a veteran of the Long March which, at the age of fifteen, he had completed with his father. He had even fought with the commandos at the battle of Lazikou Pass. The guard let him through with a nod, then herded the visitors out through the Hall of Reverence. When it was empty he closed it off and left Wu Tian alone and undisturbed.

The embalmed body of Mao Zedong, draped in the red flag of the Chinese Communist Party, lay before him in a crystal coffin. 1893–1976. The hall was silent. No wind. No cries from the square. No distant sound of traffic. Wu Tian knelt on the cold floor, his hands clasped, his eyes closed so tight that colours and not memories danced in front of him.

Wu's lips moved as he prayed for the soul of Mao Zedong, the Chairman, the Great Helmsman, the saviour of China, whose spirit continued to live and guide. He prayed for the soul of Jefferson Binsky, his friend who had found him after so many years. He prayed for the forgiveness of his daughter Po Ki, and asked that she might love him again.

He prayed for two souls joined as one, for Wu Tian and for Yu Yi who stood at the window with love in her eyes as she burned to death, and he prayed that they might be reunited in the afterlife.

Lastly, he prayed for the deliverance of Mao Zedong, for only then would China become great again, and he himself be absolved of his sins.

Chapter Nine

'Ko, please, can you turn it down, just a bit?' He must have had a new sound system put in while she was in New York, and it blared out choral music from the Cultural Revolution. Ko glanced at Sally, looking hurt.

'Most foreigners like it,' he said. He spoke in Chinese. Over the months he had been using English less and less with her. He had changed the seat covers so Sally was now sitting on a bright yellow field of wheat, made of factory-woven cloth, and right at the end by the door was the benevolent face of Mao. Except Ko hadn't measured it exactly and half the face was buried down the side, so Mao was looking at her with half a nose and one suspicious eye.

The copies of *Time* and *Newsweek* that Sally would give Ko after she had read them were gone from the back-seat pocket. Ko had been proud of them. His was the only cab in town with its own library. Even the English language *China Daily* wasn't there, all replaced by obscure Maoist magazines which Sally had only heard about from Richard and other friends who studied Chinese politics.

She pulled one out and started reading the characters. She spoke Chinese adequately, but had difficulty reading it and wrote it badly. But she made out the Red Spirit column and recognised a Mao quote from her language classes: 'We should go to the masses and learn from them . . .' She couldn't understand the two characters after that and gave up.

It was only mid-morning, but jet lag was kicking in. She stuffed the magazine back into its pouch, closed her eyes and tried to let the bumps and swings of the road put her to sleep.

Ko started talking again. 'You heard that Gorbachev's coming to Xian?'

'Yes. In May,' said Sally, eyes closed.

'I'll shit in his face if he comes to my city,' said Ko with uncharacteristic venom.

'Oh. Why's that?' Her voice was slow and dreamy.

'Shit in the Soviets' face for the way they treated Mao Zedong. They invited him to Moscow and Stalin treated him like dirt.' Ko jerked the accelerator as he spoke. 'The Soviet white turds betrayed the motherland in the Korean War. That bastard Stalin promised air cover and when our brave martyrs were being sacrificed, he ran away. And I tell you, Sally, if we hadn't fought in Korea, we would have Taiwan back by now. The Americans would not have fought to save Taiwan. Fucking Soviets.'

Sally reckoned there must have been a diatribe in a magazine against Gorbachev's visit. She tried to sleep again. Ko was getting weird anyway, turning his car into some religious Maoist shrine.

He drove into the parking lot, and Sally asked him to stop as close to the entrance gates as he could. She wanted to get to her office quickly, to make copies of the disk and then lock up for the day, get Paul out of school and spend the afternoon with him, watching videos, playing games. To do something normal. Binsky's death and her sudden return home had shaken her badly.

She moved through the shopping stalls which displayed rows of imitation terracotta warriors, ranging from thimble size to life size, silk scarves, colourful patchwork bed covers, Chinese character stamps, cat-fur hats, fox-fur wraps, dog-fur shoes, cow- and pig-leather belts with buckles which never worked, videos, postcards, guide books, and silk carpets woven with patterns copied from Iran and Kashmir, which hung on the walls next to credit-card signs.

She had been away from Xian for less than a week but the stallholders shook her hand as if it had been a year. In some small way, she had helped each of them. A phrase in English. A memento from New York. The Statue of Liberty traded for a bust of Confucius. Others she had helped in bigger ways, with medication they couldn't get in China, with books not on sale. Teaching people to love girls and boys alike, and not dump their daughters by the roadside. Walking through to the Terracotta Warrior Museum, she was glad to be back.

When she got to the carpet section, she nearly tripped as a carpet was unfurled right in front of her.

'Not today, Johnny,' she said, skipping over it so as not to tread dirty melting ice on the silk. Before he could answer, she was through the door, onto the concourse outside.

A chilly wind cut through her as she headed towards the building housing Pit Number One and she pulled Cait's cashmere scarf tighter round her neck. She slowed down, looking at the building, in awe of it, as she always was. Only an archaeologist could feel as she did whenever she got close to the building. It wasn't much more than an aircraft hangar with a slanting green-tiled roof at the front and a flight of steps. But inside, the way the light played on the warriors, it was as if you were facing a real-life army, marching in their trenches – subterranean soldiers was how some of the Chinese translations described then. Binsky had been right; anyone curious about power would have to be fascinated by a man like Qin Shi Huang.

Thinking of Binsky brought a lump to her throat. 'I'll do it, Jeff, old friend,' she whispered to herself. 'We'll share the damn honours. You and I.'

Sally hurried on, cutting down steps at the side into the basement of the building and following the badly lit corridors to her little office. No one seemed to be around, which was good. But doors were open, and there were signs of life, tea in coffee jars, ashtrays, and coats hung on doors, the smell of disinfectant and urine from the toilets opposite. Sally found her key, let herself in, turned on the light, closed the door and locked it behind her. She didn't usually lock it, but she didn't feel right. She even pulled the blind down over the narrow strip of window above her desk before she turned on the computer.

As it warmed up, she checked the special glass display case in which she kept the standing crossbow warrior she had named after her father. It was the first figure she had reconstructed.

George was protected from the breath, body heat and pollution produced by the thousands of visitors who walked past the warriors every day. Their pigmentation was fading in the filthy air, and Sally reckoned there were dozens of different types of mould attacking them. But George, whom she had rescued early on, had kept some of his original hues. Once she had proved her case she would try to get funding for anti-fungal treatment. It was expensive and it would cost a fortune to do the whole army. But inside his temperature- and humidity-controlled case, George was looking great. Sally patted the glass top.

The computer bleeped. The green-and-black screen was settling. Sally sat down, unzipped the pocket inside her jacket and brought out Binsky's disk. The file was marked Zhangtomb1. There didn't seem to be a Zhangtomb2. She copied it on to her hard disk, flipped out the original, put it back in her jacket pocket, and opened the file.

It was blank. Nothing. The copy hadn't worked. She slipped in the original disk again, opened it and looked at it at random.

In the beginning, I adulated Mao. He was the new Messiah. But after the Great Proletariat Revolution, my dream that China was a place where all people would be equal had gone. I felt sorry for those who had pinned their hopes on Mao. Ping rescued me. Did I tell you that? She was the one who saved me.

She put a blank, formatted disk into the second drive and tried copying from disk to disk. Nothing. It refused to take. She flipped the black-plastic button across at the back, tried again, sitting transfixed at her desk, watching it clunk through the process. Again nothing. She pressed the print command, but the printer jerked back and forth, then fell still again. Binsky must have fixed it like that.

The phone rang. 'Mom. The teacher says that as you've been away I can leave at lunchtime . . .'

Everything inside her had been crying out to look at the

whole disk. But Paul's voice came through stronger. The disk could wait.

Sally zipped the original disk back into her pocket and got Ko to take her to Paul.

'So what's his apartment like?' said Paul, letting go of her hand as he spotted another ice puddle to jump into in the road by their house. He was in his red down jacket, with the hood up, a scarf and red mittens.

'Well, it's . . . kinda nice. Richard's got good taste. And he's got a lovely bedroom for you when we go and stay.'

Paul stopped dead and in his excitement almost slipped, clinging to Sally's hand to keep himself upright. 'That sounds great. Much better than going up to boring old Southampton.'

'And I saw Cait and Grandad. They both send their love.' Paul's scarf had come loose and she tucked it back down his front. 'Cait gave me this,' she said, touching her own scarf.

Paul glanced at it with disappointment. 'Aunt Cait? Didn't Richard give it to you?'

Sally laughed. 'Why d'you say that?'

''Cos if he had, it would mean he loved you and then we'd be sure to have somewhere cool to stay in New York.'

Sally laughed. Seven years old and he'd figured out all the angles.

That night, when Paul was fast asleep and being watched over by Mrs Ko, Sally went back to work.

She stared at her computer screen. 'Who the hell is this person, George?' she muttered. 'Some crazy guy? A victim? A dissident?' She turned in her swivel chair and faced the standing crossbow man. 'Somewhere in China, this guy filled five cassette tapes, thirty minutes each side, according to Jeff's notes, and told this crazy story.'

George stared calmly from his sealed casket, his hair tied up in a bun and his hands poised as if he was about to lay a karate blow. His moustache was neatly combed and he had shaved to leave a tiny fashionable bush of beard just under his lower lip. Sally didn't believe in ghosts, but nevertheless she felt protected by George.

She took a swig from the flask of brandy on her desk. It had been a gift from Cage, which she hadn't used for years. Then she had started taking it with her to the tomb at night. This night would be a long one. Sally still wore her down jacket because the heating was off, her fingers poking through holes in her woollen gloves and her hair tucked underneath a red woollen bobble hat.

'You're just the right companion for a dark night,' she told George before concentrating again on the screen.

There was something about being here with the terracotta army at night when the tourists had gone and the caretakers had shut up, as if that was when the warriors came to life to rearrange their formations and wander about their territory. No statutes in the world were as lifelike as these.

'So, George, what do you reckon?' She stabbed her finger at the screen. 'Zhang Ying is not his real name. Big surprise, huh? It's the emperor's name backwards. Qin's real name was Ying Zhang, sometimes written Zheng. Qin Shi Huang means literally first king of Qin dynasty, just like Mao Zedong preferred to be known as Mao Zhu Xi, Chairman Mao. There you go, George, your history lesson for tonight.'

Sally lapsed into silence, one hand on the computer keyboard, the other fiddling with the brandy flask, reading.

I will talk about the death and then I will tell you about Ping, because Ping dragged me into the death chamber when she was told the Chairman had died.

'OK. So Ping is Mao's wife. Got that, George?'

All she was interested in was whether they would preserve the body properly. I knew, from what Dr Li said, that they were going to begin the preservation process immediately. The temperature in the room was 78 degrees Fahrenheit. Anything would rot in that heat.

Dr Li injected 22 litres of formaldehyde into Mao Zedong's body and it was a disaster. His neck became as fat as his head. His head grew bloated like a balloon. The chemical seeped out of his skin and dripped onto the floor.

'Messy,' muttered Sally. She tore open a packet of peanuts with her teeth and tipped a handful into her mouth.'

When the Chairman's body was puffy with formaldehyde, Ping giggled. I can tell you who was there, if you want. Hau Guo Feng was Mao's successor and he protected Dr Li against Ping who was accusing him of doing a sloppy job. Zhang Yufeng, Mao's favourite girl who had been a stewardess on his train. She was the only one he would listen to and she read secret documents to him, which gave her power.

'Where's this leading, George?' Sally scrolled down, trying to speed-read and get to the nub of it before morning. 'Ah, the tomb. We've got to the tomb.'

Ping sent me to the tomb in 1973 when I got back from Moscow. I was so crippled and couldn't do much but watch. You must remember this was before the army of terracotta warriors was discovered in 1974, so we knew only about the tomb. And it was two years before Mao's death. Ping was certain we could find a way in and discover the secrets of immortality. She was mad, but she saved my life, and I am grateful to her. It took us four nights to open a shaft. We only worked at night in case the farmers could see what we were doing. The main passage, the inner passage and the burial hall had been built like a maze to confuse robbers. We dug in for fifty feet and found the entrances to many halls, either four or five, I can't quite remember, and each blocked with rocks. We had to move each rock to find the genuine hall and once inside I have never seen a sight like it, and I can remember even now the sound of the weeping wind chasing us.

Everywhere we went, through the burial chambers and the decoy tunnels, were traps to ward off tomb robbers. We had to be very careful.

You cannot imagine how many chambers surround the mausoleum. Qin created in his burial ground a model of his real life empire, with hunting birds and animals, gardens for his concubines, stables for his horses and offices of state for his officials.

Sally sat with a peanut lodged in her mouth, eyes glued to the screen. She sipped some more brandy. 'Zhang Ying, if you are telling the truth . . . If you are telling the truth, I will love you for ever – whoever you are.'

Some of it, Sally had heard and read in Binsky's house. Some he had kept from her, teasing her. She leant back in her chair, and crunched more peanuts.

She let her brain whirl with ideas until she remembered the photograph of the Red Book she had taken with the probe. Was it dropped by Zhang Ying and his party as they made their way into the tomb? Had they left other things which would show her their path?

She pushed the photograph to one side and closed the brandy flask before she got herself drunk. Bits were missing from Zhang Ying's story. Why, Zhang Ying, why were you sent in the first place?'

Sally scrolled again, rubbed her eyes and was about to call it a night, when a sentence caught her attention. She opened the flask again, put it to her lips, tasting the brandy on her tongue, thinking, as she read, oblivious to everything around her.

'So is that it, Jeff?' she said. 'Is that your big secret?' Then the truth hit like a blow to the stomach and her voice dropped to a whisper, which didn't matter because there was no one around to hear. 'Is that a secret to kill someone for?'

In Beijing, Li Yi met Sally off the plane from Xian and they headed off in his limousine straight to the People's University. Beijing, with its monuments and ring roads, usually gave Sally a thrill. Long ago it had been because Beijing was greyer, less frenetic but more impenetrable than Xian. Recently it had been because Richard was there, and it was strange being in the hands of the effusive Li Yi instead. His musk aftershave wafted through the heated air-conditioning.

'Wu Tian's a nice guy, but not of this era,' said Li Yi as the car stopped and started in the traffic. He pulled his shirt cuffs down and unclipped the cuff-links. 'He doesn't like the capitalist trappings of the West. Old guard, you know. So I tend to dress down when I go and see him.'

Sally touched Li Yi's elbow. 'You are funny the way you swing from one to the other. Entrepreneur one day. Communist Party official the next.'

Li Yi beamed at her. 'One of the privileges is getting to work with someone as beautiful as you.'

'Stop it, Li Yi,' said Sally blushing.

Li Yi smiled, dropped his cuff-links into his jacket pocket, slipped the jacket off and put on a blue woollen sweater he had by his side. 'He talks about the past a lot. I think he used to be very well-connected. But whether he can verify this diary, I really don't know.'

Sally shrugged. 'I hope he can. But really I'm doing it for my professor, Jeff Binsky.' She swallowed hard. She guessed it would be some time before she came to terms with his death.

Li Yi nodded. 'You mentioned that on the phone. It sounded dreadful.'

When they were shown in, Li Yi sat with Sally in front of the desk in Wu Tian's study. It reminded Sally of Binsky's apartment, the old books in English, Chinese, German, French, the worn carpets, and Wu Tian's manner, with a courtesy and curiosity from another age, was very like Binsky's.

'Li Yi told me that Jeff had been murdered.' Wu Tian shook his head.

'In New York, yes,' said Sally. Li Yi had told her not to be too talkative.

'It's very sad. We were very close friends.' His head was lowered, and the single lamp shone on his fingernails picking at the wood of the desk. Then, after what felt like a formal silence, Wu Tian said, 'Mr Li tells me you work in China as an archaeologist.'

'Yes, I work with the terracotta warriors.'

Wu Tian's concentration wavered. 'Excuse me. I'm so rude. Would you prefer to speak in English or in Chinese?'

They had been using Chinese. She shrugged. 'Either is fine.'

'English, then. I like to practise. An old man like me doesn't get much of a chance.' He fumbled in his jacket and brought out a packet of cigarettes. He took one out, looked as if he was about to light it, then had second thoughts.

'I didn't know we had foreigners working with Qin Shi Huang's army.'

Sally smiled. 'It's the most exciting work I've ever done.'

Wu Tian switched back to Binsky. 'We hadn't been in touch for years. I wrote to Jeff in nineteen sixty-eight after my wife died. Then he contacted me just . . . let me see . . . it must have been just over a week ago. He said someone would be coming to see me. But he didn't say it would be you.' Wu Tian turned round, touched the window behind his desk, as if pushing it properly closed, then faced Sally again. 'It is so very good of you to come and see me. The young people today ignore their elders. Even at the university, they don't know the minds of the workers and the peasants.' He coughed and cleared his throat. 'Popularity is not necessarily part of good leadership. Though Mao Zedong was popular and a good leader. But Qin Shi Huang is not so popular today.'

'But he was a great leader.'

'He was indeed. What would China be without the Great Wall?' He lit the cigarette, spending time on it. 'I don't usually smoke,' he said. 'Your visit has made me smoke. It is very good of you to come.'

'Jeff asked me to.'

'Yes. Yes, I know. He faxed me.' He opened a drawer in his desk, brought out a copy of the fax and read it again. 'Yes, January the nineteenth. He wrote to me a lot after my wife died, but I couldn't reply. You must understand. China was a very difficult place then.'

'He still considered you a friend,' she said.

'Yes. I too. But I couldn't show it. To speak to you is like having Jeff with me again. It is difficult for an American to understand a country like mine. What you see in the West as betrayal, we have to accept as part of life. You take silence in the face of injustice as betrayal. But in China, if a loved one disappears, and you say nothing, you give others a chance of staying alive. Sometimes you must applaud an unjust imprisonment or an execution, show your support for the state in order to save the lives of those you love. We are constantly pulled against our own human instinct. Our silence and our applause make us complicit and the only way to move forward is to believe that we have done the right thing. To believe in China. None of us is innocent. The psychology of our whole nation is scarred.' Wu Tian paused and hummed to himself for a few seconds. 'I think Jeff understood that about China.'

'Yes, he did. He talked to me about it.'

'Did he tell you about the death of my wife?'

'Just a bit. He mentioned her when I was in New York last week.'

'Did he tell you how she died?'

'That it was during the Cultural Revolution. That a mob got out of control.'

Wu nodded. 'It was a fire. I didn't get to her in time. I brought my daughter up alone.'

'I'm sorry. I'm sure you've been a good father,' answered Sally cautiously. She glanced across to Li Yi, but his face was impassive. Sally felt unsure about what she was being drawn into.

Wu Tian nodded slowly. 'I wish you would tell my daughter that.' He looked straight at Sally. His eyes were old and watery. He wore a sad smile. 'But you know what young people are like with their parents. Mr Li tells me you have a boy in Xian who you're bringing up alone.'

'Paul. Yes. He's seven.'

'It must be difficult.'

'Sure, it can be tough. But he's great.'

'His father is dead?'

Sally laughed nervously. 'No, we separated.'

'Was he violent? Did he drink?'

'Sometimes people just don't get on.'

'You are lucky to have the choice. How old are you, Dr Parsons, if you don't mind me asking?'

'I'm thirty-three.'

'Four years older than my daughter. She's twenty-nine. She's a very clever young woman. But she doesn't respect me. Do you respect your father?'

'Uh – yes.' And Sally was amazed to find that she really meant it.

'I am happy to hear you say that.' Wu Tian abruptly got to his feet. But he dithered where he was, arranging papers on his desk. Sally could see how Wu and Binsky would have got on. They were both oddballs in their own cultures. He was one of the few Chinese who had ever talked to her frankly about the country's psychological scars.

Sally said, 'Anyway, I'm sure you didn't ask me here to talk about your daughter. Jeff wanted to know about the man called Zhang Ying, who wrote – or I should say recorded – a diary which he gave to Jeff.'

'Yes, Jeff told me about this transcription, or translation. He put it on a computer disk for you to bring to me.'

Sally rummaged through her purse and brought out the disk. She leaned forward to give it to Wu, but he didn't seem interested, so she sat back with it on her lap.

'He faxed me two pages which describe the inside of the tomb. I am probably the only person left alive in China who can tell whether it is true. Have you read the transcript?'

'Some of it,' Sally replied.

'Is there anything which struck you as being important?'

'The most significant thing for my work, if Zhang Ying can be believed, is that people have been inside the tomb.' She was being careful, trying to read Wu Tian's reaction. But as she spoke, he half closed his eyes and she could read nothing. 'It sounds magnificent, Professor Wu. Moats of mercury. Jewelled vaults. Everything just as it was described in the *Shi Ji*. But Jeff wanted you to authenticate it.'

Wu began folding a sheet of paper on his desk into smaller and smaller squares. He stopped and let it bounce open. 'Dr Parsons, after Jeff contacted me, I tried to trace this man. I believe this Zhang Ying was a masseur of Mao Zedong. Tell me, does he go into detail about Mao's last days, the death bed and his allegiance to Mao Zedong.'

'Yes. Yes he does. Quite a bit. But it doesn't seem to lead anywhere.'

'Zhang Ying was a catamite, a boy lover, who worshipped the Chairman.' Wu pressed down on the folded paper. 'Zhang Ying is not his real name. You see, Zhang Ying is the reversal of Ying Zhang.'

'Which was the real name of Qin Shi Huang.'

'Precisely. You know your history. This Zhang Ying is a prankster, I think. Maybe it is better Jeff died without knowing that. He must have worked hard on the translation. As far as we know, the tomb was badly looted. Shortly after the Emperor's death, there was a rebellion and it was broken into. You must know about it. There can be little left now.'

'I've conducted a photographic probe inside one of the outer vaults. There are treasures in there,' said Sally.

'Yes. Mr Li told me. They are broken up, I suspect.'

Sally nodded, disappointed. Wu's eyes looked everywhere except at Sally, yet his manner remained calm. 'Mr Li, why don't you see if we can make a copy of this disk, so that Dr Parsons can keep the original?'

Sally looked at Li Yi. 'You might have to de-activate a copy block which Jeff put on it.'

'Don't worry,' said Wu Tian. 'We are a university. We have all the modern gadgets.'

Li Yi, usually so cocky, got up immediately, walked backwards a couple of paces, and almost bowed before turning to leave the room. He didn't go out of the door at the far end as she had expected but through a side door she hadn't noticed between the bookcases.

'Should I send a note of condolence, perhaps?' asked Wu Tian. 'I'm sorry, I don't know much about Jeff's family.'

'Perhaps to Columbia University.' Suddenly, ashamed, she realised she knew nothing about Jeff's family either. 'That and China were his life.'

Wu Tian pulled out a sheet of notepaper. He began writing in Chinese characters, then screwed up the paper and started again in English. Sally watched quietly.

Li Yi came back in, holding two disks. Wu looked up. 'What is your view, Mr Li?' he asked in English. 'You are from Shaanxi Province. So tell us, do you believe the treasures are still inside Qin Shi Huang's tomb? And what would be the reaction of the Chinese people if it was excavated?'

Li's reply was measured and formal. 'The businessmen in Shaanxi Province wish the tomb to be opened, like the Egyptian pyramids. The revenue from tourism would be enormous.'

'I fear both you and Dr Parsons will be disappointed. The tomb has been ransacked.'

Sally was about to mention the Red Book she had photographed, so modern, so out of place among the treasures inside.

But as Wu Tian signed his condolence note, she caught his eyes again and saw something menacing there, as if the brown, bland pupils were suddenly backlit, flickering at her like the face of an irritated ghost. A sudden shiver passed through her.

Chapter Ten

From the corner of Grand and Lafayette, Bill Cage watched the Chevrolet Suburban Discoverer get lifted onto a truck and taken away. He wore a green anorak, with the hood up, its synthetic fur keeping him warm.

Cage reckoned his adult life had started on his tenth birthday when his drunken mother hurled a locket at him, the chain trailing like the trail of a meteor. Cage caught it. The locket opened on impact and for the first time Cage saw the face of his real mother. And he reckoned he was completely alone just after he turned fifteen, the night his father was jailed for fraud and officers of the court came to take him into care.

Cage ran, kept running until he knew they wouldn't catch him, running, hiding, working and fighting until he was old enough to join up. Those words of his adopted mother bounced around all the time. 'There she is,' she had screamed at him. 'The bitch. That's the little whore who didn't want you. You want a real mother? Why don't you go get her?'

Was that what had made him a bad guy? The sort of person that made Sally throw him out and get a court ban on him? Was that why he had become so half Chinese and half American that he could never work out what he really was?

Cage saw the kid drop a cigarette onto the ice. He had been watching the vehicle for a week, doing the day shift, while a fatter, bigger guy did the nights. The kid walked inside the beauty parlour. A light went on in the room upstairs and a blind came down.

Pulling off his hood so his vision was clearer, Cage crossed the road and pushed against the beauty parlour door. It was shut, but only with a spring lock, and Cage had it picked in less than half a minute. Leonard was watching him. Half a dozen of Leonard's people were on the streets around. Cage opened the door and closed it behind him.

To his right was a dark room, smelling of damp, the curtain closed. A single red light from a tiny shrine sent a glow around the room. Two coffee tables were the only furniture, one by the street window, one at the other end, both with burnt-out joss sticks on them, the ashes spilt on the floor.

Straight ahead was a narrow staircase, its carpet threadbare. Upstairs there was silence.

'Take a weapon,' Leonard had insisted. Cage had, but he wasn't going to fire on some Chinese kid, shipped to do someone's dirty work. He had killed enough like that. It was time to learn to get what he wanted without killing.

On the corner of the stairs, the light moved, a shadow passing across the crack of a half-open door. Along the narrow corridor there were two doors to the left and one to the right – the room they had watched the vehicle from. A cigarette had been dropped on the floor and trodden out in the doorway. Cage stayed absolutely still and waited. The smell of sandalwood lingered.

In the room on the right, the hinges of a window squeaked as it was opened, then a shadow darkened the doorway again. Cage dropped back, and the kid crossed the corridor. His face, just before he went inside the other room, changed expression, indicating there was someone else in there. Then Cage heard the mechanical clicks of weapons being made ready.

Cage kept his weapon in its holster. If he touched it, he'd use it. There'd be two dead Chinese illegal immigrants, and his record would be rolled out in front of the investigation. He swallowed hard, tasting bile at the back of his throat.

'You motherfucking donkeys,' he shouted in Chiu Chow, his native dialect, rough and coarse, as if he was one of them but more so. 'This place has got so many cops round it you won't ever see the sky again. How long you been in New York? Eh? You fucking pansies, speak to me. How long you been here for?'

The door opened. They drew it right back inside the room, and light flooded across the corridor. A gust of wind from the open window blew away the cigarette butt. Cage was about to speak again, when he smelt fuel. A bottle, a flame streaking from the rag in its top, curved across into the bigger room and smashed onto the floor, flames leaping out into the corridor.

Cage ran forward to the doorway, flat against the wall. The curtains were alight.

'We're seeing smoke,' said Leonard into his earpiece. 'What's going on in there?'

'Molotov,' whispered Cage. Then he dropped to the floor and switched to Chiu Chow again. 'What asshole you working for?' he yelled through the smoke. 'You step outside this house now, they'll cut you down like a fucking bamboo shoot.'

Cage used the smoke to get right up to their doorway. He drew his pistol, took off the safety, put a round in the breech, feeling as if his stomach was filling up with vomit.

'That you or them?' Leonard talking again. Cage didn't answer. Leonard should know better than to use an earpiece to a man in the middle of a shooting. He held his weapon in both hands, pointed it towards the ceiling, slipped it to semi-automatic, stood up, and started firing – fourteen rounds, no suppressor, straight off, one hell of a noise. And as he fired, he went in, pistol whipping the small kid round the face, then stomach-kicking the bigger one. He eased back the trigger. One round was left.

'Cage, answer!' Leonard shouted.

'Couple of minutes,' said Cage.

The bigger guy was winded, leaning against a wall. The kid was on the floor, bleeding from the ear. Smoke was blowing through, catching in their throats.

'Stupid little shits,' muttered Cage in Chiu Chow. 'On the floor,' he said to the bigger guy. Then to the kid, 'You OK?'

The kid nodded. A breeze turned into a gust, rocking the door; it looked as if it was about to slam shut. Cage glanced towards it, glanced back at the kid, saw his eyes and turned to the bigger guy, who had another weapon pointed at him. He was a different type from the kid, older, face harder, dead,

95

drug eyes, and there was something about them which gave Cage a chance.

Nothing else to do, he had told himself each time it had happened before. Each time, he had gone for an upper body shot because it wasn't the shooting range, and moving and firing, and doing it against time, didn't give you the luxury of killing with a round in the brain stem or wounding with a skilfully placed shot to the mid-calf, somewhere that would heal with time. After the post-mortem, if they had one, they'd tell him he'd clipped the heart or severed an artery, causing death pretty much instantly. They'd clap him on the back, because he was the guy who could do it and it didn't seem to affect him. Which is why they kept sending him back again. Every time he'd tried to put his old life behind him, Cage found it creeping back on him again. But not now.

Cage dropped his weapon. It fell loudly on the floor, and he yelled, 'You wanna kill a fucking cop, you fucking piece of shit? Pull the fucking trigger then, you cock-sucking slant-eyed pair of rat's eyes.' He stepped forward, bracing himself, but sensed the shot wouldn't come. He kicked the guy in the stomach, and took his weapon as he stumbled.

'Fuck you,' muttered the guy, doubling up, grasping for breath.

'Piss off,' shouted Cage. Holding the guy's collar, he propelled him out of the room. 'One coming out,' he said to Leonard. He turned his weapon on the kid, just to make sure. Then back to the bigger guy. 'Go down the stairs and out the door. There's twenty snipers out there, so you take one step out of line and they'll blow you away.'

Then to Leonard again. 'One coming out the front door.'

And to the kid. 'Idiot. Your friend could have died.'

'Not my friend,' answered the kid sullenly.

'Takes a lot to pull a trigger. You stay in this trade, kid, you gotta learn to read the man who'll pull the trigger.'

Leonard came on again. 'How many left?'

'One. Give me five minutes.'

He stood by the kid, letting his pistol sway back and forth over him. 'Now you got two choices and thirty seconds to decide. If you don't answer me straightaway, we'll throw the book at you. Attacking a federal agent, arson, weapons, and that's even before we get to heroin peddling. Or you give me one name, just one – the man who runs you, your dragonhead – and I'll make sure you get off lightly.'

No reaction. Cage knelt down, his face half an inch away from the kid's. 'Before you decide, I want you to know one thing about dying. You listening?'

The kid didn't move, but his eyes gave in. They collapsed on themselves and could no longer face down Cage.

'Killing you won't make any difference to anyone except you.' Cage waved the pistol over to where the bigger guy had been. 'No one would have cared if he'd killed me or if I'd killed him. No one except the two of us. Do you get what I mean? You've got to remember, the main thing about people dying is that there's always someone to replace them, even if you love them, grieve for them. With your life, you wouldn't know much about grief. It's too much of a luxury. But if you make a success here in America, you'll learn all about those things – sadness, love, regret, euphoria. These are all American luxuries. Limousines, private planes, bank accounts, trust funds. You see what I'm getting at? Thing is, as soon as someone dies, people look around for a substitute. So just think about it. If I kill you now, your wife, girlfriend, will be getting a new man to fuck. You got kids? You're probably too young, but if you have kids and I kill you, they'll get a new father. And your boss, the one you're protecting now, he'll get a new goon to watch his cars and lick his boots.' Cage stood up again. 'I tell you what, I'll make it easier for you. Life's easier when you think in extremes. You tell me his name – and tell it true because if you don't, you're dead anyway. Tell me his name and I'll let you walk. You'll be a completely free person. No trial. No cops. No nothing. All you've done is hang around a car park. So you walk. If you don't tell me, I'll kill you.' He brought the weapon up and touched his eyelid with the barrel. 'You look at my eyes, kid. Look and see if they're the eyes of a man who'll pull the trigger.'

The kid stared at Cage blankly. He must have been just out of his teens. Cage kept talking. 'It's quite simple. Either five

minutes from now you'll be having a bowl of noodles somewhere, or you'll be dead on the floor with a bullet through your
skull. And no one gives a shit except you.'

He brought up the weapon, held it in both hands, aimed it at
the kid's face. In those seconds when the kid was deciding, Cage
experienced what the junkies call the rush. Excitement cascaded
through him, and he realised that he actually liked what he did
and that he'd felt let down when he'd let the bigger guy go.

He was terrified the kid would see the same hesitation in his
eyes as he'd seen in theirs. In those few seconds while the kid
made his decision, Cage felt his stomach churn and tasted bile
again coming up in his throat. He hated himself for enjoying the
pleasure of killing and for being disappointed when he failed to
do it. You had to have killed to know that feeling.

Cage found Leonard in the workshop. The Chevrolet was on the
ramp, stripped of its wheels and chassis cover. The seat covers
were off, the roof lining cut open, the engine casing on a
wooden slat on the floor.

'Not a good start, unplugging the wire,' said Leonard, watching mechanics prise off a set of brake pads. 'The kid headed a
couple of blocks south into a Chinese restaurant.'

'Joseph Li's the name,' said Cage, making out he didn't care.
'Or Li Yok-yau.'

Leonard whistled through his teeth. 'I thought it might be but
we can't touch him.'

'What does that mean?'

'You're working in a democracy. We can't just barge in and
arrest Joseph Li who runs a fashionable chain of restaurants,
donates to political parties, finances community centres in
deprived areas, is on first-name terms with the mayor, congress-
men, senators and all those people. It doesn't happen like that
here, Cage. And besides, this car is clean.'

There must have been thirty mechanics in the workshop.
They'd been working for close on six hours and their enthusiasm
had gone. The next shift would put the car back together again
and it'd be lifted back out into the parking lot.

'Have you traced the engine casing number?' asked Cage.

'California. It was first registered in San Francisco.'

'But these are New York plates.' The plates were on the floor, under a bench, untouched.

'So? Cars cross state borders. That's why they have wheels.'

Cage drew out a pocket knife and opened the blade. He squatted down, picked up the front plate, laid it on the bench and slowly cut a line down the centre of the black letter 'T'. Then he gently opened the plastic. It was a fraction of an inch thick, but inside was a transparent polythene coating. He pierced it and brought out specks of white powder on the tip of the blade. He handed the knife to Leonard, turned the plates over and ran his fingers round the edges. 'The plates are fake,' he said. 'They were made up in China, sent over to San Francisco, put onto this vehicle and driven over here.' He took the knife back off Leonard and cut through another letter. More powder came out. 'It was never a shipment. Only a sample. Joseph Li's a smart operator.'

Leonard handed the plates over to the forensic team in the workshop and walked Cage outside, his hand on his elbow. 'You still wired?'

Cage's radio mike was turned off but he unplugged it too, to make Leonard feel more at ease. It must have been hovering below zero outside. They stood in a car dump in freezing drizzle.

'That plate? How'd you know about it?' asked Leonard.

'I've been to a place where they make them up.'

'In China?'

'In Thailand. But the Chinese do it.'

Leonard nodded. 'Let me tell you something about Joseph Li. Most of the rich Chinese who fled from Mao in the fifties were gangsters. We know them as Triads. But because Mao was a communist, we welcomed them with open arms. So they became gangsters here. Joseph Li was a big man in Xian, ran politicians, hotels, transport companies, the police – all the normal trappings. In forty-nine, when Mao came to power, he went to ground. With the help of some network, he got out through Hong Kong with his wife and two daughters in the mid-fifties. His son couldn't escape.' Leonard stamped his feet. A street light popped and went out. The overpass, filled with the evening traffic, vibrated above them.

99

'Sure Li's a crook, but until recently he had been a controllable one. Two years ago, he started trying to rebuild his empire in China. With the reforms, a lot of overseas Chinese are doing the same. He's been working through his son, Li Yi, who survived Mao and still lives in Xian.' Leonard paused. 'What I'm going to tell you next goes no further. You understand?'

Cage nodded.

'We put a phone tap on Joseph Li for a couple of weeks. One of the conversations which came out of it was between Li and his son. Li asked if it would be wise to invest in the *Hungsze Ling Yun*. How'd you translate that?'

'Red Spirit,' said Cage. 'But red in a political way, like Mao red, communist red, China red, and spirit like a ghost, or a soul, something not yet dead, still fluttering around the world.'

'Right. Li Yi, the son, was against it. He went on about China being different now. Then the father said something like, "Business and politics in China can never be separated. We must invest in the new political force." '

'What did he mean, political force?'

'The CIA ran a check on Red Spirit for us. It's a small Maoist movement which no one takes much notice of. It controls a couple of magazines. Very low circulation.'

'Who runs it?'

'Old guard communists. They didn't seem too sure.'

'But they also peddle heroin?' Cage pulled his collar up against the cold.

'Seems that way. I've been instructed to bust this racket,' said Leonard. 'But I've got to do it without ruffling the feathers of Joseph Li until right at the end.'

'So you're taking me up on my China offer.'

'You and I are going to get Joseph Li in a pincer movement. We know who he is in the US. You find out who he is – what he is – in China. What is his network? Who does he report to? How can we nail him? I don't care if it's the head of the goddamn Communist Party himself. I want to know.'

He'd done it. He'd planned it, steered it and won. 'It'll be a pleasure, sir,' said Cage quietly. Leonard touched Cage's elbow and turned him back towards the workshop. 'We'll get you

100

money, false passports, an escape route if things go wrong. The file on Li Yi, the son – have a look at it. He's a fixer and an entrepreneur, and one of the people who uses him is Dr Sally Parsons, your old girlfriend.'

Chapter Eleven

'I feel so stupid. Just tell me I'm stupid.'

'Absolutely not,' laughed Richard. 'You're not drawing me into that trap.'

'Naïve, then,' suggested Sally. After she'd left her spooky meeting with Wu Tian, Li Yi had given her back the disk. But when she put it into the computer at work, it showed up blank. Now she was curled up on her bed, the telephone resting on the pillow next to her head. She fiddled with a knotted lace of one of Paul's runners, trying to get it undone. 'Tell me I'm naïve,' she pressed.

'If I was to use any word to describe you, maybe, just maybe, I'd stretch to trusting, but . . .'

'But what?' Richard would pull a rabbit out of the hat. He had the knack of making her feel good, even thousands of miles away.

'Well, you promised Jeff you'd deliver the disk to Wu Tian and that's what you did. Just think how you'd feel if you hadn't carried out his wish just because you couldn't copy the damn thing.'

He hit the spot. 'God, I need you back here,' she said. 'And not just your body.' How much she missed having someone around, just to talk to at her own level.

'Can I go to work now?' he asked humbly.

Sally looked at her watch. It was just past seven in the evening, which meant it was just past seven in the morning in the US. 'Five more minutes. This could be the only fun conversation I have all day. How's the US–Soviet love-in today?'

102

'Imagine a young, ambitious diplomat dropping off to sleep in meeting after meeting, and you'll understand what I do every day. It was much more fun when we were about to nuke each other.'

'Come back then,' she said, surprised at how solemn she sounded.

'Another three or four days, I'll be back for sure.'

'Come now.'

'Then how could I keep you in the manner to which you're accustomed?'

'If you could see me now,' she chuckled. She shifted the telephone to another ear and turned over on the bed. 'Three or four days then. I'll fly up to Beijing to tell you all my darkest secrets.'

'You never did tell me what was on that disk,' said Richard.

Until now, he hadn't asked. And she hadn't told him because it was too frightening.

'You want to know?' she said slowly. Suddenly, the conversation was serious.

'We've got four and a half minutes left.' It was a joke, but there was an edge to his voice.

Why not? If she couldn't tell Richard, who could she tell?

'OK. There was a lot of stuff about Mao's death and burial. According to Wu Tian, this Zhang Ying was some sort of masseur of Mao's who completely adored him. So a lot of stuff about the night he died and then how they tried to preserve the body but got it all wrong with the formaldehyde and ended up having to make a wax effigy. So you don't know whether you're looking at a real Mao or a fake Mao in the mausoleum. And there was a description about how during the Cultural Revolution they sealed off Qin's tomb and found a way in. The descriptions are fantastic, Richard, the skeletons of caparisoned horses, jewelled ceilings, evaporated moats of mercury. All that.'

She stopped, tossed Paul's runner onto the floor and sat up on the bed. She wanted so much to talk about the rest, but it *was* scary, as if to tell might make it true.

'And?' said Richard. 'There's something else, isn't there?'

'Yes, there is. And, somehow, I don't want to think about it

103

but . . .' She hoped Richard would break in, but he stayed quiet, his silence pushing her on. 'Zhang Ying says after the famine in the fifties, China was bankrupt. It had been snubbed by the Soviet Union. It was broke. It was humiliated in the Korean War. Mao's dream was falling apart. So Mao apparently had this crazy idea of flooding the US with heroin, making a fortune from it and turning Americans into junkies.'

Richard laughed. 'That's what it says?'

Sally swallowed. 'That's what it says. Zhang Ying quotes Mao as saying something like, "When the British colonialists invaded China and trafficked opium to the motherland, we thought their motive was profit. Now the blinkers have been removed from our eyes, and we know that the true motivation of the imperialists was to weaken China and make the Chinese people useless with their addiction to opium." Zhang said Mao was wise enough to know how to use these tactics of war against the imperialists. He ordered that opium, refined into heroin, be shipped to Europe and America, and with the help of the "patriotic Chinese societies there" – I guess that's the Triads – it would bring chaos onto the streets and ensure that the Chinese people will never be slaves again.'

'Mao used the "never be slaves again" line at his victory speech in Tiananmen Square,' said Richard.

'No, Richard, you don't get it,' said Sally impatiently. 'Zhang Ying says it's still going on. Like now. Today.'

'In Qin's tomb?'

'Yes.'

'Mao just about eradicated opium smoking in China.'

'In China. Yes. But that doesn't mean he couldn't use it as some kind of weapon.'

'Sounds crazy.'

She'd hoped he'd say that. 'Why. Tell me why?'

'I can think of a hundred better places to run a dope distribution point. What about all the military bases? You need to be near a port or an airport. You know what, Sal?'

'What?'

'I reckon Wu Tian's got Zhang Ying's measure. He's a nutcase. And Jeff, well, Jeff was looking for one last big show in his academic career. This landed on his desk. He wanted to believe it but he, too, thought it might be bogus.'

'That's why he wanted to check it with Wu Tian?'

'Exactly.'

'So you don't think that's why Jeff was killed?' Say it, Richard. Spell it out to me.

'No,' he said with finality. 'Jeff wasn't killed because he had uncovered a dope trafficking ring.'

'Thank you,' Sally said softly.

'I've talked to homicide. An apartment on the top floor of the same block was done over. So it looks like Jeff was his last call. Another horrible Manhattan murder.'

'God, how I miss you, Richard.'

'Miss you, too. Gotta run.'

Sally lay on the bed, the telephone on her chest, digesting what Richard had said. She was right to have told him. Her mind was running wild with ideas, making herself so scared she had been on the verge of pulling out.

Chapter Twelve

'So if he wants to be my dad again, why doesn't he live with us?'
Paul gave Sally a look that told her he wouldn't give up until he
got an answer. He put his hand up to stop Sally from combing
his hair.

'It's a little complicated to explain, honey.' She shook her
hand free and kept combing. 'It's one of those things you'll
understand with time.'

'No, it isn't. Even if he's not living with us, he could come and
see me. He hasn't done that.'

'That might not have been his fault,' said Sally.

She brushed his fringe to one side. His hair was dark brown,
without any trace of her red, but it was becoming unruly like
hers. Paul was getting used to it flopping in his face. Through
the window, she could see Ko turning his taxi, pausing to allow
the chickens to scatter away from the road. 'Get your jacket on.
Ko's ready.'

But Paul slipped out from under her arms and ran into the
garden. They had risen early to fit in his meeting with Cage before
he went to school, which hadn't given him time to give milk to
Ko's litter of puppies. She hoped Ko would stay in the car,
otherwise it would turn into a big conversation about the puppies
and Mrs Ko's baby, and she would have to tear Paul away.

Which was probably what Paul was planning, because he had
run to the front of the house and was beckoning to Ko. 'You
gotta get some milk on your way back,' he shouted, pouring the
last of the milk into a saucer.

Sally went out and lifted him up by his collar, stretched out

106

his arms like a scarecrow so she could put on his coat, pulled his hat firmly down on his head, picked up his satchel on the way back through the house and marched him to the car.

As they got in, Paul said, 'I don't want to see him. Do I have to?'

'Yes, you do. Give him a chance, OK? I want you to see him before school now, then next week again for a longer time. If you don't want to see him after that, we'll talk about it.'

'I don't want to see him at all.'

'Give him a chance. For Mommy, OK? Half of you is him, and he's a good man.' She never thought she would hear herself saying that.

'So why are you with Richard and not him?'

Sally sighed.

She recognised Cage straightaway and felt a lot cooler than she expected. He was pacing up and down behind the glass entrance door of the hotel, his hands clasped first in front of him, then behind his back as if he couldn't work out whether he was a civilian or a soldier. She waved at him and he waved back, both of them making the effort to be civil.

He held the door open, leaned forward to kiss her on the cheek but she moved away and offered her hand instead. Paul hung back, holding on to her coat, hiding in it. They all stepped inside, away from the door, and Sally pulled Paul round.

'Paul, say hello to your father.'

Paul looked at the ground. Cage squatted so that he could see his son at eye level. 'Hi, Paul,' he said softly.

He hadn't seen him for four years. At three, there's a lot of baby about a boy. At seven, there's a lot of man. Cage had to look away to stop a welling in his throat as it sank in that he had lost those years with Paul and they could never be replaced.

Paul didn't move. It was an awesome judgement from child to father.

'I don't expect you remember me. I last saw you when you were three.'

Ever so slightly, Paul shook his head. But he still didn't look up. Cage pulled a package out of his coat. The corner of the box got caught on the edge of the pocket and he had to fiddle with it. Paul held Sally's hand.

'I brought you a present from New York.'

Sally recognised the wrapping from a gift store at Kennedy Airport. Paul didn't take it, but he said, 'Thanks. Richard brings me presents from New York, too.'

Sally hurt for Cage. 'Why don't we all go pull up some chairs and get some coffee?' she suggested breezily.

Cage found a table at the far end of the lobby. He put Paul's present in the middle and pulled up three chairs, although Paul splayed himself out on Sally's lap, heavy and awkward.

'Paul's on his way to school,' said Sally.

Cage tried again. 'What's your favourite subject, Paul?'

Sally kept quiet until the silence became embarrassing. 'His real favourite subject is bicycling, isn't it, hon? The Chinese bikes are a bit slow for him. I managed to get him a second-hand bike from one of the other American parents.'

'What sort of bike is it, Paul?' said Cage.

Paul buried his face in Sally's shoulder. 'Come on, Paul, answer your father,' Sally coaxed.

Cage signalled a waiter and ordered some coffee. 'Paul, do you want a Coke? Orange juice?'

'He'll have a Coke,' said Sally, talking straight to the waiter. 'C'mon, tell your father what sort of bike you have.'

'No.' It was the softest whisper in her ear. He gripped her shoulder.

'It's a mountain bike. Ten gears. Faster than a car on the bumpy roads,' Sally said. Taking herself by surprise, she reached across and touched Cage's hand. 'Sorry,' she whispered.

Cage smiled. 'It's fine. How've you been, anyway?'

'Apart from *this* thing,' she playfully slapped Paul's butt, 'fine. How about you?'

'Fine. I saw Cait in New York. She told you what I was doing here? It's good to see you, Sal.'

That was far enough. Paul was wriggling so she let him slither to the ground. She looked at her watch. 'Look, I'd better take Paul on to school. We'll try and fix something up for later.'

'How far is it?'

'Depends on the traffic. Five, ten minutes.'

'Let me go with him.'

'Bad idea,' said Sally straightaway. What would Cait say to that?

'Why not?' asked Cage, gently persuasive, like he had always been. 'Father and son alone. Might help break the ice.'

Sally ruffled Paul's hair. He was standing, holding her hand. He glanced towards the box on the table. 'Do you want your father to ride with you to school?' He squeezed her hand, but the silence remained. 'All right, young man. If you don't answer within ten seconds, I will assume that you don't want him to go with you. Ten seconds, OK? Starting from now – ten, nine, eight, seven, six, five, four, three, two, one and a half, one and a quarter, one and—'

'Sure, he can come,' Paul released Sally's hand, leapt forward, grabbed Cage's present and was about to open it when Sally snatched it from him.

'That's something you missed your chance with. You can look forward to it all day and open it tonight.'

'Maaaaawm!' It was Paul's marker whine. Not serious.

Cage was on his feet. 'What time do you have to be at work?'

'It's fine. I'll be here when you get back.' After all, it was what Cait had suggested. She regretted the way she'd said it, as if it was a chore she needed to finish.

She saw them to the car, then went back inside and poured herself another coffee. She smiled to herself, feeling unexpectedly proud of Paul, because while she and Cage were wondering which one would intimidate the other, he had managed to intimidate both of them.

She realised her hand was shaking a bit, not through fear but through some sort of excitement, like when she had first met Cage. She wondered if all women felt like that with him, or whether it was just a chemistry between the two of them. She even felt a twinge of jealousy towards women she didn't even know existed.

The attraction had begun the day they sat next to each other at language school in New York, learning Chinese. Cage was in the military, but taking night school out of work hours, and

109

when Sally asked what a soldier was doing learning Chinese, Cage grinned at her and said it was classified. Like she wasn't meant to believe him. When Sally told him she was going to be an archaeologist in China, and he said he was jealous because it was a really exciting job, she couldn't work out whether he was serious or not.

He made his move in the first week, telling her to watch his tongue movements in his mouth to try to get the Chinese tones right, and they stood there in the corridor, peering into each other's mouths, correcting tongue movements.

He didn't ask her out for a date as such. One afternoon she said she was heading to the new Barnes and Noble to look at a book on Chinese archaeology. She reckoned it would be too expensive to buy but she wanted to take a look at it anyway. Cage asked the name of the book and said he would steal it for her. She couldn't tell if he meant it. When she got there, Cage was already at the bookshelf.

'Give me fifteen minutes and meet me at the Empire Hotel,' he said. 'Take the main entrance, and I'll be in the bar just on the right.'

She gave him twenty minutes, then crossed the intersection by Lincoln Center and saw him through the window, perched on a bar stool, reading the *New York Times*. Sally tapped on the window and walked in. A bottle of champagne was sitting in a bucket, covered with a white linen napkin. He had already poured himself a glass. A gift-wrapped package, tied with a flowing red ribbon, was in the middle of the small round table.

She unwrapped it and pulled out the book, not the cheaper paperback edition but the glossy illustrated hardback, which must have cost way over a hundred dollars. 'So, did you steal it?' she said, smiling.

He lifted out the champagne bottle, wiped the drips from the bottom, and poured her a glass. 'I paid for the champagne,' he said. 'It's a difficult thing to steal.' He was cool, but a little nervous in the way he topped up her glass without letting the bubbles settle down.

The book stayed on the table, something unexplained between them. Cage took over the conversation, and by the end she was telling him most things about herself. She had never met anyone with so much curiosity. Soon, he knew all about her family: Cait, who was training in child psychology but never had a boyfriend; Helen who could talk of nothing but getting married and having kids; her long-suffering apron-bound mother; and her grumpy father who had never really left the Montagnard crossbow men in the Vietnamese mountains and whose only common ground with her was teaching her the crossbow.

Cage made her laugh when he asked her to demonstrate how to operate a crossbow on a damp napkin, and got her to reveal her lifelong dream to walk through the vaults of Qin Shi Huang's mausoleum.

Halfway through, she realised she knew nothing about him, and when she asked where he worked, he said, 'Nowhere yet. But I hope to serve my country all over the world.' Then he winked at her, so she couldn't tell if he was kidding.

'And the Chinese?'

'Look at me. I'm not exactly a Midwestern cowboy, am I? I guess I'm looking for a bit of my roots.'

Then he had called for the check, and pulled an envelope out of his pocket and handed it to her. Inside was a greetings card on which he had written, 'Dear Sally, thanks so much for a wonderful drink.' From the card a slip of paper dropped onto the table. It was the receipt for the book.

Sally laughed out loud to herself as she remembered the first joke Cage had played on her. She was just beginning to enjoy her coffee and solitude when a voice boomed at her across the lobby. 'Sally. Dr Sally Parsons. How dare you have morning coffee in the Xian Garden Hotel without inviting me?'

Li Yi walked quickly towards her with a broad smile all over his face, and Sally registered the stupid mistake she had made in arranging to see Cage in this hotel, because it was *the* meeting place of Xian.

She got up, and he kissed her on both cheeks, swung his briefcase onto the spare seat, and sat heavily in Cage's chair, casting a smell of sweet musk aftershave around the table. He leaned back, clicked his fingers loudly and kept on until a waiter scuttled over and, without asking Sally, ordered another pot of coffee.

'Am I interrupting anything?' he asked, eyeing Cage's cup and the half-drunk glass of Coke.

'Not at the moment, and if you've got my disk back for me I'll forgive your intrusion.' She had pestered him about the disk. Li Yi kept promising to deliver but it never appeared.

'Be patient, Sally, please. If you wanted to keep it, with all due respect, I must say you were a little naïve in handing it to a professor of Marxism at the People's University.'

'So why didn't you warn me?'

Li Yi smiled. 'And if Li Yi had known about the disk and not informed the correct authorities, he might have been whisked away to a labour camp in Tibet.' He casually ran a finger round his throat and dropped his voice to a whisper. 'You are lovely, Sally. So innocent that you keep forgetting what my beloved motherland really is.'

Sally bit her lip. She remembered the evasive, menacing look in Wu Tian's eyes at the end of the meeting. Li Yi was right.

She put up her hand. 'OK. Point taken. I was dumb.'

'Don't worry, we all keep forgetting that China is still a communist state.' Li Yi waved his hand around the lobby. 'Ten years ago, who would have imagined we would all be dropping by for coffee in an international hotel? But underneath this, nothing has changed. Even a document which just says Mao had a dimple on his chin or what the rainfall was during the Cultural Revolution is liable to be confiscated.' He shrugged. 'Feel for me, Sal. I have to live with it.'

The waiter returned with the coffee, and Li Yi made a show of pushing five US dollars into his hand. Then he looked at his heavy gold watch. He also wore a gold signet and a smaller ring on his wedding band finger. 'So what are you doing here, Dr Parsons, having coffee all by yourself?'

'Actually, I'm sorting out some family matters.' She smiled and put her hand on Li Yi's arm. 'My meeting will resume soon and then you'll have to fade away.'

'Busy. Busy. Busy. That's our Dr Sally Parsons.' Li Yi put down his coffee cup and looked towards the door. 'So, before anyone disturbs us, your good friend Li Yi will give you the exceptionally good news. Listen carefully. The old guard at the Cultural Relics Bureau are being fired, which means the government will soon be changing its mind about excavation of the tomb. I've had a word with one of the new archaeologists there.'

'Who?' said Sally. Suddenly, this was interesting.

'That I can't tell. But I'm ninety per cent certain they will give the green light to excavation. He was talking about bringing in the Japanese but I told him about your work and he was impressed. The Americans helped us defeat the Japanese, I said, so we should give the Americans the tomb.' He took a cigarette out of a silver case, then produced a souvenir lighter decorated with the face of Mao Zedong.

'When?' asked Sally. 'How long?'

Li Yi lit the cigarette and took time drawing on the tobacco. 'Difficult to say. I'd guess three to six months, and if it happens, you may have to work directly for us.'

'Who's us?'

'Either the Cultural Relics Bureau or the Shaanxi provincial government. It depends how I structure it. You would be a foreign consultant. It's a nationalistic thing because the tomb is such a big deal. We wouldn't want an American institute excavating the tomb. We would do it and you would be on our payroll.'

'That's fine,' said Sally. That would be better, she thought. Much better. No more New York meetings. No more Beards, Watsons and Eliots with one 'l' and one 't'.

'The government would throw a whole lot of money at it and offset it against the tourism budget.' Li Yi swallowed his coffee and looked at his watch again, just as Sally spotted Cage walking back through the door with a wave, and quickening his step to get to her.

Same wave. Same movements. How easily they had moved around each other when things were good. 'Is this Dr Parsons' date?' asked Li Yi, standing up.

'He's Paul's father.' Her voice lowered as Cage approached.

'How interesting.' Li Yi stubbed his cigarette out. It was barely smoked.

'How did it go?' Sally asked Cage.

'I think it worked OK,' Cage answered, seeming to take the measure of Li Yi. 'We discussed six different ways to get from your house to Qin's tomb.'

Sally laughed. 'That's a game I play to get him to sleep.' She turned to Li Yi. 'Cage, this is Li Yi, one of my oldest friends in China.'

Li Yi's hand was already out. 'Cage – is that your first name?'

'She's called me Cage practically since we met. For some reason, she took against the name Bill.'

'My job is to make it an easier and smaller world for American friends visiting China.' He picked up his briefcase. 'So if there's anything you need, get Sally to let me know.'

Sally and Cage sat down again, watching Li Yi meander across the lobby waving to people he knew. Cage put his hand to Li Yi's coffee pot, satisfied himself that it was warm and started pouring some for Sally. But she had put her hand across the cup. 'I'm fine, thanks. I have to get to work soon.'

Cage poured for himself, then put his elbows on his knees, looked at her. 'I'll say this once more, then I'll shut up. It's good to see you again.'

Sally didn't respond, then immediately felt guilty. 'Cait said if Paul wants it, we have to find a way to work it so you can see him. If he doesn't, then you should back off for a bit and let him get used to the idea.'

'Fine with me.' He was still looking at her, the way he used to when he wanted something.

Sally laughed. 'Cage, stop it. This is meant to be a working meeting.'

Cage shrugged. 'We're working. Like I said, fine with me.'

'How was Paul in the car?'

'Grumpy. So I said I was sorry. We talked about mountain bikes and he asked me to look at his.'

Sally didn't like that. She hoped he couldn't tell by her expression. 'Anything else?' she said.

'He also wanted to know when I stopped being a soldier.'

'Have you?'

'Yeah. A while ago. I thought it was time to get a life. Paul

114

asked if I was going to be a soldier again. I said I wasn't. He wanted to know if I was going to live in China, and I said I didn't know. He asked if I knew a man called Richard Gregg.'

'The little rat.' Sally stiffened, but couldn't help showing her pride in Paul's direct questioning.

'I said I didn't. Then he regaled me with stories about how clever this Richard Gregg was, and how the three of you got on so well together and how you'd just been in New York checking out the big apartment on the Upper West Side you were going to live in. So naturally I asked Paul if his mom was in love with Mr Gregg.' Cage picked up his coffee and took his time drinking it. He said nothing more, letting the words hang there, while Sally fidgeted, taking out a hair clip, hooking her hair behind her ear and clipping it back on.

'All right, Cage, my curiosity is killing me. What did Paul say?'

'Your son said he hoped you would marry Richard, because Richard could become a real dad to him. He said Richard was neat.'

Sally swallowed. 'Oh, God, Cage. I'm sorry.'

'He asked the fat little cab driver if he agreed.'

'Ko?'

'If that's his name.'

'And what did Ko say?'

'Ko said Richard made you happy. Is that true?'

'Sure,' answered Sally nervously. This wasn't going how she'd planned it. 'We have a good relationship.'

'That's good,' said Cage bravely. 'It's good for you. Good for Paul.' He paused. 'But then Paul said he was kidding and he'd much prefer me to be his dad and he thought you and I should get married.'

'He what?'

'He said Richard was a prissy little weasel and if you married him he'd run away.' He stared at her, his eyes piercing through.

'You're making it up.'

Cage held up his hand mockingly. 'As Ko is my witness.'

Sally was looking straight back at him, but she couldn't work out what was going on behind his deadpan expression.

'Yeah. I'm kidding.' Cage broke into a huge grin. 'He's a great boy, Sal. Well done. And I hope it works out with Richard. I mean it. You deserve it.'

Sally was blushing, trying to hide her own smile and trying desperately not to laugh. She leaned down and picked her bag up off the floor. 'I have to go. I'm already late for work.'

Cage reached across the table and lightly took her hand. 'Stay a little. Ten minutes?'

Sally pulled back her hand. 'Cage, don't.' She got up. 'Next week sometime come round and see Paul on his bike.'

Cage was on his feet too. 'Do I have to go through Cait? You know, get to you through a third party?'

Sally heaved her bag over her shoulder. 'Not necessary. Let's scrap that damn court ruling and start from scratch.'

As she walked across the lobby, Cage followed. She moved as if she didn't want him, but she hadn't said goodbye with either a handshake or a peck on the cheek. At that moment, Sally didn't know what she wanted. If Cage had turned and gone to his room, she would have been distraught. But he had caught up and was stepping ahead to open the door, and that irritated her.

Ko brought the car round, and Cage held the back door open for her. 'Are you going to the terracotta warriors?' he asked. Sally nodded. 'Mind if I join you for the ride?'

'I thought you were tracking down your parents.'

'Please,' he said. Sally leaned over and opened the other back door for him. 'Besides, we need to talk,' he added, getting in.

'*We* don't need to talk. You and Paul do.'

'Right,' said Cage, and he left it at that, keeping his distance from Sally on the shared back seat and studying the bizarre decorations in the taxi, the laminated Mao emblems which Paul and Ko had discussed like two boys collecting football cards.

The traffic was heavy and they made slow progress. Eventually, when they got to the underpass, Sally broke the silence. 'That's where they leave the babies. Ko and I find a lot, especially early in the morning. Don't we, Ko?'

Ko grunted and touched one of the cards hanging from the mirror – a photograph of Mao gazing out to sea.

'Ko's wife is having a baby soon and he's praying to the Great Helmsman for a boy.'

Cage pulled one of Ko's Chinese magazines out of the seat pocket and flicked through it, not really taking it in. 'Have you heard of this writer called Red Spirit?'

Sally shifted closer to him, looking at the magazine he was reading. 'That's *Dangdai Sichao*, Contemporary Trends of Thought. Red Spirit is usually in *Zhenli de Zhuiqiu*, Pursuit of Truth.' She looked further back in the pocket, then checked the one in front of her. 'Here we are. He has quite a following, doesn't he, Ko?'

'I think he's right, if that's what you're asking me,' said Ko in Chinese. 'No offence, Sally, but China must find its own way.'

She let it go at that and they drove in silence for a bit. Cage read the magazine and occasionally glanced out of the window. Somehow it reminded her of their language training together. Then she had an idea. 'Li Yi might be able to cut the red tape in finding your mother's birth certificate,' she suggested.

Cage looked up. 'You think so?'

'You need someone like Li Yi or you'll be waiting years to get anywhere. I couldn't operate here without him. I should have thought of it when you met him. You want me to call him?'

'If you could, Sal. Thanks. I haven't got a whole heap of time for this but somehow it's becoming an important thing in my life.'

'I'll call as soon as I get to the office.' She took the magazine from him, flicked through the pages, then tapped the Red Spirit column. 'There. The latest recycled thoughts of the great Chairman Mao Zedong: "Freedom is the understanding of necessity". I read them every day instead of my horoscope.'

'Do you know who Red Spirit is?'

'Haven't a clue,' said Sally lightly. 'I'm hopeless with the present. Try asking me about what happened two thousand years back.'

Cage laughed. 'Can we have dinner or something?' He raised his eyes towards Ko. 'You know, with Paul, Li Yi and everyone else around, it's difficult to have a proper conversation, and I think we need one.'

'You sound like Cait.'

'I'm trying to.'

'We're not getting . . .' She stopped herself, realising Cage was right.

'No, Sal, we're not getting in too deep, too soon, and I'm not trying to,' said Cage. 'But there are things unsaid that should be said, because when Paul graduates, gets married or gets into trouble, you and I are going to have to work together.'

Sally thought about it. Against her will, she knew she should agree. 'No guilt trip, OK? No excuses. No getting back together again.'

'Sure.'

'OK, then I would love to have dinner with you.'

When they got to the Terracotta Warrior Museum, Cage walked Sally towards the turnstiles, where she turned and touched him on the chest. 'You're not allowed any further. I'll call.'

Chapter Thirteen

Cage had only been back in his hotel room an hour when Li Yi rapped on the door. He walked straight in. 'Sally said you might need some help. I saw you come back through the lobby and thought I'd come up.' He double-locked the door and put the chain across.

'Thanks for getting in touch so quickly,' said Cage.

Li Yi didn't answer. He knew the layout of the room better than Cage did, he slid back the wardrobe door, opened the mini bar and took out a miniature of Johnny Walker Red Label whisky. He unscrewed the cap, poured it into the glass on top of the fridge, and downed at least half of it in one.

Cage stayed on his feet and leaned against the wall by the window, arms folded. Li Yi took out his cigarette case, took one for himself, almost closed it again, then offered one to Cage, making sure both of them understood it was an afterthought. Cage didn't move. Didn't accept or reject. Didn't acknowledge the offer.

Li Yi smiled. 'I respect you for that,' he said. He lit up with the Mao lighter. 'So what are you in Xian for, Captain William Rupert Cage?'

'I'm looking for my mother. Possibly my father,' Cage replied drily.

'Forgive my bluntness, but I like to know who I'm helping. China can be a dangerous place.' He paused while he exhaled. 'No rule of law here. Gangsters everywhere.'

'I was born here in Xian. June the eighteenth, nineteen fifty-seven. I've come back to find out who my parents are.'

119

Li Yi waved his cigarette around in an imperious way. 'So, William Cage, you are a half-caste bastard: mother Chinese; father, God knows what. Born in China three years after the Korean War ended. Mao Zedong's transition to socialism was in place. Fifteen years from then our cities were to have been of the same standard as the United States. The land reform of the Great Helmsman had been completed. The landlord classes which had ruled China for six thousand years had been eliminated.'

Cage wasn't sure what game Li Yi was playing with this historical essay of China. 'By killing two million people,' he said softly.

'Sorry, what was that?'

'Lot of bloodshed, killing landlords.'

'You were born on the eve of the Great Leap Forward, China's economic miracle to overtake the West.'

'Twenty million dead,' said Cage. 'Starvation.'

'Probably thirty million,' said Li Yi. 'Does it matter when the numbers are so big? You have read up on your Chinese history.' He put the cigarette in the ashtray and clasped his hands in front of him, preacher-like. 'And they still love him. That's the amazing thing. They love Mao. They love the Communist Party and they love China.' He tossed Cage the Mao lighter. 'Keep it. It's already a collector's item. You can get a hundred dollars for it on the black market.'

Cage turned it in his hand and threw the lighter onto the bed. 'So Sally told you I needed someone to help me cut through the red tape,' he said. 'Some things stay with you all your life, eating away at you. For me, this is one of them. If you can help, I'd appreciate it. I would also be able to pay.'

Li Yi nodded, chin in hand. 'William Rupert Cage. Adopted January 11th 1958, through an agency based in Ohio, by a childless professional couple in New York. But you, Bill Cage, didn't prove to be the remedy they'd paid for. Fifteen years later, both your adopted parents were off the rails – is that how you say it in English? Your father was jailed for insider trading and is now a broken man. Your mother wanted to be a television star but never made it, turned to drink and died five years ago. You did the sensible thing and joined the Marine Corps. From which you were discharged on June the fifteenth, nineteen eighty-eight. Your commanding officer was a Colonel Al Childs who wrote in your record that you were a good fighter but an unreliable soldier. The reason for your discharge is classified. So, where did you fight, Bill Cage?'

'That's classified as well.' Cage was having a better day than he had thought. Leonard had made his military record available, but not too available, forcing Li Yi and his associates to do a bit of work, but not too much.

'You had a reputation for surveillance work. Colonel Childs said you had an ability to blend in with any race. When you were Chinese, you could seem Chinese. When you were with Europeans, you could seem Caucasian.'

'Is that possible for any man?' said Cage.

'That's what's in your report. But you were also insubordinate and that was your downfall. Are they right?' Li Yi pushed himself off the wall and sat on the edge of the bed.

'Mr Li, I think there's been a mistake,' he said softly but with a measure of threat. 'I'm in Xian to find out who my parents are. I applaud you for the quality of your information network, but you obviously think I'm someone I am not.'

'You're a criminal,' said Li Yi bluntly. 'You washed out of the military and took to a life of crime. Back in the States, there's a warrant out for your arrest. From what I've been told, you left a man dead.'

So Leonard had fed him the shooting too, just like he had fed it to Captain Freni. But by making him a killer, Leonard had raised the stakes.

'Let me repeat myself. I want help in finding my parents. If you can help, fine. If you can't, why don't we just call it a day?' Cage walked to the door and unlocked it.

Li Yi didn't move. 'I look after Sally in this town. He stubbed out his cigarette, sat back and put his hands behind his head, the body language of a man holding power.

'What does that mean?'

Li Yi laughed. 'Relax, Bill. If I can call you Bill? It's not a threat.'

'Then why say it?'

'It's a fact.' He stood up, went to the door and pushed it shut. Cage let him. 'Have a drink.'

'No thanks.'

Li Yi topped up his whisky with another miniature, this time drinking it down in one. 'China is one big protection racket. That's why I told you. There's the army, the police, the Communist Party, the big state-run industries, the new conglomerates. And with Deng Xiao-ping in charge, the gangsters are back. The police, the courts, they're all in the pocket of someone or something. No justice. You understand me? So when I say I look after Sally, it means I protect her. I make sure she can explore her archaeological sites and raise her son – your son too – without anyone hurting her. It's not a threat. It's a fact.'

'How'd it go?' asked Sally when she called him that evening.

'Good,' said Cage. 'But he says he needs me to go to Beijing. If my father was a foreigner in the fifties, the papers would be with the Communist Party, not the local authorities.'

'Oh,' said Sally. She hadn't expected it but for some reason she didn't want Cage to leave Xian so quickly. It wasn't Cage exactly, she told herself, just that she liked having someone around from her own culture she could talk to.

'So I was wondering if we could have dinner tonight,' Cage was saying. 'Then I'll catch up with Paul when I get back.'

Sally had planned to work on the tomb, and she wasn't sure she wanted a heavy dinner with Cage. But she found herself agreeing, though it was a step further than Cait would have thought necessary. Cage picked the same French restaurant Richard had first taken her to, which didn't help. Not that, in Xian, French meant anything in culinary terms, except that it wasn't Chinese food.

When Sally walked into the restaurant and Cage enthusiastically stood up to greet her, she wished she had taken a shot of brandy.

She had dressed for the occasion, which she didn't often do in China. And she had washed and conditioned her hair, then tried to blow dry it to get it to stay back without too many hairpins. She chose a dark blue business suit with loud gold buttons, as far removed from intimacy as anything in her small wardrobe. But she did mess around with her lipstick longer than usual. Paul was engrossed in some computer game and when she said, 'You are so lucky you're not a woman,' he barely looked up, just kept playing, and Sally shut up.

While she had dressed up, Cage had dressed down in a pair of jeans with a red open-neck shirt and a colourful silk scarf which clashed with it. A leather jacket was slung over the back of the chair. His figure was too trim, his confidence too assured for him to be one of the tourists, yet his face was too alert, too curious for him to be a local Chinese.

She let him kiss her on the cheek and, once she sat down, he was attentive, keeping to light chat and handling the waiters so well that Sally started to relax. Cage mimicked Li Yi, with his cigarette case and Mao lighter, which he showed off to her as his first souvenir of China. 'You could get a hundred dollars for that on the black market,' he said with perfect intonation, then switched back to his own voice. 'Is he for real? Is that the voice of modern China?'

'He's my lifeline,' said Sally, chuckling. 'He might be a little up front, but he fixes anything I need.'

'So can he find my parents?'

Sally shrugged. 'I use him for visas and work permissions. I haven't tested him on genealogy before but if Li Yi says he can fix it, he usually can. He's proud of his reputation.'

Cage grinned. 'Then I'll be out of your hair.'

She let him pour her some wine. 'You didn't seem to care about your parentage before. Are you going through a mid-life crisis or something?'

'I cared. Just didn't talk about it.'

'I don't want to be tactless, but it must have crossed your mind. Do you think you were found on the roadside, like Ko and I find the baby girls?'

Cage brought out his locket, opened it and slid it across the table to Sally. 'You remember this? Does she look like the sort of woman who would leave a baby on the street? She's beautiful, isn't she?'

The faded photograph in the locket was of a woman in her

mid-twenties, looking dutifully at the camera, posing for an ID photograph. She wore a bland Mao tunic; her face was serious and stern. But Cage was right, thought Sally, she was beautiful. She looked in control of her life.

'Yes, she is,' said Sally. 'But they were rough times, Cage. Rougher than now.'

'I always carried it with me. Remember?'

She nodded, looked, then slid it back to Cage. He had shown it to her once, but it was after an argument and she hadn't wanted to know, hadn't wanted things to get deeper than they were. She hadn't seen it since. She felt Cage was showing her his vulnerability and she wasn't sure how to handle it.

'Why now?'

'We all get older and I have time on my hands,' said Cage.

'Have you really left the military?'

'You could say that.' He left a gap for Sally to inquire further, but she didn't take it up. So Cage went on, 'Any chance of you being in Beijing when I'm there?'

Sally thought of Richard coming back, but she shook her head. 'I don't get much of a chance to get up there. But it sounds like Li Yi can help you.'

'So I should trust him?'

'For God's sake, Cage. Don't ask me. I'm the biggest sucker in the world. I fell for you, didn't I?' She bit her lip. She hadn't meant to say that.

Cage brushed it aside, smiling. 'You got Paul from it. He's not a total loss. Work keeping you busy?' he asked, seamlessly shifting the topic clear of minefields.

'Yes,' she said. 'I work hard to try to prove I'm worth keeping here. That's why I was in New York recently.' Their relationship was too distant for her to tell him about Binsky and the tapes. Maybe next time. She thought about that and it dawned on her that she and Cage would probably end up having dinners and lunches on and off for the rest of their lives because of Paul. She wouldn't have to fight it any more, and she silently thanked Cait for pushing her into seeing Cage again.

When he asked about dessert, she ordered a sorbet because she didn't want the evening to end. She had a cappuccino, although she knew the restaurant's cappuccino was barely drinkable. When he offered, she ordered another.

'Let's do this again,' he said when they were leaving. He pulled out her chair for her and picked up her scarf which had fallen to the floor.

'I thought you were going to Beijing with Li Yi,' said Sally stiffly.

'Is that a no?'

'Richard's coming back in a couple of days.' She hadn't meant to use that.

'So Beijing and Richard equals no?'

'No. It's just that . . .' She fiddled with her hair. 'Come on, Cage. You know what I mean.'

While she was getting her sentences in a twist about how or whether to see Cage again, not with Paul, but just the two of them, Cage helped her and said, 'But you wouldn't like me not to have asked.'

To her dismay, Sally found herself laughing again. 'You're right. I wouldn't,' she said.

Sally's trade, by its nature, dealt with death. Burial sites were the workplaces of an archaeologist. Richard's return kept getting delayed so Sally concentrated on her work. After nights of preparation she was ready to insert the probe inside the tomb once again.

Sally thought in terms of soil traces, carbon dating, primary state formation, pollen traces like those found on a skeleton in Iran – a burial with flowers; the yellow crusts of tartaric acid in Egyptian jars – a cellar of wine; human tissue in a mummified human gut – cannibalism; starch residues on stone tools – the eating of root vegetables.

Human beings were first formally buried after death some-where between 40,000 and 100,000 years ago. You could tell because their skeletons showed no evidence of violent death. Nor did they bear the teeth marks of a wild animal to show they had been dragged to a final resting place. Australian Aboriginal paintings had been carbon dated back to 40,000 years ago. The eating habits of the Solomon Islanders had been traced back

27,500 years. So where she was now on the tomb of Qin Shi Huang, built 2,199 years ago, represented no significant span of time. In the great expanse of history, the Mao and Qin empires could be thought of as being of the same era; both men had the same mind-set, sophistication and brutality. In strict archaeological terms, with Mao gone and the more pragmatic Deng Xiao-ping in charge, China was only now evolving to secondary state formation.

After losing the disk, Sally had pored over the museum's own records to try to find some corroboration of Zhang Ying's account, but with no luck. There hadn't been any clear record of which parts of the tomb might have been raided in the power struggle of 206 BC, three years after Qin's death. She had tried to link the methane fires which were meant to have discoloured some of the warriors in the pits with the place of break-in. It led nowhere.

But Sally couldn't let it go. With nothing else to go on, she would use Zhang Ying. Even if he was a fraud, he had read his history and she could work with him. She decided to plot out the path which Zhang Ying and his team could have taken into the tomb. She used the electrical prod, which gave her echo soundings like a submarine. At the very best, it told her where rock formations lay just underneath the clay surface, places where it would be possible for her to drill down and use the probe camera.

A couple of weeks earlier, when she began tracking the path, she had caught sight of the tramp again, scuttling like a tortoise and shapeless in layers of cloth and rags. One night, she had taken him chicken and rice in a cheap tin lunch box and left it on a ledge of rock by the path heading up the slope. When she came down, the lunch box was there, empty and scoured spotlessly clean. A single fresh leaf had been left as a sort of acknowledgement.

For five nights running now, she had left out the lunch box. It had become a routine, comforting too, knowing that she shared the tomb with this cold, unapproachable person. That was the extent of their strange relationship; she did not try to approach him, or persuade him to approach her.

Normally this sort of project would have had dozens of people working on it. She had to narrow down an area of more than twelve thousand square metres. The north-south outer wall of the tomb was more than a mile long. The east-west outer wall was two-thirds of a mile long. Assuming that Zhang Ying had used one of the actual tomb gates as an entrance, she had five to choose from: two on the northern wall and one each on the three others. By her calculations, the best spot to drill would be over the eastern gate roughly facing her office and the Terracotta Warrior Museum just over a mile away.

She had got to know the shapes of the trees in the orchards and the way they looked at night. The orchard swept down below her, silent and empty. To her right she could make out the dark green fields stretching towards the museum. Up above were orchards again, divided by the line of steps of which tourists climbed to the top. Her eyes were getting so good she could see a night fog rising off the grassland. It would burn out with the dawn.

On the slopes of the tomb Sally set to work. She took her soundings, positioned the drill and sank it through the clay. It took two more hours to fix the air lock, then she lowered the camera.

What she saw needed no scientific interpretation. Running east to west from the centre of the burial mound towards the Terracotta Warrior Museum was a railway line. There were no broken artefacts, no murals, archers, chariots or crossbow men. Just a modern rail track in a tunnel.

First the Red Book. Then Zhang Ying's story. Now a rail track. Where she stood, the rain came down aslant hitting her coldly on the face. The slopes of the tomb were her second home, but they frightened her.

Looking down, halfway towards the road, she identified one of the old stone walls which might have marked a boundary for an outer burial chamber. At the bottom, the kiosk by the tourist entrance was visible and the houses of the village down the track on the other side of the road. At night, they were always dark and some were even shuttered up. She had never seen so much as the glow of a wood fire down there.

Then she saw the tramp again, looking like an ape on all fours, scuttling sideways. There was something about his head, the way it bobbed in and out of the body, that made him immediately recognisable. She walked down like a stalker not wishing to disturb a deer. She kept her flashlight off and moved just a few yards at a time, until she was clear of the orchard and on the main steps. Then she turned on the flashlight and Ko flashed his lights to tell her he was waiting.

The empty lunch box was in a different place to the night before. Every night it had moved about three hundred yards along the base of the hills. This time, he had put two leaves ahead of it, about three yards apart, to show her that the careful positioning was deliberate, and that the lunch box was marking out a trail for her to follow.

Exhibit 38 – Audio Tape Evidence
Federal Court, Pearl Street
Manhattan
December 16th 1989

'She's got photographs of the rail link.'
'How do you know?'
'She made a phone call.'
'I thought we would be warned.'
'She worked faster than we thought.'

'And what of Bill Cage?' Wu Tian asked.

'If we are patient, you will be able to do whatever you want with him. He's with me now here in Beijing. You can meet him and make your own judgement.'

'And he can work for us immediately?'

'Not yet. First we will implicate him. Then draw him in. We will create a situation where he has nowhere else and no one else to go to but us.'

'You have his birth certificate?'

Li Yi unclipped his briefcase and passed an envelope across the desk to Wu Tian, who didn't open it but put it neatly on his

right underneath a paperweight. Wu coughed. 'And Parsons –
she has found the railway line.'

'Yes, but she hasn't drilled since.'

'The photographs?'

'Apparently they didn't come out. There was something
wrong with the film. So she had nothing to send to New York.'

'Are you making excuses, comrade?'

'No, comrade.' Li Yi sat up straighter. 'She isn't close to
finding anything else. It is not necessary.'

'How do you know? She witnessed the shooting in January at
the museum. You told me that yourself. She has found the
railway line . . .'

'We check her office. We check her computer notes. If she gets
close, of course I will honour your command, comrade. But we
must be cautious.'

'Yes. Yes, of course.' Wu Tian fell quiet, scratching his
fingernail into the edge of the desk. 'But don't you see? She is
looking. Why else would she have ignored what I told her and
keep searching? She is like my daughter. They are all the same,
these women. They do it to make us angry. That is why they
failed to contribute towards the Great Proletariat Revolution.'

Li Yi shifted in his chair. 'Yes,' he said contritely. 'Yes, I hadn't
looked at it that way.'

'Why are you hesitant?' Wu Tian's voice was low, almost
friendly.

'It is dangerous for a Chinese society to involve itself in the
murder of an American. We already took a risk with Binsky. If
Parsons dies as well, it is . . . she is a famous archaeologist,
comrade. Everything you have worked for will be put at risk.'

Wu Tian snorted. 'We must never be cowed by the bluster of
reactionaries,' he said, quoting Mao Zedong. He took out a pen
flashlight and pointed to a map of China on the wall to the left
of his desk. The beam darted from city to city. 'Look at our
forces, comrade. Chengdu, Lanzhou, Harbin, Shenyang, Xian,
of course, Beijing, of course.' He swept the beam in circles in the
western and northern areas. 'The poorer our people, the more
they are turning to Red Spirit. I am told ceremonies are taking
place in every village, in every temple, in every commune.'

129

'Yes, comrade,' whispered Li Yi.
'My followers now are in the tens of millions.'
'Yes, comrade.'
'Then do what I say.'

Chapter Fourteen

The buses lined one flank of the car park. On the other side were private cars and taxis, parked so badly that they boxed each other in, which was why she didn't want Ko waiting there. It would drive her crazy waiting half an hour just to get out when she left.

Normally Ko would drop Sally at the museum and go off to do other jobs. But today, Sally had more equipment in the boot to take up the slopes, and she wanted to do it in daylight, before picking Paul up from school. So she stuffed a twenty-dollar note through the protective grille and asked Ko to wait.

'Keep the meter running,' she joked and Ko let out a roaring belly laugh and tapped the meter, which he had never switched on.

The girl at the ticket booth was new, sparky with punchy tourist English and teeth set in a studded brace. She had heard of Sally but had never seen her before. Once through the turnstile, Sally headed for the covered shopping emporium where she was hit by a wall of hot air. The heating system came on at fixed times which had nothing to do with the temperature outside.

Sally moved quickly through towards her office. When she got there, she closed the door, locked it as she had been doing ever since she got back from New York, and turned on the computer. It was old and slow. The file of her notes took an age to come up. Every morning, she typed in her findings from the night before.

Someone knocked on the door. She ignored it, thinking it was workmen messing around with ladders outside. Then came another knock, and someone shouted in Chinese for her to open up. The handle shook as they shoved the door hard, so that the flimsy chipboard gave at the edges and she could see a gap of light from outside. Sally hit the 'save' button, cursed at the lazy way the back-up disk whirred, while the door rattled. When the file was saved, she closed the computer down, put on her jacket, slipped the disk into her pocket and calmly unlocked the door.

There were two of them, in neatly pressed uniforms, epaulettes, their names on the pockets, guns in the holsters. A different sort of police from the ones she was used to.

'Hi! Can I help?' she offered chirpily in Chinese, standing there with a big smile, hiding her anger, and holding out her hand to shake.

They didn't take it. Didn't say anything. The one in front, a tall, fit guy with a hard-hewn face, swaggered into the room, jostling her and not caring. The second one hung back. He was smaller. His face was more alert, curious, not hostile like the arrogant guy; it had a touch of innocence, a baby face, which made him look more intelligent.

'Your passport,' said the arrogant one.

'I don't have it with me,' she lied. 'And who are you?'

'Police,' said Baby Face from behind.

'What police come barging into a woman's office like this?'

'Passport,' repeated the arrogant one, speaking in English.

'I told you. I don't have it.' Sally softened her voice, relaxed her shoulders, let her arms drop to her side, making her body language more friendly, not that there was much body language from inside her floppy jacket. 'I'm sorry,' she said in Chinese. 'I left it at home.'

'That is illegal,' Arrogant snapped in English, refusing the olive branch. 'Aliens visiting China have to carry passport at all times.'

'What do you want it for?' There was something scary about Arrogant. He had a raw edge of violence to him which Baby Face didn't have. So she turned slightly, half an eye on Arrogant, half on Baby Face, and repeated, 'Why do you need my passport?'

'Your visa has expired.' Arrogant was opening the drawers of her desk and tipping pencils, paper clips and paper onto the floor. He stuck his fingers into the soil of one of her pot plants, flicking the earth onto the floor and wiping his fingers on his tunic. 'You are in China illegally.'

'My visa's fine; it's multiple re-entry until June. And you are in my office illegally.'

'You have to come back to our headquarters with us,' Baby Face said quietly, almost apologetically. He was still by the door but had moved further into the office. Whatever happened, Sally was determined to keep the door open.

'I'll come to the police station when I finish work,' she said to Baby Face, still in Chinese. 'We can straighten it out then.'

'No. You come now.' Arrogant again, his English jerky.

'Excuse me, big boy,' she said, dripping sarcasm, though her heart was pounding. She reached past Arrogant to the phone.

If Li Yi couldn't fix it, no one could. She had been saying that for three years and it had always worked. Arrogant put out a hand to stop her. 'You need permission to use the phone.'

She glared at him. 'Why? Am I under arrest?'

'No phone call,' he said firmly.

'Then why don't you make it? Why don't you call the Head of the Foreign Investment Bureau for Shaanxi Province, Mr Li Yi, and tell him that you're holding Dr Sally Parsons of the Archaeological Institute of America against her will at the Museum of the Terracotta Warrior Army.'

Arrogant dropped back a step but kept his hand on the telephone. Baby Face closed the door. Sally, reading the name on his uniform, said in English, 'Zhao, keep that door open or I'll break your damn neck.' She smiled a winning smile, but the door stayed shut.

Very slowly, she moved the telephone away from Arrogant. He didn't stop her. She started dialling Li Yi's number. Arrogant was looking around, interested in George, the crossbow warrior, and he stepped round Sally to open the casket. Sally snapped sharply in Chinese, 'Get your hands off that! Or I'll report you for tampering with cultural relics.' Arrogant hesitated, and recovered enough just to tap the top of the glass, as if that's what he had meant to do all along.

Damn Li Yi! He wasn't answering. She let the telephone ring until the recorded voice came on. They heard it and they knew she'd failed. As Arrogant began taking the receiver from her hand, Sally's grip tightened on it. 'I'm leaving a message,' she snarled. 'Li Yi, it's Sal here. Two cops have barged into my office and want to haul me off to town. Can you get hold of—'

Thank God. The click of the call being picked up. Then a whisper. Li Yi's voice. Barely audible in English. 'Get the hell away from them . . .'

Sally swallowed and kept herself together enough to smile, hoping they didn't notice the terror which suddenly surged through her. 'Li Yi, that's great. Thanks a million. I'll give you a big kiss when I see you next.'

Smirking, Arrogant snatched the receiver from her hand and put it back on the cradle. He held out his hand. 'Passport and ID,' he said.

'He says you should call Wang Yu,' said Sally, surprised how cool she was. 'He's the boss of the museum, a big man in Shaanxi Province.' She lifted the receiver again and shoved it at Arrogant. 'Go on, call him.' He looked through her, his face close enough for her to catch his breath on her face. Odourless. Sterile. All the more frightening. She wouldn't call Wang Yu herself. He was never there. That's why the place was in such a mess.

'If you come with us it will be better,' said Baby Face, his English more studied than Arrogant's.

'Where's your authorisation?' said Sally.

'We are the police,' repeated Arrogant. He started probing again, picking up the things on her desk and looking at them. Sally's memory raced, trying to think what she didn't want them to see.

George, in his cabinet, was safe. Even Arrogant wouldn't dare touch him. 'Cultural relics' was like a divine mantra in Xian. The probe was safely on the slopes of the tomb. Other exploration kit was locked in a crate in the corner.

Arrogant picked up a framed photograph of Paul, taken when he was four, on the beach at Southampton. He was wearing water wings and Cait was swimming with him. Arrogant handled it carelessly, as if he was about to throw it down somewhere.

Sally took it from him. For a second, he held on to it. She

134

tugged it away, and he raised his hand to strike her. 'Just try it, pal,' she snapped. Arrogant dropped his hand, but he kept messing with the stuff on her desk. If she went with them, it could take hours, even days. They were like that. They would search her, search her office. Question her over a single sentence in her notes.

She turned to Baby Face. 'OK, guys, you win. Just give me a couple of minutes to pack up.'

'You will come?' said Baby Face. She could see how he relaxed, the sort of kid she might hire as a researcher. Arrogant didn't give an inch. He wanted to trash her office, slap her about. He arched his back and cupped his hand round the top of his pistol holster.

Sally sat at her desk making meaningless notes. The two policemen fidgeted. She made a show of putting papers into a briefcase, then, as if they had been keeping her waiting, she snapped, 'Come on then. Let's go if we're going.' Baby Face jumped and opened the door, waiting for her to go through. 'You first.' She faced Arrogant. 'I have to lock up.'

Baby Face and Arrogant talked in low tones. She couldn't work out what they were saying. She fiddled with the lock, her back to them. She had left the briefcase in there, didn't need it where she was going.

She spun round. 'Going to freshen up,' she announced to Baby Face.

'Do it in Xian,' said Arrogant.

'It'll take an hour to get there in the traffic.' She was one step into the Ladies when he gripped her left elbow. It was painful, even through her jacket. Sally tried to rip her arm away but he held her.

'You're not going anywhere without us.'

Get the hell away from them. She'd remember it for the rest of her life. The panic in Li Yi's voice.

She whipped the back of her hand across Arrogant's face. He fell back, eyes watering.

Sally ran. She knew the underground corridors better than they did. Thanking God for her long legs, she just kept going, putting distance between them. The corridor swung round to the right where the lights were off. Sally felt her way through the darkness to the door. She knew that it opened into a whole different warren of tunnels leading towards Pit Three. But did they know?

She pushed the chipboard door and felt the spring-held hinges give way. The voices of Baby Face and Arrogant were getting closer, but she was through and the door leapt closed behind her.

Behind her, the door opened again, the hinges squeaking briefly.

She had been through here before, when they had cleaned it up for visitors. Months earlier, she had been shown the new construction plans for humidified, temperature-controlled vaults to house the terracotta warriors. Work had begun but it would never be finished. It was too expensive to do properly. Now, there were puddles everywhere and water ran down the walls. Her jacket was cumbersome and far too hot in the damp, muggy tunnel. A beam across the wall of the tunnel told her that Arrogant and Baby Face had switched on their flashlights behind her.

She kept going, heading down, racking her brain to remember the layout. In the darkness it was difficult. Shapes appeared, like ghosts. A man smoking a cigarette? She slowed, almost asked for help. It turned out to be a slop bucket and a mop on a table. She thought she saw a fork-lift truck. Yet when she rushed past, it was a wooden cabinet. The dark and her own mind played tricks.

She was moving too fast. She knocked a plate of food off a ledge. It had been there for days and the stench was appalling. Noodles fell on her hand and she shook them off.

The tunnel went on down, curved to the left, then straightened out. Damn! A big stretch. They would see her. Their flashlights were everywhere. She could hear Arrogant's disciplined, rhythmic breathing as he chased her. He was a good runner, ahead of Baby Face.

She remembered there was a T-junction up ahead. To the left was an area which was to hold the reconstructed chariot, the one with the umbrella holder which Eliot had sneered at. The oxygen was thinner, her lungs were tight, rasping. The ceiling suddenly got lower and a cloth brushed her face. She slapped her cheeks to get it off. But it clung and she clawed it away. It was a spider web, caught up in her hair.

Two flashlights, one sweeping right, one left, silently, not shouting for her to stop, which somehow made it scarier. Her head was pounding blood. Or was it a machine vibrating through the clay?

Feeling with her hand, Sally kept to the left-hand wall. It was soft with damp and cold. Sweat ran into her eyes, making them sting. Then she found the small tunnel, the one where the workmen tossed their cigarette butts and other rubbish. It was just big enough to squeeze into, widening out but getting lower, so she had to crouch, scraping her head on the roof, until she was shuffling along on all fours, her hands sinking not into earth but rotten food, discarded paint rags. The smell was worse than anything she had ever known, suffocating her, making her choke with sheer disgust. Her fingers felt decaying chicken, clotted rice and slimy vegetables, velvety mould over everything. The crumpling of a polystyrene lunch box was deafening in the sudden silence.

Just above her, Sally heard a scampering sound. A rat's tail swished across her face and the creature dropped down on her. She felt it scrabbling on her jacket, then jumping off among the rubbish. Earth trickled down onto her head and with it came insects. They crawled all over her face, then into her jacket and under her T-shirt. She pushed herself forward on her elbows, felt blood warm on her hand, cut by a shard of glass from a broken coffee jar.

She managed to turn to look behind her. Flashlights threw erratic shards of light around her. Sally blindly clawed herself along. Up ahead, the darkness changed hue. No light, but less dark, like the way the sea changes on a black night.

She felt a wall in front. Heavy clodded clay. An end to the tunnel. The air was foul. Unbreathable. Arrogant and Baby Face were at the other end. What was it – fifty feet? Maybe seventy-five. Between them lay a carpet of food, filth and maggots. The flash of a rat's eye shone in torchlight. God, how many rats were there?

She held her breath. This is how a rat dies, she thought. Somewhere dark, hidden, stinking and underground, where no one would find it. Southampton was a million miles away and suddenly Sally wanted to be there so much. But she wouldn't die. She would kill every rat and every policeman with her bare hands before she did anything that stopped her seeing Paul again.

The flashlights went off. But they were both still there. Sally could sense them. She turned and dug her fingers into the wall in front of her. There was something else. A board? She scraped the clay away, pushed with her shoulder and felt the board give a little. Earth fell around her like a landslide. The rat ran away from her. The flashlights came on again. She could hear Arrogant and Baby Face, their voices uncertain.

She waited, dead quiet, not moving. She heard their footsteps crunch away completely. Too scared of rats to come into her tunnel. Little shits.

She pushed against the wall again, then pushed harder and it gave way. She fell forward. The air was ice-cold but thankfully full of oxygen. Sally scrambled through. Smooth concrete on the floor. A pinprick of light from above. She stood up, put her arms out in front of her and walked, one careful step at a time. She was in some sort of chamber that smelt of fresh paint. She felt her way to a wall. Smooth concrete again. She leant against it and felt for her own flashlight. It came out of her pocket along with maggots, bugs, vile things, all crawling on her hand. She was past caring.

She heard the distant throb again, way overhead. Heating? Air conditioning? Some form of ventilation? She slowed her breathing, moved her flashlight around and let her eyes adjust. The beam was weak. Damn batteries. As far as she could make out, she was in a replica of a burial chamber. There were even unfinished murals on the walls, hunting scenes with animals and a dark blue sky with stars of maroon, yellow and green.

She didn't have a proper sense of where she was in the museum complex and she had lost track of how long she had been running. It felt like hours, but according to her watch it was only a few minutes. She went round methodically with the flashlight, pushing against the wall. There must be a door. How else would they get in with their concrete and paintbrushes? She came to a metal door, not even concealed, painted white, and some joker had even put a crossbow on it, like a cartoon, with the Chinese character for poison in a bubble above the tip.

She pushed. It didn't give. Then she saw the inside lock, turned it and the door opened into a dimly lit corridor; she could hear voices far down at the end to her right. To her left, there was more light, as if there was an atrium or fluorescent lighting. She wiped the sweat and grime from her face. She must look like shit. She stepped out, listened and walked slowly towards the light. There was still the smell of dampness, but also of paint and machinery and concrete.

She worked out that the tunnels had taken her round in a huge sweeping arc to the other side of Pit Number One where the official entrance to the main museum would be when it was built. Its subterranean design would protect the most precious artefacts against pollution and humidity: the Number One Bronze Chariot with the coloured patterns on the window, the charioteers clasping the reins, the cavalry officer and his horse, the general in full armour. An enormous area, Li Yi had told her, like the Metropolitan Museum in New York, big enough to hold the treasures from the tomb when they excavated it.

She paused for a moment to brush the worst of the dirt off her clothes. She wiped her face and hands with a tissue and scrabbled in her purse for a comb to get the insects out of her hair. She remembered the way out and walked towards it confidently and briskly, as if she was going to the beach at Southampton.

Ko spotted her as soon as she came into the parking lot, and his face screwed up with displeasure as he saw that she had dragged herself through more filth than usual. His eyes glanced at the seats both of them knew would be messed up.

'Paul's school,' she told him.

Her body hurt where she was scratched, where she had crashed her elbow against the concrete wall, where she had hit her head on the rock ceiling. But the worst hurt was inside, a heaving, crashing tidal wave threatening to bear down on her, the pain of danger closing in, of a world collapsing around her.

She stared out of the car to avoid Ko's eyes which were darting around the mirror to ambush hers. He looked at his watch. 'Bit early,' he said sharply.

'Just do it, Ko,' she said wearily. 'Please.'

The air was cold and dry, chapping her lips. She ran her tongue around the inside of her mouth and tasted a lump of clay, salty and gritty. She wound down the window and spat it out. A child stared at her in astonishment from the roadside, reminding Sally how crazed and filthy she must look.

Early? Good. She would clean up properly before picking up Paul. She got Ko to pull in at a hotel a couple of miles from the warriors. One voice told her she hadn't put enough distance between herself and the police. Another voice intervened. Screw them, it said. Screw them all. If she was in trouble in China, it didn't matter where she was. She was in the land of a billion eyes.

Braving the disapproving looks of the hotel staff, she walked up to the reception desk, paid in cash for a room, picked up soap, disinfectant, shampoo, a hairbrush, toothpaste, toothbrush and T-shirt, sweater, pants, socks and scarf at the lobby shops. All were decorated in some way with the face of the Emperor Qin Shi Huang, his warriors, or Mao or Confucius.

Under the shower, she scrubbed clods of soil off her and watched the insects and the mud wash away. She was cut and scraped in more places than she could be bothered to count. The water was either too hot or too cold, spluttering out and smelling of open drains and coal fires. She washed her hair, clawing hard at her scalp.

Gradually she relaxed. She knew she was in danger but for the moment, at least, she was safe. The most important thing was to get Paul to safety.

She dried herself with two pink towels, so tiny that she had to wring them out. She struggled to get a comb through the knots in her hair, leaving it heavy and wet on her shoulders. Before she left, she leaned hard into the mirror and smiled. Whatever was going on, it was bad, so bad that she knew exactly what she had to do with Paul and with herself. She smiled. Smiled like she meant it. She had a plan. 'Attagirl, Sal.'

She picked up the hotel phone and asked the operator to put her through to Richard's number in New York. She got the answer machine, the message he left when he was out of the country. She called the embassy in Beijing to see if they had a contact number for him and was put through to Maeve, his secretary.

'Sally, Richard's not in right now. He said he'd be back before the end of the day.'

'You mean he's here, in China?' She gripped the receiver to stop herself shaking.

'No, actually he was calling me from Hawaii,' she joked.

Sally bit her lip to stop herself snapping at the girl. 'Maeve, this is personal and it's urgent. If you have a number for him, for God's sake give it to me.'

'Don't weep on me, darling,' said Maeve. 'He has one of those new mobile phones with him.' She read out the number.

What happened next made Sally wish she had never asked for it. The phone rang and Richard answered. A woman's voice next to him said, 'Darling, whoever it is, tell them to call back.'

Chapter Fifteen

'Who was that?' asked Christine. She rolled over, letting the
sheet fall off. Richard put the phone down on the dresser. He
turned to see her trailing a finger around her neck and her
breasts, deliberately tantalising. She had heard Sally's voice and
had reacted automatically to the threat of another woman.

'No one important,' Richard said lightly.

She leapt forward like a cat, her breasts against his spine and
her arms clinging round his neck. 'No, tell me. I love secrets.'

He brought her hands together, took them up to his lips and
kissed them. 'Our whole world is secrets, Miss Perfect Jade. But
luckily this one isn't classified.'

'Who was it, then?' She pulled her hands free and let them
loose on him. One second he felt as if he was being mauled by
an octopus, the next brushed by a moth.

Richard had borrowed a house belonging to another diplomat on leave. The kitchen, dining room, living room, study,
guest bathroom and bedroom were set up with listening bugs
and video surveillance, with tapes and monitors running into
another diplomatic house next door. But Richard had discon-
nected the guest bedroom. If his task was to get Christine into
bed, then he didn't want engineers evaluating his sexual per-
formance. Not that he expected her to say anything of note.
She, too, would have been trained in elementary espionage, and
once over the threshold of a diplomatic residence – British,
American, Russian, whatever – she would assume she was
under surveillance.

Christine pressed herself hard against Richard and he felt her warmth as she tried to arouse him, to blank out any impact the phone call might have had on him.

'It was Sally Parsons,' he said.

Christine drew away. 'She's your girlfriend?'

'We have casual sex. It doesn't mean anything.'

'Liar. I can tell by the way you say it.'

Richard grimaced. 'OK. She's my girlfriend.' Christine was too sharp to try to fool.

'And she doesn't know you're sleeping with a Chinese girl?'

'She does now, I suspect,' he said.

'Do you have feelings for her?' she asked.

'I'm not sure I want to talk about it.'

'So you do have feelings for her.' She bounced up and down on the bed, enjoying Richard's discomfort.

He shrugged. 'I have feelings for you.'

'Don't even try,' she laughed. 'Admit it. We both know why we're doing this. I'm a personal adviser to the general secretary of the Chinese Communist Party. You are an American official. Maybe an American spy. It doesn't matter.' She kissed him on the lips. 'When you talk to her next, you tell her that you were carrying out your nation's duty by spending the afternoon with me. What you don't tell her is that we've had a lot of fun.' She pushed herself back, the sheet covering parts of her midriff and her legs. She playfully brought it up to her face like a veil. 'Am I right?' she said.

'Pretty much.' Richard pulled the sheet away and kissed her naked stomach. 'She's in a bit of trouble. I'm a diplomat. I have to help her. She's calling back.'

Christine's face clouded and she sat up. She wrapped herself in the sheet, leaving him naked. He got up from the bed.

'Why? Is it a problem?' he said, stepping into his trousers which had been lying crumpled on the floor.

'What help does she want?'

He picked up his shirt from the back of a chair by the dressing table. 'The police tried to pick her up for something. She was damn stupid and ran away.'

'I don't understand. What's she done?'

'A man was killed in New York, and Sally was the last person known to have been with him.'

'Who did she kill?'

'I'm not sure she killed him, but strangely, he was a friend of your father's.'

'My father doesn't have any friends,' Christine said dismissively.

Richard ignored the comment. 'He was a man called Jefferson Binsky. He and your father knew each other in the mid-fifties. Long before you were born.'

'Yes. Father did speak about him. An American professor.'

'You never met him?'

She shook her head. 'No. My father admired him, though. Until . . .' She twisted the sheet between her fingers. '. . . until my mother was killed.' She twisted it tighter, making her knuckles white, then unfurled it and threw it down.

She looked up at Richard quickly and nervously, and he saw that her eyes were moist. He moved closer to her, touching her gently on the elbow, expecting her to flinch away from him. Instead, she shuffled across the bed and held him, her chest against his through his open shirt, her head on his shoulder. He knew she was going to talk, knew she was going to tell him why she had ever shared a bed with him.

'My mother was very beautiful. She was a teacher,' said Christine. 'She was an innocent. Yet I wish my own vision could be as clear as hers was. I have inherited my father's madness. I can feel it sometimes, kicking inside me like an unborn child. If she were still alive, she could help me. She had a simple purpose in life, to teach, to help and to love. I remember her telling me that. But my father and I, we hide behind other things, like our politics and our work. We use them as shields because we don't want to dig any deeper into ourselves.'

She shifted her weight, unwrapped her arms from him, sat up and took Richard's hands and rested them on her knees. 'I'll tell you what happened. It was Friday, August the thirtieth, nineteen sixty-eight. A hot day. I was eight years old and the Cultural Revolution was in full swing. My father was a sort of controller of the Red Guards for Chaoyang District, a very important job because it took much in of central Beijing. My birthday is September the second. I was to be nine, and he decided it was time to show me what the Cultural Revolution was all about. He dressed me up in a Mao tunic, gave me a little Red Book, pinned a Mao badge on me, and told me that this was the way that China could beat off foreign aggressors for a thousand years. You know the sort of crap.

'He took me to my school. Only when I got there did I begin to understand what was going on. It was the school holidays, but he told me we were going to see my mother who was running a summer school. I thought my father was taking me as a surprise for her. In fact he wanted me to see the school being destroyed. There was a mob of Red Guards outside; they seemed to have the building surrounded. I was excited, I remember, but confused. I turned to him and asked, "Where's Mum?" But I was worried because the Red Guards were waving their badges and books in the air, and shouting, "Confess, confess!" and "Down with the capitalist class!" Christine arched her back and hung her head back. 'I saw my mother at the door and started to run to her. But my father held me back.' She put her hand on Richard's shoulder and gripped it to demonstrate.

' "It's not safe", he told me, the way he said it made me feel really frightened. My mother had children gathered round her. She wasn't frightened, I could tell that, but she knew she was in trouble.'

'Why?' asked Richard.

'I had heard my father arguing with her. Something about the textbooks she was using in her science lessons.' She looked up at him. 'You know how it was. Anything written before nineteen forty-nine was banned.

'One of the children ran out from behind her. A little girl. I didn't recognise her, it was so quick. But I know who she was now. My mother tried to stop her, but she ran right into the mob. They caught the girl, covered her head with a sack, then they tied her by the feet and neck like a chicken. I could see her struggling. They threw this girl – Chen Mei – around like a football, chanting all the time. Imperialist this. Running dog that. They dropped her and they didn't care. They just picked her up and started throwing her again. My mother gathered the other children, took them all inside and shut the door.'

'What did your father do?'

'He watched. Word must have spread that this was where the action was, because more Red Guards were arriving as well as ordinary people who just came and joined in. The teachers had locked up the doors and windows. For about half an hour, it all went quiet. Even the chanting stopped. Some of the Red Guards brought out lunch boxes. I tugged at my father's hand, asking if we could go into the school and be with my mother.'

'What did he say?'

'He just mumbled, "Confess, confess, confess." I didn't know what he meant. Now, of course, I do.' Christine slid off the bed, shivered, and wrapped the sheet round her.

'Someone threw a petrol bomb. It exploded against the wall. That one didn't damage anything. It just made the bricks black. Then they smashed the windows at the front of the school with rocks and threw petrol bombs inside. Then they went quiet again, waiting. I don't know if you know, but when a petrol bomb explodes, there is a lull between the flash and when you know that it's set fire to anything. So we all went quiet until we saw the first flames appear, little flickers up the curtains. We all cheered. Yes, Richard. I cheered because my father was cheering, raising his hand in the air. I don't know if I thought it was some kind of game. I just followed him. He was my father.

'They threw in more bombs and the whole school was alight. Flames. Black smoke. The works. My father pulled me forward to the front of the crowd. They let us through because of who he was. I remember the smell of burning wood and petrol, because we were standing next to where they poured the petrol into the bottles. The rags were all ready, lying in a row on the ground like little corpses.' She wound the sheet tightly in a coil. 'Like this. Imagine this dry cotton fed into a bottle filled with petrol. Then light the end here.'

She let it go loose. 'Just above the front door was a balcony. A ledge. My mother opened it. I suppose she thought the children could jump down to safety. Smoke was everywhere. I was coughing. One of the Red Guards thrust a petrol bomb into my father's hand. He held it while the Red Guard lit it, and straightaway my father threw it. He didn't hesitate. It smashed against a wall, and the Red Guard gave him another one. Lit it for him. This time, my father aimed for the balcony, for my mother. The fire was behind her as well and the children were pushing and screaming to get out. He threw a third bomb and . . . and . . . my mother went up in flames.'

Richard stared rigidly at Christine, his hands clasped tightly together, the fingers and knuckles white.

'The flames died down, like they do. Her hair was burnt off, and her clothes. Her flesh was all red and her face was black. But, even like that, she had such dignity. Compared to those animals below her, she was a model of calm. "Take the children," she shouted. "At least save the children." My father was chanting, "Confess, confess, confess." I heard my mother, and only then did I have the presence of mind to break away from him and run towards her. It was the worst thing I could have done, because she saw me. And when she saw me, she saw my father. "Go back, Po Ki. Go back," she yelled. Another bomb exploded at her feet and then she was really on fire. She did nothing to stop the flames. And she showed no fear. Do you know why?'

'Why?' prompted Richard softly.

'Because her only weapon was to shame them into saving the children. If she struggled, they would only laugh at her. But if they saw her slowly being eaten by the fire, maybe they would stop in time to save the children. You see what I mean about her innocence. She believed that even in the most evil human beings there was goodness.'

Richard had stayed perfectly still throughout, seized by the horror of what he was hearing. 'And?'

'They watched her burn. They weren't interested in her confession. They'd started burning the school before they told her what she was meant to have done wrong. We all stood there and watched it burn, praising Mao for delivering such a glorious traitor to us. Someone picked me up – not my father – to get me away from the heat of the fire. I saw her say, "Po Ki, I love you." It was what she always used to say when she put me to bed. She said, "Love your father." I couldn't hear her, of course. But I knew what she was saying. I will never forget her face. I saw her feeling like a blind person for the balustrade. The whole left side of her head was charred and in flames. She was just burning. Then I couldn't see her any more. But I heard her when she finally broke down, a most terrible scream, a death scream. I had never heard anything like it before. She must have been in such horrible pain just before her death. I was carried away from the crowd. Later my father came for me. He was still muttering, "Confess, confess, confess," as though he was mad. Perhaps he was.'

'Why?' stammered Richard. 'Why would he try to burn his own wife? With his daughter watching?'

'That's what I've been asking myself all my life. Do you know how many unanswered whys a person can ask before it sends them mad?'

'And you . . . you lived with him after that? You were brought up by your father?'

'That's what my mother was saying. Don't you see? Otherwise, I would have ended up in a labour camp or something. Even as he was killing her, she was making sure he looked after me.' She found the corner of the sheet and ran her thumbnail down the seam. 'What do you think, Richard? Tell me what you think.'

'I truly don't know.' He put his hands round her waist and drew her towards him.

Christine stiffened and drew away. 'Sorry. Sometimes I just hate all men. It's not you. It's nothing to do with you.' She wiped away a tear and smiled grimly. 'If I was an American, I would be in constant therapy, wouldn't I?'

'That's for sure.' It was all Richard could say.

'He had betrayed her,' continued Christine. 'He told them about the textbooks. But now he hides behind Mao all the time. To him, Mother's death was just an unfortunate side effect of the revolution. It was for the greater good. If I ask him about what he really thought or felt that day, he just rants. He's memorised huge tracts of Mao's writings and just quotes them. If I say, "Did you really kill Mum solely because her textbooks were out of date?" he says, "The socialist system will eventually replace the capitalist system; this is an objective law independent of man's will . . . blah, blah, blah." Why do you think I ran away to Harvard? Why do you think I jumped into the bed of the first American I met who could speak my language? All those years ago, Richard, you gave me the escape I needed.'

'But why did you come back?'

'Because it's still unresolved. Because China is unresolved. We are the ones who have to confess now, Richard. Don't you see? Our history has to be accurate.'

'It'll never happen.'

'Zhao Zhiyang says he's keen on it. But maybe that's because he's a little in love with me. Deng is against, I think.' She lay flat on the bed, her arms behind her head.

'You've – how should I say – done remarkably well, considering.'

'Damn right, I have.' She stared at the ceiling and ran one finger lightly around her left breast. 'But what's really unresolved is me. Because in spite of everything, I do love my father. Maybe I even admire him for putting some lofty vision above the good of the family. I don't know. Was it an admirable thing to do?'

'I don't think *you* think that.'

'I have to, Richard, because I'm more like him than I am like my mother.' She sprang up, wrapped her arms round him and kissed him on the lips. 'If I weren't a selfish little bitch, I wouldn't be here with you now.'

All signs of tears and sadness had suddenly gone.

When his mobile rang, Richard was standing by the mirror and Christine reacted first. 'Don't answer it,' she said.

'I have to,' he said, reaching for the phone. He had forgotten all about Sally.

'Why? Why do you have to?' Her voice was soft, not raised, but threatening.

Richard cupped his hand over the mouthpiece. 'She's in trouble.'

Christine crawled across the bed to get to him, hooked her hand round the back of his legs and pulled him towards her. 'Get someone else to look after her,' she said, knowing Sally could hear.

But Richard was already talking.

'The Chinese police wouldn't act like freelance cowboys, Sal. Certainly not with a foreigner. Your visa's OK, is it?'

'My visa's fine.'

'Then the only thing I can think of is that something has blown up in the US about Jeff's murder. The cops there might have asked the cops here to track you down.'

'For God's sake, Richard. You said . . . It was you who put me on the plane. I didn't kill Jeff.'

'Sal, calm down. Now go and pick Paul up from school. Take him to Bob and Julie Maddox. I'll ask Bob to fly up to Beijing with both of you. You can stay with me.'

'You and your goddamn floozy.'

'If this is going to work, Sal, you've got to think straight.'

'A woman thinks a damn sight straighter when her boyfriend's not screwing a whore in the middle of the afternoon.'

Christine jumped off the bed and stormed into the bathroom but left the door open.

'I know this is a traumatic time,' said Richard smoothly. 'But concentrate on Paul. If you don't want to handle the Chinese police alone, come with Paul to the embassy and we'll give you protection.'

Just as Richard stopped talking, Christine banged down the toilet seat and flushed, so loud Sally could not have missed it. Then she said in her most manufactured English, 'Darling, who's that on the phone? Darling, stop talking and come back to bed.'

Sally slammed down the phone.

Christine, still naked, took the mobile from Richard's hand and switched it off. She held his head tightly between both hands. 'Kiss me,' she ordered. Her lips opened immediately and he felt the moisture of her mouth and her tongue.

He pushed and she gave way to his weight, falling back onto the bed, with Richard holding her, him clothed, her naked, his hands spread out against her back.

Chapter Sixteen

'Screw you, too, lady,' said Sally viciously at the phone.

When a person's world falls apart, the most dangerous thing is imagination, the images of how you will end up abandoned by all the strands which had made your life a success.

She took a minute to calm herself down, then she made another call, thankful that Julie Maddox answered and told her to come right on over.

She left the towels on the floor and her old clothes tossed into a corner of the bathroom. As soon as she stepped outside the hotel, she trembled. She thought she saw a policeman, a figure lost in the shadow beneath the peak of a green cap. But it was her imagination and she pulled herself together.

Ko was out of the car, opening the back door for her as she stepped out of the hotel. 'Let's go home,' she said.

Ko checked his watch. Didn't say anything, just frowned enough to let her know she might now be running late.

'Home, then the school. OK?'

As Ko took the short cut they used most times, they were stopped by a procession of village children coming towards them, their faces glowing in the cold, cheeks flushed red and eyes ablaze with purpose. They left clouds of breath around them, the procession half in a field and half on the road, where Ko joined the drivers queuing up to get past. But there was no honking, no impatient shouts, like there would have been in Beijing or New York.

'New bridge,' said Ko, tapping his fingers on the wheel, not impatiently but in time to the music coming from the little brass band behind.

Many of the children were no older than Paul. Sure, they were Chinese. But so was Paul – part Chinese, anyway. His father had been born in Xian. Little hands gripped banner poles, two, sometimes three on each side to carry the weight and hold the poles steady against the wind. 'Sing for the mother-land,' Sally translated one as saying. 'The Chinese people will never be slaves again,' said another.

Each child wore a bright red scarf, tied precisely to fall on the left shoulder. They walked in step, as best they could, but one boy tripped on a frozen clod of earth. He was smaller than the rest, struggling with his pole, head held high and eyes straight ahead until he fell. He was hauled straight up into line so swiftly that he hardly missed a step.

Sally had seen processions like this many times before. She had even played her part as the clumsy foreigner. But this time it looked different. Ko's window was down, letting in a blast of cold air. In the euphoric faces of the village children, she saw their future: the implacable rigidity and obedience of Arrogant and Baby Face.

The memory of the silky female voice in the room with Richard made her shiver too. She tried to shake it off, to share Ko's enthusiasm and watch the brass band. She recognised the music from a Maoist opera. The children sang perfectly, like a choir. As they passed, Ko edged forward. Their music filled the car. Ko, deep in thought, was massaging a tiny plastic figurine of Mao, painted in bright gold.

The new bridge was little more than a raised culvert, part of the irrigation system of which the village was so proud. Ko put his arm out of the open window and dropped a roll of notes into a bright green bucket, far more than Sally had slipped him during the day. He stopped the taxi to chat to a tall elderly man dressed in a blue Mao suit with a red armband identifying him as the local Party steward. When they set off again, Ko said, 'They agree. They'll shit on Gorbachev's voodoo forehead if he comes to Xian.'

Ko's wife wasn't around when Sally got back to the house,

which was good because Ko wouldn't be delayed. They were running late. Sally packed Paul's overnight bag, trying to remember what he liked. She would clear the place later. Paul would get his model airplane, his atlas, which she knew he loved, *The Lion, the Witch and the Wardrobe*, which she knew he had read and loved but couldn't remember how long ago, and a Superman comic he had got from the kids of richer parents.

She changed her clothes again, putting on jeans, a thick green corduroy blouse, a red fisherman's sweatshirt she had bought with Cage in Cape Cod years ago, and the leather boots she used for digging. She did it all quickly and automatically, willing herself not to think, fighting off a creeping urge to stop and cry.

Three cases were packed, and Paul's football rolled loose on her bed. As she walked outside, she spotted his bike in the garden and called out to Ko. 'We need to put the bike in your trunk.'

Ko was smoking, the car door open, his podgy legs hanging outside, too short to touch the ground. Ko grinned. 'Where are we taking to play?' So he was back to bad English.

'Please. Just put the goddamn bike in the car?'

She was taut again, like piano wire. Fed up with Ko, his Mao watch, his Korean War, his parroted ranting against Gorbachev. And Ko could tell. He fetched the bike from the garden silently and put it in the boot. Then he fetched the bags and football, put them in too. The boot wouldn't close, so he tied it down with rope and they drove off without another word.

Classes had just ended. Another five minutes and Paul would have been driven home by one of the American families.

The school wasn't the best place for Paul. He was brighter than most of the other kids. His academic potential was just coming out. There weren't enough children to challenge him, no real peer groups, and the teachers were mostly the wives of American and Europeans who had been posted to Xian by their companies – engineers, foremen, families from small-town America who came out for a couple of years to bank money and then go home again. When Paul was only four it had been fine, but seven was an important age, when the brain started to consolidate and character was formed. Cait had kept on about it. Cait, the child psychologist, knew about these things.

The school was an ugly, two-storey building of concrete breeze blocks with small windows, the glass carelessly splashed with white paint. Sally could see Paul in his classroom, his arms outstretched, swooping round the empty room like a fighter plane.

She got out of the car. A blast of wind caught her wet hair and she moved with a skip to get inside. Paul skidded out of the classroom to meet her. 'Hey, why've you brought my bike?' he demanded.

'We're going to a new place to ride,' she managed.

Paul checked the bike out first and saw the bags in the trunk under the back wheel. He slunk into the car. 'You're going away again, aren't you?' he said quietly. He wrapped his arms round Sally's neck and drew himself towards her.

'Just a couple of days,' said Sally, stroking Paul's hair and signalling for Ko to move off. 'I have to go to Beijing.'

'Mrs Ko can look after me.' Paul's voice was faint. Resigned. A child, submissive, but questioning.

'Not this time, honey.'

'Hi, I'm Bob Maddox. Glad you made it.' A wave from behind the gate of his house. Long strides towards them. Blue shirt, open-neck collar. 'Sally. Dr Sally Parsons, right? You work with the terracotta warrior army?'

Maddox was a businessman in his mid-thirties. His whole manner, filled with homespun security, signalled to Sally as a safe landing. 'You gave that great talk on the Emperor Qin Shi Huang a year or so back. Julie found it really interesting; she's become a bit of an expert on the guy.'

Sally got out of the car with Paul. Ko opened the boot to get out the bike.

'Keep that stuff in there,' said Maddox. 'We're heading across the road to that old colonial house there.'

Sally closed the cab door and grabbed hold of Paul's hand. Maddox crouched down. 'Hi, Paul. So you're going to be with us for a couple of days?'

Paul stepped back, his face creased with disapproval. 'Head

up, Paul,' said Sally. He dropped his chin to his chest. 'Please, Paul.'

Maddox pointed behind him. 'That's our house,' he turned back to look across the traffic, 'and this one we're going to is where we look after the kids. We've been here two years in August. August the second, to be precise. And loving every minute of it.' Maddox looked at Ko. 'If we could get him to do a U-turn, get the gear out . . .'

'I'll go with Ko,' said Paul, tearing himself away from Sally. He scampered over and climbed into the back seat of the taxi.

Sally shrugged. 'You got kids, Bob?' she asked.

'Uh, no. Not that we're not trying.'

'Kids are tough,' said Sally.

'Tougher not having them,' he said. 'Now watch that green light way up by the bridge. When that goes to red, it'll be safer to cross, though it's not foolproof, and you head for that traffic island just to our right.' They crossed chaotically, lane by lane, careful with patches of ice.

'That's why Julie and I set up this system,' Maddox said once they were on the pavement. 'There wasn't enough room in the compound, so we rented a house just across the road and set up a nice little place for the kids. It helps us because we love having them, and it helps the parents because it means the wives can travel with the husbands sometimes. Keeps the relationships healthier.'

Ko managed the U-turn with Paul as they were crossing and pulled up at the gate. Paul opened the door, ran up the path and through the wooden front doors.

'He can go now,' Maddox said, nodding towards Ko.

'He's fine. He'll wait,' Sally said quickly. She wished Maddox wasn't so chatty. She needed to drop Paul and get on her way before the whole of the Xian police force tracked her down. But Maddox was in no hurry to get inside.

'Maybe a dozen families in Xian managed to keep their old lifestyle after the communists took over.' He raised his voice above the noise of the traffic. 'One of the survivors still lives here. She's an incredible woman. Still calls herself Violet, and talks about the Red Guards as Mao's louts. To us, anyway.

Don't expect she does to the Chinese.'

The house had three storeys, with dark wooden outside beams, turret rooms with tiny windows on the top floor, and a huge window stretching down two floors, the stairwell behind it. It was an amazing example of colonial extravagance, squeezed between a drab modern apartment block and a line of low-rise shacks.

'Violet is the only surviving member of her family,' Maddox went on, 'and up until she was in her thirties she was the toast of Xian society. The Japs dragged her father off around nineteen thirty-nine and she never saw him again. They beheaded her mother after raping her in front of Violet. You really should spend an evening with her, and she'll tell you all this. She survived the Japs, the Nationalists, the Maoists and whatever else life has thrown at her.'

'I'd love to,' said Sally. 'But I think we'd better move on now. I have a plane to catch.' She looked at her watch.

'Oh, sure,' said Maddox, walking on. But he still kept talking. 'The house was divided up for nineteen families. Violet managed to keep a room and has lived there ever since. Julie and I love her.'

The house was behind a low wooden picket fence, painted white, and there was even a red mailbox on the gate, with the name of the house proudly painted on it.

'Park View, huh?' Sally observed.

'We're standing in what used to be a sweeping driveway, and the gate to the estate would have been way down towards our compound. This road was just a track.'

Through the big window, she saw Paul running up the stairs. She quickened her step, walking through heavy wooden double doors into the hall which was clearly used as a playroom. An old, chipped, wooden rocking horse was on one side, an inflatable bouncy castle on the other, toys all over the floor and children's watercolours taped to the wall. The colours brightened up the dark panelling of the hall. The cries and laughter of children were everywhere, like it all made sense.

'They've got the communist families living in one wing of the house, and there's an orphanage on the other side which we help to run,' Maddox was saying. 'We raise money back home. Doesn't cost much to keep it going, and Julie gets involved in helping American couples adopt kids from here. Mostly girls, as I suppose you know.'

'Are you going to do that?' asked Sally, hoping that if she hit the personal, Bob would stop talking and let her get away.

'Are we going to do what?' said Maddox, walking forward to start the rocking horse. He brushed his hand down what looked like real horsehair. Sally guessed it was from the original house, a survivor of the Japanese and the Red Guards.

'Adopt,' said Sally.

'We're still trying for our own. But it's tempting. They tug the inside of your hearts, these kids. One morning, just after we got here, Julie and I had to meet some people off the train from Beijing. We got the time of the train wrong and arrived at the station a couple of hours early, before dawn. We found these two bundles, just dumped there, in the freezing cold. That's what gave Julie the idea for the orphanage. Some nights, you know, Julie and I just drive around town looking for abandoned girls. Best place to find them is on the ledges at the end of the underpasses. I guess the parents think it gives them some protection from the weather. Some weeks we pick up two or three.'

Sally said nothing, not telling him that she and Ko did the same thing.

Paul came bounding down the stairs, his face so alive with excitement that Sally felt good for the first time in days. He threw himself at her, making her step back to keep her balance.

'Did you ever see a place like this, Mom?' he yelped. 'Am I staying here? Promise?'

'For a night or three,' said Sally. 'If that's all right with Mr Maddox.'

'They have a trampoline upstairs. A real trampoline.' He unwound his arms from Sally's shoulders, dropped himself to the floor as if he was climbing down a tree, ran across the hall and scrambled onto the rocking horse.

Maddox smiled. 'See. Nothing to it. He couldn't be in better hands.'

A door opened to one side of the hall and Julie came out. She was a tall woman, taller than Maddox, thin as a rake, in a beige, woollen one-piece dress, slightly too big for her. She wore no make-up or jewellery, and her brown hair hung way past her shoulders, dulled by the bad Chinese air. She made no attempt to style it. Julie Maddox was a woman who had made her choices and would live with them. Life had dealt her Bob Maddox, childlessness and Xian, and she was doing her best to make it work.

'Sally Parsons,' she said. 'I have wanted to meet you for so long. I just think you've done the most fantastic things with your life.'

'Not as fantastic as you helping me out with Paul.'

'He is going to have just the funnest time here,' Julie Maddox enthused.

Sally trusted Julie completely. She was the type who would give her life for someone else's kid.

She hugged Paul. 'Mommy's off to Beijing now.'

Paul was more interested in kicking the horse to full speed. 'Bye,' he muttered.

When they got to the door, Ko started the car. Sally turned and saw Julie Maddox watching her watching Ko. She smiled. Julie smiled back. It was a woman's look. Understanding. Julie had given her the greatest gift – the safety of her son. Ko was pulling round. The lights were red behind him, giving him a clear quarter mile in front. It was time to go.

In a second, she was in the car among the smells of the seats and the Mao cushions. 'Just drive, Ko,' she said.

Ko put his foot down. She looked round, through Ko's back window, through a transparent picture of Mao in a tractor factory. Julie and Bob were out there, their hands on Paul's shoulders, both waving to her, hands linked, like father, mother and son, bidding her goodbye.

She sank her head into her hands and cried, deep sobs, not caring that Ko could hear.

Sally got Ko to stop off at a petrol station on the edge of the built-up area of town before the stretch of airport road began.

Inside, the office was hot, and a fan blew straight into her face. She called Richard. By the way he answered, abrupt, snappy, she could tell she had wrecked his day. One little thing, but she felt good about it.

'Where are you?' he said.

'None of your damn business. Why not just tell me what the hell is going on?'

'I checked and there's a problem with the trowel. One of the district attorneys has asked why you were ever let out of the country.'

'Because you put me on a goddamn plane, that's why.'

'And if I hadn't, Paul would either be in the care of the embassy or out of school and in the US.'

Sally, quietened. 'Point taken,' she conceded. 'But where does that leave me now? Am I a felon?'

She didn't even listen to his answer. As she thought of his infidelity, she felt incredibly calm, even light-headed. 'Listen, Richard,' she interrupted. 'Let's handle this face to face. I'll see you in Beijing.' Sally put the receiver down very gently and pressed money into the manager's hand. Ko was outside, filling the radiator with water. He rushed and fumbled when he saw her. 'Take your time,' she shouted across the forecourt.

She wiped her forehead. 'You know my friend Li Yi?' she said, leaning on the roof while Ko worked. He nodded. 'After you've dropped me at the airport, can you find him? Wherever he is. Tell him I'm on my way to Beijing.'

Ko nodded again. Kept working, wiping oil off his spark plugs.

'Ko, are you listening?'

He stood up straight, unlatched the bonnet prop and dropped it down. 'I find Li Yi and tell him you need help, right?' Ko smiled and held the back door open for Sally to get in.

Chapter Seventeen

The envelope, unsealed and unmarked, lay between them, a corner over the edge of the desk pointing towards Cage, who did not lean forward to pick it up. He did not even look at it. To do so would be to show interest.

The man in front of him seemed frozen in time, but his mannerisms and looks were deceptive. Despite the creases in his face and the fragility shown in his hands, the way he held the pen, the knotty movements when he opened papers, and the twisted way the cupped fingers lit a cigarette, he exuded enormous power. Cage had rarely seen it before in a man who looked so physically weak.

His clothes were frayed and shabby. The colour had faded in many washes, and holes had been patched with bluer and brighter cotton. The jacket, although freshly ironed, was indifferent to fashion, with the top button undone because the room was dry and stuffy.

Cage refused to sit and towered over Wu Tian, who didn't seem to notice or care, did not take affront at Cage's dismissal of the envelope. Nor, when Cage spoke in English, did he seem bothered by what he said. Wu's desk lamp threw out just enough light for the two men to see each other. It was a neutral light, favouring neither. The rest of the long, narrow room was pretty much in darkness. It was late at night, and even the outside lights of the university campus had been switched off. The room was like a museum, like the house of a dead grandfather.

Cage sensed Li Yi's presence; he could not see him. He was standing, maybe fifteen feet back, against a bookcase to the left with a mah-jong table between them. Every now and then, Cage heard his weight shift.

'My experience is that the less that gets written down the better,' said Cage.

'Your experience?' said Wu.

'Yes.'

Wu left the envelope where it was.

'I can show you who your mother and father are, just like this,' Wu said, clicking his fingers surprisingly loudly for a man who used his hands so awkwardly.

'Is that what's in the envelope?'

'Maybe. Why don't you look?'

There was no way Cage would show any weakness at this stage.

'Professor Wu can give you what you want before the night is over,' said Li Yi, stepping away from the bookcase. He moved like a nightclub bouncer, but Cage didn't plan to confront him. Instead he made a half-turn to get him into view.

Wu drummed his fingers on the desk. Then he got up and opened the window behind him, struggling a bit with the old metal, pushing it a couple of inches before it was stopped by filthy wire mesh. Rust fell off and Wu brushed his hands together like a schoolteacher getting rid of chalk dust.

It was the first time Cage had seen Wu on his feet. For all his pudginess, filled-out cheeks, pale colour, he was surprisingly agile. Wu stood behind the desk, each hand placed either side of the blotting pad, fingers spread.

'Forgive me if Li Yi offended you with his bluntness. He is not a cultured man. I asked him to invite you here because I wanted to meet you. And I want you to do something for me. You came to China to see your son and his mother, whom you love.' He lifted his right hand just an inch, enough to stop Cage interrupting. 'You came also to find your real parents. I will tell you how I know that later. But love of your sort is a terrible thing, especially if there is a child, who might later reject you.' Wu rested his hand back on the desk, then he seemed to have another thought and he sat back down, moving the light slightly so that it shone on him more than on Cage. 'You can sit or remain standing. I have things to tell you and you should listen.'

Cage shrugged and pulled up a canvas collapsible chair from the mah-jong table. 'I'm listening,' he said.

'In the United States, you are apparently wanted for shooting a man. You are also in trouble with the military. I am not threatening you. But I know some of these realities and I am offering to remove those things which are stopping you from moving forward. Should our police choose, they will arrest you, and hand you over for deportation to the United States. There you would be taken into custody and could remain in jail for a very long time. I have the power to stop that happening. But why should I? What relationship do I have with you which would make me do that?' He looked up, beyond Cage, a signal for Li Yi to melt back again towards the bookcases.

'Go on,' said Cage.

'I want you to do something for China. You are, after all, half Chinese. It is not a big thing and once you have done it we will have a relationship. We respect each other already. But we have no mutual debts. No gifts have passed between us. After we have accumulated gifts and debts we might even come to like each other and that would make me happy indeed. You have a strong character. Sometimes too strong, like your mother . . .'

'You knew my mother?' said Cage.

'Indeed. And your father. You have your mother's intelligence and you have your father's thoughtfulness. Once you are aware of these things, you will be more balanced as a person. Sally, Paul and your heritage will fall into place. I can help you with all of this. Indeed, I want to help you and in other circumstances I might have done it without negotiations. But I need help from you, a very small thing. It will take half a day at the most.'

Cage stood up, walked to the desk, picked up the envelope and pulled out the sheet of paper inside. It was blank on both sides. A hoax. In another place, at another stage of his life, he would have gone for Wu, who was smiling, but not jeeringly, more as if the trick had served to give Cage a better understanding of the situation. Cage put the paper back into the envelope.

'You wanted to see how much I cared,' he said.

'Correct.'

'What's to say you're not all bullshit?'

'I don't know if they are still alive. We are checking up. I believe that, like all of us, they were both damaged by the Great Proletariat Cultural Revolution. Only the strongest of us made it through.'

Wu Tian brought out a photograph from a drawer in his desk and handed it to Cage. It was an enlargement and the photographic paper was too big to support itself. It flopped down, and Cage had to hold it up with his forefinger. The photograph was of a beautiful, calm and gentle face, austere because of the framing, the official nature of the picture. But it was the face of his mother, the same picture in the locket he had had all these years.

Cage swallowed hard. Wu Tian would notice, but he didn't care. If he had come to China to find his mother, here she was. 'Who was she?'

'She was a rebel, like you, which is why the Cultural Revolution swallowed her up.'

'It killed her?'

Wu shook his head. 'It broke her, as it broke millions. But, as I said, she may still be alive.'

'My father?'

'We don't have a photograph.'

'Describe him.'

'He was a fine man. An idealistic man. But he was a foreigner, and you must understand that it is delicate, even now. So first I will explain why I need your expertise.'

He spoke in Chinese to Li Yi who unrolled a map of Beijing and laid it on the mah-jong table. Wu instructed Li Yi again, this time with an edge in his voice and Cage saw both their façades slip. For a second, one was master and the other was slave. Li Yi hauled back a bookcase, old rollers creaking on tired, brittle metal, to reveal a second, larger room. He switched on lights. The fluorescent bulbs buzzed like a ship's engine, throwing out different light around the study. There was a conference table, a dozen or so chairs, a map of China marked up with coloured push pins, even a small podium and a side table with bottled water and soft drinks. It smelt rusty, a muddle of humidity, dryness, damp, and trapped air.

Li Yi brought the map to the conference table, flattening it down with his hands. Like a flunky he opened a bottle of water and poured out two glasses for Cage and Wu Tian who had followed him into the room.

'On May the fifteenth, President Gorbachev is visiting China,' began Wu. 'It is an historic event, and we in China are very keen that the visit goes smoothly. However, Mr Gorbachev wants more than we are willing to give. He wants a strategic partnership between the Soviet Union and China to counter the power of the United States. We tried that in the nineteen fifties and they let us down. Did you know that Stalin promised us full air cover if we went into Korea? He pulled out at the last minute, leaving us to swing in the wind. We took half a million casualties. Chairman Mao's son Anying was among the dead. The Chairman mourned his son like a true father. I'm telling you this so you understand why we will never trust the Soviets again.'

Wu walked round the other side of the conference table until he was standing next to Cage, unnaturally close. Cage smelt the soap of the freshly laundered tunic and the tobacco from his breath. He felt Wu's hand touching his elbow.

'The Americans don't want us to get close to the Soviets. Never mind *glasnost* and *perestroika*. They want China just the way she is. They would even prefer it if Mao Zedong's thought still prevailed. In those days China was distant, mysterious and independent.' Wu's hand moved from Cage's elbow to his shoulder, fingers spread, resting lightly.

'Because there are many of us who do not want to become closer to the Soviets, we have agreed to hold talks with the Americans before Gorbachev arrives to see if we can strengthen our relationship. The Americans wanted them held in Washington, but we objected because of the press. So now they're taking place in Beijing.' He took his hand off Cage's shoulder and smoothed down the map again.

'This is your first visit to Beijing?' he asked.

'I expect I passed through it on my way to the US when I was a baby.'

Wu's finger hovered over the middle of the map. 'This is the Forbidden City. Right next to it, to the west, is Zhongnanhai, where our leaders live and work, except for Deng Xiao-ping who lives behind the compound. To the south, is Tiananmen Square with the great monuments built by Mao Zedong. The Great Hall of the People, here. The Museum of Chinese History and Revolution. The Monument to the People's Heroes. And at the southern end the Chairman Mao Memorial Hall.' Wu traced an imaginary circle round the area.

'Insofar as a nation has a soul on earth, this is the soul of China. Her history and her future.' Wu took a step to the right. Cage stayed where he was, his eyes good enough to pick out the detail. 'Here is the San Li Tun compound where many of the foreign diplomats live, and over here is the Zhao Long Hotel. It's no five-star hotel. It is used mainly by downmarket package tours or by the richer local people. So no particular attention is attracted when it is completely taken over for a conference. This hotel is the venue for the negotiations between America and China. They are being held in absolute secrecy.'

The hotel was on the corner of two main thoroughfares. It looked larger than most of the buildings around it. Across the road to the north was an apartment block, then the buildings of embassies.

Li Yi appeared with photographs, which he spread out on top of the map. They showed the hotel shot from an overpass, down the northerly thoroughfare, with the hotel on the left; from a rooftop of the apartment block across the road, looking down onto the sweeping driveway and the glass doors going in; from ground level, the lens elevated to capture a car coming in to drop off passengers. There were also photographs taken inside the building: the coffee shop; the reception desk; round to the left, into the darkness of a bar; another shot from the bar out into the lobby. And so on. They were all positions for a hit. Places from which a gunman or sniper could work and escape.

'Interesting,' said Cage, sliding the photographs around and examining them.

'Many people don't feel betrayed by the Soviets like the Chairman did. Like I do. Mao knew the truth, but one man's thought, however brilliant, cannot be everywhere. Many people were educated in Moscow. They believe China is re-making herself in the image of the United States and will do anything to stop it.' He flattened his hand on the table. 'They will try to disrupt these negotiations. We believe they may do something terrible which would damage our relationship with America for many years to come.'

'Like what?'

'Kill the American negotiators.'

'And my role?' asked Cage calmly.

Li Yi answered. 'Your file says you are an expert at building defences. You survey buildings and discover their weak spots.'

'My file says that, does it?' Cage didn't want to be drawn yet.

'The Cambodian army headquarters in Pailin, nineteen eighty-six. The Cambodiana Hotel during a regional conference, nineteen eighty-seven. The Soviet listening station at Ban Sop Bau in Laos, nineteen eighty-eight. In each of those cases you successfully devised a way through the building defences. Wu Tian tapped the map. 'Our men are trained, but they do not have your experience. The hotel is not being closed for another few days. Go and look at it, and let us know how a gunman could get through, and how we could stop him.'

Two men trailed Cage from the university campus, but he spotted them and lost them with no difficulty. Then he diverted to the China Traders' Hotel, where it was unlikely that Wu would have put a trace on the phones, and he called Robert Leonard.

'The Teochiu hit an Italian restaurant way up on Fifty-second Street last night,' said Leonard. 'Two guys dead. One expected to die. They're not important. But it was a long way out of Chinese territory. The Castellos asked to talk but didn't get an answer.'

'To do that, they have to know they have someone very powerful behind them,' said Cage. 'Wu wants me to carry out a security check on a hotel where the US and China are carrying out some secret talks. You know anything about it?'

'What are they talking about?'

'The Soviets. With Gorbachev coming, the Chinese are playing us off against the Soviets. So we're trying to cut some new deals with them, before Gorbachev gets here.'

'I thought Wu hated us.'

'He says he hates the Soviets more. Says he's heard some pro-Soviet Chinese are planning to wreck the meeting. He doesn't trust the Chinese security guys to do their job properly and asked me to have a look.'

'I'll check it out,' said Leonard. 'Keep in touch.'

Cage started by checking out the apartment block opposite. He got in by showing his American passport, took the elevator to the eighth floor, then the stairs to the roof. The door was padlocked; the chain had rusted over and the lock was stiff. Cage had brought with him a tiny can of oil, and after using it he was able to pick the lock.

Once on the roof, he checked for other entrances, but found none. Then, keeping low, he moved to the edge to see what sort of shot a sniper would have at the hotel foyer. No way. The angle was too steep. The more acute the angle, the trickier the shot would be. From here, a marksman would have to fire from a raised position, and he would be exposed to the surveillance teams sweeping the rooftop with binoculars. Besides, two trees blocked the line of sight.

A sniper would prefer a target on a podium, or on a slow walk, being greeted by people, giving enough time to anticipate movement, to follow the head, wait for it to settle, and fire. From where he was now, across the road, it would have to be a back of the head shot or, failing that, an upper body shot, through the back, because the target would be out of the car, facing the entrance to the hotel.

A shot at the car, though, would be different. Traffic moved slowly, hampered by the trucks and broken-down vehicles on the main roads. Vehicles turned in from under the overpass, drove two hundred yards west, then turned left again into the hotel entrance. Even if the car had a clear run, it would have to slow to cross the bicycle lane. That was a possible shot, but not a good one. And if the car had darkened windows, target identification would be impossible.

The apartments in the building were diplomatic quarters, Venezuela, Burundi, Costa Rica. If he had had a clearer remit, Cage would have gone into each one and looked at the lines of sight from the windows, maybe finding one on a lower trajectory, with a clear path between the trees. But he had already dismissed the building as too difficult. The whole idea of such a quick shot, from car to foyer, was one which any professional marksman would have dismissed as well.

That left taking out the whole car. The range was fine for a rocket-propelled grenade, but it would mean standing with no cover – a crude way of doing things.

Cage locked the roof door and took the stairs down to the ground floor. Outside the diplomatic compound, he walked slowly towards the big junction. There was an embassy directly opposite the hotel, crenellated, with ivy hanging all over it. But when he saw that it belonged to Sweden, he factored it out. No Chinese marksman would operate from the Swedish Embassy.

The quickest way to get across the cycle lane was to just go and let the cyclists swerve around him. They did so stolidly and without anger. He took his time walking round the driveway of the hotel. Drivers called him from the taxi rank, wanting his business.

A stretch Lincoln Town Car was parked in the driveway. The driver's-side tyre was almost flat, and the car was dirty, frozen mud discolouring the cream paint, as if it hadn't been out for some time. Cage walked past, flicking up the handle to check that it was locked.

A Jaguar was pulled up by the hedge on the left, with a driver waiting inside it. What the hell was an expensive British car doing in Beijing?

The fountain water spurted out irregularly, sometimes shooting up, sometimes not making it at all. He stood behind it and took in the scene, trying to feel where a shot would come from. But he got no sense of it. He waited for a taxi to draw up and watched how the passenger got out, fiddling with her money, her gloves too bulky to handle the notes, so that she just gave a wad to the doorman and let him handle it.

The inside of the hotel was pretty much like the photographs he had seen. Straight ahead, a coffee shop, a white piano on a podium, silent with no player, and a buffet display at the back. To the left was the reception desk and beyond that a dark doorway that led to a bar. To the right were two elevators.

If Wu was right about sealing off the hotel, anything attempted inside would have to be by one of the staff. Or by someone lying up inside for a number of days. A guest? How thoroughly did they check the place? If you knew a building like this it would be easy enough to hide out in it. You could hide for forty-eight hours, pissing into a bottle and eating so little you didn't have to crap. The assassin would have to be Chinese to move around after the cordon was put up. He would have to get IDs, the password for the day. It was a possibility, although the hit itself would have a hint of suicide about it.

The lobby was busy enough for Cage to walk in unnoticed. He went to the elevator and rode up with two other occupants who got out on the fourth and eighth floors. Cage got out on the twelfth, left the lift quickly and headed down the corridor. He slipped through the fire exit door and was immediately hit by the smell of decaying food. At his feet was a room service tray with mould growing on the rice.

He headed up. The staircase was littered with hotel bric-a-brac. He had to move a mattress aside to get up to the fourteenth floor. On the fifteenth, boxes were piled against the fire door and he decided to keep heading for the nineteenth and then the roof. Unlike the building opposite, the door was clean, well-oiled and opened with the push of a bar. Cage eased the bar down gently, then opened the door an inch to see if there was activity on the roof. He couldn't tell for sure, but it seemed empty, so he stepped out confidently.

Two engineers adjusting a satellite dish looked up, took Cage for a tourist and resumed work. Cage walked over to the western edge of the roof, but there was nothing at the back of the compound that seemed threatening: a cluster of low-rise houses, an oblong five-storey building, and slightly to the south an alleyway which led out onto the cycle track of the Third Ring Road.

He waved at the workmen. They waved back and Cage walked over to check out the front of the roof which looked down on where he had just been. This would give a clear shot at any car slowing and coming in the driveway. If the car had darkened windows, the windscreen would be less tinted than the side and back windows and would give the shooter a clear line of sight to the target. But the shot would have to go through glass. Car and target would be moving. The only way to get a certain hit from this angle would be to rake the vehicle with automatic weapons fire, something like a 7.62mm, or a rocket-propelled grenade.

The trouble with the roof was that it would be checked out. Checked again and again. Then, if the Chinese were doing their job properly, they would have spotters up here, two on each side, one with binoculars and one with a rifle. There would be eight men to neutralise. Too many. Not a good spot for an assassin.

Cage let himself back into the hotel and went down to the top floor. A hundred men could search the hotel in about an hour, including places where people could be hiding out. Every room would be checked, doors and air-conditioning vents taped, two guards on each floor, another for the service lift and more if there was a second bank. They would need floor plans. All ducts, waste shoots, toilets would have to be ticked off against it.

He took the stairs all the way down, stepped outside and walked quickly down the driveway to the entrance. A car drove the wrong way down a cycle lane, and the cyclists braked and lifted their bikes out of its path. No gesticulations of anger. Cage crossed the cycle track, then ran across the road, weaving between a black Mercedes and a coal truck, and ended up next to an orange telephone box, with broken glass, the phone ripped out. He looked back towards the hotel.

He had had tougher ones than this to crack before. He took another long look at the hotel compound, and saw how it could be done. It was, as usual, laughably simple.

Chapter Eighteen

Stephanie Cranley spread the photographs on the table, while the audio tape of Richard's afternoon activities with Christine played in the background. She and Richard were alone in a chamber that resembled a diving capsule, inside the American Embassy. They sat either side of a table covered with green felt, and Richard had to keep his head bent so as not to strike the curving plastic walls.

Twenty years earlier, Stephanie Cranley would have been stunningly beautiful. She was still an attractive woman. Today, in her early fifties, she was wearing a maroon wool suit, hair cut short in a way that, on a woman with less prominent bone structure, would have aged her. But in Cranley's case it gave her a commanding presence.

Had Sally been there she would have recognised Cranley as Hazel Watson.

When she had told Sally she was with the State Department, Cranley had not been lying. The FCA, Federal Containment Agency, for which she worked, was funded by the State Department, the National Security Agency and the Central Intelligence Agency. Only the most senior personnel knew it existed. Its job was to identify potential threats to US interests and to deal with them at the earliest stage. In Washington, there was an understanding that the FCA would go where other agencies feared to tread. Cranley was its operations director.

She took off her jacket and sifted through the photographs like a croupier. They were a sequence taken every few seconds.

Richard, halfway through the afternoon (at 4.03.01 a.m. according to Eastern Standard Time, twelve hours earlier than local time), went to the bathroom, and made the mistake of closing and locking the door.

4.03.15 Christine was getting out of bed, dropping the sheet to the floor.

4.03.20 She was looking around the room, expertly.

4.03.35 She was squatting, naked by the door, dabbing at a shadow of sawdust under the lock.

4.03.43 She was peering through the window.

4.03.50 She had seen a cable leading to a lens planted further up.

4.03.56 She was smiling, stark naked, fresh from sex, posing for the camera, tongue out, hands splayed over her stomach pointing down between her legs.

4.04.01 Her hands were brushing round her buttocks and up to her breasts.

4.04.09 Richard, also naked, was back in the room.

4.04.14 Christine was bounding back onto the bed, hauling Richard down, hands clawing down his back, drawing blood, doing things the boys on the surveillance shift would fantasize about for weeks.

4.04.15, 4.04.20, 4.04.25 . . . she was play-acting for the cameras, with Richard as her prop.

'Our fault she found the cable,' Cranley said unconvincingly. 'Sloppy workmanship.'

'You said you wouldn't,' said Richard. 'I mean, we took out the bedroom system . . .'

'I'm surprised that you're surprised,' Cranley said drily. She brought the photos together and put them in front of her. She smiled. 'Apart from that, we thought you did well. We detected an intimacy, and that's all we really need. If you're on the other side of a negotiating table, better to have slept with the enemy than not.' She glanced at Richard. 'Sally called in the middle. What happened there?'

'What the hell do you expect happened?' replied Richard angrily.

Cranley stabbed a finger at him. 'Your personal life is not my concern. Our role is to ensure that Gorbachev does not want to do business with China. If we successfully sabotage his visit, then our operation will have been a success. And frankly, Richard, I don't care who you have to sleep with to achieve it.'

Cranley unfolded a map. Half of it showed a layout of the Zhao Long Hotel. The other half concentrated on the network of roads and alleys sprawling out from the compound. Cranley indicated the area of the driveway.

'Arrivals, here at nine a.m. We wanted to host it in Washington, but they insisted on Beijing because there would be less chance of a press leak. They're probably right, so it's fine by us. Our negotiating team comes by car in from the embassy, down here past the San Li Tun market, and makes a right turn into the Zhao Long. We travel in two separate cars. They're fielding Liu Huaqiu, the deputy foreign minister for US affairs, but we don't have an assistant secretary of state until Richard Solomon takes up his post in June. So we're not sure yet whom we'll send.' Her pen landed at the doorway of the hotel, marking the paper.

'Christine will be attached to Liu like glue. So you will travel in the lead car. The two other negotiators from the US Embassy will be in a car which comes in five minutes later. The numbers are small because the talks are meant to be informal and workman-like. Technically, the US State Department is the lead agency because of the special classified status of the FCA.

'As soon as you arrive, you will be shown up to . . . here.' The pen stabbed again, this time the room plan for the hotel. 'The talks themselves are in a corner suite overlooking the Third Ring Road, which has an anteroom with comfortable chairs, coffee and soft drinks. You'll have five minutes of small talk with Christine and Liu. This is your opportunity to break the ice with him.'

Richard nodded but stayed quiet.

'Christine remains your key,' continued Cranley, 'because she has the ear of General Secretary Zhao Zhiyang. You have to show her and the Chinese negotiators that you also are the key. Your travelling in the lead car will help. But you have to go further than that. Our acting assistant secretary – or whoever it turns out to be

– will let you step inside the anteroom ahead of him. You should sit down before he does. You must speak out of turn. You must interrupt him. He'll play along. You'll be wired and we'll have our people over at San Li Tun, measuring your success.'

'OK,' said Richard slowly. 'And what's on the agenda? What are we negotiating?'

'Leave that to the two negotiators from the embassy.'

'Christine will know. I have to know.'

'We're taking a leap in the dark. We're shutting up about democratic reform. We're offering preferential trading terms. Human rights, Tibet, democracy – all that crap – are off the menu. New beginnings, we're calling it. Deng Xiao-ping's China can develop how it wants, jail as many damn dissidents as it wants without a single gripe from us, just so long as it doesn't get into bed with the Soviets.'

'Voters back home won't like it.'

'It's been authorised at the highest level,' retorted Cranley.

Li Yi didn't meet Sally, but he sent a car and gave her one of his lavish apartments overlooking Beijing, with views of the pastel rooftops of the Forbidden City and the dark, sombre monuments of Tiananmen Square. Sally stood on the wrap-around balcony looking over tourist China, so high above it that the screech of the traffic was no more than a background hum.

She was called back in by the telephone. It was Li Yi on the line. 'Welcome to Beijing,' he gushed. 'I'm so sorry I wasn't there to meet you, but busy, busy Sally – she never knows what she's going to be doing next.'

'What did you mean?' Sally said straightaway. 'What did you—'

But Li Yi broke in, stopping Sally from repeating his panic warning *Get the hell away from them*. 'No need to go into that now. We must remember where we are.'

Sally paced the apartment, looking down on Beijing. Finally, she fixed herself coffee, then tore a single sheet of paper off the pad on the desk and neatly wrote down the things she had to do.

At six in the morning, she called Cait in New York. Her sister had just got home through the Friday night rush hour. When

Sally told her what she wanted, Cait simply said, 'I'll get back to you within an hour.'

While Sally waited, she took out the photographs and the notes she had made on the tomb. She worked on them until Cait called back.

'Right. This is what I got,' she said. 'Nothing about Binsky's murder for some weeks. He had a very small private funeral and has been buried near Columbia University. The last mention you got was in the *New York Post*, the day after the murder. The "noted archaeologist" who was the last friend to see him alive. End of story. I also talked to a crime reporter on the *New York Times*. He told me for sure, if the police wanted to talk to you that badly, he would have heard about it and they would have run a story.'

Sally spent another two hours working on her notes, studying the paths that could get her into the tomb. She fixed herself a light breakfast of fruit and noodles, then with a half-full glass of water in her hand she rang the embassy and asked for Richard Gregg's office – not him, but his office.

She spoke to Maeve, shouting through the glass, which she held next to the mouthpiece. She felt stupid. It was something Cage had taught her as a joke years ago – how to disguise your voice on the phone. It distorted the frequency so much that even the voice recognition machines couldn't identify anything through it. Sally spoke Chinese, mixed with bad English, and found out that Richard wasn't due in until mid-morning.

Then she called the embassy's information department. It was a Saturday. The embassy was open for the morning.

'Hi, this is Sally Parsons, the archaeologist from Xian.'

The receptionist's tone leapt from bored to deferential. 'Dr Parsons. How great to hear from you. We get so many people asking about your work here.'

'Thank you,' said Sally. 'It's very kind. You must be new in China.'

'I've been here only a couple of weeks. My name's Susan Masters. How can I help?'

'Firstly, welcome to China. And secondly, are there any messages for me? Sometimes people leave them with you guys.'

175

'Are you expecting anything particularly?'

'Not really. But when I'm in Beijing I generally ring to check.'

Sally heard the tapping of computer keys. 'Nothing here that I can see. There's some references from a few weeks back . . . Oh my God!'

'What's wrong?'

'It's just about Professor Binsky's murder.'

A rush of adrenaline swept through Sally, but she stayed cool. 'Yeah, any movement on that?'

'Just says you were with him shortly before he died, and it has your number in Xian if the detectives want to talk with you.'

'Nothing else?'

'Not that I can see. Is that it?'

'I've got some down time this morning to hang out and read up on American culture. If it's OK, I plan to come by this morning and catch up on some magazines.'

'Sure. That would be great.'

On her way to the embassy, Sally checked into a small, discreet hotel, where the rooms were acrid, worn and cheap and no one took much notice of her. Her purpose was to leave her credit card, notes and her passport in the hotel safe. She didn't quite trust Li Yi not to search the apartment while she was out.

Susan was a bubbling blonde in her mid-twenties. Sally sat on the chair opposite her desk. 'You know, I left my passport in the hotel room,' began Sally, 'and the guard gave me such a hard time with my photo ID from the Archeological Institute.'

Susan giggled. 'It's really great to meet you in the flesh.' She pushed her chair back and stood up. 'You know what gets me?'

'What's that?'

'It's that you're so normal. That you have the same hassles with passes that we have. I'll get you a coffee.'

Sally laughed. 'I take mine with cream and no sugar.'

Susan disappeared into the little kitchen round the corner.

'Do you know if Richard's in yet?' said Sally loud enough for Susan to hear.

'Richard Gregg?' She leaned back round, her face lit up at the prospect of sharing some of Sally's personal life. 'You go out with him, don't you?'

Sally flicked back her hair. 'Actually, we're getting married,' she said. It wasn't quite not true, so she didn't completely despise herself. 'He proposed to me in New York.'

Susan brought back two cups, passed one to Sally, put her own down on the desk and clapped her hands together. 'That's great news.' She sat down, then repeated herself. 'That's really such a good thing to hear.'

'Thanks.'

They briefly sat in silence, Sally letting Susan share in her faked happiness.

'Listen. We had a fun night last night, just the two of us,' said Sally. 'And you know how it is I would so much like to surprise him. What do you reckon I pick up a copy of the *New Yorker*, the *New Scientist* and the *New York Review* and read them in his office, so I'm waiting, all wifely-like, when he gets in?'

Susan grinned. 'I wish I had some guy to do that for.'

'Can you take me there? This place is such a rabbit warren.'

'Sure.' Susan started punching in Richard's extension. 'I'll check with Maeve.'

'Why spoil it? Let's just turn up.'

A flicker of indecision flitted across Susan's face. Sally could see that Susan was remembering the rules, the indoctrination, the security lectures from her training.

Sally turned on her best smile. 'You never get the man you want and the job you want by sticking to the rules.' She jumped to her feet. Susan hesitated, then stood up too, taking a quick sip of her coffee before leading Sally down the corridor.

Through the secure door, the first person they saw was Malcolm Mackie, Susan's boss. It was a long corridor with plenty of sizing-up time. Susan slowed her pace nervously. But Sally walked on ahead, long legs taking her forward, arms outstretched. 'Malcolm, how's it going? How's things?' They had met a year or so back, and she kissed him on both cheeks. Mackie looked uncertainly at Susan for a second, and Sally said, 'We're off to see – guess who?'

'So you guys are still an item?'

Sally was already moving beyond him. 'Listen out for either violins or fireworks, and you'll find out.'

The way the corridors curved round, Sally soon recognised where she was. Richard's office was towards the end, and Maeve sat outside with another secretary who worked for the guy next door. Sally stopped, turned round, her hand to her mouth. 'Oh God, Susan I forgot the magazines. You couldn't run back and get someone to bring them to me, could you?'

'That someone would be me.'

'Do you mind?'

'It would be a pleasure. Now that Malcolm's seen us, I don't feel like I'm bending the rules.'

Sally waited for Susan to disappear, then quickened her pace. She swept round and through the door. 'Maeve, how's things? Richard said for me to wait for him in his office.'

Maeve was small, slight-framed, with cropped black hair, up front and bright. 'He didn't mention it to me,' she replied, not unfriendly but cautious.

'I guess he wouldn't if he didn't even tell me he was back in Beijing.' She winked and hooked her hair behind her ears. 'I just left him. Not left him, as in separated. But left him, like after spending the night and a lazy morning in his apartment. But that's off the record.' By the time she said that she had one foot in Richard's office, and Maeve had made no move to stop her. 'Susan's coming by in a minute with some magazines.'

'Susan?'

'Works in USIS, the information section. She's new. With Malcolm Mackie.'

Maeve nodded. Sally went in, leaving the door ajar. When Susan arrived, she asked her to close it behind her as she left.

The phone rang in Richard's real office, two floors down in the basement of the embassy. He was listening to the tape of Christine's story about her father, taking notes.

'Richard, it's Christine. Stop whatever you are doing and listen. Because what I am about to tell you is very important news.' She was totally professional, as if the afternoon in bed had never happened.

Richard turned off the tape-player so Christine couldn't hear her own voice.

'Hu Yaobang is dead,' she said.

The Chinese tended to assume everyone had the same intimate knowledge of their leaders as they did. It took Richard a couple of seconds for it to register. Hu Yaobang was a former general secretary of the Communist Party, an avowed Marxist, yet a leader widely believed to have wanted a freer political system.

'When and how did he die?'

'A couple of hours ago. He was on the crapper and had a heart attack. They'll love him for that. Hu the human, if you'll excuse my English pun. Think about it.'

'I'm thinking.'

'He's a popular hero, Richard. Remember what happened when Zhou En-lai died? They came out onto the streets. The wreaths in Tiananmen Square reached sixty feet up the sides of the Monument of the People's Heroes. Two million people were out there, cursing Mao and his mad wife. Richard, listen to me, this is what they are going to do with Hu. Think about it.'

'It doesn't affect the negotiations,' asked Richard cautiously.

'It might help them. Watch the universities. The students will use this to demand more freedom. Deng Xiao-ping will have to listen.'

Richard thanked her, then brought out one of his many books on modern Chinese history and looked up Hu Yaobang. People loved him because he had rehabilitated thousands who had been persecuted by Mao. If Mao was the glorious Emperor, Hu was the human face, the leader of compassion. Richard glanced at his calendar. It was 15 April 1989. In exactly one month, on 15 May, Gorbachev was due to arrive.

He was about to turn Christine's tape on again when Maeve rang. 'Sally has just arrived,' she said. 'She's in your room. What do you want me to do?'

The door eased open, Richard talking to Maeve. 'If Washington calls, put them through. Otherwise, hold my meetings.' He turned to Sally with a smile, brushing the lapels of his jacket. 'Sally, you did fly up. This is great. What a wonderful surprise. A *fantastic* surprise. Maeve told me you were here. She fixed you some coffee? We have the most stunning Javanese coffee. I have

179

it sent up from the embassy in Jakarta.' He was still smiling when he clicked the door shut. He moved to kiss her.

Sally closed up the *New Yorker* she was reading, tossed it beside her on the couch and stood up and put her hand out to stop him. 'Don't touch me,' she said harshly. 'Are you fucking Maeve as well?'

Richard hesitated, lost his stride, just a fraction but noticeably. 'Unnecessary, Sal, unless you want me to ask if you are fucking your ex-boyfriend, Bill Cage. I'm told he's running round China with some sob story that he's looking for his parents.' Richard stretched out his left arm and ran an imaginary violin bow across it. 'I can hear the melancholy music now.'

'Don't be a shit, Richard, it's above you.'

Richard sighed. 'All right. I'm sorry. And before I say any-thing more and before you snap back at me again, I want you to know that I love you, Sally Parsons. I want to be with you for the rest of my life.'

'Save it.'

Richard drew back, running his finger along the edge of the desk as if checking for dust. 'I won't say I can explain about Christine,' he said. 'But one day I *will* tell you what happened, just as one day you'll tell me what happened when you met Bill Cage in Xian. If you remember, you did say you would never see him again.'

'Nothing happened.'

'Isn't it better if we just concentrated on sorting out this problem with the police?'

'I've sorted it.' Sally wasn't going to ease the pressure. 'I checked with the police in the US and what you said was bullshit. They don't want to talk to me.'

'What I said was a guess, Sal. But I *do* think I've nailed it down now.' He pressed the intercom on his desk. 'Maeve, bring in the William Cage file, will you?'

'Cage?' said Sally, unable to hide her surprise.

Maeve knocked and brought in a thin file, only one or two papers in it. Richard stood behind the desk and pulled out one sheet. 'OK, now, Bill Cage is wanted by the NYPD for a shooting in Manhattan.'

Shooting? What shooting? But she stayed quiet.

'Apparently Cage was caught up in some drugs bust just before coming out here.'

Sally sat down. She thought of the joking, courteous Cage flirting with her across the dinner table. 'I don't believe it,' she whispered.

'Hear this out. The NYPD wants Cage for the shooting. They hear he's in China. Some bright spark cop says he has a buddy in China, someone he met on an exchange visit or an international conference or something. He calls him and says Cage is easy to track down through his son who's living with Sally Parsons in Xian. By the time this message gets down to the local precinct in Xian, the orders are to go and bring in Sally Parsons.'

Everything Richard said sounded horribly credible. 'Cage seemed very relaxed when I saw him.'

'Cage used to work under cover for the special forces, Sally. I don't know if he ever told you that. He'd be able to carry off a meeting with you and Paul with no problem at all.'

'So it was all a sham?'

'Look, I don't know.' The edges of his lips twitched and then his face broke into a spontaneous smile. He walked over to her, gently pushed strands of hair over her ears and kissed her on the forehead. 'It's been difficult for both of us.'

Automatically, Sally touched his hand, then she remembered that woman's voice and quickly drew back and moved away. 'I need to know exactly what's going on,' she said sternly.

'We can make a formal diplomatic representation on your behalf through the foreign ministry,' said Richard, stepping back and trying to ignore her snub. 'It's Saturday today. I won't be able to get an answer on this until Monday. And you'll have to stay in Beijing.'

Sally nodded. 'You don't think it's about my work on the tomb?'

Richard shook his head. 'I don't, Sal. Jeff's disk has been pretty much discredited and everyone's known for weeks that you've been poking around up there.'

Then she couldn't stop herself. 'Richard, I need you around. I need your support . . . but I'm not going to say thanks and everything's fine, because it's not. You haven't told me who she was.'

'She was someone working on this Gorbachev visit with me.'

'Chinese?'

'Yes. And Sal, if I could tell you how sorry I am . . . Looking back on it, she was probably ordered to seduce me.'

'Will you see her again?'

'She's on their team. But . . . Look, Sal, after Gorbachev's visit, after May the fifteenth, I won't see her again, ever, not even across a negotiating table. I want us back in the US and Paul in a good school and I want us to stop leading these long-distance lives.'

No. Not yet. However much she wanted to. Don't soften. 'But you didn't even tell me you were back in China.'

Richard held his hands in the air. 'It has been really busy. I wanted to get this wrapped up and then give you a call. It's not as if we were both in Beijing. Whether I'm in China or not, we're still a thousand miles apart.'

Sally swallowed. Her hair had fallen over her face but she let it stay there. She hated not knowing whether to trust him or not. She was his lover and he had been unfaithful to her. Right now she was finding it so difficult to separate that from the help he could give her. Tears were gathering and she didn't want Richard to see them.

Chapter Nineteen

'For China it's excellent accommodation,' said Li Yi, driving Cage into the university campus. 'Only the top visiting foreign academics get to use it.'

'I've never been compared to an academic before,' Cage replied.

Once inside the apartment and alone, Cage removed a frosted slat from the window, took a small bathroom mirror off the wall, and removed another mirror hanging in the living quarters of his suite. With thick tape, he secured the small mirror to the ceiling and propped the other on the desk, so they worked like a periscope and he could watch the two men posted outside while he worked.

They were standing on either side of the main door to the block, one floor below. Unlike many of the security guys he had seen around, they carried weapons in their holsters.

A heavy glass chandelier hung from the ceiling. The cleaners only ever got to the lower part of it, which was sparkling. The upper glass was yellow-grey like a sandstorm. Instead of an overhead light, spot lamps were recessed into the ceiling, and the dimmer switch didn't work properly, so they were on all the time, flickering and making it difficult to concentrate. Cage reckoned the cameras would be somewhere up there. He found a third mirror in the bedroom, laid it flat on the desk, and turned the spotlights on full. For good measure he strapped his pocket flashlight to the desk lamp and turned it on full beam, so the hidden camera would be shooting its pictures in strong light. Unless Chinese technology was generations ahead of US technology, there was no way the film would pick up what he was writing.

Cage worked with a pencil on a pad of plain paper. He sketched from memory, using one sheet for each possible option for an attack. He drew a diagram of the hotel and maps of the locations around it, such as the apartment block opposite, the overpass and the climb down from the roof to the alleyways behind.

He was deliberately vague about the weapons that could be used. He wasn't up to date on Chinese rocket-propelled grenade launchers, or their long-range rifles, sights and lenses. So he stuck to types, vehicles, guns, rockets, escape routes. On the final sheet of paper, Cage listed in priority the options a trained saboteur or assassin would choose.

It took him the whole afternoon to finish his scenarios. He copied them and slipped one set in the envelope the guards had given him; the other set he folded up and put in his pocket. He tore ten more sheets from the pad so no indentations remained, ripped them into tiny pieces and flushed them down the toilet.

Cage unrigged the torch from the lamp and turned down the spotlights. 'Finished,' he said to himself in a loud voice, knowing it would be picked up by whatever bugs were in the apartment. Seconds later one of the guards went inside the building.

The guard was a kid, with blood-red cheeks and the toughness of the countryside, pretty much like the one watching the Chevrolet in Manhattan. The hand he held out for Cage's envelope was callused, the thumb and forefinger twisted so badly that he would have difficulty firing a gun. He didn't smile. Didn't say anything. Cage shook his head and said in Chinese, 'I will deliver it to your boss personally.'

'No,' said the boy. Just one word. No fear. No anticipation. No expression.

Cage slammed the door in his face, looked up to the ceiling and said, 'You want it, I deliver it. You don't want it, I flush it down the toilet. Five minutes.'

It took ten, but Li Yi himself was at the door, wearing an expensive cashmere overcoat and black matching scarf. 'The boss wants you to meet him a little way out of town. Do you mind?'

184

'Not at all,' said Cage. 'I'd love a drive into the countryside.'

They climbed into Li Yi's black Audi, which smelt of some kind of air freshener. The driver was no more than thirty, but his face had lived far longer, his nose so bent it must have been broken at least twice. His right hand was scarred with a knife cut between the thumb and the forefinger. Further up his wrist, half hidden by the cuff of his tunic, Cage spotted the insignia of the Wo Shing Wo society, once famous for collaborating with the Japanese occupation of Hong Kong and now better known for its collaboration with the Teochiu in heroin trafficking. Li Yi called him Mok.

They set off, heading north. It took twenty minutes to leave Beijing behind and reach the fields, which were showing the first green of summer, and the river which foamed with pollution, carrying debris and litter in its slow-moving waters.

They turned off down a road lined with high pine trees, their trunks painted white. They had to slow for potholes which scraped the car's exhaust. The first sign of a village was a small trundling tractor, piled high with children, moving at little more than walking pace. Further along, a cart loaded with logs, pulled by two donkeys, made its way even more slowly.

Li Yi told Mok to pull up. 'We'll walk from here,' he said to Cage.

Outside the city, the temperature was lower by several degrees, and Cage reckoned they had an hour at most left of daylight. It was chilly and he wished he had brought a sweater. He followed Li Yi, keeping behind him, fast-paced past the tractor, then the donkey cart. Then the kids came out, as if from nowhere.

Li Yi had sweets ready and tossed them left and right, enjoying showing off to Cage. The children clawed the ground, fighting over them. From their sores, spindly legs and running noses, Cage guessed it wasn't for fun. These were hungry children who weren't getting even basic nourishment.

'I thought it was one kid per couple,' said Cage.

'Not here,' said Li Yi. 'The boss wanted you to see this. The real China.'

The kids followed them as they approached the first houses of the village, low-slung and made of contorted mud-brick walls with dirty red-tiled roofs. Paraffin lamps shone from inside some. Others had flickering lamps powered by small generators.

They came to the end of a queue which stretched through the whole village. It was an orderly line of at least a hundred people, hands clasped in front of them or behind their backs, or fidgeting with worry beads. They weren't talking. As Li Yi and Cage walked past, the whole village was strangely silent. Even the children hung back, sucking their sweets and wiping their noses.

A few heads turned to look at them as they passed, and Cage picked up a humming sound, a mass whispering, a chorus of breath, but he couldn't work out what they were saying. Li Yi strode ahead impatiently.

Cage saw the lanterns and the façade of the temple. At first he thought the sound was more people cheering somewhere in the distance, then he realised it was a recording of a speech accompanied by cheering, played over speakers rigged up to lamp posts around the temple door. The people here were eager, trying to push through or at least get a look inside. Those who went in covered their faces against the heavy incense smoke which drifted out onto the street, mixed with the smells of a chilly night and coal fires.

As soon as Li Yi and Cage approached, guards came out, not with holstered pistols this time but with automatic rifles slung over their chests. Li Yi and Cage were both pulled into the temple. The sweet-smelling smoke caught in the back of Cage's throat, making him cough.

Inside, the mood was different. It took some time for Cage's eyes to adjust to the incense smoke and the dim light. The room was packed, a crush of people swaying back and forth, with the voice and cheering being played over and over again, each cycle lasting a minute. The people recited with the voice, but when the cheering started, they fell quiet, heads lowered. A few shook their arms above their heads.

The room was not large, about the size of a small village hall, and the carvings suggested it had been the local Taoist temple, but the gods had been removed. The focus at the far end was a golden-coloured statue, incense burning around it.

As Cage edged forward, the crush of people became disciplined once again, lining up to file past the statue. Each held three or four joss sticks between flattened hands and they walked one by one to bow three times in front of the statue. Posters hung from the ceiling, which was decorated with a mural of the galaxy, dark blue and black, with glittering gem stones, rubies, sapphires and clear diamonds, representing the stars of the northern constellations.

Then, through the smoke, Cage saw that the statue itself was not of Buddha but of Mao Zedong, standing on a black plinth, overcoat swept back, tunic neatly buttoned, mole on chin, mouth benevolent but serious, body round but not running to fat, high forehead and receding but plentiful hair, brushed back, and his hands clasped calmly behind his back. His figure was a mixture of uncle and Buddha, god and general. Around the plinth were trays of earth filled with burning joss sticks. As each person passed, they became so focused on Mao that a frenzy set in. The last time Cage had seen such a thing was with the Khmer Rouge in western Cambodia; before that, in the Philippines in the cult worship of Ferdinand Marcos. Cage stood back and watched. Li Yi had vanished.

'The Chinese people, comprising one quarter of all humanity, have now stood up.' Low cheering. The loudspeaker was inside the statue, as if the words were coming from Mao himself, and the cheering was played through other speakers around the room. 'Ours will no longer be a nation subject to insult and humiliation.'

People began to pray. Quickly. Rushed. Only seconds to get their message over. Their eyes watered, movements became jerky and inhibitions were thrown to one side. The statue itself was not sacrosanct. It was mauled, stroked and touched, as if it had the gift of healing, as if it had been given the power of the laying on of hands.

A young man, poor, his face wretched, fell to his knees, then prostrated himself fully, kissing the ground at the bottom of the plinth.

A woman, hard to tell her age, with a ragged, lined face, tore off her tunic, to reveal a pair of shrivelled breasts. She climbed up, hauling herself onto Mao's feet, pressing her breasts against his belly, shouting for him to give her milk. Milk to feed her children. Already two children had died, two boys, from malnutrition. She rubbed her hand on her creased belly, then rubbed it on Mao's belly. She only had a daughter left. But a daughter was no good. Would Mao Zedong bless her with a son?

Another woman followed, young and fresh-faced, dressed more smartly than the others, as if her blue Mao tunic had come from the designer shelves of a department store. Only when she tried to stick the joss sticks in the box did Cage see how ill she was, trembling and weak, with sweat pouring down her face. She brought out a razor and ran it down the back of her hand, drawing blood so quickly that it dripped onto the floor. She tried to climb onto the statue, but didn't have the strength, and others came forward and helped her up. She sucked in the blood and stretched up to kiss Mao's lips, letting the blood drool out of her mouth onto his. She ran her bleeding hand right down his body, pleading as she went. Her blood was rotten with cancer, she said. She was only nineteen, but she was dying and they said nothing could be done. The leukaemia would kill her before the autumn festival. She lost her balance and fell, cracking her head hard on the floor before anyone could catch her. Then she was gone, spirited away by a guard.

A hand on Cage's elbow. It was Li Yi, back again, guiding him to the right of the statue and to the door through which the worshippers went when they had finished. Neither man spoke, the atmosphere was too concentrated for that. Once out of the main room, the power of the incense lessened.

The people, queuing by a door on the left-hand side, took no notice of the two men pushing through them. Their eyes were on a television screen rigged up over an archway in the corridor. Cage couldn't work out whether it was Mao proclaiming the People's Republic in 1949, or one of the deranged hero-worship sessions in Tiananmen Square during the Cultural Revolution. Then he realised it was a montage of both with the soundtrack running underneath it; the camera shots were both panoramic and close-up on individual faces, not unlike the faces in the temple.

Li Yi knocked on the door and opened it without waiting for an answer. There was another queue, more pensive and casual, the atmosphere more like a doctor's waiting room than a temple. Li Yi led Cage through yet another door that opened into a vast office, dark but for two lamps on either end of a wide wooden desk at the far end. It was a narrow room and decorated almost exactly like Wu's office at the university. Between the light from the doorway and the light on the desk there was darkness, giving a sense of a journey, of pilgrimage.

Cage followed Li to the far end of the office. The areas to each side of the desk were also swathed in darkness, like the wings of a stage. On the right, two folding wooden chairs were open and they sat down.

Wu himself was dimly lit; most of his face was in shadow, the lamplight falling only on the top of his head. Cage saw that the way he sat mimicked Mao Zedong, not enough to be accused of impersonation but enough for these disciples to accept that the spirit of Mao lived on, an all-powerful, all-wise and kind figure who would steer China once again back to an era when the peasant had been king.

'Keep them out for a moment,' said Wu to Li Yi, who crossed the room, told the queue of devotees outside to wait, bolted the door from the inside and stood with his back to it, arms folded.

Wu turned to Cage. 'These people are helpless under the new government,' he said. 'You see how the dollar ideology has left them with nothing, not even their pride. They have to work eighteen hours a day just to eat. The mental institutions are filled with people who can't take it. Yet what you are witnessing is what you Americans call the China miracle.'

'Yes, it's interesting,' said Cage tactfully.

Wu Tian pursed his lips and rubbed his forehead. 'I understand you have written up your report.'

Cage drew the envelope containing his notes out of his coat pocket and walked to Wu's desk, standing in front of it like one of Wu's supplicants. Wu turned behind him to a secretary, who handed him a sheet of paper. He put it on his desk, his hands clasped on top of it.

'Do you read Chinese?'

'Some.'

'This is your birth certificate from the Xian municipal archives. The copy is not good. We are trying to get the original so we can read your mother's name clearly. Your father, as a foreigner, is not mentioned at all on it. Nor does it contain your mother's whereabouts, occupation, address or any details like that. But soon I should have for you the Communist Party documents being held here in Beijing.' He held out the sheet.

Cage took it and looked at his birth certificate. He saw the characters of his mother's name. But they were too blurred to read. Her date of birth was clear: 12 March 1930, making her twenty-seven when he was born. Just seeing these details on a form, and a thumb print next to his mother's date of birth, the twirling pattern from the hand that would have held him all those years ago, was enough to jolt him. Surely she would have held him if only for a moment. Or had he been taken straight from her?

I want to know more, he thought. I want it more than anything. I can't leave it like this. She would be fifty-eight now. Easily still alive. Maybe married again with other children. Brothers and sisters. Nephews and nieces. A blood family. I have to keep going. Whatever it takes, I must fill this emptiness, end the anger. A man needs to know his own blood. His mother. His father.

But Cage didn't let his face reveal any of these thoughts. Anyone looking at him would have been forgiven for thinking he was bored, not even holding the birth certificate properly, as if about to drop it into a rubbish bin.

His expression changed only slightly when a scream from outside cut through the room over the monotonous cycle of the Mao Zedong video. Not a wailing scream like the devotees in front of the altar, but a scream of anger and for help, and not from behind him, where they were thronging the temple, but to his right where people went out after Wu had granted them their wishes.

Mok came in through a side door, crossed the room, opened the main door and shouted. There was another scream. A woman's voice weakened to a whimper, then went quiet. Wu merely looked down at his desk, waiting for it to end.

'Soon, you say?' said Cage, ignoring it. 'You'll get the details soon?'

Wu pulled out a red handkerchief from his tunic and dabbed his forehead, then his neck. Li Yi poured tea for him. Mok came back in, saying nothing.

'Yes. Soon we will know who they are, where they are and if they are still living,' said Wu Tian.

Cage took his drawings and notes from the envelope and laid them on Wu's desk. He briefed Wu on the possible methods of attack and the target areas as quickly as he could, wanting to get the hell out of the temple. Out of the village. Back to the city. Cities he could handle. But he knew from Cambodia, from the Philippines, from Angola and Laos, that villages were the most dangerous places because everyone was on the same side. And in this village, whatever the hell its name was, they were all crazy, violent, vulnerable, which was the most dangerous type, especially when run by a man like Wu Tian.

'You've been most helpful to the Chinese people,' said Wu.

Cage shrugged. 'That's the afternoon's work. But I'll let you know if I think of anything else.'

Wu glanced across at Mok, and Cage caught a ripple of uncertainty in Mok's eyes. Cage didn't like Mok's face, the broken nose, the scar above the right eye, the blank, brown eyes. Here in the village, far from anywhere, where every devotee was blindly loyal to Wu's cult, it was a dangerous face to have as an enemy.

'Li Yi, take Mr Cage back to the guest apartment,' said Wu. 'Feed him, give him anything he wants. If he wants to call home, open up an international line.'

Mok opened the side door, the one with the scream behind it, and led Cage out into an alleyway. The first section was covered by the eaves of two buildings. Down towards the street, the alley gave way to open ground, covered with rubbish that had been dropped or blown in. Mok paused deliberately to let Cage catch up, then turned, so Cage could see as well.

The young woman was dead. Cage had seen enough dead people to know. The blood lay in pools, and ran thickly down the body. Dogs were sniffing cautiously, keeping their distance, the body too warm to touch, its flesh too freshly killed even for the dogs. She was the city girl with leukaemia, cut up by knives. Wounds criss-crossed her belly and her entrails were spilling out onto the ground.

Further on, Cage thought he saw another body, maybe two, piled up against each other, but he couldn't be sure. By the wall sat two men, young, matchstick thin, chewing on chicken legs and stuffing lettuce and rice into their mouths from polystyrene cartons, using knives speckled with blood as their cutlery.

Cage moved on, as if he had seen nothing, forcing himself to look as uninterested as he had when reading the birth certificate. He saw Mok watching him, caught the expression of self-satisfaction, of a sadist in charge of a man who had now seen too much.

Cage's disgust was tempered by years. His bewilderment had been hewn down into an understanding of sorts. Some leaders needed to kill to survive; Hitler, Stalin and Mao were the most notorious. But there were many others in Africa, Asia and Europe, the focus on tribalism, cultism, shamanism, nationalism, whatever they chose to call it. Cage knew they all worked in the same way: a maniac, his devotees and the power of killing.

Who was that woman? A member of the middle class so riddled with cancer that she would go anywhere for help. And Cage had been allowed to see her body in order to draw him further in.

Chapter Twenty

Sally was jotting down notes on her work on the tomb when Richard rang.

'First the good news, and then the good news,' he said breezily.

'I'll take the good news first.' Cooped up in Li Yi's apartment, Sally found it hard to be as upbeat.

'Strictly, I shouldn't have done this, but since it could be important to your work, I thought I could get away with it. These negotiations I'm working on – I put Jeff Binsky's disk in as a small concession the Chinese could give us, like a goodwill gesture. Wu Tian's now been told he can give it back to you. You can't blame him. He was just doing what any Party official would have done. But if you drop by his office tomorrow afternoon he'll give it to you.'

'Thanks,' she said casually, determined not to let him sense her rush of excitement.

'Don't I get more than thanks?' laughed Richard.

'You'll get more than thanks when I know you're not seeing other women.'

Richard didn't falter. 'And I was right,' he said. 'They *did* mix you up with Bill Cage.'

'Thank God for that,' said Sally. She was relieved, but her reaction was more complex. What about Cage? What about Paul's father? She was relieved and sickened.

'I'm checking to see how the screw-up happened,' Richard was saying.

'It doesn't really worry me. Like you said, screw-ups do

happen,' she said, trying to maintain her distance.

'Are you seeing him?'

'Cage? Nothing's planned. He doesn't even know where I am right now.'

'This is a professional call, Sal. Cage shot someone during a drugs raid. You really don't want to be involved with this guy.'

Sally snapped, 'Don't you think I know that?'

'Just let me know if he tries to contact you.' Richard's voice was calm and professional. If he had any feelings about Cage's previous relationship with Sally, he didn't show it.

'Of course I'll damn well let you know. You're the only lifeline I've got right now.'

'Look, I've got one hell of a schedule tonight and tomorrow, but I should be clear tomorrow evening.'

Sally quietened. 'Can we get together?' She wished she didn't sound so needy, so all over the place, one minute yelling, the next pleading.

'Let's try,' he said sympathetically. 'But you're in good hands at Li Yi's place.'

'Just wait it out, huh?'

Exhibit 38 – Audio Tape Evidence
Federal Court, Pearl Street
Manhattan
December 16 1989

'I thought you should let your boss know that his daughter will be at the negotiations.'
'I'm sorry, what negotiations?'
'At the Zhao Long Hotel. Just tell him.'
(Line cut – **Transcriber's note**.)

'We have to stop it. Your daughter . . .' said Li Yi. 'In twenty minutes she'll be at the hotel.'

Wu Tian coughed. 'I know,' he said calmly. 'She even showed me the letter from the American she is fucking while she sells my country to him.'

Li Yi listened to the rustling of Wu's sleeve against the

mouthpiece. He heard the phlegm in his throat. Then Wu Tian said, ' "Every communist must grasp the truth: political power grows out of the barrel of a gun." Problems of War and Strategy, November the sixth, nineteen thirty-eight.'

'But your daughter will die,' urged Li Yi.

'Could you come and join us? We need to clarify the pieces to be shipped to Xian.'

'Your daughter, comrade. Your daughter.'

'How is Tiananmen Square?' asked Wu. 'Are the students still gathering for the funeral of Hu Yaobang? I will need to go there. When Mok has finished, send him round with the car.'

Bill Cage emerged from the cab as a frail old man, attempting to stand upright but forced by age into a stoop. He shuffled, apparently slowed by some leg injury, and squinted as if from failing eyesight. To any passer-by, the limping old man was a veteran of old China, a man who had paid his dues and should be shown respect.

'We want you there,' Leonard had said, when Cage had called in from yet another hotel lobby. 'Things don't match with the intelligence we're getting at this end.' Leonard wasn't a man given to hype and the way he talked had jolted Cage. There was no 'I', but 'we', meaning the FBI, meaning that Cage was their agent in China and the charade about him resigning, about him being on his own, was over.

The caps he had applied to his teeth and the wax lightly rubbed into his skin gave his face a look of age and poor health. His hair was slightly greyed and he had covered his fingertips with a thick lacquer to conceal his prints.

He mumbled to himself as he walked. The rooftop snipers would see him. The watchers, the police, the security guards might note him. But with his age and apparent senility he would be ignored.

Two motorcycle outriders, lights flashing, turned in, followed by an Audi with darkened windows. The cycle lane was busy and the car had to slow as it entered the forecourt of the hotel.

Cage crossed the road slowly, stopping between lanes to give him time to look at the hotel forecourt. Two extra guards were posted on either side of the main doorway. Two others were on the gate. From the roof, he caught the reflection of the sun in binoculars. The Jaguar was gone. There were only three taxi drivers instead of the dozen or so before. The stall which sold soft drinks and cigarettes, just up from the taxi stand, was gone, and the homeless under the overpass had been moved on.

'Do you want some tea?' a friendly taxi driver called. Cage lifted his head ever so slightly, a hand too, to acknowledge the kindness. He shuffled on.

He got as far as the junction and paused. He stayed among the criss-crossing bicycles and pedestrians while the lights changed twice. Then he recognised Mok by his broken nose and his wiry, twisted shape. Mok stood, wearing a padded Mao jacket, black leather cap and jeans, beside the broken telephone box, staring at the door of the Zhao Long Hotel.

Hotel staff came out and opened the back door of the Audi. A middle-aged Chinese man in a dark suit stepped out, straightened his tie and smoothed down his hair with his hands. A woman, attractive, self-assured, in her late twenties or early thirties, got out of the other side of the car carrying a thick leather briefcase, like a portable office. She walked round to join her boss.

They chatted just outside the glass doors, near the limousine, pointing at the erratic fountain, sharing a joke. Then they went in, staying just inside the foyer.

Cage was fifty yards from Mok.

Mok didn't move. But he shifted his weight slightly. Cage had seen it before in men, the telltale sign that their adrenaline count was going up. Cage got closer, causing Mok to glance round, to register an old man approaching. Cage tried to work out Mok's line of sight, but before he could pinpoint it, Mok moved away from the phone box.

The American cars approached from the other direction. No outriders. Flags flying on the hoods. Two Town Cars. American drivers, not Chinese. They stopped at the traffic lights. Mok straightened, eyes hard and focused. The Chinese negotiators came out from the foyer, just the two of them. The woman on the right, without the briefcase; her boss on the left, no coat but a blue scarf round his neck.

The lights changed to green and the little convoy moved forward. Mok moved just a step, his eyes shifting from the cars to the hotel and back to the cars again. Cage noted the watchers up on the roof. But they had seen nothing. The world around him was relaxed.

Mok's hand shifted inside his coat and Cage, a decrepit figure, hunched and broken, rose to his full height like an uncoiling spring. The American driver didn't see what Cage was doing; nor did Christine Wu, her boss, the taxi driver, or the guards at the gate of the hotel who had stepped out to block the cycle track so the American cars could make the turn.

Cage moved so fast that Mok didn't know what hit him, a flying tackle, Cage's shoulder against Mok's legs. They both fell heavily, Cage on top, his arm up to knock Mok's hand out of his jacket.

Mok was holding a remote. Nothing fancy. Probably a radio control for a toy car. Cage smashed it out of his hand sent it skidding along the pavement. Both men scrambled to their feet. Mok's fist caught Cage above the ear, and shock waves blurred his vision. Then Cage saw the gun, and caught Mok's wrist, twisted it, got him to drop it and head-butted him right between the eyes. Head-butted him again, kneed him in the stomach, and broke free.

The American lead car turned into the hotel. Cage opened the remote, ripped out the batteries, then swivelled and smashed the plastic box into Mok's face.

Mok didn't fall. Hell of a fighter not to fall with a blow like that.

Their eyes met for a split second. Mok dived for the gun on the pavement, bending to scoop it up and fire. His eyes were ridiculing, truly laughing, and Cage knew what it meant. He left Mok. The gun could look after itself. Cage hurled himself into the road, and for the first time the Americans, the guards, and the roof snipers noticed him.

Someone opened fire. Mok? Another crack. Cage weaved, dodged the cars, jumped the fence dividing the lanes, banged on bonnets to get across, and pushed past the guard at the entrance.

He saw what Mok had been looking at. He had written it in as an option in his report to Wu. He ran past the fountain, his voice breaking into a scream, his whole persona changing, old man to athlete. The Americans were out of the car, both climbing out the same side. They didn't seem to have heard the shots. A youngish guy in a suit was shaking hands with the Chinese girl. He looked round and saw Cage, who yelled in English, '*Bomb! Bomb! Inside! Now!*'

Cage barged into the woman, arms round her, pushed her through the glass door, hitting it open with her forehead. He hurled her down into the coffee shop.

The concierge stepped forward, not understanding what was happening. Cage screamed at him, switching to Chinese, '*Cover! Take cover!*' Through the door, he saw Mok across the road with the gun. In all the mass of people, only Cage and Mok knew what was going on.

The Lincoln Continental lurched up like a whale. The bonnet was ripped off and hurled into the fountain. The windows shattered all at once, glass spraying like shrapnel across the forecourt as the driver's seat spun into the air. The car lifted off the ground, throwing shock blasts out, killing the taxi drivers and the gate guards.

Out in the road, cyclists crumpled on top of each other and a truck ploughed into the wall enclosing the hotel grounds. The Lincoln was in the air, turning in appalling slow motion, crashing down on its side. Fuel spilled out, sluicing along the ice, and then caught fire. The flames trailing back to the tank blew up the car for a second time. The blast blew in the glass door, flinging the concierge against the wall, upturning the tables and chairs and shattering the mirror at the far end of the coffee shop.

Cage held Christine beneath him, hands wrapped round her head, pushing her into the floor, feeling her tremble as the bomb did its work, feeling her body tense, relax, tense again.

Then he let go, because it was over.

After the roar, came the silence. So quickly. Quiet. Not even the whimper of a voice. Absolute calm, as though the world were resting.

'Thank you.' Softly. In Chinese, a trembling whisper from underneath his shoulder.

He rolled off her and stood up. 'You OK?' He offered his hand, and she held it as she got to her feet, unsteady. Shouting started outside, and a chunk of plaster crashed from the ceiling. Reflections of the flames danced in the glass that was left in place. Outside there was panic, but to Cage the voices were far away.

'Thank you,' said Christine again, but more formally, like a guest to a waiter, confused by an old man who moved with the agility of a wild animal. She shifted her glance. Cage turned and saw Richard stumbling towards her.

Cage reverted to old age, hung his head, hunched his shoulders and shuffled away. Around him people were beginning to move and whimper in pain and shock, the first soft voices after an explosion.

'Are you all right?' Richard asked Christine.

'Yes. Yes, thank you.' She pointed to Cage, whose back was to her now. He kept his head turning erratically, as if disorientated, to keep her in view.

In the smashed mirror, behind Christine, Cage saw the fragmented image of a motorcycle and a pillion rider with a machine pistol, a sudden movement out of sync with everything else.

They came fast, leaping across the cycle lane, into the forecourt and round the fountain, the rider's foot on the ground, revving, twisting the wheel to get it round. An uninjured guard, quick to notice, but not quick enough, was shot down. Those who recognised the sound of small-arms fire knew what was happening.

Cage spun round. 'Get down! Hit the floor! Again!' he yelled, mixing Chinese with English.

'*Down!*' Cage shouted at Christine in Chinese and he hit her behind the knees, making her crumple to the floor, as gunfire smashed into the wall just above their heads. The motorcycle leapt deafeningly into the foyer, bouncing and crashing over the bodies on the floor. The pillion rider had two machine pistols. Dead calm, he picked off the concierge, a waitress, someone on the stairs to the Chinese restaurant. Then the bike roared off again, round the foyer as if it was a circus ring, filling it with noise and fumes.

Cage crawled away from Christine. The gunman saw him, fired and missed. Cage moved again. Another burst. Cage rolled a third time, almost as if he was taunting him. Cage knew how tricky it was to ride pillion and hit a moving target. That was why he had put the car bomb at a higher priority than a motorcycle hit in his report to Wu.

'Shit for brains, Cage!' he muttered bitterly and twisted backwards. Leonard had got it right. He had blown it. His desperate eagerness for Wu's information about his parents had caused him to end up in a stinking, deafening death trap, carpeted wall-to-wall with the wounded, dying and dead, and it was his own fault.

Cage grabbed a lump of ceiling rubble and threw it at the bike. The rider revved and swung round to come back at him again. Cage picked up a thin wooden leg broken off a coffee table and a foot-long shard of mirror glass.

He leapt towards the bike, to draw fire away from Christine and to give the gunman as little space for a shot as possible. The back wheel skidded. The rider straightened up and came for him again. Cage threw the table leg like a spear into the front wheel of the bike. The wood splintered and snapped, but it did its job. The bike's back wheels shot up into the air, throwing the two men over the handlebars.

As they hit the ground, Cage was on top of them. He rammed the glass into the neck of the gunman, severing the artery, and grabbed the machine pistol. It was restricted by the shoulder strap, but Cage yanked it far enough to let off a burst into the rider. Then he spun round in a full circle, to check that no other threat was out there.

Christine was crouching against a wooden dumb waiter, a line of bullet holes inches from her head. Richard was huddled, foetus-like, behind the door of the bar. The two Americans were getting up. Others stood, bewildered and shaking in the foyer, bodies bleeding around them.

Cage looked at the faces of the killers. Just kids. Uneducated peasant killers from the countryside. Couldn't even ride a motorcycle properly.

Christine was getting up. 'Who are you?' she stammered, blood leaking down her face. He must have hit her really hard against the door.

He slipped away, through the mêlée at the front of the hotel, where oil, ice, fire and smoke were mixing with the screams of hurt and hysterical people, the panic of cyclists and the horns of trucks and cars.

Cage walked through it all and vanished.

Exhibit 42 – Audio Tape Evidence
Federal Court, Pearl Street
Manhattan
December 16th 1989

'Wu Tian was responsible.'
'Do you know for sure?'
'Absolutely. He was trying to kill his daughter.'

Chapter Twenty-one

Unaware of the bombing, Sally locked up Li Yi's apartment and caught a cab to Wu Tian's office at the university, asking the driver to wait. Mok opened the door and Wu Tian got to his feet as Sally walked into the study.

'Dr Parsons, thank you for coming to see me again,' said Wu. 'I know you must be very busy with your work.' He walked round the side of the desk towards her. Only a couple of small lamps lit the room, which seemed even darker and gloomier than before.

'Thanks for solving the problem with the disk, Professor.' Sally held out her hand, but Wu didn't shake it. Instead he beckoned for Mok to come over. 'Fetch the computer disk we have for Dr Parsons,' he said. Mok slid round towards a door to her right. 'Can I serve you some tea?'

She clutched her bag, standing in the middle of the room, determined to get out as soon as she could. 'No. I really have to run. There's a taxi waiting outside.'

Wu nodded thoughtfully. 'Yes, yes, of course. But I wonder if I could persuade you to stay.' As he came closer to her, Sally stiffened. The door latch clicked and Mok reappeared, but he wasn't holding the disk. 'I want to show you something next door. As an archaeologist, you will understand. We are trying to recreate old China.' His hand was on her elbow. Mok held open the door and Wu guided her in.

Sally drew breath at what she saw and stepped forward without encouragement from Wu. The room contained a strange mix of the political and the religious. On both sides, against the wall, were statues of Taoist gods, generals and goddesses, garishly coloured and adorned with jewellery. There seemed to be no order to them. A recumbent Buddha, plated with gold, rested his head on a hand with ridiculously long fingers. Next to him stood a dark wooden cross, well over ten feet high, with the figure of a wretched Christ, blood congealing on the palms of his nailed hands.

The middle of the room was taken up with a floor-to-ceiling statue of Mao Zedong, sitting on a chair, acting as a gatekeeper. His legs were crossed and his eyes gazed down at the floor which was decorated with another image of Mao, a gold-painted mural of his face. It was the same reproduction as Ko had in his taxi, but it was thirty feet long and twenty wide, so that wherever you walked in the room, you were stepping on a section of Mao's image.

To the right of the statue was an equally large standing jade figure with an erect penis and small rounded breasts with tiny green nipples, youthful, poised, both man and woman. The ceiling was painted with blue skies full of angels, some fornicating, some giving birth, some wounded and dying, droplets of their blood mixing with the stars and moons. Incense burned all around.

Wu Tian let go of Sally's elbow and dropped back. Sally turned and saw Li Yi in the doorway, talking to Wu. Li Yi glanced across at her. 'Stay where you are, Sal,' he muttered quickly, his eyes darting around the room. Then he whispered in Wu's ear. The mask came down again, the ashen face and the hard eyes.

Mok noticed too, and came alongside Wu with a cigarette. Wu took it and let Mok light it for him. He drew on the tobacco, turning the cigarette in his finger.

'Are you certain she's still alive?' he said to Li Yi.

'She was saved by a beggar.'

'A beggar,' he repeated. 'Stay with Dr Parsons.' He signalled for Mok to follow him back into the office. The door closed.

'What's going on?' whispered Sally.

'I'm not sure,' said Li. 'Just stay with me. I know why he wanted you to see it. He wants you to understand.' He pointed. 'That's a replica of Mao's bedroom.'

At the end of the room was a huge bed. Half of it was covered with books, some opened, some closed with slips of paper as bookmarks. The walls on either side had alcoves of altars to Mao Zedong, each with a portrait and a bowl of water with floating lotus leaves and red candles already lit, the flames throwing strange shadows around the room.

A naked girl, barely out of her teens, scuttled out from behind a curtain on the left. She had full red cheeks, and an air of fear and obedience about her. She looked like the children Sally had seen in the parade outside Xian, of peasant stock, illiterate, uneducated, privileged to serve the pleasures of her master.

The girl pulled back the bedcovers, making sure not to disturb the books. Two more girls appeared, fully clothed in Mao tunics. One joined in preparing the bed, the other took a small bowl of water, hung it from a bucket, cut up a mango and dropped the peel into the water.

The girls began to sing a soothing lullaby. Three more appeared, one in a Mao tunic, another in a white lace night-dress, and the third wearing only loose-fitting red panties. Then a man appeared. He was dumpy, middle-aged, and one of the girls took off his spectacles. Slowly, all three girls undressed him. Two men came forward with a sponge, towels and a steaming bowl of water. They washed him down, letting the water drip on the floor, towelled him dry and draped him in a red silk shawl. The girls' voices turned into repetitive chanting.

Girls kept coming and going. Those in Mao tunics stayed fully clothed, the others dropped their clothes beside the bed and climbed onto it, arranging themselves in a circle.

Sally turned to Li, who put his finger to his mouth to stop her speaking. 'He's one of Wu Tian's provincial leaders,' he whispered. Sally had to lean over to hear him. 'It's the greatest gift Wu can give them – an evening in the style to which Mao was accustomed. Mao believed the mango created an elixir which would prevent him ageing. That's why they're using mango peel.'

Sally stared at him, her eyes frantic with questions.

'This was all part of Mao's search for immortality.'

'No,' she said, grabbing Li Yi's arm. 'I mean, what are we

doing here? Why did you tell me to get the hell out when those two thugs tried to arrest me?'

'You've heard of Red Spirit?'

'Ko talks about him all the time.'

'*This* is Red Spirit. The movement to revive Maoism in China.'

Sally held Li Yi's arm tighter. She was speechless. As Li Yi kept talking, pointing at things like a museum guide, she tried to get a grip on herself.

'He calls all these people Group One,' Li Yi was saying. 'The name Mao used for his entourage.'

Sally wasn't going to be distracted. 'The police who were after me, were they Red Spirit?'

Li Yi nodded glumly.

'Then what am I doing here?'

'I'm going to try to get you out. Until then, try to look calm.'

A masseur by the altar poured the heated water with the mango peel into a cup. A girl took it and the cup was passed from girl to girl to the bed. Two naked girls knelt on either side of the plump man. One massaged his back through the red silk shawl. The other lifted the bowl to his lips and tilted it so he could drink. Water dribbled down onto his shoulders, and a third came forward to lick it off. He giggled, and the girls giggled. Then a book was presented to him, opened at the correct page. He rubbed his eyes and let the red silk fall off his shoulders. He sat naked and cross-legged on the bed, reading. His body was old and flabby, but somehow it emanated power.

Li Yi guided Sally behind the Mao statue. 'Listen to me, because Wu will ask,' he said hurriedly. 'You have to understand the Chinese people. Mao was a sacred figure. Anything he touched became a sacred object. People who had touched Mao did not wash their hands for weeks so others could touch them too, and pass it on. Wu is giving this man that power by allowing him here from whichever impoverished part of China he comes from. Somewhere in the north, by the looks of it. Wu Tian understands it all so brilliantly. All over China he has created leaders in Mao's image.' Li swept his hand around the room. 'What you are seeing now is being replicated in temples and universities all over the country.'

'It's horrible,' said Sally vehemently.

'It's a cult. We Chinese live and die by them. If you understand Qin Shi Huang, you will understand this.'

A girl pulled the red shawl off the bed, like an unwanted sheet. The man lay down on his back, his legs slightly parted and his eyes closed. The girls, four of them, humming softly, stroked him with massage oils, heated by the altar candles, each concentrating on a section of his body.

'Mao never washed his genitals,' said Li Yi. 'Taoist sex manuals state that a man can replenish his *yang*, that's his longevity and strength, by soaking up secretions from the vagina. Mao used to say he washed himself inside the bodies of women. But watch. I bet this fellow's impotent. Most of them are.'

One girl was sitting astride the man as another tried to give him oral sex. One of the men, also naked, stroked his forehead, and two girls massaged his feet, all of them bizarrely singing a Communist Party song.

Neither Sally nor Li Yi noticed Mok slip back into the room, not until he appeared in front of them and hit Sally across the face with the back of his hand.

Two hours later, Sally was encircled by a hundred people, three or four deep. The women were on the inside of the circle. The men who had massaged the man and prepared his oils were behind the women, and the outer circle was formed by the bodyguards, foot soldiers from the mountains.

Sally was on her knees, her arms pulled behind her back and tied with red rope. A white pointed hat was on her head and a placard hung from her neck emblazoned with the Chinese characters for 'liar'. Her coat was torn, slashed with a knife.

A girl stepped out of the circle round her and kicked Sally in the ribs. Determined to keep her balance, she swayed but didn't fall. Her head was lowered, eyes to the floor, staring at the wart just beneath the lower lip of the gold-painted Mao mural. But her head was not hanging. And she would not fall over. She was *damned* if she would show any weakness.

The girls were sinister and sickening. They were Wu's sex maidens, wearing Mao tunics, waving copies of the little Red

Book, *Quotations of Chairman Mao Zedong*. They yelled and spat at her, jumping forward to kick her. 'Eliminate Sally Parsons!' they screamed. 'Eliminate the anti-China criminal! Expose the red-haired foreign devil! Expose the imperialist United States!'

Eventually they quietened down, out of breath, and a man started up from the circle behind the girls. 'Comrade Mao Zedong is the greatest Marxist-Leninist of our era.'

Another, a woman this time, recited: 'Mao Zedong thought is a powerful ideological weapon for opposing imperialism and for opposing revisionism.'

Then another woman: 'Mao Zedong thought is the guiding principle for all the work of the Party, the army and the country.'

Then Sally's tormentors sang: 'Mao Zedong is the reddest, reddest sun in our hearts. Hold the banner high for Mao Zedong thought . . .'

Sally knew what was happening. This was a 'struggle session', just as if it was the Cultural Revolution all over again. They had given her the dunce's cap and tied her in the airplane take-off stance, arms wrenched right back and forced above her head. God, how her arms ached! Next they might cut off her hair, half starve her, beat her with clubs and throw bags of human faeces at her.

Each time they slapped her head, she forced herself to look up again. The next attacker was no more than fifteen, her face filled with blank violence. The girl spat in her face. 'Liar! Whore and liar!' she screamed, pulling viciously at Sally's hair just for the hell of it, then skipping back as if she had just performed her lines for the school play.

Others slapped her round the head and shoulders, some so gently it was just a brush, others as hard as they could against her ears and temples. Strangely, the pain led to clearer thinking. What was it Jeff had said? *I craved to be ruled by a man like Qin so that I could judge my own character*. Did Jeff want to go through *this* so he could have a leader to hate? Or a leader to love? It was neither. Jeff just wanted to escape from the blandness of America. Love or pain didn't matter to him.

The toe of a boot cut into Sally's ribs and for a second, as pain seared through her chest, she lost her balance. She gasped for breath, coughing, the incense-filled air catching badly in her throat. She braced herself for another kick.

'Confess. Confess. Confess.' The mindless voices were marching towards a crescendo. Oh, what the hell! She let herself topple over. Her tormentors cheered, as if she had taken the first step towards being accepted by them.

Lying on the floor, Sally became aware that a film show had started up; panoramic scenes were being projected onto the wall, of peasants in a field, waving their spades and hoes like flags. Mao's face beamed through it and images flashed up of harvests, factories, demonstrations and a nuclear explosion. She looked at the faces screaming at her, the madness in their eyes, their hands clawing in the air, the saliva on their tongues.

Sally closed her eyes, filled no longer with fear but with regret, believing now that she would never get out alive.

Chapter Twenty-two

Bill Cage paid off the taxi driver in the tourist area near Tiananmen Square, dumped his beggar's clothes and bought a new lightweight jacket. The green shirt he had worn underneath was crumpled but clean; the crease in his trousers had kept its shape. He pulled out a tie, put it on and recovered his passport and money from hidden pockets.

He was still cursing his own muddled judgement. The prospect of finding his mother had disorientated him. Now he faced the truth. An attack had been made on the lives of US government personnel, and he had drawn up the plan for the attackers. He had let himself be duped like a rookie, and he wasn't going to call Leonard until he had answers.

The taxi dropped him a little way from the gates of the university and Cage walked briskly through the campus to his apartment. Only one guard was outside, not the older guy, but the boy, hardly down from the mountains. Cage waved, revealing a packet of cigarettes, and beckoned the boy inside.

As soon as the boy was out of the light, in the darkened stairwell, Cage caught him in a neck lock with one arm and stuck tape over his mouth with his free hand. He took his pistol from the holster, and held it to the kid's head.

'Undress,' he said in Chinese and stepped back.

Shaking, the boy unbuttoned his tunic and trousers and took them off.

'Get back under the stairs,' said Cage.

The boy stumbled backwards. Cage bound his hands and legs and left him there trussed up. The boy's uniform looked a

209

little short but adequate. Cage ran up the stairs to his apartment, key ready. He walked in and threw the uniform onto an armchair.

The blow from behind caught him on the back of the neck and his feet were kicked from under him. He fell heavily to the floor but managed to roll and get to his feet again. The older guard stood over him, foot back for another kick, except Cage threw his full weight at the man. As they crashed backwards, the attacker's head shattered the glass of the cabinet, the thin glass cutting his neck.

Cage stepped back, the pistol out. Blood streamed from the guard's throat, and the fight had gone out of him.

'Idiot,' said Cage. 'Lucky it wasn't an artery.' He threw the guard a cloth to clean himself up, keeping the gun on him while they both caught their breath.

It was late afternoon. Outside, Cage could see students going home, filing out of the campus whose crumbling buildings and Marxist concrete gave it a grey, brooding air.

There was no fear in the guard's eyes, only resignation. 'Where's the fuel?' Cage snapped in Chinese. The guard looked blankly at him. Cage pointed to the paraffin heater. 'Where's the fuel kept?' he repeated.

The guard nodded towards a cupboard by the door. Cage opened the cupboard and found a can of paraffin. He went to the kitchen, got two empty soft drink bottles and poured paraffin into them. 'That's good. Stay cool,' said Cage to the guard as he worked. 'People do stupid things when they're bored. They get stupid and they get killed. You want to know what I'm doing? I'm doing the most simple thing in the world for a man to protect himself.'

Cage detected a perverse curiosity in the guard. The man wasn't worried about his own fate, only interested in Cage's skill in making a petrol bomb. Cage tore a strip from the sheet on his bed and stuffed the cloth into the neck of the bottle, sealing in the fuel but keeping the end dry. He undressed, and put on the younger guard's uniform. It was small, as he had thought, but it would be all right. Chinese uniforms never seemed to fit. He checked himself in the mirror, slipped the two petrol bombs into the pockets in each trouser leg, then ordered the guard to put on the clothes he'd just taken off.

Cage dialled the university operator. 'Hello, can you put me through to Wu Tian, head of the Department of Marxism? Thank you.' More ringing. Cage waited, watching the guard dress.

It was Li Yi, not Wu Tian, who came on the line. 'Sally is here with us,' he said quickly as soon as Cage gave his name. In the background, Cage heard chanting, chilling and monotonous, like in the village where he'd also heard the scream of the girl before she was killed.

'I'm coming across,' he said and ended the call.

He tested the mechanism of the pistol and said to the guard, 'I'm going to have this weapon on, without a round in the breech, because I don't want to kill. But if I ever get to the point where I have to bring in that round, you're going to die. And no one's going to give a shit except you.'

The afternoon sun cut through the buildings like a searchlight and Cage approached Wu Tian's building with the light behind him and the guard in front, dressed badly in Cage's clothes and his hands tied behind his back. 'I have the American,' he shouted in peasant Chinese.

The guard outside Wu Tian's building couldn't see properly against the sunlight, only the figure being clumsily pushed towards him. 'He's sick. Get the door open,' said Cage impatiently. As the guard hesitated, Cage yelled, 'Open the fucking door or you'll go home and find your mother fucking a donkey.'

It was a shabby wooden door, paint flaking, a narrow side entrance. The guard knocked. He waited a second and knocked again.

'I said open it, not knock on it,' shouted Cage. From inside he could hear chanting.

Abruptly, the sunlight vanished behind a cloud. The guard dropped his hand from his eyes as he recognised his friend, in Cage's green shirt, and Cage behind in the security uniform. The guard reached for his pistol. Cage pushed his prisoner to the ground, dropped down himself and pulled the trigger. The weapon clicked, but no round exploded. In that split second Cage had forgotten he had no round in the breech.

Cage threw himself against the wall and the guard's shot went past him. His hostage was paralysed with terror, the two security men facing each other and Cage pressed against the wall. Cage spun out, shot out the lock of the door and kicked it open.

Often only a millimetre, a second, something very small, lies between the success and failure of a military action. What was it his report said? That he was a good fighter but a bad soldier? Cage stood in the doorway, gun in his hand, not knowing what the hell he should do next.

He slammed the door behind him and fired a second round in the air, stopping the chanting dead. Silence hung in the room, then he heard Sally's voice in the sudden quiet. 'I love Chairman Mao Zedong. I love Blue Apple. I love Jiang Ching.' Everyone was still. 'In our great motherland,' she continued, 'a new era is emerging in which workers, peasants and soldiers are grasping Mao Zedong thought.'

Cage moved forward. Li Yi appeared from the back of the Mao statue, looking out of place in his tailored two-piece suit.

'Stop. Listen.' It was a woman in the crowd, her head bobbing back and forth like a woodpecker as she spoke. 'Listen to what the foreign woman Parsons has to say about the Great Helmsman and his beloved wife Jiang Ching.'

'What has the imperialist bitch got to say?' shrieked another voice.

'Speak. Speak,' yelled voices from the mob.

A girl ran forward and kicked out at Sally, her foot passing inches from Sally's head. Another mimicked a punch from the other side. But they didn't touch her. Sally rocked back and forth on the floor, trying to gather enough momentum to get back up on her knees. 'Once Mao Zedong thought is grasped by the broad masses, it becomes a spiritual atom bomb of infinite power,' she managed.

Cage was at the outer circle of the crowd. If they came for him, he would kill. But their eyes were closed, their arms held out in front, each with a copy of the Red Book held between the right thumb and forefinger. Sally spoke in English. 'Cage, just join in. Chant.'

Cage took it up, repeating in Chinese. 'The spirit of Mao is an atom bomb of infinite power. Infinite power. Infinite power.' He held his pistol up, safety off, hammer cocked, finger inside the trigger guard. He'd made the decision now to kill if he had to and he tasted bile in the back of his throat. 'The spirit of Mao is an atom bomb of infinite power,' he repeated, moving through the circle. 'Infinite power. Infinite power.'

They kept chanting while he untied Sally's arms, removed the placard and the dunce's hat, and helped her up. Her face was bleeding. The bruises would come later. But she managed to smile at Cage. 'Never took you for a damn Maoist,' she said under her breath. Then she sang out, 'We live under the great red banner of the spirit of Mao.' As the crowd took up the chant, she hissed, 'What's with the uniform?'

'We live under the great banner of the spirit of Mao,' Cage shouted. Then, 'Walk in front of me and straight through them.'

The front line of girls let them through. The men behind gave way as well. But the outer circle of bodyguards stood fast, arms folded. Cage and Sally stopped.

Mok was by the door with one of his girls, holding her roughly, her arm twisted behind her back. He unbuttoned her tunic with his free hand, became impatient and tore it off. He rubbed his hand over her breasts, all the time looking at Sally and Cage. The girl's face was blank, her eyes glassy.

'Give up. Sally, get him to drop his weapon. Please, I beg you.' It was Li Yi, walking slowly towards them. 'Anything you do could endanger the girl's life,' he said in English. 'Mok is under orders to kill any woman he wants. Like the one you saw, Captain Cage, at the village ceremony. Wu Tian equates every woman with either his wife or his daughter. That young woman at the hotel bombing was Wu's daughter. He knew she would be there.'

Cage bluffed. 'Until he releases us and lets her go, I'm staying right here. And I keep the gun.'

Li Yi wasn't taken in. 'Everyone in this country is a prisoner. If he releases her she will just flutter back into her cage.' Li Yi threw something at Cage. 'Here, Wu wanted you to see this.'

His throw was high and silver glinted against the ceiling lights. It was a locket. Cage caught it with his free hand and flipped it open. It was the same face, with the same calmness and kindness, but a different picture, a happier moment, a holiday snap, with mountains in the background. It was only the second picture he had ever seen of his mother.

'He'll let you go now because he knows you'll come back,' said Li Yi.

'Is she alive?' asked Cage softly.

Li Yi shrugged. 'He knows. I don't. Tell him, Sally. Tell him that I have never lied to you.'

Sally was silent.

'He's angry because you saved the life of his daughter. I thought he was carrying out a political assassination. I was wrong. He wanted her dead.'

Mok twisted the girl round. She screamed out and he hit her with the back of his hand.

'Captain Cage, you go,' said Li Yi. 'They'll let you through. Sally, you have to stay. While I am here, you are safe. You have my word on that.'

'We both go or we both stay,' said Cage

'For God's sake, both of you. The law here is on the side of power, not justice.' Li Yi's eyes flickered. Cage recognised fear in his face. He turned and saw a shaft of light from the office, Wu's shadow across the doorway.

'Get down,' Cage whispered to Sally. He drew a petrol bomb out of his pocket and lit it with the Mao lighter Li Yi had given him, all in one swift motion, and hurled the bomb towards Mok. The bottle smashed behind him, throwing up a sheet of flame.

Cage pulled out the second petrol bomb, lit it and tossed it towards Wu. It crashed onto the chest of Mao's statue and flames engulfed his face. That explosion was enough to break the circle. Some fled. Some rushed towards the fire. Cage grabbed Sally's hand, jerked her to her feet and broke through the line.

Cage wrenched open the door and he and Sally ran out. Behind them, the gold paint over Mao's face bubbled and blackened. Above, on the ceiling, a video showed school girls in Tiananmen Square waving their little Red Books in praise of the Great Helmsman Mao Zedong.

Chapter Twenty-three

Cage led Sally straight out of the university campus, holding her hand, making sure she walked quickly. Outside the gates, he went to the first taxi in the line and got in.

'Tiananmen Square,' he said. As the driver pulled out, Cage looked out of the back window, but no one seemed to be following. After a mile, he paid off the driver, took Sally through a side street into a warren of alleyways and out onto another main road, where he hailed another cab.

'Kun Lun Hotel,' he said. They didn't talk. Sally's hair was over her face and she didn't bother to push it back. Blood was clotting on her right eyebrow and she sat with her hands clasped on her lap, her head rocking from side to side.

It was only after Cage switched cabs again, with an instruction to go to Jiang Guo Men Wei, that Sally said, 'I've got a place we can go. No one knows about it.'

Cage hung back while Sally picked up the key at the reception of the cheap hotel she had booked into. Such an age ago, it seemed now. The room was rundown but spacious; it smelt of old tobacco and cheap cleaning fluids and overlooked a traffic junction bustling with food stalls and bicycles.

'You're clever to have got this,' Cage said.

'I got it for the safe-deposit box,' Sally said as she walked in.

Cage helped her fix up the cut above her eye and another on her cheek, where Mok had hit her. Her ribs hurt from being kicked, so Cage tore up a sheet and put it round her like a bandage.

'What were you doing there, Cage, dropping by with gasoline bombs in your pockets?' she asked.

'Later.' Cage didn't want to be drawn.

Sally couldn't help herself. 'And I heard you had a shoot-out with some cops in New York.'

Cage, taken aback, stopped work on the bandage. 'It was a set-up,' he said softly.

He finished the knot, then checked out the room professionally, running his hands up the curtains and under the tiny windowsill, pockmarked with cigarette burns. Sally had never seen him work like this before.

'It's fine,' he said. 'We can lay up here for a couple of days.'

Cage showered while Sally called Paul who was full of stories about trampolines and rocking horses and didn't even ask when she was coming back.

Thankfully, the room had two single beds. Cage lay on one of them and drifted off to sleep. But Sally was too wound up. She needed to calm herself and the only way she knew how was to work, to retreat into the comforting rituals of her craft.

She drew a map of the tomb and its surrounding areas. She worked meticulously, as her scientific training had taught her, concentrating on drawing the detail from memory, and eradicating from her mind the horror she had just been through.

She began with the three pits of the terracotta warrior army to the east of the mausoleum and traced the route she believed the underground railway track would take, across the fields where skeletal bones of Qin Shi Huang's workers and horses had been thrown up by the ploughs of farmers. She marked the villages around the mound: the lower and upper Chen villages to the south; the Dong village to the west; to the north-east a village called Mao; then just to the west and slightly further north, another Mao village. And in a direct line to the outer wall of the tomb was Zhang village. Whether this was significant was anyone's guess.

She worked at the little desk, a beer mat wedged under the leg to keep it from wobbling, conscious of Cage sleeping behind her. Right now, she didn't want him in her world. Maybe that was how it had been from the beginning; she pushed him out because he could never belong there. She paused in her work to pin her hair back tightly and watch the dawn peak its way through the pollution. Then she examined her map critically and began to add every tiny detail about the tomb which she could remember.

Sally was a good archaeologist, clawing her way through the past until she found the truth. Sometimes she would examine soil for hours before determining where it was leading her. She could run her fingers along a calligraphic drawing and imagine the life which had surrounded the artist. Now, she was pushing herself further into the tomb than she had ever gone before.

The six man-made caves – or 'five-pointed rooms', as they came out in translation on the map – marked the outer gates of the burial area in a rectangular protective cordon. Further in, more gates formed a square round the burial mound. She drew contour rings to define the shape of the mound itself, and to show where the outer chambers she had photographed lay in relation to the rest. She wrote in the Chinese characters for the village names and marked the pomegranate trees, the rutted track she used for the probe, the tattered souvenir stalls at the bottom of the path.

When she was satisfied with the detail, she studied the names. One village named Zhang. Another named Mao. A diarist named Zhang. An emperor named Zhang, or Zheng, which meant 'correct' or 'upright'. Which might mean nothing, or everything. China was not the Chinese name for the country. The word came from Qin, the name of the First Emperor, Qin Shi Huang. China First Sovereign. But the Chinese called their own country Middle Kingdom or Central Country. Before that it was *Tian Xia*, 'everything under heaven'. China *was* the world. *Wu Tian* meant 'power under heaven'. All the power in the world. A fitting name for a Chinese emperor.

'Qin Shi Huang' was the name form Sally used for the First Emperor, but she could also have used 'Qin Shi Huangdi', the form given to emperors once they had died. The origins of the 'di' were first found on Shang oracle bones, some of them four thousand years old, referring literally to the bundle of firewood used to burn sacrificial meat to the ancestral spirits of the rulers. The 'di' came to mean deity, and an emperor would be accorded the 'di' at his death.

Sally rubbed her eyes and leaned back, wincing as her bruised ribs objected to the movement. She remembered Li Yi's words before she fled Wu's shrine to Mao – *While I am here, you are safe. You have my word on that.* Did his word count for anything where her safety was concerned? As she pondered his role in Wu's ceremonies, another name occurred to her: Qin Shi Huang's reforms were pushed through by a chief minister called Li Si, although some scholars argued that the 'Si' was his title, and that his real name was Li Yi. 'Qin devoured his enemies as a silkworm devours a mulberry leaf,' Li Si had said.

Sally bit the end of her pencil between her teeth. Was Li Yi Wu Tian's meticulous planner, his chief minister, his fix-it factotum, the moderator, the key to controlling Wu's insanity?

Wu Tian, if that was his real name, had a vision of creating another Chinese empire with Mao as its figurehead. Did he have the popular support to succeed? Was he expressing the real aspirations of the Chinese people – the poor, the dispossessed, those with no hope except to follow a false god? Or was the mantle of power passing to the students, the ones marching on the streets and scheming at universities to exploit the death of Hu Yaobang, the human face of modern China, the leader who died while shitting?

Sally looked out of the window at the confusion of morning shadows over the Beijing skyline, the strong sun playing with clouds, blue skies and layers of pollution. She dug the pencil lead into the paper. She sensed the answer to Wu Tian lay in the past, at least before 1976 when Mao died. Or maybe in 210 BC when Qin died.

Sally put on her coat, wrapped Cait's scarf round her neck, wrote Cage a note and paused with her hand on the door. Her emotions, as so often when it came to him, were conflicted. She was half afraid he would wake, yet she wanted him to before she left. He slept.

From a booth in the lobby she called Ko. He had thrown out

Time and *Newsweek* for Chinese Maoist magazines. He had peeled off the 'I love New York' sticker and replaced it with Mao gazing through a bountiful harvest. Was Ko a follower of Red Spirit?

Ko himself picked up the phone. She could tell he was surprised to hear from her. She started brightly in English, 'Hi, Ko, how's things out there?'

Ko answered in Chinese. 'Mrs Ko is delivering June the tenth.'

'Is she OK?'

'She's fine. It will be a good birth. We're going to ask him for a son.'

'Sorry, Ko, I'm out of the loop. Who are you asking?'

Ko almost whispered it. The Red Spirit. Red Soul.

'Who's that?' said Sally softly, knowing, but wanting to hear it.

'*Mao Jingshen.*' Energy of Mao. 'Many people are travelling here to witness the coming,' said Ko. 'The oppressed peoples and nations will only triumph by strengthening their unity and persevering in their struggle.' He was speaking in his slogan Chinese again.

'I should be back tomorrow or the next day,' she said. 'I'll give you a call to pick me up.'

'It might be difficult. My elder brother is coming from Xining. He is suffering from cancer of the nose. My nephew is bringing him. His factory has closed and he has no money. My cousin in Gansu is coming to ask the Red Spirit to bring rains to his farm. His mule has died and there is no money to buy another. My cousin from Chongching is arriving soon. He has a tumour in his brain.' Suddenly he switched to English. 'Comrade Sally, he can help you, too. You have no father for your son. It is not right. He will find you a father.'

'Who is "he", exactly, Ko? I don't get it.'

'But you know, Sally. You must. What were you doing on the tomb all those nights? I am so proud to work with you. You were helping us prepare. But I have told no one.'

'And he will come?'

'Yes. We have heard he will come from the tomb. The tomb contains the power of all China. We will all be going there.'

A shiver ran down Sally's body. 'See you soon, Ko,' she said as lightly as she could. 'Look after Mrs Ko.'

When Sally hung up, she stayed in the cubicle, her face to the wall, numb with confusion and fear. She could think of only one person who could help her and she had reached a point where she had to break through her anger against him. Were her instincts wrong? After Cage, it had taken a lot for her to trust a man enough to be intimate with him. Richard had broken that trust. But that was sex, and this was different. She needed now to trust Richard with her life.

Chapter Twenty-four

Maeve let Sally into Richard's office without any questions. Sally let her hair hang over her face and kept Cait's scarf round her neck to cover the injuries. But, from the way Maeve looked at her, Sally was pretty sure she noticed.

'Don't worry, it wasn't him or the bedpost,' she managed.

Maeve smiled and left. Minutes later Richard appeared.

'Are you all right?' he said straightaway. 'Maeve said it was an emergency.' He shut the door, then pressed the intercom. 'Maeve, stop all calls until further notice. Absolutely everything.'

Sally stayed where she was. She felt as cold as a statue of ice. 'Wu Tian didn't have the damn disk for me. I walked into a cult orgy and was damn near killed. And what was Cage doing there, Richard? What the hell was he doing there?'

Richard sat down next to Sally on the sofa. 'My God. You were hurt.' He started brushing her hair back, but Sally pushed him away. 'Who did this? Cage?'

Sally took off Cait's scarf and threw it across the room. 'No, it wasn't Cage. It was Wu and his . . . I don't know what to call them. I was in some Cultural Revolution struggle session.'

'It was Wu?'

'You sent me to Wu. Cage rescued me, he got me out, and I need to know what's happening.' Sally couldn't look at him because of the moisture in her eyes. She swallowed hard. 'I need to know, Richard.'

'I told you, Sal. I don't know much about Wu.'

'Yeah, right.' She would stay confrontational. She couldn't collapse in front of him. 'I know there are things you can't tell me. But just about Cage and Wu, bend the rules a bit. For old time's sake. OK?'

Richard sighed. 'Wu, I don't know. But like I said, Cage is a crook. He was thrown out of the Marine Corps after he lost his temper and shot up a village. I'm not allowed to say where it was exactly. Back in the States, he became a petty criminal and drifted into drug trafficking. We lost track of him, which was a mistake and now he's involved with the Triads. His coming out to find his parents is bullshit. He's actually setting up a narcotics link between here and the US.' Richard tilted his head back against the wall. 'That's it, Sal. I didn't want to tell you right now. But that's what Cage is all about.'

'Thank you,' she whispered.

'And that's why I asked you not to see him again.'

'Well, I have seen him,' she said quietly. 'So what now?'

Richard stood up and paced the office, his hands holding his chin. 'It's been a hell of a week. You wouldn't have heard about it in the press, but someone tried to blow up the hotel where we were meeting the Chinese.'

Sally glanced at him. 'What happened?' was all she could manage.

He shook his head. 'We don't know. But I missed death by a hair's breadth. And there have been huge demonstrations over the death of Hu Yaobang. The government's accusing them of poisoning people's minds with new ideas of freedom.'

'Li Yi said Wu Tian was Red Spirit – you know, that Maoist movement.'

'Li Yi said that, did he? What else did he say?'

'He made out that Red Spirit had a big following.'

Richard shook his head. 'Impossible,' he muttered. 'Mao's cronies are either dead or in jail.'

'There was a guy who Li Yi said was one of Wu's provincial leaders. He was getting a blow job.'

'You serious?'

'Except he was impotent and nothing happened. Then they threw me into a struggle session.'

Richard sat down again next to Sally. He held her hand and she let him. 'Now, very slowly, tell me exactly what happened.'

She told him and ended with a shrug. 'Not much else. Wu Tian wanted to hold me there, or something. Cage persuaded him otherwise.'

'Where's Cage now?'

'With me.'

'I think it is best that you and Paul get out of China for a while. Why don't you take an embassy car to the hotel, get your stuff and come back here? We'll get Paul flown up from Xian and I'll put you both on a plane to New York tonight. The demonstrations around Tiananmen Square are going to get worse. We've heard that tanks are being sent to the city perimeters. We don't know what will happen when Gorbachev arrives. You can never tell what's happening in China, but if Wu is stirring things up, China is not a good place to be.'

Sally knew that to get so close and then to run would grate on her for the rest of her life. She would never regain her peace of mind. But to stay would be madness. She let Richard push back her hair and kiss her on the forehead. 'OK, fix it,' she smiled. 'I'm going to the library. I need to be alone. Read some magazines.'

'How does a girl get a cup of coffee round here?' Sally said, breezing into Susan's office in the embassy.

'You'd never believe what's happening out there right now,' said Susan excitedly. She was standing at the window. Sally joined her.

'Look, you can just see them through the gate. There are thousands of them and they're breaking through the police lines, heading for Tiananmen Square. They're shouting about how they want democracy. Scary, isn't it?'

'Beijing seems to be going stir crazy,' said Sally.

Susan put her hand to her mouth. 'My God, that bomb – wasn't it terrible? I mean, Richard! He's OK, isn't he? I know it's meant to be a secret, but everyone in the embassy's talking about it.'

'He's fine. A lucky escape,' said Sally.

'I heard a beggar saved him.'

'He's fine,' she said again, ending the conversation. Richard hadn't mentioned a beggar. She dropped her bag onto a chair and draped her coat over it. Suddenly she realised something was missing – Cait's ochre cashmere scarf.

'Susan, look, I left my scarf in Richard's office,' she said. 'Could you swipe me back in with your pass?'

'Sure,' said Susan, smiling.

Sally walked back down the corridors to Richard's office. Maeve wasn't there, but she couldn't have gone far because her pass was on the desk. Richard's office door was open; she could hear his voice, and was about to step inside when she heard what he was saying.

She froze, leaning against Maeve's desk for support, her stomach churning. Richard was speaking in the soft, creepy tone he used on the rare occasions when they disagreed.

'My guess is she'll lead us to Cage, and we'll have them both by the end of the day . . .' Richard's hand was in the door, as if he was about to close it. 'I'm not sure she was ever too fussy whom she bedded . . .'

Sally stepped behind Maeve's desk, trying to stay out of sight.

'If we have to, we have to, whether it involves Sally Parsons or not . . .'

Then instead of closing it, Richard opened the door. 'Stephanie, you *are* watertight. Maeve, can you—' He looked up, saw Sally and stopped dead.

Sally forced a smile. 'Forgot my scarf.' She laughed nervously. She peeked round his shoulder and pointed. 'There it is. On the floor.'

'Can you hold?' Richard said into the receiver. He picked up the scarf, handed it to Sally, and tapped the receiver, as if to emphasise that he was working. 'See you soon,' he whispered, kissing her on the cheek.

She walked as quickly as she could, out of the embassy, through the compound gates and into the road. Then she cut down an alleyway on foot, her mind all over the place but her instincts kicking in to fight her confusion and her shame at her own stupidity and naïvety.

She had believed in Richard. An easy mistake. But she had really loved him. She did really love him. Love didn't vanish just like that. You couldn't just cut it off at the neck and kill it. *I'm not sure she was ever too fussy whom she bedded*, he'd said. No man would say that about a woman he cared for.

But the truth was, he probably never had.

She slowed down. At the end of the alley was a wall of green police uniforms, and just behind them were rows of cyclists clogging up the pavement, heads craning to see over the policemen's heads. She heard chanting from the streets, police sirens, shouting, and glimpsed a placard with Chinese characters for 'democracy' emblazoned in red. There was no traffic and litter blew across the empty road. A gust of wind brought a discarded leaflet to her feet. It showed a picture of Deng Xiao-ping with a black line drawn across the face.

As she pushed her way through the cyclists, a hand fell on her shoulder. 'Not this way,' said a policeman. 'Subversives.' She was the only foreigner around and he spoke in English.

She did what he said, then cut back and walked straight through another police cordon. It was smaller and there was traffic on the road. The police parted and let her through. It was then that she spotted the embassy car fifty yards from the entrance of her hotel. The driver, an American, was standing up, the door open, head turning, scanning the streets. Two more Americans were just inside the hotel's shabby lobby.

A taxi swept by, making her jump back. Then it pulled up and she heard Cage's voice. 'Sal, get in.' But the driver was a wiry old Chinese guy, grey face, fingers curled up and hooked on the wheel. The window was down. He leaned across and opened the passenger door. 'Get in, for God's sake, Sal.'

The police had noticed him. A whistle blew, and two men in green uniform and peaked caps moved towards them. Sally scrambled in and closed the door.

'Head down,' said Cage. 'Head down.'

He waved at the police and set off, past the hotel. Sally's head was between her knees as if she was being sick. Cage's hand was on her shoulder, gently, just enough to make sure she stayed there.

Exhibit 47 – Audio Tape Evidence
Federal Court, Pearl Street
Manhattan
December 16th 1989

'They've gone.'
'Where?'
'That's why I'm calling. Trains, airports, taxis – you've got to watch them all.'
'Why? So you can send them to their death?'

Chapter Twenty-five

Cage had booked four berths, two each in adjoining compartments, to ensure the privacy they needed. Four bunks were in each, with a connecting washroom between, so they had no need to go anywhere else in the train for the eighteen-hour journey to Xian.

Once on the train, Cage locked the doors to the berths and sat Sally by the window. 'When did you last eat?' he demanded.

'God knows.' She sat with her eyes closed, her mind empty. Cage was in charge now. She heard him rummaging in a bag.

'Here, get some food inside you,' he ordered, handing her a sandwich. She ate it hungrily, while watching the fields of northern China speed by. Having Cage around made her feel safe. She had to end it – whatever it was. She didn't care who Cage had killed, he had been there when she needed him. Overhearing Richard's conversation and the sight of the embassy car outside the hotel were enough to convince her who was on her side.

'All right, Cage,' she said. 'There comes a time when the mother of your son needs to know what the hell's going on. I reckon now's the time.'

Cage sat on the chair across the window table from Sally and peeled an apple with a penknife. 'Richard Gregg's your new boyfriend, right?'

'Was. I think we just split up.'

'Tall, slim guy with a kind of aristocratic, or I could say arrogant, face, although if I did you might think I was being petty and jealous. Wears expensive clothes, cuff-links? Silk ties, brogue shoes, blue eyes and a good head of hair?'

'Sounds about right.'

'Does he work for the American government?'

'He does.'

Cage passed Sally a slice of apple. 'You saw him just now?'
Sally nodded.

'Did he say he nearly got blown to hell by a car bomb?'

Sally was about to put the apple in her mouth, but stopped.
'Yes. Yes, he did. Then he said . . . no, *he* didn't, Susan the
receptionist in the embassy library said he was saved by a beggar.'

'That was me.' Cage grinned. 'Same guy who picked you up in
the taxi.'

Sally slipped the apple into her mouth and chewed it very
slowly. 'That was you?'

Cage nodded.

'Like I said, Cage, there comes a time, so just explain.'

'I'm working for the FBI.'

Part of her wanted to believe him. Part was uneasy. 'I thought
you got thrown out of the Marine Corps?'

'And the FBI took me on.'

'Why? I mean why were you thrown out?'

He cut another slice of apple. 'You don't want to hear—'

'I do.'

'—and I don't want to talk about it.'

'No. I want to hear it. I need to believe you.'

Cage put the knife on the table and looked straight at her. 'It
was somewhere in south-east Asia. We – American troops –
were not meant to be there. Kids with guns were shooting up a
village, and my commanding officer was letting them, so I beat
him up, stopped the killing, but too late, and got kicked out for
disobeying orders and striking a senior officer.'

'You got thrown out for saving lives.'

'They were the wrong lives.' He stood up, steadying himself
on the bunk against the pitch and roll of the train. Sally needed
to keep going, to get the whole story. 'So how come the FBI
took you on?'

'Narcotics,' said Cage bluntly. 'I'm here to help bust a narcotics line between China and New York.'

Sally looked away, out of the window. 'So the search for your mother – is that bullshit?'

'No. But it's not everything.'

She couldn't reply. She had to give herself a few seconds. Cage brought out his two lockets, opened them, cleared away the food packages and laid them on the table. 'Sal, my cover had become my reality. Li Yi threw this to me just as we were getting out. Remember?' Sally looked at him and nodded. Cage picked up one of the lockets. 'This is a completely different picture of my mother.'

'So you think they know where she is?'

'I'm convinced. If I walk away from this assignment, sure, I can live with it. But if I walk away from her now, having got so close, how could I forgive myself? What do I say to Paul when he asks? How could I forget her?'

'The reason I went to see Wu Tian yesterday was to pick up a disk,' Sally told him. 'On it was a strange story about the tomb of Qin Shi Huang and how Mao had used it in the sixties and seventies to store heroin. Apparently, he had a crazy idea of poisoning the US, like the Chinese had been poisoned by British opium.'

'Wu has read this?'

'I guess so.'

Cage whistled through his teeth. 'So that's it,' he said under his breath.

'That's what?'

'The Teochiu Triads, the main traffickers, have a new type of pure heroin which is so powerful you get the same rush smoking it as injecting it. So it means no syringes and no AIDS. They've used it to muscle in against the Mafia in the New York narcotics trade. We managed to trace the Teochiu links back here . . .' He gently took her hand. 'To Li Yi, in fact.'

Sally gasped. 'To my Li Yi?'

'And finally to Wu Tian.'

They were both quiet for a few seconds, then Sally laughed. 'And I just walked in and gave them the evidence which blew their little secret.'

'Before Mao came along, Li Yi's father – a guy called Joseph Li – used to be Triad boss in Xian. Wu helped him escape in the fifties. The father is now one of the most powerful Chinese gangsters in New York and Wu Tian's calling in the favour by asking him to be his distributor.'

'So that's what it's all about,' said Sally softly. She now had the full explanation, but she was still hesitant. 'You've heard of Red Spirit, haven't you? We talked about it in the taxi.'

'Of course. Why?'

'Li Yi told me it was a huge movement with supporters everywhere.'

'Possibly. Funded by Wu's drug money. We know that Wu's connected with it.'

'Would Richard have anything to do with it?'

Cage thought for a moment. 'If the US thought Red Spirit was powerful enough to destabilise the Chinese government, yes, he would.'

On the journey to the station, Sally had told Cage some of what had happened with Richard, but not all. 'Help me with this,' she'd said. 'This is exactly what I overheard Richard saying to someone called Stephanie. One: ". . . if we have to, we have to, whether it involves Sally Parsons or not." Two: ". . . Stephanie, you *are* watertight." He spoke as if I was a player.'

Cage shook his head. 'Impossible to say. I'll check up on Stephanie when we get to Xian. He leaned down to the floor, picked up the bag and brought out a pack of black hair dye and a pair of scissors. 'Now to some practicalities,' he announced.

Sally looked at what he planned to do with horror. 'Oh no,' she said. 'I won't cut it, Cage. I'll dye it, but not cut it.'

'Chinese hair is thin and straight. Yours is—'

'I know, it's a thick, floppy mess. But I'll put it under a hat.'

'It'll be safer if we cut it.'

'No.' And suddenly Sally found she was laughing.

'OK. Into the washroom, and sweater off,' he said.

Sally leaned over the sink as Cage poured bowl after bowl of warm water over her head until her hair was ringing wet. Then he squeezed dye out of a tube and worked it well into her hair, wearing a pair of polythene gloves supplied with the dye pack.

It's like the old days, she thought. Like the times they had fun together.

231

'Sorry, this isn't Fifth Avenue,' said Cage. 'We've got big facecloths instead of towels.' He laid four of them round her shoulders before she sat up. 'Now you have to sit with your hair cold and clammy while the dye sets in,' he instructed.

'Yuk.' Sally touched her hair and felt the stickiness. 'In my bag, there's a mirror. Let me have a look at myself.'

Cage held the tiny mirror in front of her. 'Oh my, God,' Sally shrieked. They both burst out laughing. She felt Cage's hands on her arms, and didn't know what to do. So she kept laughing.

'We've got to do the eyebrows. I'll make you look worse than Groucho Marx.' He squeezed dye out of a different tube, specially for eyebrows. 'Close your eyes tight.'

He expertly massaged the dye into her eyebrows, then gently dabbed her face dry. 'All right. Open now.' He held the mirror in front of her again like a hairdresser.

'That's better.' She bit her lip, turned round and looked up at Cage, touching his hand. 'But I'm surprised at how unthorough you are.'

'And what do you mean by that?'

'Well . . . supposing they strip search me?'

Cage let out a bark of laughter.

He washed out the basin and then joined Sally at the window table again.

'You followed me to the embassy?' she said. 'I can't believe it.'

'You think I'd let you even step outside the room by yourself?'

'And you used me to get to Li Yi.' She glanced at him but didn't meet his eye. She wanted to know, but couldn't face another betrayal.

'No,' he said quickly.

'What was it then?'

He took her hand. She didn't respond. 'I asked Cait to clear the way for me to see you way before I knew about Li Yi,' he said.

Sally looked at him. 'You did?'

'I did.'

It was way past midnight when Cage climbed onto the top bunk in the same compartment. They talked some more, mostly about

232

Paul and about the past, keeping to safe ground, until they fell asleep to the gentle rhythm of the train.

Sally didn't sleep well. Restless, jarring dreams came to her.

Paul was cycling through a village where the kids all lay dead. Wu Tian was there, smiling, laughing, beckoning. Sally ran towards Paul, reaching out, trying to stop him. But he didn't recognise her because she had dyed her hair. When she caught up with him, her hand went straight through him. Her son was only an image, but an image which kept pedalling.

She ran and ran and found she was running to the rocking of the train. She woke up, feeling exhausted and alone. It occurred to her that perhaps the empty space in her life was of her own making.

She got up, poured herself a glass of water, then climbed up to be with Cage. She lay next to him and put her hand inside his shirt to feel his warmth. She took his hand. He was asleep and she pressed their hands against her breasts. They stayed there for a moment, but then he woke with a jolt and uncurled his fingers from hers.

'What's wrong?' she whispered.

'Nothing,' he said. 'But let's not make it wrong again.'

Sally climbed back down to her own bunk. She closed her eyes and for a few minutes concentrated on the tomb, and on how to find the strange storyteller who called himself Zhang Ying. Then she fell asleep, restful now. By being rejected, she felt she had made some kind of peace with Cage.

Bill Cage lifted his head so he could see the darkness out of the window, and tried to fill his mind with the emptiness of the night.

Chapter Twenty-six

'It might not seem so to you, but I am a very lonely man.'

Wu Tian's eyes were grey and filmy, and his voice sounded tired. Li Yi couldn't read him. Wu sat behind his desk while men dismantled the statues and altars in his bedroom. He talked amid the banging and scraping of boxes, work he had ordered, but he appeared to be oblivious to it.

'Loneliness has a fascination for me,' he said. 'It gives a man time to look himself in the face. You might accuse me of running away. But we all run away from something, don't we? Even great men. What were we doing in the Long March, if not running away?'

'You are right, comrade,' said Li Yi. 'You are always wise in these matters.'

'Those demonstrators in Tiananmen Square, they don't understand their own country. You watch, comrade, soon they will deface the picture of our Great Helmsman and they'll build the Statue of Liberty in its place.' He lit a fresh cigarette from the butt of the one he had almost finished.

'Red Spirit will prevail, comrade. Your foresight has been incredible.'

Wu Tian nodded, acknowledging the compliment. He stood up, more frail than usual. Mok flitted across from the dark doorway behind his desk and gave Wu his elbow for balance.

'Make sure it is all packed properly,' Wu Tian instructed Li Yi. 'There are treasures here.' He smoothed down his hair, adjusted his tunic and waved his hand around his study. 'Who shall I leave all this to? It is terrible that a man does not have an heir, that there is no one to put flowers on his grave and to visit his sarcophagus and pray beside his body. How can a daughter betray her father so?'

'Your daughter is . . . she may return,' said Li Yi hesitantly.

Wu shook his head sadly. 'But I can't accept her, don't you see? She has betrayed the revolution.'

Li Yi tried again. 'In Xian, you will have the children of the Red Spirit. They will praise your leadership in creating a new era for the motherland.'

Wu Tian nodded and steadied himself on Mok's shoulder.

Stephanie Cranley poured herself a cup of green tea. 'You are very clever, Richard, which, of course, is why I had you transferred to me. You are more clever than I am, and turbulence rages in your soul. You are overkeen to prove you are better than your father. He was a distinguished diplomat who worked face on to the world, as it were. You have chosen the secret world, so there will never be a way of comparing your work to his.' Cranley sipped from the cup and looked up at him. 'Your brother, Michael, he's a lawyer, isn't he?'

'Corporate law. He's doing very well.' Richard was sitting behind his desk, opposite Cranley.

'You'll never be able to show your success like him,' she said. 'You'll never be paid like he is. Your accolades will not go beyond this agency. If you are seeking reputation, you must follow your father's footsteps.'

Richard sighed. 'Stephanie, it's fine. I'm not sure this is the time for a therapy chat.'

'I'm glad you used that word, Richard. Therapy calms troubled waters, and your waters seem to be very troubled at the moment or you wouldn't have asked to talk to me.'

'The bomb, that was—'

'I'm not talking about the bomb.' Her tone was silky, yet contained traces of sarcasm and threat. 'This is a one-strike-and-you're-out business, Richard.'

Richard pressed his hands on the desk. 'Stephanie, nothing has changed. I wanted to inform you that Wu is now heading to Xian. It is exactly as we had planned.'

'Except that the FBI will soon know exactly what we – or
should I say – you – have been doing.'

'And what have we been doing? We identified a political group
in opposition to the ruling Communist Party and encouraged it.
What's new in that, Stephanie? We do it all over the world.'

'Except we don't fund politics with dope peddling. I don't
care what you do here, Richard, but when the FBI gets involved,
I get involved.'

'We're not involved in—'

'Then why did you bed Sally to use her as your unsuspecting
mole on the tomb? Why did you recommend that we shut her
down after the Gorbachev visit? Why did you get the institute to
send her the probe so she could get a camera in there?'

A flicker of doubt crossed Richard's face. Then he leaned
back with his hands clasped behind his head, and spoke with
more confidence. 'You knew what I was doing, Stephanie. I had
your authority. We'd worked together to make sure Washington
kept its eyes off China for the first six months of this year. We
had no ambassador here. James Lilley has only just taken up his
post. There is no assistant secretary of state. Gaston Sigur left
office on February the twenty-first. Richard Solomon's not due
to take over until June the twenty-third. That gave us – and I
mean 'us', Stephanie – the freedom to develop Red Spirit as we
wanted. And let me remind you how it's worked out. Right now,
Wu Tian will be heading for Xian to activate Red Spirit. Wasn't
that the plan? Isn't that how we want it to work? Red Spirit
comes to life and Gorbachev realises China is too unstable for
any utopian Sino–Soviet alliance and he ducks out of it.
Collapsing Soviet communism, returning Chinese Maoism –
what else does the US want except to become the only super-
power left in the world?'

'A fine analysis,' said Cranley softly. She had been listening
with her chin in her hand. 'Except the demonstrators in
Tiananmen Square seem to have done our job for us.'

Richard laughed. 'Even the Federal Containment Agency
can't unravel things that quickly.'

Cranley smiled, but didn't reply.

'A Red Spirit would have appeared,' continued Richard, 'even if we hadn't created it. There's too much anger at Deng Xiao-ping's reforms.'

'I don't think either of us needs a lesson in politics.' Cranley paused, leaned forward. 'This is about getting found out, and it seems Bill Cage and Sally Parsons have everything they need to get you found out. The press, Congress, the people who elect our president – they would not understand your brilliance, Richard, and I can't afford their disapproval.'

Cage got off the train first to make sure the station was safe. It was heaving with people, but no one was waiting for them. No one was trailing. They got a cab and as soon as they were on their way Sally told him her plan. She knew it would lead to argument, which was why she had kept it from him on the train.

'I want you to drop me at the tomb, go and check on Paul, then book into the Golden Flower Hotel. It's less conspicuous than the Xian Hotel.'

Cage's reaction was predictable. 'Sal, you're crazy. No way am I going to let you out by yourself. You go to Paul.'

'Not yet. We need to end this,' she said firmly.

'But it's not safe.'

'Nothing's safe until it's ended,' she snapped. 'I know what it's like out there.'

She was short-tempered. Trying to prove herself. Why? Why not relax and let Cage take charge? Because she had tried that before, and when she'd needed him, he hadn't been there. Sally had always worked alone, in the lab, in the pit, on the slopes of the tomb. If her instincts were right, if she went back alone again, he would be there, the man whose head bobbed in and out of his clothes like a turtle. She was sure he was the key to ending it.

'Please, Cage. You go and check on Paul. If I knew you were doing that, it would settle me.'

'OK. But if something happens, I want to know how to find you.'

'Go up the main tourist steps to the top of the tomb. About two-thirds of the way up on the left, I'll break off two branches of a pomegranate tree. You'll see a path with rutted tracks.

Head down it about a hundred and fifty yards and there'll be a
heavy piece of equipment under a black plastic cover. That's my
base. So if you really need me, head there.'

'OK,' said Cage slowly. 'I've got a false South Korean passport. I'll book in under a Korean name. Let's say Kim Chong,
working for a company called Gold Star Electronics.'

'Why Korean?'

'South Korea and China have no diplomatic relations, but
there are plenty of tourists. So no one can even begin to trace
the name.' He pressed into her hand the locket Li Yi had thrown
to him. 'And since we're splitting up and since you're the mother
of my son,' he said under his breath, 'I want you to keep this.'
He shrugged and smiled, embarrassed.

'Give it to Paul.'

'No. When the time's right. I have one. I want you to have
one. Less chance of both of us getting run down. Tell him I
might have been a lousy man to you but that I tried to be a good
dad.'

'Thanks, Cage.' She swallowed hard, not able to hide her
emotion. 'It means a lot.' Sally wrapped her arms round his
neck and kissed him on the lips. She broke away wiping her eyes.

Her dark hair tied back, Sally walked up the steps to the top of
the tomb in the late afternoon. It was hotter than she had
expected. The north Asian summer was harsh and unforgiving,
bringing gritty dust on the winds, then still, dry air which
sucked the water from the human body.

As night fell, Sally watched the silhouettes of the mountains
and the last of the sun on the roofs of the villages below, the
names of which had become so alive and human to her. She had
rarely been on the tomb at dusk. Usually, it was far into the
night when she came, and villages were sleeping.

The tomb itself was busier than usual. Just to get to the steps
she had to walk through clusters of people camped out; blue
tunics, rough ruddy faces, callused hands and usually dulled
faces alive with hope. *We will all be going there*, Ko had told her.

'Welcome, welcome,' they shouted to her as she climbed up.
The first one shook her hands, not noticing the white skin. After

that she kept her hands in her pockets and wished she was six inches shorter. But they rubbed her elbows and chatted to her. She heard '*Mao Jingshen*', spirit of Mao, several times, with an expectant look of shared joy in their eyes, something she had never seen in China, not in Ko, not in Li Yi, not even on the faces of the terracotta warriors.

There must have been several thousand encircling the tomb, setting up for the night, lighting fires, preparing meals and laying out sleeping blankets. Oil lamps flickered through open windows in the houses below, reminding Sally of the first ever photograph she saw of China, historic and idyllic.

Sally left the path and stepped into the orchard. Cage would never make it through all this, but she broke two branches of a tree, just as they had agreed, then walked quickly on down the path, looking for a lunch box left among the pomegranate trees.

It was four months since she had first seen the extraordinary man, fleeing from the beam of Ko's headlights. He must have watched her all those nights. He did not seem threatening. Perhaps he was cautious, unsure of her, wary of direct contact. But for some reason he was keeping watch on her, and Sally wanted to know why.

She stopped at precisely the spot where she had made the probe which had found the rail track. The drill was still there, hidden under a bush and wrapped up in thick polythene, just as she had left it. Sally inspected it with her flashlight, her hand cupped over it to contain the light. She felt around it with her free hand. Nothing. He hadn't touched it. She traced the path where she'd left the lunch box. But he'd left no signals for her, no stones, no leaves, no lunch box.

She sat on the ground, leant against a tree trunk and opened the rice and chicken box she had brought for her supper. She ate it slowly, chewing out the flavour as if she was on rations. Then, exhausted, she fell asleep.

He came just after ten, waking her gently with a tap on her shoulder and squatting in front of her, his face barely visible and his head bobbing up and down inside his coat. He made no attempt to speak to her, but simply offered her a lunch box with cold chicken leg and rice. When he saw that Sally had just finished her own, she detected a flash of disappointment.

'Zhang Ying? Are you Zhang Ying?' Sally whispered.

He said nothing. He was tiny, no more than five feet tall. On the right-hand side of his face was a dark blotch, like a birthmark, which ran down to the edge of his upper lip. He had a straggly black-and-grey beard. His head was wrapped in a blue cloth, and he wore woollen gloves with holes cut out so his fingertips were free.

He pointed up and over to the far side of the mound, touched Sally's shoulder and beckoned for her to follow.

Scuttling along the ground in front, crouched and hunched, Sally could see he was clearly the victim of some terrible deformity. He knew his way through the orchards, down the slopes, along the drainage ditches on the flat ground of the rice fields at the edge of the mound. He was always ahead of her, but sometimes he stopped and stroked his beard, waiting for her to catch up. Sally followed, her stomach knotted with excitement.

Chapter Twenty-seven

Cage watched Sally head off up the tomb and melt into the crowds. He could have trailed her. He felt he should, but her clever gift to him was Paul, and he headed for a shopping emporium where he bought a jacket, trousers, a tie and a new pair of shoes. He booked into the Golden Flower Hotel under the name of Kim Chong, working for Gold Star Electronics. After showering, he spent time removing wax and powder from his face and hands, and washing the grey out of his hair. He blow-dried it and put on his new clothes.

He took another taxi to the Maddoxes' house, but paid off the driver a block away when he saw a police cordon.

He recognised the house from Sally's description of it, with its pointed eaves and the huge front window which dropped down two floors at the front. Toys were scattered on the lawn and he knew straightaway the place had been ransacked. As he got closer, he saw broken windows on the ground floor and burnt paintwork. A rope with red rags hanging from it was stretched across the garden gate, which hung on its hinges. Pedestrians and traffic slowed as they passed, and Cage took his time, not so slow as to be noticed, but time enough for him to examine methodically what might have happened. He tried to remain composed, but he felt as if he had been punched in the stomach.

The fire, he could tell, had been pretty much contained. He cut down a small street a block away, then doubled back along an alley that ran behind the back of the houses. A hundred yards along, he jumped the fence into what looked like a factory yard. He ran straight to cover, looked around, and climbed over another fence. Now he was on the property next to the house where Paul should be, but there was a wall about fifteen feet high, with barbed wire on the top, between him and it.

The fence back into the alleyway was lower, with a gate in it, held by a small padlock. Cage picked the lock and eased the gate open. Far down on both sides were policemen, their backs to him. Closer, standing perfectly still and upright, leaning on a walking stick, was an elderly Chinese woman.

She turned, alerted by the sound of the gate.

She must have been well into her seventies but retained a serene elegance. She wore a light-blue dress with lace at the cuffs and neck, and a straw sun hat which cast a shadow over her face.

'They kidnapped a little American boy,' she announced.

'Who?' Cage was abrupt. He walked towards her, keeping against the fence to lessen the chance of the police seeing him.

'They'll want a ransom.'

'How do you know?'

She let out a little laugh. 'I know the gangsters. Communists, Nationalists, Japanese. Warlords. I know them all.' She pointed ahead with her stick. 'This is my house. I've lived here all my life. My name is Tang Qing Ling. In the old days of the foreign concessions, they called me Violet.'

'The boy's name,' pressed Cage. 'What's his name?'

'Paul. He's the son of Sally Parsons, the archaeologist. He'd only been with us a few days.'

He clenched his fists. 'How do you know it's him?'

'I know all the children, and Dr Parsons is quite well-known. She's been working on the tomb, you see. There are rumours about that tomb among the locals. In nineteen seventy-six, two weeks after Mao Zedong died, the tomb was sealed off. The people of the villages around the tomb were evacuated, and for a few days none of us knew what was happening there.' She spoke with confidence, her accent that of the old landed classes. Once she would have been very beautiful.

'Can you get me in? Into the house?'

'I can, but then you will get caught up with the police.' She turned slowly to Cage and looked at him closely. 'You are looking for that little boy. Why else would you jump over garden walls? Are you his father?'

Cage turned away from her. Then back again, trying to shake images of dead children from his mind, of thugs with guns who did most of the world's killing. Violet gazed at him with compassion.

'The men who took the boy and set fire to my house were members of a splinter gang of the Teochiu Triads.'

'Damn it! How do you know?'

'The tattoo on his wrist.' She paused, took two unsteady steps towards him and rested on her stick. 'They are all the same. You look like a tough young man to me. I saw your son's face, before they put the sack over his head. He's tough too. Be proud of him. Julie Maddox is distraught. The Americans are not like us Chinese. They aren't used to these things happening.'

'They're getting used to it,' he said softly.

'I thought she might come. Not you.'

Suddenly Cage understood. 'Is that why you were waiting?'

She ignored his question. 'You need help. You mustn't do something stupid like go to the police.'

'No,' Cage replied patiently. 'What should I do?'

'The Teochiu are in control here. Their insignia is two palm leaves – I think they're palm leaves – close together like this.' She cupped her hands in front of her. 'My father used to pay them protection in the thirties. But why they set fire to the house,' she shook her head, 'God only knows. That's what we do in China. Make violence because it's easier than doing anything else.'

'And they want ransom?'

'I expect so.'

'Did they tell you that?'

Violet smiled. 'I am an old lady who knows the rules. Where are you staying?'

Cage told her.

'I was kidnapped twice,' she recalled. 'When they wanted something from my father.' She tapped him on the elbow, and pointed to the policemen. 'Don't get caught up with the police,' she repeated. 'You should leave now.'

Cage didn't move. To leave this place would be like abandoning Paul. Yet he trusted this frail, elegant woman and he needed to find Sally. 'I will tell his mother,' he said. 'I'll be back at my hotel four hours from now.'

'They'll wait. They won't kill him straightaway.' She took off her hat and pushed back thin strands of hair. 'But don't show your anger. Do what they say or they might do something like this.' The area on the right side of Violet's head where her ear should have been was crossed with two red scars and flaps of useless skin. 'They did it on the first kidnapping. No anaesthetic.' Her eyes were watering. 'Go now. Go to your hotel and wait.'

Back in the hotel, Cage called the American Embassy in Beijing from his room and didn't care who traced the call. He wanted to be found. He wanted confrontation. With Paul kidnapped, he needed someone to hit, not hours of waiting in an anonymous hotel room.

'Mr Gregg is in a meeting,' said Maeve, not even offering to take a message.

'I'll stay on the line while you tell him that the man who saved his life at the Zhao Long Hotel wants to speak to him now.'

'That'll be very difficult.'

'He's in the embassy?'

'I believe so.'

'Then get him on the line . . .'

'I'm afraid that would be impossible.'

'. . . or I'll make sure he's dead two days from now.'

Maeve hung up. Cage called back and started speaking as soon as she picked up the line. 'You put that phone down again and, like I said, I'll kill Richard Gregg. Tell him it's Bill Cage.'

When Richard came on, he said, 'Captain Cage. It's been a long time. I believe I owe you my life. But then I believe you planted the bomb that almost took it.'

Cage ignored Richard's sarcasm. 'Wu Tian has kidnapped Paul. Wu Tian is your man, Gregg. Like Thomas Ford and Ta Sot, Ken Son and all those other butchers in Cambodia were your men.'

244

'Your histrionics are unhelpful.'

'I'm in the Golden Flower Hotel in Xian. You will find Paul. You will have him at this hotel by six tomorrow morning. If you fail, I'll do what I should have done to Ford. I'll kill you.'

By the time Cage left the hotel to find Sally, it was well after dark. As his cab approached the tomb, he saw more and more people camping by the roadside, illuminated by the flames of their camp fires. Makeshift altars had been erected on stools and tables, draped in red cloth, with sickles and stars. Passers-by threw in money and leant down to kiss statues of Mao Zedong.

At the foot of the tomb, Cage had to step over people rolled up in sleeping blankets. On the steps they slept sitting up, heads on each other's shoulders, and Cage climbed up around them. He found the two broken branches of the pomegranate tree and was soon following Sally's path. He reached the probe, but there was no Sally. He scrawled a note and taped it to the polythene cover. 'Room 710, Golden Flower Hotel. Urgent. Paul is missing.'

Chapter Twenty-eight

Every so often, he would turn to check she was following and beckon her along. He didn't speak a word. Sally found herself being led along paths on the side of the mound, criss-crossing areas she knew and some she didn't until they arrived at the entrance of a long, narrow cave, lit by a single candle flame shielded in a bamboo case.

Sally saw flickering silhouettes dancing around the walls and people – she was sure they were people – crouched or lying down, dark shapes under the low ceiling. Beyond them the cave was unlit and in darkness.

Her mute guide rocked excitedly from side to side, then signalled for her to stay just inside the entrance.

As her eyes became accustomed to the dimmer light, she saw that the people inside were actually on their knees, hands clasped as if they were in prayer. On the wall was a simple cross, two branches of a tree strapped together with tape or wire. Underneath was a table, covered in a cloth, with a smaller cross in the centre, a bowl next to it, the candle and a book, or a box – the flickering light wasn't good enough to see clearly.

'Who are you all?' she asked in a whisper.

Clothes rustled and heads turned towards her, eyes just as curious as hers. The mute shuffled back to her and tugged at her elbow for her to move further inside.

'Do you live here?'

The mute nodded. But none of the others answered. She expected the familiar smells of decaying vegetation and stale air. But the cave was spotlessly clean. It was difficult to tell how many there were. Twenty? Maybe more if they stretched right down into the darkness.

The mute pulled out a stool for each of them. They sat side by side. For the first time Sally saw how terribly deformed he was and why his figure was so contorted.

'What happened to you?'

He put a gnarled finger to his mouth, indicating she should be quiet. He rustled under the stool and brought out a Bible. She noticed three fingers missing on his right hand. The other two were curled up on themselves. He pushed over the pages, like a child who couldn't fully coordinate its limbs, until he got to the title page. It was in English. He was holding the King James's Authorised Version of the Bible.

He stabbed his finger to emphasise his point, then turned the pages to the place he wanted. He pushed the Bible into Sally's hands.

With her finger on the page to keep the place, Sally turned back to the front, staring to see if there was an inscription, something to tell her how a battered Bible had got here. 'Nanjing, 1928' it said in English, followed by a name in Chinese characters which she couldn't make out.

She flipped the pages back again and looked up. On the left-hand side of the table, a man, in a clergyman's cassock, with a tattered white dog collar and purple cape, held a Bible in hands held open like a lectern. 'And when the chief shepherd shall appear, ye shall receive a crown of glory that fadeth not away,' he read in Chinese. The candle lit half his face, and the faltering light threw up a huge shadow of a man, hands and book on the wall of the cave behind.

The light was just enough for Sally to read the text as she listened to the Chinese. The silence and intensity of the congregation made her feel an incredible peace, as if her own Christian culture thousands of miles away had suddenly been shipped into Shaanxi Province. The people around her all seemed to be deformed in some way. As her eyes improved she could see that many were without limbs or were otherwise horribly injured. Those lying flat on the ground had slabs of wood on wheels by their side, presumably their only means of getting around. Some had walking sticks next to them. Others fumbled about, unable to see.

When the service was over, the congregation shuffled further down inside the cave. They helped each other, moving painfully slowly. A pathway had been smoothed along the floor for those who needed to wheel themselves along. The more able carried with them stools and the altar table. The clergyman, taking the cross from the wall, was the last to go and, as he joined them, they began singing a hymn which echoed round the walls. A wedge of light appeared right at the end, sending out a beam which lit them up as they moved through.

Sally turned urgently to the mute who had guided her here. He held her hand. He was surprisingly gentle. She pointed towards the light. 'Are they going into the tomb?' she asked.

He nodded, then flattened his hand on her shoulder, telling her to wait.

Sally worked out that she was in one of the four entrances Zhang Ying might have used to get into the mausoleum. The cave was like a tunnel. The rock had been hewn out by hand, and the floor concreted over.

'Who are you?' asked Sally after they had sat in silence for a few minutes. 'Are you Zhang Ying? Did you record the tapes?'

He lowered his head, his expression sad. After a few moments he got up awkwardly, using Sally's shoulder for support, and shuffled further into the cave, leaving Sally alone.

Then came a voice. No person, no shape was attached to it, only the words straining out of the darkness.

'I am Zhang Ying, Dr Parsons.'

Immediately, Sally knew that the mute was only a messenger, and that she was now listening to the same rasping voice she'd heard in Jeff Binsky's house.

She strained her eyes, but there was a sea of blackness around her and she realised that Zhang Ying had no intention of being seen. She stepped forward.

'Don't look, Dr Parsons. I am not a pretty sight.'

'You are the person who made the recordings?'

'You have done good work. We have been watching you look

inside the tomb. I had hoped you would know Jeff Binsky, and you did.'

'You knew him?'

'Oh yes, and we know that you know about the tomb.' The voice wavered. Sally heard a stick scraping on the concrete, and saw movement in the blackness. Without thinking, she stepped forward again, and Zhang Ying melted away. 'Please, I am not ready.'

'I'm sorry,' said Sally gently.

'All of us here are victims of the Cultural Revolution. The Red Spirit movement wants to return China to those times. I knew how they were doing it, but I had no way to tell the world except by sending Jeff the tapes.'

'You asked who we are,' the voice creaked on. 'I will tell you. We are Christians – Catholics and Protestants. All of us have a deep belief in God. Some of us have lived in these caves since the Cultural Revolution and have become part of them. There are people like us all over China. Buddhists and Muslims as well, hiding from the forces which try to destroy us. Your guide, the man who cannot speak, was a great student poet from Shanghai. Tao Chian. You won't have heard of him because his work was destroyed. It was so clever and questioning that they cut out his tongue and vocal chords and threw him from an upstairs window onto the street.'

Tao was nowhere in sight and no one else was with her, yet she felt safe in the blackness.

'And you? What happened to you?'

'I was in a fire. They saved my life in Moscow.'

'What fire? When?'

'During the Cultural Revolution, the Red Guards came and burnt anything they found. I was engulfed in flames, just for a few seconds, but it was enough. My body, my lungs, my skin are all irreparably damaged. All these people have their own stories of fires and beatings and killings.'

Sally thought she saw the shadow of an arm reaching out, but then it withdrew.

'I was saved by Mao Zedong's wife Jiang Ching. It was she who sent me to Moscow for specialist treatment. I stayed there for five years. Recovering from burns is a long process. It gave

249

me life, but I am still hideous, which is why you must listen to me from the darkness.'

'So that is why she called you to Mao's death bed.'

'Yes. Mao was obsessed with immortality and Jiang Ching was obsessed with her own future. With Mao dead, she was nothing.' Zhang Ying tried to laugh, but it became a cough. 'She was right,' he went on when his throat had cleared. 'She's in jail now. Did you listen to my tapes?'

'I heard some and I read Jeff's translation.'

'He translated? Good. So you know the story.'

Suddenly, the security she had felt in being with Zhang Ying drained away. 'You mean it's true? The heroin trafficking?'

'Yes. It's true.'

Sally felt around the wall of the cave, found a patch of even ground and sat down. 'Your descriptions of the tomb were very detailed. I'm sure that's why Jeff thought it was authentic. You talked of the weeping wind.'

'We watched you, Sally. We knew he had the railway. We know some of the places he's storing it. But not all of them. We don't know if he has refineries here. We hoped you would find something which would give us answers.'

'Did I?'

'Yes. You showed us the way to the main entrance of the tomb.'

'Facing east toward the terracotta warrior army.'

Zhang Ying lapsed into silence. Then he spoke, hesitantly and so softly that Sally couldn't hear.

'Sorry?' Sally said. 'I didn't get that.'

'I asked about Jeff. How is he?'

Sally put her hands on the rock face. It was cool like marble. 'Jeff's . . . I'm afraid he passed away.'

'Passed away?'

'Someone broke into his house and killed him. It was the night he gave me your recording.' She clasped her hands to her face. 'Oh my God, that was why.'

Zhang Ying coughed, a sickly, coarse hacking from far inside the lungs. Then he went quiet. There was a scuffing to one side, and the mute was back. He sat down next to Sally. Zhang Ying spoke again, his voice faltering and sad. 'Yes, I fear it might have been. My tapes were his death sentence.'

'Don't blame yourself,' said Sally.

'Thank you.'

'How did you know Jeff?'

His next words took Sally by complete surprise. 'We were lovers.'

'Lovers?'

'Lovers in the days of Maoist China, when to kiss and be in love could mean a labour camp.' Sally craned her neck to try to see him. Zhang Ying laughed, rasping, cracking, deep. 'You assume I am a man.'

'Yes. Yes of course.'

'My ruined voice disguises my gender. My real name was Yu Yi. I am the wife of Wu Tian, who tried to burn me to death. I saw him throw a petrol bomb at me, and my daughter watched me go up in flames. I fell backwards off the balcony and a child saved me by throwing blankets over me. I never saw my family again. In Moscow, I yearned to be back with my daughter, but as the years wore on, Yu Yi slowly died and I became Zhang Ying, too deformed, too horrible to be a mother again. It is better that my daughter believes I am dead.' Yu Yi's voice shifted as she moved. Sally thought she saw a bundle on the ground, perhaps clothing, but she could make out no face. Yu Yi, barely distinguishable from the rocks around them, kept speaking.

Wu Tian and I were both brought up as Christians and educated in mission schools before the revolution. We had a vision of creating a better China. Wu Tian changed, of course. Maybe it was because he knew I could never love him as I had loved Jeff. Do you know what I mean, how a woman can only ever love one man?'

Sally swallowed hard and felt Tao touch her elbow. 'You . . . and Jeff?' she muttered.

'Don't be surprised. Why do you think I sent him the tapes? Tell me, did he ever marry?'

'No. No, he didn't,' stammered Sally. 'The last time I saw him, the day he was killed, he talked . . .' Sally checked herself and started again as that late afternoon conversation flooded back to her. 'Yes, I think he did speak about you, with great love. He asked if I ever felt I belonged to China. Then he said he loved the contours of her land, her vicious rivers and the unyielding harshness of her countryside. "I loved her because she was so different," he told me. The way he said it, I think he must have been talking about you. Did you tell him you were Zhang Ying?'

'I didn't. I was afraid he would be married. What would have been the point of stirring up all those emotions?' Yu Yi fell quiet for a moment. 'Besides, we had a child – a little boy.'

'A little boy?'

'Yes. It was wonderful and dreadful. Jeff was a foreigner. When I became pregnant, I was determined not to have an abortion. I couldn't abort a child created with a man I loved so much. Yet I knew the child would be taken from me, and he was, in the summer of nineteen fifty-seven.'

With trembling hands, Sally reached inside her coat and touched Cage's locket. Cage was born in June 1957, the same month Jeff left China. It all fitted.

'Why? Why would they take your son?' she asked.

'I was a school teacher and a member of the Party. A relationship with a foreigner was illegal. I kept the pregnancy hidden under my Mao tunic for as long as I could. But when I became too big, there was only one person I could turn to for help. Wu Tian and Jeff were best friends and Wu managed to get my baby adopted through an American agency. But he had to name Jeff as the father, and Jeff had to be deported. He both betrayed me and saved me,' said Yu Yi. 'I would never have forgiven myself if my son had been killed or brought up in a labour camp. Yet to lose both my baby and his father at the same time . . . it was almost too much to bear.'

Sally listened to the painful, rasping voice and felt appalled by what she herself had done to Cage, removing his son to China, out of his reach, forcing him to negotiate through a third party for permission to see Paul. She brought out the locket and clasped it in her hands. Jeff had known that pain. She remembered how his expression had darkened when she'd asked him why he had left China. Had he ever tried to find his son in America?

'I married Wu,' Yu Yi went on, 'and I loved him, but not like I loved Jeff Binsky. I could never love another man in the same way.'

'So Wu turned against you?'

'He turned against himself. He tried to make the revolution a more powerful force than human love. While the revolution made him feel like a king, his wife made him feel a lesser man, because you can't fake love. You just can't. And eventually the only way he could find his release was to get the revolution to kill me.'

'By burning you to death,' Sally whispered.

'For weeks he had been criticising me for using the old textbooks. We didn't have anything else, but he said it was better to use nothing than teach the word of capitalism. So I asked him, "Is the law of gravity different in Beijing and New York. Does an apple fall differently from a tree?" He answered with a quotation from Mao. He was doing that more and more. Whenever I tried to discuss something, he would retreat into Mao.' She paused and cleared her throat. 'His world couldn't live with primary school logic because his was an illogical world. Mao was trying to push society against the laws of nature.'

Sally nodded in the darkness. 'That's what Jeff said. Exactly what he told me.'

'What did he say?'

'Something like instead of people loving their parents, Mao demanded they betray them to the mobs. Instead of bringing up their children, parents were asked to hand them over to the Communist Party.'

'Yes. We talked about that. And my husband believed it was right. He was swept along with the revolution. He didn't understand that actually he was driven by his own emotions.'

'What do you mean?'

'The day he sent the Red Guards to my school was the eleventh anniversary of his declaration of love for me. August the thirtieth, nineteen sixty-eight. My baby born with Jeff would have just turned eleven. My daughter with my husband was about to turn nine. He had to kill me in front of our daughter, to show there was no shame in what he was doing. In his mind, it wasn't him who threw the petrol bomb, it was the revolution. The higher cause swallowed up his wife for the greater good.'

'But why didn't you confront him? See your daughter again?'

'It was better to let him think I was dead. It gave him the release he needed. If he wasn't rid of the bitterness, I was convinced my daughter would be next.'

Sally took a deep breath. 'I have a friend who is looking for his mother. This is her picture.' She leaned across to Tao and gave him the locket. He limped off, not far, maybe thirty feet into the darkness. A lighter flared, showing two heads together, looking at the photograph, just for a second. Yu Yi's head was covered, her features impossible to make out.

'Do you know her?' whispered Sally.

'Come here,' said Yu Yi. 'Come closer to me. I want to feel you.'

Sally got up and walked slowly towards the voice.

'That's far enough.'

Sally stopped. She felt the locket being pressed into her hand. Cloth and skin briefly brushed her.

'Please, step back now.'

'Is it you?' Sally asked under her breath. Her head was spinning. She put her arms behind her, felt her way back to the wall and leant against it.

'I'm sorry, I don't know her,' said Yu Yi with finality. 'I wish it was me. But it is not.'

Deflated, Sally slipped the locket back into her pocket.

'That little boy who comes with you sometimes, is he your son?' asked Yu Yi, her tone brighter.

'Yes. His name is Paul.'

'And the man searching?'

'Paul's father.'

Tao touched her elbow and guided her forward again. Sally felt her hand being grasped, felt the damaged tissue and mis-shapen fingers. Dawn was breaking and light was flowing through the entrance of the cave, but Yu Yi managed to stay in shadow. Sally saw the shape of a face, but nothing more.

'Go now,' said Yu Yi. 'We have to stop my husband. He is

clever. To the masses, he is just a writer, a columnist. No one has actually seen him or heard him speak. To his lieutenants around China, he is the paymaster. He delivers money. They deliver devotees, the poor, the uneducated, the excluded. He gives them something to belong to.'

'They are outside now,' said Sally. 'They're coming.'

'So I've been told. He knows he will either succeed or fail in the next few days. The demonstrations in Tiananmen Square are helping him as well. If his forces join up with the forces among the students, there will be war. The army will be divided, the people will be divided, the regions will be divided. We have to persuade those people outside that they are chasing a fantasy and they must go home.'

Chapter Twenty-nine

Amid the uncertainty he faced, Richard Gregg knew two things: that Bill Cage would carry out his threat to kill him and that Christine was his key to getting Paul released. He finally tracked her down through her office to the Great Hall of the People in Tiananmen Square. She was part of the Communist Party leadership negotiations with the students who had now taken over the square.

Richard got his driver to drop him as close to the square as possible. There must have been tens of thousands there, with trucks still ferrying demonstrators in, not just students, but worker's groups, trade unions, a cross-section of China's disgruntled society.

The sky was black with rain and the crowds whispered about the Mandate of Heaven and dark portents of approaching calamity.

Richard made his way towards the Great Hall of the People, treading through the rubbish, broken glass, cigarette butts and squalor of the demonstration. Deafening slogans pounded out from loudspeakers strung up around the Monument to the People's Martyrs in the middle of the square. 'Down with Deng Xiao-ping,' a voice shrieked into the microphone. 'End his hooligan government. Kill Li Peng.'

Richard stepped gingerly over mattresses where the students slept, using each other's bodies as pillows. He pulled out his diplomatic pass and jostled his way past the Western television crews trying to get access to the Great Hall of the People. The meeting had just broken up. Students emerged at the top of the steps, defiant, punching their fists in the air. 'They don't under-stand the power of our movement,' shouted one student leader. 'They're too old and they've been in office too long.'

Richard ran up the steps into the Great Hall, trying to catch Christine. He spotted her pushing through a side door, cutting across and down. She was running. Someone shouted after her to come back. She dropped a pen, which rolled at her feet on the steps. She didn't bother to pick it up.

'Christine!' Richard shouted.

She turned, saw him and froze, her face full of confusion, then kept going into the crowd.

'Po Ki,' yelled Richard again, using her Chinese name. But his voice was drowned out by the racket from the speakers. Christine kept running towards the Forbidden City. Richard was faster, jumping over people, not caring if he trod in their lunch boxes or spilt their water bottles. He grabbed her elbow. She shook herself free. He caught up with her again, spun her round to him and slapped her face. 'Christine! For Christ's sake! Do you want to listen to me or spend the next ten years in jail?'

She caught her breath and held her hand up to her face. 'Fuck you, too!' she spat.

Richard kept hold of her elbows, aware that dozens of people were now watching them. 'Christine. Stop it. Get a grip on yourself.'

'They fired me. Zhao Zhiyang's about to be fired.' She struggled free of him and swept her hands around the square. 'The students don't know it, Richard. Li Peng was wearing a grey Mao suit, just like Dad. They're so innocent, these guys. They can't tell from his eyes what he's going to do. I know. I've seen that look before.'

'On your father's face,' said Richard, his voice gentler. 'When you were a child.'

Christine started walking again, but slowly, allowing Richard to keep up with her.

'Listen,' he said, 'if the army moves in here, you and anyone connected with reform will be on their hit list.' He pointed up at the portrait of Mao above Tiananmen Gate. 'China's going to revert back to him.' He caught her shoulder and made her stop.

'What do you suggest I do?' she said.

'Stop your father doing something terrible. Only you can do it.'

'I have no influence over him.'

'You've tried to help here, more than anyone else. But it's too big for any of us. But with your father, you can help. He's kidnapped a little boy and is going to kill him.'

'Why should I help you?'

Richard put his hand under her chin to make her look at him. 'Because if you do, I will get you US residency.' He pointed around the square. 'You can have a life away from all this chaos.'

Christine softened, but asked, 'And why should my father listen to me?'

'You're the only person in the world he cares about.'

'Crap.'

'It was he who planted the bomb that nearly killed us.'

Christine's face darkened. 'My God. Did he know I would be there? How can you say I'm the only person . . . It doesn't make sense.'

'He needed to kill you to *stop* caring about you. Just like your mother.'

Sunlight streamed into the room, showing up the dust and the emptiness of her father's study. The door was hanging open and she knocked on it gently. 'Father?' she said, stepping just inside. The narrow room had been stripped. The books, the carpets, the desk – all gone. The rooms to the left and right were empty as well. 'Father, it's Po Ki,' she said again.

Wu Tian appeared wearing an immaculately pressed blue Mao suit with a Mao badge pinned below the left lapel. 'Why aren't you with those pansy traitors in Tiananmen Square?' he asked.

'They're going to lose. Zhao Zhiyang will be fired. Deng has accused him of joining the side of turmoil.'

'Good,' said Wu, pulling down the cuff of the tunic and smoothing back his hair. 'And you will lose your job as well and be sent to prison. So you have come to your father for help.'

'That's right,' lied Christine. Her passport with the stamp in it was taped firmly to her inner thigh. She knew Richard would put a block on the visa if she tried to use it before Paul was freed. 'But there is something else.'

'Why should I help you? You've been a bad daughter.'

'I know. I'm sorry. I was wrong.' She stepped further in, repulsed by what she was about to do. 'But the little boy your men have kidnapped has done nothing wrong.'

Wu was taken aback. His expression changed, unable to conceal his surprise.

Christine used it to her advantage. 'I don't know why you have taken him, but I beg you to release him.'

'Why should I act against the wishes of the state?'

God, how she loathed him! 'Father, this is nothing to do with the state,' she said gently.

'It will not save you from prison. Why do you care about a little boy?'

'Why have you taken him?'

'That is none of your concern.'

She wound her arms round his shoulders. Wu stiffened. Christine pulled him towards her in an embrace. 'I am your daughter. You are my father. Do this for me and we can love each other again.'

'We cannot until you learn to love China, until you accept why your mother had to die.'

'I do,' whispered Christine. 'Now I do.'

'You came to me saying you were marrying an American.'

Christine shook her head and buried it in his shoulder. 'I only said that to upset you. There is no lover. You have shown me the true China and how it should be. The love between father and daughter is unconquerable.'

Clumsily, he returned her embrace. 'Do you,' he stammered, 'do you really understand me?'

'Yes, I do,' she whispered. 'I was wrong.' She stepped back from him, wiping a fake tear from her eye.

'I am going to Qin Shi Huang's tomb. You must come with me,' said Wu Tian, straightening out his tunic. 'Come with me and I will free the little boy. With my daughter by my side, I have no need for him any more.'

Deng Xiao-ping, cigarette between his fingers, was watching CNN broadcasts from Tiananmen Square. The foreign press were in China because of Mikhael Gorbachev's visit, yet the Soviet President had been unable to get to the main entrance of the Great Hall of the People because of the demonstration in the square.

Deng had been hunted and purged. He had killed, had commanded battles and had helped carve China into what it was today. Now, in his mid-eighties and his country's supreme leader, he found himself facing one of its darkest moments.

In front of him were confidential reports from other cities – Shanghai, Tianjin, Harbin, Lanzhou, Wuhan, Changsha – detailing protest after protest. A thousand miles away near Xian, probably the most threatening of them all was taking place. Tens of thousands were making the journey to the tomb of the Emperor Qin Shi Huang, praying for a return to Maoism.

Deng dropped his cigarette into an ashtray and walked into the adjoining reception room where he took the armchair allocated for him in the centre, with a spittoon by its side. Around the room were the Communist Party elders.

'Imagine for a moment what would happen if China fell into turmoil,' he began, slowly looking around the room at the men he had known for decades. 'If this was a problem confined to Tiananmen Square, my opinion might not be so resolute. But from Shanghai to Kunming, from Hohot to Lanzhou, demonstrators are on the streets. Many people are going to the tomb of Qin Shi Huang because they believe Mao Zedong is going to come to life again there. In Chengdu, I hear that the Rose Empress restaurant has burnt down and people have stormed into a hotel for foreign guests. All of their demands are different. Some want Chairman Mao. Some want President Bush.

'If China falls into turmoil now, it would be far worse than the Cultural Revolution. There would be civil war, with opposing factions controlling different parts of the army. Blood would run and refugees would flow out of China not in millions or tens of millions but in hundreds of millions. This would be a disaster on a global scale. So China mustn't make a mess of itself again. A nation that cannot agree on its destiny is a very dangerous place.'

Chapter Thirty

Cage saw the pistol through the spyglass of his hotel room door. When he opened it, a hand shoved his shoulder, pushing him back inside. A second man came in and shut the door behind him. They were the same two policemen who had chased Sally through the tunnels.

Cage put up his hands, looking Arrogant in the eye, and stepped back to give both men space to move in. Baby Face searched him, pulled the revolver out of his jacket pocket and gave it to Arrogant. 'You want to see the boy,' he stated.

'Why do you think I'm being so nice to you?' replied Cage.

Baby Face opened the door, and Arrogant dropped his weapon to his side. The three of them walked to the lift. As they crossed the foyer, Cage saw Violet sitting at the bar. For a few seconds their eyes locked. She seemed to be mouthing something at him, but before he could read it, Arrogant had hurried him out of the door and into the car.

Mok hadn't spoken one word to Paul. He had made him dress in a little blue Mao suit but had not treated him badly. After delivering him to the farmhouse, Mok delegated Paul's safety to his men. His orders were to keep Paul unharmed until Wu Tian arrived at the tomb.

They had taken him at night while he was asleep, put a sack over his head and bundled him into the back seat of a car. Paul had felt as though he couldn't breathe. He had coughed and thrashed his arms about, until a hand pushed him down onto the floor and kept him there.

262

Terrified and unable to see, Paul had counted the minutes, folding a finger into the palm of his hand every sixty seconds. He had done two hands and was three fingers into a third when they turned off the road to the right. The track was bumpy. Feet pressed harder against his back to keep him down.

'Stop it, you're hurting me,' he yelled through the sack, and the pressure eased.

Two men had lifted him out and walked him into the house. He could smell the freshness of the air, and wood smoke. They allowed him to keep the hood off, as long as he stayed inside the house. He was pretty certain he had been driven out of Xian to the west, which meant he was close to the Terracotta Warrior Museum where his mother worked.

When he felt safer, Paul told them the food was lousy and that he needed his school books, a football, a new T-shirt and jeans, crayons, paint and paper, and a bicycle. They got everything he asked for, except the bicycle.

It was mid-morning now and Paul was painting a picture of the house he had been kidnapped from, with the trampoline, rocking horse and huge garden at the back. One guard was cleaning a pistol and smoking. Three other men were sitting around, their weapons on their laps.

'You're not going to shoot me, are you?' said Paul in Chinese to the man cleaning his gun. His lined face looked as if it had seen a war.

'If you misbehave, I'll have to,' said the guard, not looking up from his work.

The guard tore off a strip of tape, turned another magazine upside down, unclipped the magazine in the gun, bound the two together, and clipped it back in again. Paul didn't take his eyes off the man.

Paul remembered seeing a newspaper picture of a man carrying a gun like that and he'd asked his mother what it meant. But she was busy at the time, running here and there around the house tidying up because Richard was coming. 'I don't know anything about guns,' she had snapped.

'You don't know anything about bicycles but we talk about them,' he had shot back.

'Bicycles aren't guns,' she had said.

'Come on, Mom. All I want to know is why they put sticky tape on the thing that holds the bullets.'

She stopped puffing up the cushions and tidying the room but she didn't look at him. 'If you want to know about guns, ask your father,' she said.

She'd looked at him so weirdly, he had realised then that he'd better drop the subject. But now that he was hostage to a man with a gun, he had a chance to get an answer. 'Why do you put that tape on?' he asked the guard.

'You concentrate on what you're doing.'

'My dad knows more about guns than you do.'

'Is that a fact? Then what does he say about putting the tape on?' The guard ran a cloth over the weapon, laid it on the table and looked at Paul.

Paul wished he'd asked Cage when they were in the taxi together going to school. But if you see your dad once every four years, you can't remember to ask him everything. He didn't dare look back at the guard. He should have kept his mouth shut. He wetted his paintbrush and got back to the picture.

'You going to tell me what your dad says?' asked the guard.

'I'm concentrating on what I'm doing,' mumbled Paul. He didn't think they would shoot him. He closed his eyes tight shut and mentally counted Ko's puppies. While he was doing it, he heard the rumble of a truck coming down towards the house. All he wanted to do was go home. It didn't matter whether his mom knew about guns or not.

The truck stopped. All four guards picked up their weapons and went outside. Paul left his picture and crept to the window to see what was happening.

The truck was full of soldiers, sitting back to back. Four jumped to the ground, their weapons pointed at the guards.

Paul stared motionless for a moment. It was as if the guards had forgotten about him. He was pretty sure he could get from the house to his mother's office, and absolutely certain that he wanted to see her.

He slipped back to the kitchen, where there was a door. He opened it and ran out of the house, round the side and headed straight up the slope behind into an orchard. He crawled further and further up until he could see over the roof of the house.

The shouting below got louder and one of the guards was gesticulating with his revolver. Then there was an almighty crashing sound as one of the soldiers fired into the air. Paul fell to the ground and gripped hold of a tree. He had never heard gunfire before. Everything went quiet, and when he peeked again, the guards were lying flat on the ground, their faces in the dirt.

'Your activities here are illegal,' he heard one of the soldiers say in Chinese. 'We are here on the direct orders of the army commander.'

Two soldiers kicked open the door of the house and went in. One came out through the kitchen door and looked up towards Paul. But Paul was flat on the ground, hidden by a tree.

He tried to stop himself breathing. The man looked around but didn't seem to be searching for anything in particular. He walked to the front of the house. Paul's guards were being forced to climb onto the back of the truck at gunpoint. For a moment, Paul thought about running out and telling them who he was. But the gunfire had frightened him, so he hid, watching the army truck disappear down the track. Then, his heart in his mouth, he went back into the house. It was strange, being so empty. He wetted his brush again, turned his picture over and wrote 'TOMB' in English on the blank side of the paper.

Paul started to walk. At the tomb would be people he knew. They would help him find his mother.

Cage was brought to the house shortly after noon. Baby Face, who had driven, kept a weapon on him while Arrogant got out of the car. Arrogant looked up at the house where the door swung open, then down at the dirt track that bore the tyre markings of a military vehicle. Cage could tell from his face that something was wrong. Arrogant went into the house. He reappeared a few seconds later round the back. 'The boy's gone,' he said flatly. He scraped his foot in the tyre marks. 'The army has been here. They must have taken him.'

'Taken him where?' snapped Cage. 'Who's taken him?' Cage

wanted Paul more than anything. He wanted time with his son, he wanted to talk to him about those empty years when he had grown from a toddler to a boy and Cage hadn't seen him at all.

Arrogant got back in the car next to Cage. 'Drive back,' he said to Baby Face in Chinese. 'We'll check with Mok.'

The mention of Mok decided Cage. Until then, he hadn't quite been able to read the two cops.

Cage waited until Baby Face had set off, the speedometer flickering up to thirty kilometres an hour along the track, with a ditch on the right and a steep drop on the left.

Suddenly, Cage knocked Arrogant's weapon arm into the air, rammed his body against him and opened the right side door. Arrogant half fell out. Cage wrenched Arrogant's pistol from him, then kicked his legs so he landed clear of the car on the track. Baby Face braked.

'Keep driving,' yelled Cage, leaning forward, making sure Baby Face saw the pistol pointed at him. But he had misjudged the young policeman. Baby Face opened his own door. He fell out in a controlled roll and came up firing his weapon into the car.

'Shit,' muttered Cage. The engine was still running, the car sliding forward towards a bridge and a dry river bed. Cage threw himself over into the front seat as two shots crashed through the bodywork. Cage got his right hand to the accelerator and his left onto the bottom of the steering wheel. He was steering blind.

He gave the accelerator one last shove and hurled himself out. He landed on the stony hillside. Ahead, the car gathered speed, tipped over the edge of the slope then turned on itself and crashed into rocks on the edge of the river. The fuel tank caught fire. A ball of flame shot into the air, subsided, then another huge explosion sent fire and debris flying, setting light to grass and trees.

Cage heard footsteps on the small stones behind him, turned and fired, sensing more than knowing his target. Arrogant fell back, hit, lost his balance and tumbled down the hillside.

A pall of smoke covered the burning car. Cage crawled towards it, knowing that Baby Face, the smarter one, was up there somewhere. He took a lungful of breath and swallowed to clear the bile collecting in his throat. Then, plunging into the black reek of burning oil, he clambered back up onto the road. Baby Face had taken cover, expecting Cage to be somewhere else.

Cage fired, hidden by the smoke, hitting the ground a couple of feet from where Baby Face was. Baby Face fired back, but he couldn't see his target. The Cage shouted, 'Drop it.'

Baby Face let off another shot. Cage returned fire, just inches from him. And Baby Face dropped his weapon.

Cage emerged from the smoke, his clothes and face blackened. He held the pistol in both hands, levelled at the centre of Baby Face's chest.

'Hands on your head. Turn round and walk back to the house,' commanded Cage. 'Your friend is dead. So don't mess it up.'

When they got to the house, Cage asked, 'Is it booby-trapped?'
'I don't know.'

Cage couldn't see anything. No wires. No freshly disturbed ground. No planks of wood or pieces of metal on the ground to conceal landmines. But that didn't mean it was safe.

He ordered Baby Face in first, keeping him in sight, gave it ten seconds and followed. He saw Paul's painting kit, but no picture.

'Where is he?'
'I don't know.'
'Where is he?' Cage shouted.

Baby Face shook his head. 'I tell you, I don't know. Our instructions were to bring you to him.'

'What do you think happened?'

'We are police, not military.' He pointed out of the side door. 'Those tracks are from a military vehicle. It means soldiers were here.'

'Whose soldiers?'

'The soldiers are loyal only to Beijing.'

'And you?'

Baby Face pushed back the sleeve of his uniform to reveal the cupped leaf emblem of his Triad society.

'The fucking Teochiu,' muttered Cage.

'Fucking Teochiu,' repeated Baby Face in English. 'If the soldiers came here, it means Beijing ordered them to. The army's been sent to break us up, us and the students in Tiananmen Square all at once.'

'And Paul? The boy?'

Baby Face shrugged. 'If the soldiers came, he's safe. They'll take him to his parents.'

Cage said nothing. He wanted to scream that he, Bill Cage, was Paul's father. But that would be a weakness, something he couldn't afford. Just then, as Cage's mind raced, he saw the picture. It had fallen to the floor. He picked it up, read the message TOMB, and thrust it in front of Baby Face.

'Right. Take me there,' he demanded.

A gentle hum started up from the back of the house, seeping around them. Cage couldn't pinpoint what it was. A vehicle? Aircraft? Insects in the woods? Gradually it became louder, swelling like cheering from a sports stadium. Baby Face went outside, Cage followed him, the gun still levelled, but knowing that the time for killing was over.

Now they could distinctly hear human voices, hundreds of thousands of them, echoing and cascading through the country-side around, getting louder and louder, like a slow, rumbling roll of thunder.

Chapter Thirty-one

The crowds stretched as far as Sally could see. Where there had been newly green fields, there was now a canvas of blue tunics and dark heads all the way to the Terracotta Warrior Museum and beyond. The road along which she and Ko had driven so often all those nights was blocked with vehicles abandoned when they could get no further, and devotees were filing around them. As Sally emerged from the cave, she saw she would have to walk three, maybe four, miles before she could get a taxi, if there were any around.

Police were trying to keep people off the burial mound itself. Sally was inside the cordon and the only way she could go was up. She followed the path back to the probe. Immediately she saw Cage's note, a fresh white piece of paper stuck with brown tape to the polythene. *Room 710, Golden Flower Hotel. Urgent. Paul is missing*.

Paul missing? What did he mean? Sally tore off the note and ran back down the path towards the only people she could trust – the cave-dwellers. She scratched herself against the tree branches and lost her footing on the dry ground, slipping, cutting herself. But she remembered how she had followed the mute, and kept to the same route.

The cave was empty. She went inside, walking deep into the darkness. All signs of human life had been stripped from it. Only the smooth concrete on part of the floor told her she was in the same place. She felt her way to the end, where she had seen the shaft of light. But she couldn't find the entrance.

'Yu Yi, Yu Yi,' she cried out. 'Help me. For God's sake, help!'

Silence. She left a note and ran out into the daylight, her lungs drawing in the summer air, her leg muscles tearing as they propelled her up, higher and higher through the orchards. If she could get to the top, she could find a way out. Somehow she had to get to Cage, to the hotel, to wherever she could find Paul.

She caught her breath, resting for a few seconds against a tree trunk, wishing she had never brought them to China, had never been enthralled by the damn tomb. She never wanted to see it again. She pushed herself up from the tree and started running again. She went out onto the main steps used by tourists, and looked down. The mass of blue tunics, dotted with banners, statues and flags rippled to the horizon like the sea.

Cage and Baby Face walked up to the hill above the farmhouse. From there they saw the extent of the crowd. The burial mound rose like an island above the flood of devotees. People were still arriving from all directions, gathered around altars and pictures, chanting and waving their arms in the air.

'They are waiting for the tomb to open,' said Baby Face.

Cage was close up behind Baby Face, the pistol still against his back. 'Get us through,' he said. 'One sign that you're trying to escape and I'll kill you.'

They walked down into the crowd, which parted obediently at the sight of Baby Face's uniform. They stepped around families cooking meals and people sleeping, several under a single blanket. The further they went through the crowd, the worse the stench was. Closer to the tomb, where people had been for longer, bodies were crammed together.

'Keep moving,' said Cage.

Baby Face smiled, but not sadistically. It was more an expression of acceptance. 'This has gone too far for me, too,' he said. 'Deng cannot let this happen. But he can't stop it either. He can move against the people in Beijing who want democracy, but not against those who support Mao.'

'Who do you support?' said Cage.

'I'm Teochiu. Who are you?'

'Let's just say I know your bosses in New York, so keep walking,' said Cage, nudging the barrel harder into his back.

'I'm as keen to end this as you are. Only if you are Chinese would you know how dangerous this is.'

When they reached the base of the tomb, Baby Face began an argument with the police guarding the entrance to the steps. They wouldn't accept his police pass. Then he lifted his sleeve to show them the tattoo of the Teochiu, cocked his head back in the direction of Cage and said, 'He's Teochiu, too. From New York.'

And suddenly they were through, once again in open space, heading towards the probe where Cage had left his note, with the steps almost to themselves.

Paul slipped in the mud, scrambled to his feet, but still couldn't see out from the crowd. He kept bumping his head on elbows and legs. He could hardly see any sky. How was he going to find his mother? He tried shouting for her, but it was too noisy, too many people, chanting, ringing bells and playing tapes.

The good thing was he could twist and squeeze between everyone because no one cared about a child. They all seemed in some crazy daze anyway. He kept heading up the side of the burial mound. He reckoned if he could get high enough to look down, he would spot her red hair.

'You can't go through.' A policeman took him by the shoulder and pushed him back. Paul fell face down. He wondered why he wasn't crying. Sometimes when his mom was around he'd cry at least once a day, if he fell down, hurt himself, specially if someone had pushed him down like the policeman. But right now crying didn't cross his mind.

He wiped a clod of mud off his face and before crawling back he watched how the police worked, in fours, with gaps between them. They were getting bored and talking together.

Paul crawled as close as he could to the police line and waited for what felt like hours. He heard that song, 'The East is Red', through a tinny speaker at least three times before he saw his moment – all the police in front of him were concentrating on lighting their cigarettes.

He sprinted across the line. One of them saw him but a moment later he was in the undergrowth, out of sight. Paul thought the policeman would chase him but instead he turned back to finish getting a light. Paul crawled further away until he felt safe enough to get to his feet and run.

He was hardly breathing he was so excited. How would he tell his mom about what he'd done? That was the trouble with just having a mother. She would fuss over him and tell him not to do it again. Bur a dad – he could really tell a dad about how he escaped from the Chinese policemen.

By the time he got to the top of the steps no one was taking any notice of him. Lots of people had got through the cordon, lots of children, too. But it wasn't crowded like below. A strong wind blew dust up everywhere and the board for the tourists with the map on it rattled about.

He stared down, but all he could see were people with black hair. There was no sign of his mother. Paul could see the museum, but how could he get there? He knew it was a mile and a half across the fields, and the thought of squeezing through a mile and a half of legs made him swallow hard, sit down and work out what he was going to do next.

He kept thinking about what his dad would have done. Not Richard who was going to be his dad, but Bill Cage, his real dad, whom Mom didn't like. Paul found he was kind of proud that his dad had gone off for all those years, because he knew about guns.

Halfway up the steps, Sally looked up in despair, then down at the crowds, and kept walking. She walked to think. Normally she would go to the police. But the police had tried to kill her. She would call Li Yi, but she didn't have a phone, and anyway, how could she trust him? Maybe Cage was around. Maybe he was back in the hotel waiting for her. She checked to see if anyone was carrying a mobile phone, but they hadn't properly reached China yet. She felt exhausted, but she just had to keep moving, moving up. Perhaps from the top she would be able to see a way to get back to Xian – and a telephone.

Then she couldn't go any further. She stopped, almost at the top, not wanting to get there and find herself defeated yet again. Her arms hung down by her side. She lowered her head and let the tears come, hoping that once they had finished she would have the strength to carry on.

The woman was tall like his mom and she moved in the same way. But what was she doing dressed like Ko? And with black hair? And why were her shoulders slouched, as if she was vomiting?

Apart from all that, she looked more like his mom than anyone else he'd seen, so he might as well give it a try.

'Mom! Mom!'

The high-pitched voice was unmistakably Paul's. In English. Sally looked up, her eyes blurred. There was Paul leaping down the steps towards her. Sally ran forward as he jumped down at her, two steps at a time, then missed his footing and almost knocked her over.

She held him, hugging him. 'Honey, I'm sorry. I'm so sorry.' She wiped her eyes so she could see him properly.

It was just like Paul had thought. His mom was upset; not proud of him. 'I escaped, just like in the movies. Wham! Wham!'

'But you're OK. You're OK. How did you get here?'

'I'm fine. I chased the policemen until they were so frightened of me.'

She pulled down the collar of his jacket, not knowing what to say. 'And how did you get dressed up like this?' she blurted out.

'How did I get dressed like this? What about you, Mom? Why's your hair all black? It looks gross! I nearly didn't recognise you.' Then, when Sally hugged him again, Paul couldn't stop his tears either.

From far below, Cage recognised the familiar movements of a woman he had known intimately. She was bending down and hugging her son. Then she took his hand and they began climbing to the top. He paused to watch them. After one hell of a bad day, the world was suddenly coming right. For the first time he was looking at Sally and Paul as his life. From a distance, amid the mayhem, there was something suddenly perfect about it all.

'Sal,' Cage yelled out. The wind was too strong and the hum

from the crowd too loud for the words to carry. 'Come on. Move it,' he said to Baby Face, and they set off in a jog to catch up.

'What the hell?' muttered Baby Face and stopped. In a second, Cage saw why.

Four men had come out of nowhere and were dragging Sally and Paul rapidly into the orchard. Cage only caught sight of Paul being scooped up, of Sally flailing and a hand being slapped across her face.

Cage flinched. From the way the hand moved and the body turned, he was pretty sure he was watching Mok at work again. He began to run – but he knew he was too late.

Sally was pushed to the ground and a sack put over her head. She was forced face down, legs splayed out, while hands searched her all over.

'Paul,' she choked. 'You OK?'

'Yeah.' His voice was muffled, barely audible. 'It's what they did to me before. You'll think you can't breathe but you'll be OK.'

They were taken down a gradual slope in the direction of Yu Yi's cave, but then the descent became steeper. Sally was being pushed along, hands gripping her elbows, in a forced march. Paul was in front of her, snapping in Chinese at his captors. 'You hurt me and my dad will come back and kill you.'

Soon they were on flat ground. Sally listened to the chanting of the crowd. 'The Great Helmsman will come again. The Second Coming to the Middle Kingdom.' The claustrophobia of the hood and the stench of waste and rotting food made her want to retch. She coughed, then tripped on a tree root and started falling, but her captors propelled her on.

The path turned sharply, almost doubling back, and then she felt the cooler air of one of the caves. A door opened, metal on concrete, and she was shoved inside, into air-conditioning and strong lighting. She could sense people around and heard men muttering in low voices.

'Wow, Mom I can't see a thing,' whispered Paul through his hood, 'but we're inside the tomb, aren't we, Mom? Actually inside?'

'Take these goddamn hoods off us?' Sally yelled to no one in particular.

No one answered. A rumbling sound came from what Sally judged to be the direction of the Terracotta Warrior Museum. As it got closer, she realised it was a train pulling up and she knew exactly where she was – on the eastern side of the tomb, about to be taken by underground railway to the museum.

She and Paul were made to step into one of the train's three small carriages, each of which took four people. Tunnel air rushed past them loudly as the train gathered speed. The journey didn't take long. The train stopped and they were helped out. None of their captors spoke. But the grip on her elbow eased and Paul reached for Sally's hand. He held it tight, his defiance subdued.

Their hoods were loosened and taken off. The sudden light was harsh. Paul rubbed his eyes. Sally squatted down and held him. 'I'm OK, Mom. Honest, I'm fine,' he whispered.

When she looked up she recognised she was in the chamber through which she had escaped from Baby Face and Arrogant. A hundred yards back was her own office, with crossbow warrior George in his humidity-controlled case. Overhead was the shopping emporium.

Mok was talking on a radio. 'Through here,' he said in Chinese, the first words he had spoken. Sally and Paul were led through a door in the wall into a lavish office. Wu Tian sat at a desk in the corner, underneath a poster of Mao, with statues of his other gods around him.

Guilt ran through Sally as much as fear. Paul was with her, prisoner of a demented monster because of her blind ambition.

'Good,' said Wu, standing up and rubbing his hands. 'Dr Parsons has arrived with her son.' He turned to Mok. 'I knew once we had the boy, the mother would follow.'

'What the hell are you playing at?' snorted Sally, trying to break free.

'Mom, what's happening?' Paul squeezed her hand harder.

'The next few hours will tell us what is happening,' Wu answered calmly. 'The spirit of Mao Zedong will be revealed to the people and China will find its way again.'

Wu's desk was empty, as if it had just been moved in. No notepad. No paper. No files. Just framed photographs on the walls of Mao, including one of his body lying in a sarcophagus in the Tiananmen Square Memorial Hall. To the left was a small table with a kettle, cups, napkins and a packet of Chinese biscuits. Next to them was a telephone.

Wu walked out from behind the desk and up to Sally. He brushed her cheek with his hand and she felt the coldness of his signet ring. 'You have changed the colour of your hair. You knew I didn't like it. You did it for me.' He moved to stroke it and Sally stepped back.

'And your son. He is very handsome. He must love me so much to come to see Uncle Wu.' He patted Paul on the head. Paul recoiled. Sally lunged forward to push Wu away, but he was ready and slashed her across the face. She stumbled and fell.

A door on the other side of the room slid open next to Mok, and Christine came in. She glanced at Sally, but she could have been looking through her to the wall beyond. She moved towards her father with great confidence and an inner calm that acknowledged no fear. She was a commanding figure, a sudden rival to Wu's authority. She walked across to Paul and put a hand on his shoulder.

'Go to your mother,' she said in English.

But Wu stopped him. He beckoned Mok, who took Paul to the side.

Wu reached up and touched Christine, who took his hand in both of hers and brought it up to her face. 'Father, I owe you a debt of gratitude. The sacrifices you have made for me are more than any daughter could have asked for.'

Wu gazed at Christine. His mouth opened and closed, trying to speak, but nothing came out. Then he stood up and father and daughter embraced, as if there was no one else in the room.

'You understand the higher aims of the revolution,' said Christine. She quoted from Mao: ' "We must have faith in the masses and we must have faith in the Party." '

Wu Tian wiped a tear from his cheek. 'On the Question of Agricultural Cooperation, July the thirty-first, nineteen fifty-five. Truly, you are my daughter returned.'

'We must let the boy go back to his parents,' said Christine. 'Just like your daughter has come back to you.'

In the middle of the floor, Sally scrambled to her feet.

Mok's eyes were darting everywhere around the room, the faithful servant, watching out for his master, guarding his hostage child. Mok's men shifted around, keeping to the walls, leaving the centre of the room to Sally, Christine and Wu.

Wu pointed to Sally. 'She cannot leave. Ever. She knows the secret of the tomb.'

'But the boy knows nothing,' said Christine calmly. 'Let Mok take him out. Li Yi will make sure he's safe.'

She walked across the room and talked directly to Mok. 'Let the boy go,' she said softly. But Mok's eyes shifted from Christine to Wu and when Christine spoke again, everything changed. 'Free the boy. My father doesn't understand the situation.'

'What don't I understand?' bellowed Wu. 'Why are you talking to Mok?'

'Father, free the boy, please. For me.'

'Come, boy. We can watch a picture show together.' Mok brushed past Christine, walking Paul back to Wu.

Sally put out a hand, as if to bar Mok's way. 'Paul, don't—'

Mok let Paul go, took two leisurely steps towards Sally and hit her in the solar plexus, doubling her up. He stepped back, smirking.

Paul cried out, turning towards Mok, his face filled with terror and confusion. He stood wavering between Wu, Mok and his mother who was gasping and heaving air into her lungs, trying to stay upright.

Wu moved quickly across the room and hit Christine across the face. 'You little bitch. You've been lying to me all the time.' He grabbed Paul by the shoulder and hauled him back behind his desk. He sat Paul on his lap, flicked a switch to dim the lights and projected a photograph onto a white section of the wall.

'Now, boy, we can look at our snapshots,' said Wu.

Sally recognised it immediately – Richard in bed with a Chinese girl. She stared at the naked woman wrapped round her lover, and then suddenly remembered who else was watching Wu's picture show.

'Paul. Close your eyes!' she shouted.

When she used that voice Paul knew there was no negotiation. Sally got a glimpse of Paul squeezing his eyes shut, putting his little fists across them, and Wu laughing at her.

Christine looked at the changing photographs projected onto the wall and the fight seemed to drain out of her. Her father had won; this was the final humiliation.

Sally's eyes moved from Christine to the pictures and back to Christine again, and the cold truth cut through her. The Chinese girl with Richard was Wu Tian's daughter, the same girl standing here dressed in a Mao suit. Sally looked back up at the wall. The picture there now was of Richard on the phone, Christine still naked, and a time and date code on the bottom told her that he was taking the call she had made to him.

In the next picture, Christine was on top of Richard, facing the camera, his hands clasped round her back, pulling her down towards him. In the third picture, time coded five minutes later, Richard was sitting on the edge of the bed, with Christine astride him, her head thrown back.

'Just keep those eyes closed, honey,' said Sally coolly. Paul splayed his fingers across the top of his face.

'You are a good mother, aren't you?' Wu jeered. 'Not like my daughter and her mother who fucked Americans to get children.'

That was Mok's cue to punch Christine in the face. He kept hitting her until she collapsed on the floor, blood streaming from her nose and mouth.

'Fucking bitch,' whispered Wu. 'Whore of your mother's womb.'

Christine tried to struggle up, but Mok kicked her in the stomach and she toppled over, writhing. Mok's men pulled Christine to her feet and dragged her out of the office, through a door to the side. She managed to turn and her eyes met Sally's for a fraction of a second. Even now, her inner serenity was there for Sally to see.

From outside, Sally heard Christine's scream, a long, haunting sound of pain. Then Mok came back. 'It was hidden under her cunt,' he said, throwing Christine's passport onto Wu's desk.

278

Wu held Paul with his left hand and slowly turned the pages with his right. 'So I was right.'

'Yes, comrade. There is an American visa in it.'

Wu came to the visa and gazed at it. Sally dug a fingernail hard into her wrist, anything to get her mind away from him. Wu massaged Paul's shoulders with his free hand.

Chapter Thirty-two

'We can't get inside from here,' said Baby Face. 'But I know a way in from the museum. It might work.'

Cage let him lead.

'Wu has a vault where we store the heroin . . . Police! Police! Make way,' he shouted to a mob of peasants. He kept talking. 'Wu Tian has his own quarters in there and behind is a way into Qin Shi Huang's tomb.'

'Would Paul and Sally be there?'

'I expect so.' He stopped and pointed. 'See that green, right on the horizon, blending with the blue? That's the army. They'll ring this place and contain it.' He turned back and faced Cage. 'My orders are that if the army does not side with Red Spirit, the Teochiu will pull out. You can put away your gun now. We'll move faster without it.'

Cage lowered his hand, but kept the gun by his side, following Baby Face as he moved through the crowd. 'Orders from whom?'

'New York. I'll do what I can to get you to the boy and his mother. Then you're on your own. But when it comes to busting the Teochiu, remember some of us are honourable people.'

Baby Face walked faster, heading due west across fields which had been churned into stinking mud, thick with refuse. The faces of the people in the crowd were rapt and blank, straining towards the tomb, lips moving in chants and incantations, hands passing around statues and books.

The Terracotta Warrior Museum was closed, the parking lot empty, turnstile booths shut, the banners welcoming President

Gorbachev ripped down and left hanging from their poles. The few people there seemed to know Baby Face. They called out and waved to him. 'The army's moving in,' Cage heard them say.

'Will they shoot us?' a woman asked Baby Face.

'Not here,' he said. 'In Beijing they will. But not against Red Spirit.'

Baby Face vaulted over a turnstile. Cage followed and they ran through the deserted shopping centre and out to the pathway leading to Pit Number One. Baby Face cut down the steps which led towards Sally's office, headed down the corridor in the opposite direction to the way he had chased her, and stopped at the entrance to the underground museum.

It was clean but not yet finished; cans of paint and trestles had been left around two large glass cases. One contained a covered chariot with four horses and a terracotta general in full armour and gown, his hands clasped in front of him.

Baby Face pointed to it. 'In there,' he said. 'There's a way in through the chariot.'

Suddenly, Baby Face's head turned crimson as his skull was destroyed by a burst of gunfire. Cage dropped. There was no cover. Out of the corner of his eye, he saw the gunman on the other side of the glass case. He had only three rounds left in his weapon.

Cage stayed down and rolled, then sprang to his feet and leapt up against the glass, smashing it with his shoulder. He crashed into the terracotta general and fell in a welter of glass and blood on the other side. He hit the ground and fired twice, both rounds high, one hitting the gunman in the throat and one somewhere in the upper chest.

Another gunman landed inches from Cage. He recognised the broken nose, the cruel eyes. Mok smashed Cage in the face and moved back, getting ready to fire. Cage dropped down onto the broken glass as a line of bullets cut through the air above him. He lay there, pretending he was hit, and listened to Mok's footsteps crunching through the debris towards him. He heard the click of Mok changing ammunition clips. Cage had one round left. When he fired, he wouldn't be able to see.

'Fucking half-breed piece of shit,' said Mok, getting closer.

Mok's footsteps were inches away. Cage attuned all his senses to making a split-second judgement, the moment when the pretence would end and Mok would go for the kill. Cage slowed his breathing. The cold metal of Mok's gun barrel brushed the hairs on his neck.

'Turn over,' said Mok.

Cage let him press it closer, knowing Mok would want him to feel pain and fear. Then he felt the weapon tighten; the moment had come, the trigger was being squeezed. Cage turned knocking back the gun, ramming Mok's torso. He shot him point blank in the forehead.

He picked up Mok's weapon, an AK-47 with two magazines taped together, and took two more magazines and two grenades from the dead man's jacket pockets.

He heard voices from down the corridor, the clatter of military equipment, men reacting to gunfire. Cage kicked in the glass case surrounding the chariot, and the priceless terracotta figure shattered like a flower pot. He pushed it off the plinth, just as a burst of gunfire splattered the concrete above his head. Cage threw himself down onto the rubble, pulled the pin of a grenade, and hurled it down the entrance corridor.

The explosion sent a tornado of debris and shrapnel over Cage's head. He brought out the second grenade, then paused, stopped by a sudden, ghostly silence. His face was pressed down against the rubble, and when the dust cleared he saw that a panel on the side of the plinth had recently been screwed back into place. Tiny scratches on the screw-heads caught the light and a few splinters stood up. Baby Face had been right. There was a way in.

Cage opened the panel. There were steps going down, and fluorescent lighting. It was so quiet he was pretty certain Mok's men weren't down there.

He climbed down the steps and found himself in a wide, white corridor with a red ceiling decorated with golden stars in clusters of five. He walked cautiously along, gradually becoming aware of murmurings, stifled moans and whimpers. The corridor swung round and stretched away ahead of him. What he saw stopped him dead in his tracks.

Along the walls were huddled bodies. At first Cage couldn't tell whether they were alive or dead, but as he approached, he realised they were both: the dying left with the dead. All were young women, some crouched, their hands in their mouths, shaking and whimpering. Most had been stripped naked, the slashes of Mok's knife on their necks and down their backs. Some looked at Cage through wild and glazed eyes. Others just lay in heaps, too weak to move.

The smell of blood made Cage choke. He had never seen such horror. But he had to keep going. As he walked, stepping over coagulating blood, he wondered where the first shot would come from.

'Please.' The voice was distinct. He turned. 'Please, I'm alive.' She managed to lift her head, and he recognised the face of the girl he had saved in the hotel bombing. She was naked and her arms were tied behind her back. There were tiny cuts all over her shoulders, breasts, legs, stomach and face. She had been left, like the rest of them, to bleed slowly to death over as many days as it took.

Cage knelt down and freed her. Next to her was a dead woman dressed in a Mao tunic which he ripped off the body. He used it to cover Christine as best he could and stem the worst of the bleeding. She was ashen, but her eyes were moving normally. He had caught her in time. He helped her sit up. 'Who did this. Was it Wu?'

'He let Mok do it.'

'Why?'

'My father thinks I betrayed him,' she whispered.

'Wu is your father?'

'Yes. He killed my mother. He tried to kill me . . . All these women – he thinks they are me.'

'Where is he?'

'Through the door. Be careful. Mok—'

'He's dead,' said Cage.

Christine blinked, taking in the news.

'The little American boy. He's through there too.' She managed to lift her arm to point, then dropped it on Cage's hand.

'Is the door locked?' asked Cage.

283

'I don't know.' Her eyes flickered. 'He'll kill everyone. Go.'

'I'll come back,' he said, trying to sound convincing.

He clipped a new magazine into Mok's automatic and walked to the end of the corridor. He pushed against the door. It didn't give. He could hear voices on the other side, but they were too muffled for him to work out what was going on. He felt up and down to see if there was a keyhole or a combination lock. Nothing.

Cage stepped back and rapped on the door with the barrel of the gun. The lock was turned from the other side and the door swung open, but as soon as the guard saw Cage he tried to slam it shut again. His reactions were slow and there was a dopiness in his eyes. Cage put his foot in the door and hit the guard round the jaw with the gun butt. He spun round and crashed to the floor. Another guard across the room raised his weapon to fire, and Cage reacted instinctively, aiming for the upper body, two rounds, mid chest, and killed him. He turned and put a round in the right lower leg of the guard on the floor. A third gunman stared at him, weapon lowered, back pressed against the wall, his eyes veering back and forth. Without Mok, he was useless.

As soon as Wu saw Cage, he moved with the speed of a man twenty years younger. He grabbed Paul and put a pistol to the boy's head. There was no part of Wu's body Cage could be sure of hitting with an unfamiliar weapon.

Sally coiled herself to rush at Wu.

'Don't think about it, whore,' he whispered. She froze, rigid with tension. Paul was shaking with terror, but there was also a glow of hope: his father had come to save him.

'It's over, Wu,' said Cage. 'The army's outside. They're breaking it up.'

Wu tightened his grip on Paul's neck. 'You may look Chinese but you're American shit, like the rest,' he snarled. 'The army will help me. Don't try to understand my great country. I have sacrificed my wife and daughter for the revolution. The revolution is everything.'

Wu walked backwards, away from his desk, dragging Paul with him, then shuffled sideways and stopped.

'Good little boy,' he whispered. 'Good little boy.' He jerked Paul round, reached back and opened the door behind him. 'The lying bitch tricked me.' He pushed Paul through.

'Mom! Dad!' Paul's cry echoed as the door slammed shut behind Wu.

Sally screamed and ran over to the door, but Wu had already locked it. She and Cage were alone in the room, except for the guard, shivering against the wall, and the one on the floor with a flesh wound to his leg.

Sally turned to Cage and yelled, 'Do something, for Christ's sake!'

Cage didn't look at her. He went over to the guard against the wall, slapped him on the face and got no reaction. Cage pulled his sleeves and saw dozens of needle marks around the inner elbow. 'Strung out on heroin,' he muttered.

'What are you doing? Get in there,' shouted Sally. 'Shoot the lock out.'

'No,' said Cage. 'If I do that, he'll kill Paul.' Think, he told himself. Think only of logistics. No emotions. 'You work here. Is there another way in?'

'There is,' said Sally. 'But I have to go alone.'

'No way.'

Sally shook her head. Cage's coolness was helping her think more clearly. 'Cage, listen. I can end this. You tried to help us, but it didn't work. So, please, do as I say.'

'Sal, we haven't got time. We go together.'

'Supposing I don't make it? Supposing I'm wrong? Then Paul is dead, isn't he?' She shook her head angrily. 'No, Cage. You stay here. Wait a decent interval and then get through that damn door and get Paul back for me. He's your son, he's worth two chances, isn't he?'

Cage picked up the dead guard's AK-47, checked the magazine and put two spare ones in his pockets. 'I'll come with you as far as the exit. It's not a pretty sight out there.' Cage tied up the guard, opened the door, then turned to Sally. 'This is really horrible,' he warned her. 'Just keep walking.'

As soon as Sally saw the corridor of bleeding, dying women, she spun round to look away. She fumbled in her pocket for a handkerchief and held it up to her mouth. Cage's hand was on the small of her back. 'Keep going. Just keep walking,' he ordered.

There was a low wailing and her ankles were brushed by hands reaching out for help. The only woman on her feet was Christine, leaning heavily against the wall and wrapped in a blood-soaked Mao jacket.

Sally slowed down, reaching out to take Christine's hand. 'God. Did Mok do this to you?'

Christine squeezed her hand weakly. 'Go. Just go. I'll be all right.'

I yearned to be back with my daughter . . . Sally remembered Yu Yi's words. . . . *but as the years wore on* . . . *It is better my daughter believes I am dead.* Sally looked at Christine with compassion. 'Stay here. You have everything to live for. We'll be back,' she said.

Cage took Sally up through the opening into the museum and she saw the chariot she had spent years reconstructing, now just broken and scattered shards of terracotta. There was Mok, a red-black spot in the middle of his forehead, slumped dead amid the broken treasures. There were more bodies in the corridor where Cage had thrown the grenade and they trod over them until Sally stopped and pointed to a door.

'This is it,' she said. 'The shopping centre is up there.'

The door was unlocked. He opened it slowly. Daylight streamed in. He looked out, nodded and turned back to Sally. 'You sure you'll be all right?'

'No, Cage, I'm not sure. But it's our best shot and that young woman back there needs help.'

Outside, it looked deserted. As she ran, she looked back at Cage standing at the door, his eyes scanning back and forth for her. Minutes later, she was heading across the fields, pushing her way through the crowd, barging through the police cordon, screaming at them in Chinese like a mad woman until she reached the slopes of the burial mound. She ran through the trees, over patches of loose stony ground, along the criss-crossing paths. At Yu Yi's cave, she stopped, hanging on to the rock face to catch her breath.

She heard a familiar scraping sound behind her, and Tao, the mute, came out. He took her inside the cave, far into the darkness.

'Wu Tian has my son,' she panted. 'He's taken him into the tomb. If you know a way in, you must show me. Please.'

'Yes. We will help.' It was Yu Yi's familiar voice. 'We have been ready since we saw your note.'

'What do you mean, ready?' asked Sally.

From behind Yu Yi came a slow shuffle of people.

'We knew we would have to stop him one day,' said the pastor in English, walking out of the shadows. He was no longer dressed in his cassock but in a pair of grey overalls. He held a flashlight, switched off, in his right hand. 'My name is Pastor Tang. My church used to be in Nanjing, but now it is here.' He spoke in the clipped tones of an English schoolmaster. He seemed to have escaped injury. More people came out of the darkness.

'Wu has got men and guns,' Sally told them. 'What can you do against him?'

'Wu has guards,' the pastor replied, but they are all heroin addicts. Some of them he keeps down there permanently.'

Two of the cave-dwellers were carrying crossbows. One was a tall man with receding grey hair and glasses, a scar stretched down his face. The other was a woman, her hair neatly clipped back, the sleeves of her tunic rolled up. She noticed Sally's curiosity.

'Our weapons are reconstructions of the originals which we found inside the tomb,' she said proudly. 'And I assure you, Dr Parsons, they work.'

Sally gazed at the scene around her. These were the crippled, the injured, the scarred victims of the Cultural Revolution, gathering in this dark catacomb to take on their oppressor.

'Are you coming in with us?' A child's voice, in English, a little hand tugging at her clothes. Sally looked down at a girl's face, a little older than Paul's.

'Tell me,' Yu Yi's voice again, 'how is my – husband?'

'He's crazy,' Sally said. 'He has mood swings. One moment he is charming. The next he is a sadist. I have just . . .' She stopped

287

herself. The corridor of women was too terrible to describe. 'He is a mass murderer.'

'The mood swings would be because of the mercury.' Yu Yi's voice was calm. 'There are no rivers in there. They have long evaporated.' She paused. 'But the mercury is in the atmosphere – only in the mausoleum, not in the outer chambers. We can't smell it or see it, but Wu has spent many days in the tomb and it must have affected his nervous system.'

'What about Paul? Is that where Paul would be?'

'We expect so. But don't worry. Your son won't be there long enough to be affected. And my husband won't kill him if he can keep his fantasy alive.'

There was a rattle of sticks, crossbows and other equipment being readied.

'Let's go,' said Tang. 'Follow us into the tomb.'

The mute reached up to take Sally's hand. She let him lead her, following his crablike scuttle as, ahead of her, the band of people slid open the door of the tomb.

Inside were dozens of flickering candles, throwing shadows back into the cave and lighting up those going in: reflecting off a pair of spectacles, a crucifix hanging from a neck, catching on a crushed cheekbone, a limping peg leg, a quiver of crossbow bolts.

In the outer vault, Tang tested his flashlight then turned it off again. The pathway was clear, but on either side was debris, and about a hundred yards in, Sally saw the first terracotta warrior, decapitated and missing an arm. This was the chamber she had photographed four months ago. As they moved through an archway, she stepped over the fallen rafter, and bent down and picked up the copy of the Red Book with its plastic cover. Somewhere in the darkness above must be the tiny hole she had drilled on that freezing cold night.

The mute tugged at her elbow, indicating that she should crouch down as they moved on through a low, wide tunnel into another vault.

Sally gasped at the sight in front of her.

Candles high up on ledges illuminated the whole chamber. Straight in front of her were the first skeletons, not laid out as she was used to seeing them on burial sites, but sitting, crouching, curled up, their clothes decayed to shreds. These must have been the original workmen, killed in cold blood or left to die when they had finished their work, in order to preserve the secret of the tomb. On the ground lay their tools – hammers, chisels, blunt knives – just dropped where they fell. To her right lay the rib cage of a horse and its skull, the bit still in its teeth. The leather harness, remarkably preserved, hung to the ground. A chariot behind it was on its side but intact, its shaft strapped to a terracotta horse which had fallen over, taking the chariot with it.

As the procession moved on, the shuffling footsteps echoing all around, they came to a rank of twenty-four coffins, arranged in four lines of six. In each coffin was a skeleton, gracefully laid out, and with it a musical instrument, a zither, a triangle, a flute, pan pipes, a decayed drum and something that looked like a banjo or a violin. Behind the coffins, on a raised platform, were the stools where the orchestra had sat. They must have played Qin Shi Huang's body into the tomb, and kept playing until they were too weak. Then, knowing their fate, they must have stepped elegantly into their coffins and died.

On the other side of the vault were the remains of a bed, on which lay a skeleton, curled up, like a foetus. Sally was drawn to the figure. A gold bracelet hung off the wrist bone. A necklace of jewels had dropped into the rib cage. Shreds of silk clothing still covered parts of the skeleton. On the ground was a wooden foot massage roller, and more tattered fabrics. This was the bed of a concubine, soothed by orchestral music and relaxed by massage so she was in prime condition to give satisfaction to the Emperor.

The mute tugged at Sally's hand again. She could sense the heightened tension among the cave-dwellers. Pastor Tang stopped in front of two huge wooden doors, reinforced with bolted bands of metal. The cave-dwellers stood two abreast in front of it.

'We have been gradually descending,' said the woman with the crossbow. She pulled back the string of her weapon and inserted a bolt. 'The next chamber is the mausoleum.'

In there were the dried rivers of mercury, the poisoned cross bolts and Wu Tian with Paul.

'Be careful,' Sally said under her breath. 'For God's sake, I hope you know what you're doing.'

The woman took a step towards her, and Sally could see that her lips were scarred as if they had been burnt. 'We have waited many years for this day.'

'Where is Yu Yi?'

'She has gone in by another way.'

When Sally started moving forward to join the ranks of cave-dwellers, the mute held her back.

The pastor pushed on the heavy door, and this time there were no candles on the other side. Electric spotlights high in the ceiling shone down into the middle of the mausoleum, casting a dim and uncertain light everywhere. As the doors swung wide, gunfire erupted. Sally heard the familiar swish and thud of crossbow bolts, followed by more bursts of gunfire. She broke free of the mute and, keeping to the wall for cover, ran up to the door. The bodies of two of Wu Tian's men lay on the ground. Two more were firing aimlessly, strung out on drugs, as Pastor Tang had said, their shots going nowhere, and seconds later they were cut down by the crossbows.

As suddenly as it began, the fighting stopped.

Ahead of Sally was a dry ditch which must once have been one of the rivers of mercury. Two plinths stood on the island on the other side. On one was a gold coffin, on the other a glass sarcophagus in which Sally could see a yellow robe decorated with red and blue flowers, a robe Qin Shi Huang had been described as wearing. The face, too, was clearly visible – not the face of Qin, but of Mao Zedong, distorted through age but unmistakable, his body clothed in the First Emperor's robe.

Behind the sarcophagus, Wu Tian stood on a platform, holding an automatic, dressed like Mao Zedong in sweeping coat and baggy trousers. He had arranged his hair to recede like Mao's. He had Paul with him, spot-lit in the little silk suit of a Chinese emperor. Paul saw Sally but kept quiet.

A great hush enveloped the mausoleum as everyone registered that Wu was there. Wu, with the child, had all the power. His eyes darted around the immense space. The scrape of a shoe, a moan from one of the wounded, a drip of water from high above, every sound was amplified in the silence. Somewhere, far away, Sally thought she heard the rumble of the train.

Then Wu Tian spoke, slowly and deliberately. 'I have your son. He will become a child of the new China.' He brought out a cigarette from his tunic, rolled it around in his finger, and put it in his mouth. He fumbled for his lighter, flared it, lit the cigarette and drew hard. Wu coughed. It echoed around the chamber, sounding like the coughing of patients in an asylum.

His body shook, and Sally thought it might be the affect of the evaporated mercury. But then she realised he was laughing under his breath. He stopped and pulled Paul closer to him. 'It is my duty to restore the confidence of the Chinese people.' His voice was measured, but his hand shook as he raised it again to draw on the cigarette. 'You have come to stop me. I hold this child, so you will not succeed. For me, the sacrifice of one boy to improve the lives of millions of boys is a good thing. But for you . . . for you, you snivelling, whining cowards, you will let me succeed just to save this urchin's life.'

'What do you want?' Sally whispered.

'What do I want?' mimicked Wu Tian. He pointed towards the east gate. 'It is what they want. Those loyal Chinese people outside. They want their great leaders who are here in this mausoleum to rise up and unify the nation again. And I, Red Spirit, have the power to give them that.'

Sally caught a flash of light in the corner of her eye. It was a torch beam behind Wu. Cage was standing there. It must have been him on the train. By his side was Christine, looking pale but on her feet, most of her cuts bandaged and dressed in another, cleaner tunic. Wu hadn't seen them. Cage turned off the torch and held Christine steady.

'Soon my provincial leaders will be allowed in with the delegations to witness the rebirth.' Wu pushed Paul's head down so he was staring at Mao's face in the sarcophagus. 'They will see our Great Helmsman Mao and our First Emperor Qin blended into one. They will see Red Spirit as the new Mao, and they will see this little boy as the reincarnation of Qin Shi Huang.' He stroked Paul's cheek, hooked his finger under his chin and lifted his head. 'There is nothing any of you can do against me with your toy weapons. My followers are outside. Millions of them. You are powerless.' Wu pressed a switch and floodlights came on, lighting up the podium, reflections dancing off the glass of the sarcophagus, and showing the terror in Paul's eyes.

'It's OK, honey,' called out Sally. 'Everything will be just fine.'

She wished Paul would answer. But he didn't. He was trembling, his head forced up by Wu, weeping quietly, too frightened to even wipe his eyes.

All around, the cave-dwellers watched, motionless. Pastor Tang was like a statue, resting on his staff. The crossbow woman stood with her arms by her side. Closest to Wu was Tao, who was squatting, his head bobbing ever so slightly. Near to Sally was a tiny man with a withered right arm and one eye missing. He had two crossbow men on either side of him. But their weapons were lowered; they could not fire without risking Paul's life.

Then suddenly into the stillness came a piercing, inhuman scream, beginning like a ripple but filling out, hanging in the atmosphere and bouncing around the walls. Sally shivered against its power. Wu looked confused. Then the scream came again, stripping the mask of confidence from his face.

The scream stopped, and the echoes were suspended in the air for a moment before they, too, faded. Wu was still, his eyes dulled as if they were being filled with shadows from twenty years ago.

Then came the voice, gentle but assured. 'The last time you heard that, it was my death scream. I was dying in the fire.' No one could see her, but Yu Yi's voice dominated the mausoleum. 'My name is Yu Yi. I am the wife of Wu Tian, the liar and the coward who makes prisoners of little boys.' Her voice, louder and louder with the echo, grew with authority. 'Stop what you are doing. This is your wife whom you thought was dead. If you harm that child, you will answer to me.'

Sally strained to see her, but in the places where Yu Yi might be there was only darkness.

'Yu Yi?' Wu Tian whispered.

'You tried to kill me. Then you tried to kill our daughter.'

Wu Tian dropped his cigarette to the ground, smoothed his collar and fiddled with the Mao badge. With his right hand he held Paul by the shoulder.

'Is it you, Yu Yi? Is it really you?'

'Yes, it's me,' Yu Yi said implacably. 'I didn't die. You . . . you *nothing*,' she hissed.

'Forgive me, Yu Yi.' Wu Tian seemed crushed by the terrible truth confronting him. 'It was for the revolution,' he tried. 'How could I stop the revolution?'

'Liar,' Yu Yi shot back. 'You couldn't stomach the fact that your wife had loved another man and regretted ever loving you. Don't talk to me about your pathetic revolution. I saw your eyes. I saw you look at me when you threw the petrol bomb.'

For a moment Wu Tian loosened his grip on Paul, but then he checked himself and pulled him back. 'Yu Yi, you must understand that I had no choice,' he whimpered.

'Oh, yes, you did. You had a choice but you were too much of a coward to make it. Now, you have another choice. Let the child go.'

Wu Tian was quivering, his hand squeezing Paul's shoulder. 'You and I . . . It should have been you and me. Not the Chairman. I loved you, but you wouldn't love me back.'

'So you tried to kill me.'

'The Chinese revolution is great, but the road after the revolution will be longer.'

'Mao Zedong, March the fifth, nineteen forty-nine, Report to the Second Plenary Session. So you're still reciting that rubbish to defend your evil.'

'You are really Yu Yi,' said Wu Tian, leaning forward, keeping Paul against him. 'Where are you? I must see you. Are you a ghost or a reincarnation like our Great Helmsman? I must see you.'

'I'm no ghost and you make me sick. Too stupid to think for yourself. Too frightened to do anything except recite from the dead.' Yu Yi strained her voice. She seemed to spit out the last words, but her voice was wheezing and her energy was fading; some of the words were not completely clear.

'No. No. No,' screamed Wu Tian. 'You must love me. You must adore me for all millennia. Our daughter, I gave her chopped minced pork every day for her school lunch, just like you would have wanted.'

'Mother?' The new voice sent a fresh chill through the chamber. Wu Tian's eyes flickered round behind him, and he saw Christine, shrouded strangely by the light, moving, defenceless but fearless, towards him.

Tears were streaming down Christine's face. 'You're alive. My God, you're alive!'

In that moment, as Wu Tian's head turned in confusion between Yu Yi's voice and his approaching daughter, Paul made his escape, ducking away from Wu, scrambling over the sarcophagus, jumping the ditch and flinging himself towards Sally.

'Down, Paul! *Get down!*' Cage screamed, and Paul dropped to the ground just as Wu Tian fired at him, and missed. Sally and Paul ran back into darkness.

'Fucking bitch wife. Like your whore of a daughter,' Wu yelled, firing the gun blindly towards the area where Yu Yi had spoken.

Two cave-dwellers darted out, one from each side, crossbows ready. But Wu Tian spotted the quick movement and shot them. One fell into the shadows, the other in the light.

Cage could not open fire at Wu, Christine was too close. Wu Tian, agile, moving with surprising speed, threw himself down from the podium. Cage ran down towards him, but a shot rang out from somewhere else, not Wu, and Cage fell.

Sally had never experienced anything like the feeling she had when she saw his sudden collapse. A deluge of emotion created a pit in her stomach – fear that Cage might be dead, dread that Yu Yi's power over Wu Tian was gone. She knew that if any of them were going to live, he had to be stopped.

'Stay here. Don't move,' she whispered to Paul. She edged along the wall in the darkness and reached the cave-dweller who had fallen into the shadows. She recognised him from the church service, his spectacles smashed and blood pouring from a head wound. Sally picked up his crossbow and took three bolts from the quiver.

'Have I killed that whore bitch of a daughter yet?' taunted Wu Tian. 'The revolution does not tolerate traitors.'

The more he ranted, the more unpredictable he became. Sally stayed against the walls, out of the light, moving round until she was behind Wu. He was still looking out towards where the crossbows had been fired.

'Yu Yi, my love. Where are you?' he whispered.

Sally spotted the flitting shape of Paul. Wu must have seen it too. His head jerked round and raised the gun. 'Haven't I killed that half-breed urchin yet?'

'Are you going to try to murder us all?' Yu Yi's voice was stronger, clearer, trying to make herself sound like she used to.

'My love.' Wu Tian was turning back and forth.

Paul tripped and fell. A beam of light hit his face. He put his hand up against it and began scrambling to his feet. He caught sight of Wu Tian, the automatic levelled towards him. 'Mom, Mom . . .' he cried. Then, as Wu Tian's finger tightened inside the trigger guard, Paul's voice became a howl of animal terror, a cry for mercy.

'Noooooo . . .' Sally screamed at Wu, and in the same second positioned herself just as her father had taught her: feet at right angles, crossbow to shoulder, chin steadying, finger firm on the squeeze, breathe out and fire.

The bolt caught Wu Tian on the shoulder, knocking him back, causing a burst of gunfire to hit the jewelled ceiling. His free hand caught the side of Qin's coffin and kept him upright. He brought the gun down, steadied it, his eyes searching wildly for his target. Sally didn't move, knowing that if Wu Tian didn't die now, this would never end. He fired, cutting up the ground in front of her. But Sally stayed exactly where she was. In her head, she heard her father's voice, giving her instructions. Don't change position. Reload. Keep your feet still. Crossbow up.

She fired again.

The bolt hit him just above the heart. Wu Tian fell back, his hand grasping for the coffin, and his tumbling weight took it with him, skeletal bones inside flying loose as everything crashed into the dry ditch. Sally ran over to Paul, hauled him to his feet and held him as tight as she could.

Chapter Thirty-three

The mausoleum was filled with an awesome quiet.

Holding Paul, sitting on the cool earthen floor, Sally looked at the murals of stars and hunting animals on the walls, and halfway up on ledges hewn out of the rock saw kneeling terracotta archers who must once have been armed with poisoned arrows to protect Qin's body. She saw, also on raised ground, skeletal remains, but jumbled up, with no human or animal shape to them. Then finally her eyes rested on the fallen coffin. The body of Wu Tian was half crushed by it, lying in the ditch.

Tao came up to her. 'Is he dead?' asked Sally.

The mute nodded.

'And Yu Yi?'

Tao's disfigured face broke into a smile.

'Here, Paul, help me up.' She managed to get to her feet, then she remembered Cage.

'Paul, where's your dad?'

'I don't know,' said Paul weakly.

She spotted Christine, took Paul's hand and walked towards her.

'Cage is hurt but fine,' said Christine. 'The bullet scraped the right side of his head.' She pointed to Cage on the other side of the podium. His right shoulder was bloodied, and he held a handkerchief to his head.

'Cage,' shouted Sally, her voice echoing, surprising her. When he looked up, she let go of Paul's hand and ran towards him. 'Cage. You bastard. You lovely bastard,' she cried. 'I thought

297

you were dead.' She threw her arms round him, her hair all over the place, getting in the way when she tried to kiss him. 'Never, ever let me feel like that again.'

'Are you OK?' he whispered.

'I'm fine. I'm fine.'

'You should have seen her, Dad.' Paul's voice, demanding to join in. 'I bet she could outshoot *you* any day.'

'Make sure you tell your granddad that,' quipped Cage.

Tao touched Sally's shoulder and pointed towards a dark crevice. 'I second that,' said Yu Yi. But still she wouldn't let herself be seen.

'Thank God you're alive,' said Sally.

'It takes more than an angry husband to kill me off.' An attempt to laugh came out more like a grating whisper. 'My voice almost let me down.' She coughed. 'I have had too many cold winters here. I don't have the strength I used to have.' She coughed again. 'Po Ki, my daughter. Come towards me. Tao will show the way.'

Tao led Christine forward. 'Mother,' she whispered. 'It really is . . .'

'You saw me in the fire. Now come and see the result.' High above in the ceiling a dim light illuminated most of the wall but Yu Yi was sitting under an overhang of rock which hid her in its black shadow. 'Sally, come, too,' she said. 'Bring your son and his father.'

They caught up with Christine. Tao beckoned them forward, and for the first time Sally saw her, so crumpled with illness yet still so defiant.

The only part of her body that had survived unscarred were her legs. Her mouth was stretched open and twisted. Her face was blotched and badly discoloured and the left side from the chin to the eye socket was crushed and still stained crimson red. She had no hair, and no cloth to cover her head. Her left arm had been amputated above the elbow. The hand on the right arm was mottled and livid, the fingers bent like claws.

'You are so beautiful,' Yu Yi said to Christine. Her voice was even weaker than before. There was sadness in it. She looked at them. Only one eye seemed to work. The mute held Yu Yi's left stump, gently massaging it. 'I want to see *you* more clearly,' she said to Cage. 'Come closer.'

Cage stepped forward, but Yu Yi held up her right stump. 'Stay where you are. I can see you better with a little distance. Sally told me about you. I had a son like you who was taken from me.'

Cage turned quickly to Sally, who shook her head.

'No, I am not your mother. But I have seen her photograph,' said Yu Yi. 'We are about the same age. I want you to know that I have never stopped loving my son. And you must look at me to see what she might have endured by giving birth to you. She would not have abandoned you and if she was able to see you now, she would be proud.'

Cage ran his hand up and down the metal of his gun, feeling more at ease with it than with the turmoil of his emotions. 'Stay quiet. Stay quiet,' he said softly. 'We'll get you to a hospital.' He couldn't think of anything except saving her. He was Cage on the battlefield, working out logistics in order to keep sadness and anger at bay.

'Hospital. No,' replied Yu Yi. 'Now go, all of you, and leave me with my daughter.' She coughed, and Christine was on her knees beside her, wiping the saliva from her mouth.

'Who cut you like that?' said Yu Yi. 'Was it him?'

'It was one of Father's men. But don't fuss, Mother . . .'

'Of course I will fuss. You're my daughter.' This time the cough racked right up from the bottom of her lungs. Her eyes closed in pain and opened again. 'We can't rest yet. Help me. There is one last duty I have to perform.'

A moment later Yu Yi was ready. Christine held a microphone to her mother's mouth and when Yu Yi spoke, her words were carried on the public-address system rigged up by Wu Tian right through the tomb and beyond it to the mass of people around the burial mound.

'Go home. Go home. There is nothing here for you,' Yu Yi said decisively in her ruined voice. 'In a few minutes you will see us on the hillside. We are not the spirit of Mao. There is no such thing. We are not a reincarnation of Mao, nor are we his sons or daughters.' Yu Yi's voice faltered. The Tannoy system made her sound even more frail; the struggle for breath, the rasp of damaged vocal chords were amplified and echoed painfully through the mausoleum.

But she went on. 'Soon, you will see a group of old people, an ugly sight. We are the victims of Mao. You will see the scars and deformities we carry with us. We were beaten, imprisoned, starved, humiliated, tortured and torn from our families. We were burned, thrown from windows, beaten by Red Guards. Look at us and you will understand why the spirit of Mao must never return to this country. Then go home to your villages.'

Pastor Tang led them out, carrying his stave. The main entrance to the burial mound faced east towards the Terracotta Warrior Museum. It was a set of double doors, twelve feet high and set back into the hill in a clearing among the pomegranate trees. The cave-dwellers passed Sally on the way out. The crossbow woman shook her hand. Others embraced her. She watched their descent towards the crowds and then went back inside.

With the door open, natural light made its way in, and she looked around at the expanse of the mausoleum. It must have been ten storeys high and two hundred, maybe three hundred feet across. Each section of the walls and ceiling was decorated with some vision of Qin Shi Huang's life. Suddenly, she had an urge to laugh. Three years ago she had set out on a quest for archaeological discovery and she had ended up fighting a drug trafficker.

She headed with Cage and Paul to the ditch. She wanted to see Wu's dead body first. Qin, Mao, all of them could wait. But Wu she wanted right now. They jumped down into the shallow trench and stood, gazing at him where he lay, twisted by the momentum of her last shot. One hand was round the bolt in his shoulder, and his head was tilted down, the expression on his face one of surprise at what had happened. Blood was still soaking into his Mao tunic.

'Don't look, honey,' she told Paul, but it was only an afterthought, as they had already been standing there for a few seconds.

'If you hadn't killed him, Mom, I would've,' he said.

She knew she should be amazed at all the treasures around her. But all she saw was sadness and desperation. Yes, the tomb was as described in the ancient writings of the *Shi Ji*, but it was also a pathetic monument to the folly of men trying to live beyond their allotted time. The bones of the great Emperor Qin Shi Huang had lain strewn in a coffin like paper clips, all his possessions, his concubines, his animals just a scattering of decay around him.

But Mao was different. The sarcophagus was practically undamaged. Just one area of glass on the top had broken and a piece had fallen onto the body inside. Mao's face appeared before them, blotched just behind the right ear and with a discolouration from the bottom of the left eye to the chin. It hadn't been concealed by the make-up which Sally could now see lit up by the spotlights: thick powder on the cheeks, lipstick slightly smudged on the lower lip, mascara on the eyelashes – unless they were false eyelashes – and congealed dark dye round the roots of the hair, which looked as if it had been glued on.

Cage put his hand through the glass and touched the cheek. 'It is the body,' he whispered.

'And in Tiananmen Square . . .'

'Is the wax effigy. Mao's body must never have been there.'

Sally looked at the preserved corpse of Mao and thought for a moment about the forensic testing, writing the papers, making the arguments, winning the scholarly prizes and being challenged by rivals who wanted to pull her reputation apart. That would be if the Chinese ever let anyone near it. Which they wouldn't because this was China. The tomb would be closed again. No word of Wu Tian would reach the outside world.

'Let's go and have a look outside,' she said and the three of them stood at the door which Tang and the procession had just passed through.

She adjusted her eyes to the sunlight. The army was now on the hillside and soldiers were clearing a passageway for the cave-dwellers. It was a dignified procession, the cave-dwellers walking slowly two abreast, with the more able-bodied helping the disabled. There was no leader, no emblems of their cause, no crucifixes, statues or images of gods. They walked silently along

301

a farm path, keeping their beliefs to themselves, cheered by the crowd because the devotees needed to believe in something, even an odd, bedraggled bunch of old people who had hid out in caves for years and were only now emerging back into the real world.

The tiny man with the withered arm and one eye stumbled and a soldier moved in and lifted him onto his back. Other soldiers helped as the cave-dwellers, disorientated and weak, found they couldn't make the journey. By the time the procession had reached the flat farmlands, it was a mix of cave-dwellers and troops, of green and ragged dull blue, of young men with weapons by their sides and frail people with walking sticks, eyes squinting against the sun.

A group of soldiers nodded to Sally, Cage and Paul and went past them into the tomb to begin the work of bringing out the bodies and the heroin. Sally found herself following the procession of cave-dwellers, holding one of Paul's hands and Cage the other, all of them lost in their own thoughts. Paul skipped as if he was in the school playground, but his face was drawn and puzzled. Sally kept looking around for Yu Yi and Christine. But there was no sign of them and the Tannoy was silent.

Just as they reached the bottom of the mound, she turned back again towards the mausoleum and saw Tao scuttling towards her, his mouth open in a cry which would never be heard.

Epilogue

As Sally walked into the restaurant for lunch, Richard got up with a smile. She rushed forward and kissed him on the lips, gave him a big hug and brushed her finger down his face. 'My God! You survived,' she said breathlessly. 'I kept calling the embassy and they said you had been pinned down in Tiananmen Square.'

Richard kissed her again. 'It's good to know someone cares.'

'Cared? I was worried sick,' she said, unhooking her bag from her shoulder and hanging it on the back of her chair.

'So how long are you back for?'

Sally held up her hand. 'No, you first. I want to know everything.'

'I thought you weren't talking to me any more.'

Sally touched his hand. 'Things went a bit crazy, that's all.'

A waiter poured champagne, and Richard raised his glass. 'Let's drink to us.'

'To us,' repeated Sally, clinking his glass. She took a sip. 'And to your bravery,' she added and put the glass back on the table.

'All right,' said Richard. 'But I wasn't that brave. I was holed up in the Beijing Hotel until the embassy staff came and got me out. We knew the tanks were there, but frankly we didn't expect them to open fire like they did. They shot anything that moved. It was dreadful.'

'I saw that lone guy on TV stopping the line of tanks. Incredible!'

Richard took a long drink and Sally filled up the glass for him again. We all underestimated Deng Xiao-ping. We had forgotten that he had come to power through the bullet.' He

303

smiled grimly. 'I know it's a cliché, but it's true.'

'But what about Gorbachev and all that?'

'Came to nothing. No one will deal with China now. Killing those students has made the country an international pariah. She's about as isolated and weak as she's ever been.' Richard held up his hand to call a waiter. 'Let's order,' he said.

Sally leaned across, pulled his arm down, and entwined her fingers in his. 'There comes a time in a girl's life, Mr Gregg, when a man just has to submit. So what we are going to do is order more drinks, get very drunk then go back to your place and fuck ourselves stupid. Do I make myself clear?'

'Perfectly,' said Richard quietly.

'And while we're drinking,' whispered Sally, 'I will tell you in explicit detail exactly what I am going to do to you once we climb into bed.'

Richard lifted his glass to take more champagne.

'I will give you so much pleasure that your afternoon Chinese doll will seem like a sack of mud in comparison.'

Richard grimaced. 'You're not still sore about her?'

Sally shook her head and squeezed his hand again. 'Brave men in foreign lands with native women can be a big turn-on.' They both laughed out loud. Sally topped up their glasses, then said, 'But tell me, what was all that about anyway?'

Exhibit 109 – Audio Tape Evidence
Federal Court, Pearl Street
Manhattan
December 16th 1989

'No, Sal, it's not the champagne talking. I really want to settle down. I mean, it's . . . no, no more . . . well, just a drop . . .'

'No point in ordering if we don't drink it.' (Laughter)

'We could always take it home . . .'

'I'm enjoying this. You know, in all those months we've been intimate, we've never had a chance to talk like this.'

'I'll drink to that.'

'To us.' (Glasses clinking)

'To us.' (Pause) 'I want to settle down with you, Sal.'

'You said that already. And there comes a point when a girl has to be told why.'

'I love you.'

'That's the champagne talking.'

'I told you that before.'

'Maybe. But your life . . . Richard, it's too complicated for me. Cage asked me to come back when he saw me in China, and I said no. I left a relationship with him when I never knew what he was doing. I won't get into that again.'

'I'm leaving it. It's damn well finished.'

'Leaving what? What's finished?'

'Give me some more . . . Thanks . . . You know if we get them to give us a silver spoon and we put it in the top, the champagne will stay alive.' (Laughter/giggling)

'What's finished?'

'The job.'

'The job? What will you live on?'

'No need to worry about that. You know I've got a brother who earns big bucks as a corporate lawyer. Well, I tell you, Sal, my bank accounts will make him look like a pauper by the time I'm finished. I've just bought this place on the Upper East Side and you and I and Paul are going over tomorrow so you can choose just exactly how you want it decorated.'

'So how do you afford it?' (Barely audible)

'Your friend Li Yi . . . You know, Sal, all I want is to throw you onto the bed and peel your clothes off. Right now.'

'What about Li Yi?'

'I'll tell you because I'm finished. You know, Sal, I don't want this fucking job any more.'

'I've never heard you swear like that before.'

'Because you've never seen the real me before. Look at me, Sal, look at the man in front of you and tell me whether you can love him and be his wife for ever and a day.'

'I want to more than anything, but you must let me know all of you. There can't be any secret sides.'

'It's nothing new, Sal. Like in Indochina in the sixties, the CIA ran an airline called Air America which flew out opium

*from the Laotian hill tribes. It got refined in Saigon or Hong
Kong, then it was sent over to the States, courtesy of Air
America. We did it to let the tribes earn some money and
stay on side against the communists. So I was just carrying
out an honourable US tradition, trafficking narcotics to
bolster national security. We needed Wu Tian to destabilise
China, so I started this little operation for him. Every time it
was my turn to be the diplomatic bag courier, I flew out Wu
Tian's heroin. It just went straight through with no customs
checks, and Li Yi's dad, Joseph Li, sold it. I'd go back with a
pouch full of money to fund Wu Tian's Red Spirit campaign.
On the way, Li Yi would take his cut and I would take mine.'*
'You creamed it off?'
*'Let's just say a State Department salary is not very reward-
ing.'*
*'I can't believe you've been so . . . so . . . I don't know . . . but
at the end of the day I can't believe you've been so damn
practical and clever.'*
'Is that a compliment? You mean you're not shocked?'
'Shocked! I'm so proud of you, Richard. Let's drink to it.'
(Glasses clinking)

They stumbled in each other's arms to the front door of
Richard's apartment, laughing and fumbling around for the
keys.

'I'll fix some coffee,' slurred Richard when they got inside.

'Like hell you will!' said Sally, feigning anger. 'I don't bed a
man who's drinking coffee. Fix us a couple of brandys, get
upstairs and get your pants off, while I make myself ready.'

As Richard staggered into the kitchen, Sally slipped back out
of the front door and into a Lincoln Town Car parked by the
sidewalk. She unclipped the radio microphone from the top of
her panties and handed it to Robert Leonard who was in the
back seat.

'Well done, Dr Parsons,' he said. 'You got the trafficking, the
money, his motive. Everything we need. With this and what Bill
uncovered, Joseph Li will be behind bars for a very, very long
time.'

'Joseph Li?' Sally turned in her seat. 'What about Richard? And what about Hazel Watson or Stephanie Cranley, the woman you said was Richard's boss?'

Leonard answered without looking at Sally. 'Joseph Li is the big fish, and Cranley wasn't peddling narcotics.'

'Richard was.'

'Pull up here,' Leonard said to the driver. 'I have to get out. The driver will take you on.'

Sally put her hand on Leonard's elbow. 'Cage said you were a straight guy, so tell me. What happens to Richard?'

'Richard's being posted to Paraguay. For him it'll seem like a jail sentence. Cranley stays where she is. In our trade, people like Cranley and Richard are watertight, Dr Parsons. Don't ask me why. They just are.'

It was a brilliant June afternoon and the car dropped Sally outside a small Chinese restaurant near Columbia University. She walked in and stopped for a moment to look at three people sitting at a table, chatting, digging into a banquet of dishes, unaware of her. She drew a deep breath.

Cage spotted her first. 'How'd it go?' he said, getting up and pulling out a chair for her.

'Oh, not bad,' said Sally, sitting down. 'Richard asked me to marry him.'

Paul and Christine stopped eating.

'And?' said Cage.

'I told him I'd think about it,' she said nonchalantly.

Paul slapped his chopsticks on the table. 'Maaaawwm, how could you? You said he was a shit.'

'Paul, language,' reprimanded Sally. 'But . . .' She paused while she picked up the chopsticks and put them back in Paul's hand. 'It turns out that Richard's got to go away for some time.'

'You're not going to wait for him?' said Paul.

'Maybe,' said Sally, smiling. 'But he's likely to be gone for a few years, so I might get a bit impatient.'

'So it worked?' said Cage.

She glanced over and caught Cage's eye and couldn't help resting her hand on top of his. 'Half worked,' she said softly. 'Sometimes even to get it half right you have to be a full on bitch.'

307

'Now that sounds a real mean thing to say, Mom.'

'Why don't you tell Sally your news,' said Christine, smiling at Paul who was popping a prawn into his mouth.

'Ko called,' he said with his mouth full. 'He's had a baby. Or rather Mrs Ko has.'

'That's great,' said Sally. But she didn't dare ask about the sex. Cage was grinning at her. Christine's face was deadpan.

'It's a boy,' said Paul.

'Thank God for that.'

Christine whispered to her, 'He's also adopted a baby girl from the orphanage . . .'

'And they're calling her Sally, after you, Mom.'

After the meal, the four of them walked a few blocks to a discreet cemetery. Paul carried a small bunch of flowers and laid it on a fresh grave. In a frame, next to the gravestone, was the photograph Cage had carried in his locket all those years.

The family stood in silence in the warm, light evening, celebrating the lives of Yu Yi and Jefferson Binsky.

Author's Note

Red Spirit is a fictional story set against a late twentieth-century backdrop. Few figures of modern history are as fascinating as Mao Zedong. Therefore, I have used situations which did happen with some real-life characters, such as Deng Xiao-ping and Zhao Zhiyang, as part of the novel. At the time of writing, the legendary tomb of Qin Shi Huang near Xian had never been excavated despite many attempts by archaeologists to get permission. A wax replica was made of Mao Zedong's body after his death in 1976 because of fears that preservation with formaldehyde would not work. The CIA is widely believed to have assisted in the growing and transporting of opium in Indochina during the Vietnam War. Soviet President Mikhael Gorbachev did visit China in May 1989 and Chinese troops did kill demonstrators to end the Tiananmen Square protests in June 1989, while in Xian and other cities protests were ended without bloodshed.

Some of the institutions such as the National Cultural Relics Bureau in Beijing do exist. But Sally's Archaeological Institute of America and Richard's Federal Containment Agency are fictitious, although most governments do have secret units responsible for deniable operations.

I drew on much published material but three books in particular should be mentioned. *The Private Life of Chairman Mao* by Zhisui Li, which described scenes surrounding Mao Zedong's death and the embalming of his body; *The Tiananmen Papers* compiled by Zhang Liang which recounted conversations within the Chinese government before the 1989 Tiananmen Square killings; and *The Dragon Syndicates* by Martin Booth which portrayed the global threat of the Chinese Triad organisations.

My thanks to William Fu, Farooq El Baz, Liz Jensen, Nancy Langston, Cait Murphy, James Miles and Justin Morris for their invaluable help along the way. A special thanks to Mary Sandys for her work on the text and to Jonathan Mirsky for the loan of books, documents and glimpses of character.

Humphrey Hawksley